Since 2004, internationally bestselling author **Sherrilyn Kenyon** has placed over sixty novels on the *New York Times* bestseller list; in the past three years alone, she has claimed the No.1 spot seventeen times. This extraordinary bestseller continues to top every genre she writes within.

Pro aimed the pre-eminent voice in paranormal fiction by critics, s helped pioneer – and define – the current paranormal trend ptivated the world and continues to blaze new trails that blur l genre lines.

more than 25 million copies of her books in print in over 100 , her current series include: The Dark-Hunters, League, Lords , Chronicles of Nick, and Belador Code.

Visit Sherrilyn Kenyon online:

www.darkhunter.com
www.sherrilynkenyon.co.uk
www.facebook.com/AuthorSherrilynKenyon
www.twitter.com/KenyonSherrilyn

Praise for Sherrilyn Kenyon:

'A publishing phenomenon . . . [Sherrilyn Kenyon] is the igning queen of the wildly successful paranormal scene'
Publishers Weekly

'Kenyon's writing is brisk, ironic and relentlessly imaginative. These are not your mother's vampire novels'
Boston Globe

'Whether writing as Sherrilyn Kenyon or Kinley MacGregor, this author delivers great romantic fantasy!'

Sherrilyn Kenyon's Dark-Hunter World Series: (in reading order)

Fantasy Lover
Night Pleasures
Night Embrace
Dance with the Devil
Kiss of the Night
Night Play
Seize the Night
Sins of the Night
Unleash the Night
Dark Side of the Moon
The Dream-Hunter
Devil May Cry
Upon the Midnight Clear
Dream Chaser
Acheron
One Silent Night
Dream Warrior
Bad Moon Rising
No Mercy
Retribution
The Guardian
Time Untime
Styxx
Son of No One
Dragonbane
Dragonmark

The Dark-Hunter Companion

Dark Bites

Also by Sherrilyn Kenyon:
League Series

Born of Night
Born of Fire
Born of Ice
Born of Shadows
Born of Silence
Born of Fury
Born of Defiance
Born of Betrayal
Born of Legend

The Belador Code

Blood Trinity
Alterant
The Curse
Rise of the Gryphon

Chronicles of Nick

Infinity
Invincible
Infamous
Inferno
Illusion
Instinct
Invision

By Sherrilyn Kenyon writing as Kinley MacGregor: Lords of Avalon Series

Sword of Darkness
Knight of Darkness

BORN OF DEFIANCE

SHERRILYN KENYON

PIATKUS

First published in the US in 2015 by St Martin's Press, New York
First published in Great Britain in 2015 by Piatkus
This paperback edition published in 2016 by Piatkus

1 3 5 7 9 10 8 6 4 2

A CIP catalogue record for this book is available from the British Library.

ISBN 978-0-349-40276-5

Printed and bound by CPI Group (UK) Ltd, Croydon, CR0 4YY

Papers used by Piatkus are from well-managed forests and other responsible sources.

MIX
Paper from responsible sources
FSC® C104740

Piatkus
An imprint of
Little, Brown Book Group
Carmelite House
50 Victoria Embankment
London EC4Y 0DZ

An Hachette UK Company
www.hachette.co.uk

www.piatkus.co.uk

To the world's best fans! Thank you all for taking these trips with me into so many worlds and realms. To my family and friends for their hours of fun and for putting up with me during those hours when I'm a mindless zombie while lost on deadline. And as always, to Robert, the best agent ever! And to Monique and my entire SMP team and all the tireless hours you put into every book. Thank you so much! I love and appreciate all of you!

BORN OF DEFIANCE

PROLOGUE

"You can't win against Vested, mongrel dog. You might as well go home to your mum and cry like the little bitch you are."

Talyn Batur barely caught the nasty retort that scalded his tongue. Then wondered why he bothered, since both he and Duel Odelus were fighting to kill each other, anyway.

Yeah, okay. I'm an idiot.

Just not a rude one.

Duel punched and kicked like lightning.

Moving as if he lacked bones *and* a spine, Talyn dodged and ducked, then delivered a staggering blow to Duel's ribs. Duel stumbled back. Talyn scissor-kicked, turned, and hammered his famous double punch into Duel's face and a head butt to his forehead.

Stunned, Duel reached for him.

By the methodical, sluggish way his opponent reacted now, Talyn knew it was time to finish it.

"Kiss my mongrel ass, Vested," Talyn growled, then swept Duel's feet out from under him and pinned him to the bloody mat.

Within a few heartbeats, the victory alarm rang, and was quickly drowned out by the thunderous sounds of those cheering his win, as well as those damning him to hell for it.

The ref pulled Talyn up by his arm to present him to the crowd.

"Undisputed! Undefeated! *Unbelievable!* The new Zoftiq Vested Champion of 8560! The Iron Hammer! Talyn Batur!"

Drunk on adrenaline and victory, Talyn struck his chest and glared defiantly at the arena that was packed with screaming fans as he fought down the raw bloodlust that was pounding through his entire being. A bloodlust that still wasn't nearly appeased. Over sixty thousand Andarions were here tonight to watch him bleed—and that didn't even begin to count the tens of millions who were watching from home. Some betting that he'd win.

More hoping his opponent would gut him in the goriest way imaginable.

But as his breathing calmed and the pain of his match set in, one reality hit him even harder than the blows of his felled opponent.

Out of all these tens of thousands who surrounded him, not a single one was here for him, personally. While those who were rejoicing his victory would go home to celebrate tonight, he'd take his shower, change clothes, and return to his spartan military barracks. Alone.

Tomorrow, he'd get up and go to work, like any other day.

The unconscious Vested bastard at his feet was right. In all the universe, Talyn only had one person to tell about his win.

His own mother.

How pathetic and worthless was *that* reality?

I really need a life.

Since his mother was off on a summit meeting with the Andarion tadara and under strict comm silence, he'd have to wait until tomorrow night to do even that much. And he knew she wasn't watching or listening to the event. She never did. It wasn't that she didn't care. She just didn't want to know about his fights until she was sure he was still alive, and not lying dead on the Ring floor.

End of the day, Talyn Batur—*the* celebrated athlete of his entire generation—had no one, in this massive arena packed to capacity with Andarions and aliens, who gave a single shit about him, except his manager and his trainer.

It was something he'd lived with and accepted the whole of his life, but never had it burned more than it did right now as he looked out at the thronging mass of Andarions who were here with friends and females. Two things, because of their stringent bloodline laws, he'd never known, and would never have.

The ref finally released his arm as they dropped the barricaded cage walls and carried his opponent away on an air stretcher. They were both bleeding profusely from the wounds they'd given each other over the last three and a half hours. While Duel Odelus had done his best to kill him, Talyn had only fought to win.

That had always been his priority. Screw the carnage. He wanted victory.

Respect.

Most of all, he just wanted to get laid.

Well, not right now, because he could barely move. But once his mobility was restored, it'd be nice to have a female kiss his boo-boos for once.

Wiping the blood and sweat from his brow with his forearm, he returned to his side of the Ring where his manager and trainer waited to congratulate him. Their words were meaningless. He hadn't gone into fighting for the praise.

Only to advance his military rank as fast as possible, and to keep his ass out of trouble.

He fought because it was all he knew. All he was good at.

The sole thing that gave him any real pleasure. Because *here,* in this Ring, he could unleash the pent-up fury he was forced to bite back whenever he stood on the other side of those cage barriers.

Talyn took the towel from his trainer's hand and dodged the reporters as he made his way through them to his dressing room. He'd let Erix deal with them. His trainer lived for this shit. Talyn would rather have his head split open than skillfully bypass the questions he didn't want to answer, from Andarions he couldn't stand. Andarions who didn't think he was fit to breathe their air.

His manager, Erix, was in his glory as he went from post-fight interview to interview, bragging about his skills in training Talyn over the years.

Yeah, right . . .

More correctly, it was Talyn's fists and willingness to stupidly open a vein, either his or someone else's, whenever he was under attack.

Pulling the bloody mask from his face and fang-guard from his mouth, Talyn passed the security agents and headed to his locker room. Unlike Duel's finery, his was a shithole. The barebones, barely furnished back room that was provided for mongrel dogs to shower and dress in. No frills. Utterly hideous.

Just like him.

Ferrick, a grumpy, potbellied, middle-aged Andarion who barely reached Talyn's shoulders, joined him in the dressing room. He was grinning so wide, his fangs were exposed and his white eyes gleamed with delight. "Next time, kid, I need you to kill your opponent. We're talking major bonus payout. We'd be rich."

Talyn snorted. "*You'd* be rich."

"Yeah, okay, I'd be rich. But I have four daughters in university with upcoming unification ceremonies. You've got to help me. Next fight, rip out the trachea and beat your opponent with it. I can get some serious mileage from that. And credits out my ass."

Reaching for his towel, Talyn raked him with an amused stare. "How about I make your wife a rich widow instead?"

Ferrick laughed. "That threat would hold more impact if I didn't know how much you hate dealing with others, and there's no way in Coreła's thorny hell you'd ever set your own fights. Or deal with the media."

"I'm not sure *I'd* bet *my* life on that . . . were I you." Talyn headed for the showers.

"Think about it, kid! Just one death. One! Slow and painful is better, but at this point, I'd take a quick, painless one."

Shaking his head, Talyn turned the shower on, and washed off his mask first. After Ferrick left to deal with reporters, he undressed, shoved his shoes and dirty shorts into his duffel, and showered. There was no maid service or attendant on the lower side of the Ring. Everything was self-serve. Which was fine by him. Like Ferrick had said, he preferred solitude to bullshit company.

Or worse, sycophants to his face, assholes at his back.

The water stung against his wounds and bruises. But he was used to that, too.

He'd just finished showering when his military armband went off to let him know that he was due back for check-in. Picking up his jacket, he paused to finger his major's stars on the epaulette, and the honors and medals he'd won over the last four years. Tomorrow, he'd put in for rank advancement. With a win like this, and given his service record, it should be guaranteed.

If he were a fully Vested Andarion, there would be no doubt.

Four weeks ago, it would have been a damn good probability, too. But that was before Colonel Chrisen Anatole had been transferred in as his CO.

Now . . .

His comm link buzzed with the special armada tone.

Talyn put it in his ear and answered as he finished dressing. "Major Batur."

"Major? Where are you?" the lieutenant snarled in the snottiest of tones.

Again, fury rose high as Talyn bit back a nasty set-down. A Vested officer would be able to verbally slap the lower-ranking lieutenant. If he tried that, *he'd* be put on report. It wasn't his place to question or correct his so-called betters. "On my way back to post."

"You missed your check-in."

Talyn choked. "Not possible. My band just went off. I have leave until midnight."

"No, sir. You don't. Check your orders."

Talyn pulled them up on his link, then cursed. "I reviewed them before I left. My curfew was midnight." He ground his teeth as he saw that Anatole had reset his time *after* his fight had started, knowing there was no way Talyn could see it until he violated it.

"Regardless, you are now AWOL. Report to Provost on your return."

"Will do." Talyn hung up and gathered his gear. So much for celebrating. Violating check-in wasn't something the Andarion military took lightly. It was one of their strictest policies and held some of the worst punishments for anyone dumb enough to do it.

His rage mounting, he limped his way to a public transport and got in. He swiped his military ID and sat back while it drove him back to base.

Trying to keep his thoughts off what was waiting for him and the boiling anger over the injustice of it all, he watched the small monitor, and listened to the media commentator reviewing the night's fight results.

"Talyn Batur is not only the youngest to ever win the title, but is *the* first Andarion in Ring history to take the Zoftiq title in both the Open *and* Vested leagues. We know the Iron Hammer is celebrating his unprecedented and historic victory tonight. Sources say that he was spotted in his dressing room with a number of beautiful females, all vying for the Hammer's attention. And I'm sure he's giving it to them, even as I report this."

He snorted derisively at the announcer who continued to cover the fight highlights.

Wish I lived the life they think I do. . . .

Honestly, Talyn felt just like he had the very first time he'd ever fought a match. Sick to his stomach. Aching. Tired. Wrung completely out. He'd won that night, too. Only there'd been no reporters to cover it. Rather, he'd walked home afterward, in the rain, to an empty, run-down apartment, and made himself a can of soup. Done his homework and tucked himself into bed before his mother came home and saw the bruises on his face that would have forced him to lie to her about what had caused them.

She'd have reamed him solid for daring to fight at that age. For that matter, she reamed him now after every match for being stupid enough to step into the Splatterdome. She couldn't stand to see him hurt.

If only he had a choice about it.

"Nothing ever changes," he breathed. Yet as he looked out at the Andarions on the street, he wanted it to.

Desperately.

All his life, he'd played by the rules. Done what he was supposed to, and got his teeth kicked in by everyone around him. Literally and figuratively.

He was done with it.

I just want to be normal. To have what other Andarions took for granted. Anonymity. Family.

A welcoming female in his bed.

Equitable job opportunity.

But those were all elusive bitches, who teased him to the brink of insanity.

Sighing, Talyn glanced down at his reset orders and wanted to give Ferrick the fatality fight he craved.

From the moment the royal-blooded Anatole had laid eyes on him, the colonel had hated Talyn for his lack-Vest caste. Like most everyone else Talyn had ever met, the bastard didn't even try to hide it. He went for Talyn's jugular with psychotic glee, as if it was his divine right to punish Talyn for only having a single maternal family bloodline.

Let it go.

Yet truthfully, he was tired of doing that, too. At this point, he was craving blood to a dangerous level.

Pulling out his link and needing a distraction from thoughts that were bound to get him arrested, he started gathering information on his next fight opponent.

Channel it, dumbass. That was what he was best at. While his mother might hate what he'd chosen to do with his life, fighting kept him semi-leashed and sane.

Most days, anyway.

Narrowing his eyes, he made himself pay attention to the words on his link. He was on the fighter stats page when an annoying ad popped up. As usual, he moved to close it. Until his gaze fell to the gentle face of an angel who seemed to be smiling for him, personally. While she wasn't the most beautiful female he'd ever seen, there was something about her that called out to him. A soft, kind heart that was lacking in most.

Damn, she was . . .

Sweet. The kind of female who made a home worth fighting for. The kind who could lift a male's spirits . . . along with a number of other things.

Time for change, Talyn. Time to take something for yourself.

He'd just won the biggest fight of his career. Had claimed a title very few ever did. Had done what no other Andarion had *ever* done . . . he'd won it in both leagues.

Vested *and* Open.

Just shy of his twentieth birthday.

Now, it was time he fought for the one thing that mattered most.

His life.

I'm not a mongrel dog. And he was done with being treated like one.

CHAPTER 1

Felicia Orfanos hesitated as she caught sight of the massive male who waited for her in the small, dimly lit room. A full seven feet in height, he was ripped like a bodybuilder—with a *massive,* muscled build. She'd never been this close to anyone with a physique like his.

Holy gods . . .

Strange, he'd seemed chunky in the photo he'd submitted with his application. But there was nothing *over*weight about him.

Nor did he appear shy or bashful. Never mind socially awkward. Things he'd been dubbed by the answers he'd provided on their required questionnaire.

"Fierce" and "terrifying" were the only two adjectives that came to her mind as she swept her gaze over his confident male stance. He had all his weight on his left leg, and his muscled arms crossed over his chest as he stared at the wall with a stern expression that was absolutely chilling.

Lethal.

Even though he was dressed in black street clothes, it was a warrior's pose. His black hair was a mass of tiny braids he wore back from his face, letting her know that at his age, with *that* hairstyle, he was still in the military. Another thing that hadn't been disclosed in the file her agency had given her.

Not that it really mattered. Obligatory military service was required of all fully Vested Andarion males and females upon graduation from primary school or university. Given that he was here to buy her services at his age, he must come from some seriously high-caste parents. And he must have gone straight into the military instead of university upon his graduation.

He turned slightly as if sensing her presence. The moment his white eyes focused on her hooded form, she felt a small electrical charge rush over her.

Gracious. He was gorgeous! Granted, all Andarions were, but he was exceptionally handsome and well built. Every inch of that light caramel skin begged for a bite.

And his entire demeanor changed instantly as he realized she was the one he'd come to meet. Now, he looked like the bashful, unsure male their personality evaluation had proclaimed him.

Something that made her smile. How could he be made nervous by *her* when he was the only thing threatening in this room? He even dwarfed the security guard, who eyed him with obvious fear and respect for his gargantuan size. Yet this male reminded her of a skittish schoolboy at his first boy-girl dance.

"Felicia," the broker said as he stepped forward to greet her. "Meet your prospective patron."

With a deep breath for courage, she lowered her hood and smiled at him.

Talyn felt his throat go dry instantly as her wealth of dark brown curls sprang out from the cloth to frame an adorable oval face. She was even more beautiful than she'd been in the pictures he'd seen. And a lot more petite than he'd expected. She barely reached the middle of his chest. While she was athletic in build, her limbs were so thin compared to his, they appeared frail. So much so, he was afraid to touch her lest he accidentally break something. And just like in her photos, her silvery-white eyes gleamed with kindness and warmth.

Biting his lip, he glanced to the guard and broker, wishing they'd leave them alone. But because she was an unwed virgin, there was no chance of that.

"Would you care to sit?" Talyn asked her respectfully.

"Sure. Thank you."

He pulled a chair out for her. She moved with the fluid grace of a dancer. Her every gesture was a thing of absolute beauty. Sitting across from her, he tried to think of something witty to say.

Nothing came to mind.

Just don't drool on yourself. That was all he'd need to make her run screaming for the door.

She glanced about nervously before she spoke. "So what exactly are your terms? I know you wrote that my duties would be light, but can you elaborate?"

He felt heat creep over his face as she got right down to business and he cringed at having to explain it in front of witnesses who already knew he was desperate. Otherwise, no male his age would be here, dealing with *them*. Or be willing to pay the exorbitant fees they demanded.

Because of his lack-Vest, bastard status, they were gouging the shit out of him, and he had no choice except to take it in whatever orifice they dictated. But there was nothing he could do.

Not if he wanted Felicia.

And that he definitely did. She was so much more than he'd ever hoped to find. Honestly, he was still stunned and humbled that she'd agreed to meet with him, given his questionable lineage.

Clearing his throat, he kept his gaze on her sweet face, and forced himself to ignore the condescension and censure of her broker. "I only have two nights a week free. And only for three to four hours each, not counting the hour it takes to get from my barracks to the condo. So you'd only have to be with me three hours at most on those two nights." Which probably delighted her to no end. Most patrons required a lot more of their companions.

Uncomfortable, Talyn rubbed at his neck. "I . . . um . . . I have a curfew to meet so there wouldn't be any overnight visitations, unless I'm at liberty. Which is just once a year, and only for a week. I've already had this year's liberty so you don't have to worry about that for another twelve months. Even then, it's negotiable. I know you're still at university and need your days free to attend classes, and most nights to study. I'm good with all that."

Felicia frowned at what he was telling her. Was he serious? This was more than she'd ever dare to dream. "That's really it?"

He nodded.

She couldn't quite wrap her head around her good fortune. Something bad had to be wrong with him.

One possible flaw definitely came to mind.

"And how . . ." She cringed at the thought of what she needed to ask. But she knew from her mother, and other companions and instructors that she had to ask it before she consented to him. It was the primary concern all females in her profession had. One that maimed and killed a good 10 percent of them a year, and it would explain why such an eligible male was here, looking for one of her ilk and not negotiating for a noble wife.

With a deep breath, she forced the embarrassing question out. "How kinky and violent are you during sex?"

He actually turned bright red. "I would *never* harm a female off a battlefield, and even then, I wouldn't do so unless she was armed and after me. Nor would I ask you to do anything that makes you uncomfortable, in *any* way. We can leave all the details of *that* up to you."

"Really?"

Visibly cringing, he nodded.

She sat forward and tried to figure out if he was lying to her. This was really too good to be true. And it wasn't uncommon for males to lie to get what they wanted. She knew a number of females who'd gotten themselves into scary situations with males who'd seemed sincere and decent, only to find out, too late, they weren't. "I honestly have to say that I'm a little confused. If that's all you want, it would be significantly cheaper for you to visit a house of assignation than contract with me."

He bristled. "I have more than enough money to pay your contract fees, tuition, and upkeep. Believe me. Your broker has crawled my ass and accounts with a subatomic scope."

"I didn't mean to insult you," she said quickly. "I just don't understand why you'd ask for so little, given the high cost." And given how handsome and young he was. To hell with their stringent blood laws. What female wouldn't do him for free?

Contract or no contract.

This was one male worth a jail sentence.

He glanced to her broker before he spoke. "I want a companion, not a prostitute."

She was still baffled by this. If that was what he wanted, why not contract for marriage?

But that was none of her business. He was absolutely gorgeous and polite. Sweet, even. She couldn't have asked for a better patron. And he was definitely better than the last male who'd tried to contract her.

You can't do any better than this, girl. You know that. This was the kind of male most females prayed to marry. To have one as patron . . .

Unheard of.

"Very well, then." Felicia swallowed in trepidation of what was next. "Would you like to inspect me?"

She had to bite back a laugh at how bright his cheeks turned this time. She'd never seen anyone blush so profusely. His caramel skin practically glowed.

And to think, *she* was the virgin in the room.

Once again, he glanced over to the guard and the broker, then shook his head. "I wouldn't do that to you in front of them. I've already seen your photos, and that's not the most important thing to me, anyway."

"May I ask what is?"

"That you were as kind and gentle in person as you seemed to be by your profile answers and photos."

Her heart swelled at his bashful answer.

She reached across the table and touched his hand before she offered him a smile. "Should we try a standard six-month trial?"

He finally returned her smile. "I should like that. How long do you need to move in?"

"When would you like for me to start?"

"It's entirely up to you. I have a fully furnished condo within walking distance of your school, as your contract stipulated. All I need to do is have you added to the security and paperwork. Everything for the condo is billed directly to me. You won't have to worry about anything."

He was so unexpected. So preciously sweet.

She only hoped he stayed this way.

Please don't be a lie. She'd had enough of lying bastards in her life.

"Day after tomorrow, then?"

He nodded.

Her broker stepped forward with his e-tablet. "Excellent. I have the papers already drawn up. Read over it and sign them. I'll post them immediately, and the two of you can be about your business."

Still a little nervous, Felicia was stunned that her patron hadn't tried to negotiate anything. Rather, he'd agreed to every term she'd wanted. Right down to giving her all daylight hours so that she could continue with school . . . and a weekly maid service.

He hadn't even balked at providing her with a place to live near her school—which was some of the priciest real estate in Eris. A small studio apartment was over four thousand credits a month. For that matter, she couldn't even afford to live in the university dorms. They were almost as much. All the other patrons she'd considered had flat-out denied that request.

She signed the contract and waited for him to finish reading through it.

Once he signed it, he handed her a small card. "That's the address to the condo, and the number for my link. If you'll give me two hours' notice, I can meet you there, and make sure that you get in without any problems. Security's really tight for the building so you'll be very safe there, alone. The downside is that even if I tell them you're coming, they might not let you in without me there to verify your identity, and sign the paperwork to have you added to my lease as a licensed cohabitator."

That was a nice bonus. In truth, she'd been a little afraid of living alone. Eris was a major city, with over ten million

Andarions living in it. As much as authorities liked to deny it, it wasn't uncommon for lone females to fall prey to vicious predators. It was the primary reason she'd wanted a short commute to school. "Then I'll see you in two days."

"Two days," he repeated before he stood. "I shall look forward to it."

As he started for the door, she rose. "Um, may I ask one thing before you leave?"

"Sure."

"What's your name?"

He gave her a shy smile. "Talyn."

What a beautiful, proper name. It suited him. "Thank you, Talyn."

Inclining his head, he took his leave.

Stunned by it all, Felicia couldn't believe that she'd been lucky enough to find a patron so young and handsome. One who didn't seem to want to treat her like his property, and demand that she serve his every perverted whim.

Unlike the last revolting beast who'd almost assaulted her in front of her broker and guard. If not for them, she'd have been raped in this very room.

You know you can't trust him. Males lie. Her mother had beaten that into her head from birth.

And yet, Talyn seemed honest.

They all seem like that, daughter. Until they rip out your heart and feast upon it.

She refused to allow her mother's poison to infect her.

Glancing down at the card in her hand, she frowned as she finally saw the address of her new home. With a gape, she looked to her broker. "Is this correct?"

"Brooksyn?"

She nodded.

"Then, yes. That's the address we verified. He owns the entire top floor of the building. It's a twenty-room flat, with an indoor pool and fully functional gym."

Felicia was aghast at that. "Twenty rooms?" Seriously?

"Yes. It's positively palatial."

Especially in Eris. No one had homes that big, as a rule. Except royalty.

Or a mighty War Hauk.

"And he doesn't live there full time?"

"No. He's an officer in the armada. They require him to live in the barracks. He has a strict curfew and if he misses too many, they'll strip his rank."

"And what rank does he hold?" Deputy commander?

"Major."

That only confused her more. While majors made fairly good pay, they didn't make enough to afford a twenty-room condo by her school.

He must be royal-blooded. That was the only logical explanation.

"Has he a wife?"

Herun shook his head. "Nor is he pledged to any female. We screened him thoroughly."

Her head spun at the news. "What's wrong with him, then?"

"He has no paternal lineage, whatsoever. He's the bastard

son of an Outcast. No one on his father's side would even adopt him."

Ouch. No wonder Talyn was willing to pay so much for a companion. There was no other legal way for him to have an Andarion female as part of his life. And to pair himself with an alien female would lower his caste even more.

Which, given how low it already was, would be quite a feat.

It wouldn't matter how high his rank or how pure his mother's bloodline. No family would contract their daughter to a male without *some* paternal lineage. Especially not one whose father was such an Outcast that no one else in his entire family would adopt his son to protect him.

Just what crime had his father committed for his shame to taint his son so thoroughly?

A bastard herself, she knew exactly how harshly Andarions treated children like them. But at least she knew her father's lineage and he allowed her to count it, even though her parents had never married. While being a half-Vest limited what choices and careers she had open to her, it was nowhere near as bad as being a solid lack-Vest.

Not to mention, she was female and that automatically put her in a better caste than his, since maternal lineages were the higher valued in Andarion society.

Her heart aching for him, she lifted her cowl and returned to her small cell that had been her home since she'd begun her companion training.

She glanced around the small, spartan room.

While her mother hadn't been thrilled with her choice to

do this, she'd understood that it was the only way Felicia could go to her expensive university without crawling to her father for the money.

Or marrying into a family with a matriarch who'd treat her and her mother like sub-sentient creatures—because Felicia was bastard-born.

Her mother had kindly offered to take out loans for her. But Felicia had refused. Her mother's health had been ailing these last few years, and she didn't want to stress her mother any more. Nor force her mother into the indignity of being scrutinized by a loaner or marriage broker. Her mother had suffered enough indignities in her life.

Indignities Felicia hadn't fully comprehended until her own training had given her a whole new respect for what her mother had been put through because of her father.

Her mother must have been out of her mind as a young Andarion.

Felicia still cringed every time she remembered the humiliating inspection and certification process her agency had insisted on before they'd even list her profile on their site. It'd been a solid year before they'd offered her up for "adoption."

As bad as her training had been, it was nothing compared to the rude, insufferable males she'd interviewed with, who'd wanted a young companion they could parade around like some show dog on a leash.

Worse, her time to pick a patron had been running out. Had Talyn waited one more day to call for a meeting, she'd have been forced to accept Lord Arux's offer. She cringed at the mere thought. He'd refused 80 percent of her requests and had been completely unreasonable and offensively rude.

Grateful it hadn't come to that, she swept her gaze around her meager belongings. Two days? It wouldn't take her two hours to pack her things.

But in two days, everything about her life would change.

Everything.

She shivered as that reality went through her. The only thing of value she owned was her virginity. Once it was gone, so was any negotiating power she currently had.

Closing her eyes, she prayed that she'd made the right decision. If Talyn was lying to her, she would be no better off than her mother had been.

Yes, she had a six-month probation period with him. But once they slept together, she'd be downgraded to a used whore.

And since he had no paternal bloodline or social standing, she wouldn't even be able to use that as a way of upping her value.

She would be ruined in the eyes of their society.

God, what have I done?

"So . . . did you turn him down or agree to adoption?"

Felicia turned at the sound of Glycie's voice in her doorway. Tall, well stacked, and gorgeous, Glycie always made her feel like an ugly slug in comparison. They'd gone through several classes together, and had both been listed for adoption on the same day. While Felicia had had a few interviews since being listed, Glycie had a staggering amount of males to choose from. So many that the agency had given her extra time to pick the richest one, with the best offer.

"I signed."

Glycie gasped, then hugged Felicia while giggling with excitement. "Oh, congratulations, sweetie! How was he?"

"Respectful and young."

Eyes wide, Glycie shouted the good news down the hallway for the others to hear. It was something they always did whenever a companion was adopted by a patron.

Fresca tsked as she came into the room with a slow, sauntering walk. While she was every bit as beautiful as Glycie, she was an utter condescending bitch.

To everyone.

Rumors said that it was what kept her from being in the top tier of companion prospects . . . which only made her all the more bitter and biting. "Please tell me you didn't contract with the animal that just left here."

Felicia frowned at her hostility. "Why would you say that about him?"

Rolling her eyes, she stared at Felicia as if she was mentally defective. "Even *you* can't be so stupid as to not know whom *he* is."

Insulted by her snide tone, Felicia stiffened. "He's a major in the armada."

"And he's been the Open league Zoftiq champ for years now. He's killed I don't know how many males in the Ring. Brutally." Her white eyes turned even darker and angrier.

"When they allowed that ruthless bastard to fight in the Vested league, which they should have never done, he left my cousin with a permanent limp, limited use of his arm, and almost killed him. My cousin said he was like a rabid dog, unleashed. All the years he's fought, he's never seen a worse animal. There's no fighter more feared in the Ring than Talyn Batur. And you signed with him? Are you insane?"

"She's right," Rynara agreed as she joined them. "I was his first choice for companion, but I wouldn't even meet with him. Turned him down flat as soon as I saw his name. Last thing I want is to be in a room with someone so violent and cold-blooded. Never mind at his complete and utter mercy. Just the thought of it gives me chills." She shivered to further illustrate her point.

Fresca nodded in agreement. "I've heard he's so huge in size that he's split some of his past lovers in half. Left several unable to bear children."

"I heard he's been banned from most whorehouses for acts of perverted violence." Rynara patted Felicia on the arm. "You poor thing. You should have done more research on him before you accepted."

With sympathetic fear in her eyes, Glycie bit her lip. "Maybe you can get out of it?"

"I already signed." Felicia's breathing turned ragged as they went on and on listing Talyn's flaws.

What have I done?

If one-quarter of what they said was true, she'd be maimed in a week.

Or dead.

Sick to her stomach, she tried to think of some way to end this.

Excusing herself, she went to her broker. He was in his office, at his computer, with a gleeful smirk on his face. "Herun?"

He looked up with an arched brow. "Did you lose the address already?"

"No . . . um . . ." Felicia hesitated. "Have you posted the forms already?"

"Of course. I told you I would."

"Can we rescind them?"

His other eyebrow shot up. "Why would you want to do that?"

"I just learned some things about the major that I didn't know before."

Sighing, he shook his head. "It's done. Honestly, I don't know how you can complain. No one else would pay so much for *you* or be so accommodating to your outrageous demands. It's not like you're the prettiest companion here. You barely made the second tier of our offerings. For that matter, I was worried we'd ever recoup the money we spent for your training. Instead of complaining, you should be damn grateful he's delusional about *your* questionable status, and willing to overlook it."

Heat stung her cheeks at his needless and cruel reminders.

Herun turned away from her. "Now, if you don't mind, I have other contracts to draft."

Mortified and humiliated, she wanted something smart to say back to him. But the truth he spoke cut her to the bone.

She couldn't think of anything other than the fact that Herun was right.

No one else had wanted her.

"You're too short. Too muscled. And look at this frizzy mop of hair. . . . I don't know how we'll make you presentable to anyone." She could still see the sneer on the image consultant's face as she reviewed Felicia's "attributes." The only reason they hadn't cut her hair was the fear that it would be even messier with a shorter style.

Completely heartbroken, she headed back to her room and cursed herself with every step. *What have I done?*

Consigned herself to hell.

She was her mother's daughter, after all. Taken in by a handsome liar. She'd seen what she wanted in him, and hadn't done enough research.

Now, she would pay for it. And if the others were to be believed, she'd pay with her life.

CHAPTER 2

Nervous and afraid, Felicia cringed at the sneer on the doorman's face as he stood in the elegant, ornate doorway, blocking her from entering the posh building. Maybe she should have worn something other than old shorts and a light, thin shirt. . . .

Since she was moving, she hadn't thought anything about it, but now she wished she had.

Not like I'm nervous enough about being here. After her friends had left her with their dire predictions on how long she'd live before her patron killed her in bed with his enormity, or outside of it with his cruelty, she'd spent hours researching Talyn Batur.

There was a *lot* written about him. None of it particularly good or personal. And nothing about his military record. In fact, she couldn't find any confirmation of his military service at all. Rather the articles she'd read only went into his bloodthirsty fighting skills in the Open Ring. She'd seen countless photos of him bloody and thrilled after a fight. It was like he had a sick sense of glee from the brutality of it all.

Which did nothing to allay her terror.

Every article and broadcast she'd come across confirmed the cold-blooded ferocity Fresca and Rynara had accused him of. He took pity on no one. He was savage and ruthless. Fierce and terrifying. Unstoppable. Invincible. When he entered the Ring, he dominated it.

And no opponent walked out on two legs.

While she couldn't find anything that said he'd actually killed anyone during a fight, all experts agreed that the Iron Hammer was the most feared and ferocious Andarion to ever enter the Splatterdome.

And he was the first to truly own the brutal blood sport.

Since everything she'd found had only scared her more, and her agency refused to allow her to back out of the contract, she'd finally stopped reading before she panicked and did something stupid.

Like leave the planet forever.

Swallowing hard, she met the doorman's glare.

"Can I help you?" Could there be any more disdain in his tone?

"I . . . um . . . I'm supposed to be moving in here today."

The look he raked over her body called her a liar. "Are you with your parents?"

She wanted to jump into a hole and vanish forever.

"Felicia?"

Standing up on her tiptoes, she looked past the doorman's

shoulder to see Talyn, who must have been waiting for her in the lobby. Dressed in his major's red and black formal attire, he was breathtaking. A strange warmth flooded her at the sight of him, even though she was more afraid of him than she was the rude doorman. "Hi."

And that one word totally changed the doorman's demeanor toward her. "Here, *mu tara*. Allow me to help you."

"It's all right, Starrin. I've got it." Talyn took the box from her hands. He glanced out toward the street. "Where's the rest of your things?"

Now it was her turn to blush. "This is everything I have."

Instead of judging her, he smiled kindly. Something that was completely at odds with the horror stories Fresca and Rynara had filled her with.

"Then let me take your pack and I'll show you upstairs." He gently pulled her rucksack from her shoulders and led her past a long, shiny desk of tough-looking security guards. Each of them eyed her as if they were committing her features to memory.

A huge burly male approached them. "Is this our new tenant? Tara Orfanos?" he asked Talyn.

"It is."

She felt a rush of delight at the respect in his tone. Something she definitely wasn't used to or expecting. Most tended to treat her like the doorman had on her arrival. Because she was very small and woefully shy for an Andarion female, it invited others to push her around and treat her like a child.

"Excellent. I'll make sure everyone is familiar with her." He smiled. "Welcome to the building, Tara Orfanos. If you need anything at all, my name is Aaron. I live here on the ground floor and am head of security." He inclined his head to Talyn. "I've already assured Major Batur that I will personally see to your safety, as he was quite adamant that no harm befall you, lest he make our future mobility quite impossible and painful. While I'm not as ferocious as the major, I am quite accomplished at my job, and will make sure no one bothers you."

Felicia smiled at the male even though his words did nothing to lessen the fearful knot in her stomach. "Thank you, Aaron."

He opened the elevator doors for them. "Good afternoon, *mu tara*. Welcome to your new home. I know you'll be happy here, and if you're not, let us know and we'll make sure that you are."

Felicia bit her lip at his kindness. "Thank you, again."

Talyn pulled a shiny black card out of his pocket. "You'll have to swipe the card to reach our floor." He showed her how then handed it to her. "After the swipe, it requires a hand scan." He pressed his hand to the panel. It lit up before the elevator moved.

"So you don't press a button for the floor?"

"No. It knows where you live by the handprint. As soon as you're squared away, I'll call the manager and he'll get you entered into the system. Whenever you have visitors, you'll have to notify security. Then you can either meet them in the lobby, or security will escort them up. But only if you're home. If you're not, they'll have to wait for you in the lobby. Like I said, the security here is very serious about the safety of their tenants."

She glanced up at the camera in the corner. Not to mention the hand-carved mahogany wood and gilded ceiling. "This is much nicer than anything I expected. Thank you for letting me live here."

He shifted the box in his hands. "No problem. Since I can't visit very often, I wanted to make sure you were completely safe. I, um, I don't know if you cook or not, but I had them stock the kitchen for you, just in case. There's a grocery across the street and I worked it out with the manager to deliver anything you need or want. All you have to do is call them with your order and they'll bring it over. Or if you pick it out, they'll deliver it and charge my account. There's also a deli and full restaurant on the first floor of the building, and a small convenience store that's open twenty-four hours, even on holidays. Just charge the condo and it'll go to my monthly bill."

She gaped at his thoughtfulness that belied the ruthlessness she knew him capable of. Surely a beast wouldn't go to this amount of trouble for a paid companion. Would he?

For that matter, her own father and brothers wouldn't go to this length for any of the females in their lives. Especially *her*. They barely acknowledged she was a member of their family, and then, only when required by law.

"Likewise, I don't know if you drive or not, but there's a transport for you in the parking garage. The number for it corresponds with the condo address. It's yours, too. If you can't drive or don't want to, I have the number for a chauffeur service and they'll be more than happy to provide a driver for you. Also a protective detail should you have to study late at school. They just need a twenty-minute heads up to get someone to you. I'd prefer you use their service than take any chances with your safety."

Stunned, she couldn't think as the door opened into a bright, elegant hallway.

No, not hallway.

Foyer.

Holy crap . . . was this really her new home? Eyes wide, she stared in awe of the palatial estate.

Talyn led her into the condo that was finer than anything she'd ever seen in her entire life. Seriously. It even made her father's expensive home look like a dump.

And it was huge! Open and airy, it had a breathtaking view of the city. The furniture was elegant and *high* end. Leather sofa, fully vided wall. Rich, hand-carved tables and expensive vases and flowers. Marbled floor, mahogany paneling, and a gilded tray ceiling.

She half expected some snotty female to come out and yell at her to wipe her feet.

Or leave before she tainted it.

Talyn smiled as he saw her gaze dancing around in appreciation. The sheer joy on her face was worth every precious credit the place had cost him. The last thing he'd wanted was for her to regret choosing him as her patron when she could have chosen anyone—even an aristo.

He set the box down on the dining room table and placed her rucksack beside it. "This is *your* home, Felicia. You can have friends over whenever you like. I only ask that you keep our time for us. I'm not real big on company. Ever. No one should bother you, looking for me. If the media does track me down here, tell them to contact my manager, and if they don't go away, report them to Aaron and he'll take care of them."

She frowned at him. "The media?"

He felt heat creep over his face. "Yeah. They want interviews sometimes. Ferrick handles all of that."

Before she could ask him for more details, he picked up the intercom and contacted the manager to come up and add her to the system.

His bracelet buzzed.

She frowned at the pulsing noise. "What's that?"

He held his arm up to show her the black band on his left wrist. "My military tracker. It's letting me know that my lunch time is almost up, and I have to leave in order to get back to my post for check-in. Otherwise, I'm AWOL, and that's highly unpleasant."

"Oh." The sudden sadness in her eyes touched him a lot more than it should have.

He picked up the link from the counter and handed it to her. "My personal number is already programmed in, under three. If you need anything, day or night, call me or Aaron. He's number four. Or you can use the house system. The driver service is five. If I can't answer, leave a message and I'll call or text as soon as I'm able." He headed for the elevator.

"Talyn?"

He paused.

She closed the distance between them. Looking up at him, she gave him the sweetest smile. "Thank you for everything." She stood up on her tiptoes to place her cheek against his.

Talyn swallowed as a wave of desire tore through him and set his blood on fire. It wasn't helped by the sudden image in his mind of her in the small underpants she'd worn for her agency photos. Felicia had the sweetest ass he'd ever seen on any female, and he lived solely for the day he could peel her clothes off and sink himself deep inside her.

The scent of her floral perfume filled his head and set his senses spinning. Worse, her soft riot of curls brushed against his skin, making him so hard that he was sure it would be obvious to anyone who glanced in his general direction. He hungered so much for her that it took everything he had to pull away.

But if he didn't go right now, he wouldn't be able to return to her for weeks. "I'll see you in five days?"

She gave him an adorable pout. "Is that your next liberty?"

He nodded.

"That seems like a long workweek."

She wasn't kidding about that. Prior to Anatole's appearance, his life and schedule had been much easier to manage. Now it sucked to extremes.

"Beauty of the military. They own my sorry ass." He winked at her.

"Five days, then." She pressed a light kiss against his lips that did nothing to settle the heat in his blood.

Hard and aching, he forced himself to leave her, even though all he wanted was to stay with her for a while longer. She would definitely be worth the write-up and punishment.

His breathing ragged, he took one last look at her before he stepped into the elevator to return to work.

Felicia didn't move until Talyn was gone from her sight. An inexplicable pain hit her as she felt his absence like a physical blow. How weird. She barely knew him. Had only met him twice, and not even for a total of half an hour.

But no one had ever been so kind to her. So thoughtful or concerned. He didn't treat her like a paid whore.

He treated her like a treasured wife. Like she mattered to him. Something that was completely at odds with what her friends had told her to expect. And it was definitely not what she'd learned from her research.

Then again, they didn't know him. At all. The reporters were speculating, and none of her friends had ever met Talyn. They were commenting on rumors, too.

You know better than to listen to those.

The heartless monster they'd warned her about wouldn't have gone to *this* length to make her comfortable and safe.

Tears filled her eyes as she looked around the massive condo he'd provided for her. Housing in Eris was *so* expensive, and that included the cheapest sections. Not even in her wildest dreams had she ever allowed herself to envision such a place as her residence. She'd expected something small, hopefully clean, and without vermin.

This . . .

Laughing, she ran through the huge open rooms, amazed at how beautiful they were. How elegant.

Until she came to the master bedroom.

Her jaw went slack at the humongous bed that faced the most

incredible view of the city she'd ever seen. She could even see the outline of her school from here.

The tray ceiling above was trimmed in gold and painted to look like a celestial sky. An ebony ceiling fan was suspended over an ornate, hand-carved platform bed. A matching settee was to the right of an elaborate dresser. But more intriguing than that was a huge bouquet of flowers, and a wrapped present on the bed that had her name on it.

Almost afraid to see what it contained, she approached the flowers first and took the card from the small envelope.

Felicia,

There's a wallet in the dressing room table with charge accounts for your use. If you don't like the decor of the rooms, please let the manager know and they'll redesign the condo for you. Don't hesitate to make it yours. Your happiness, safety, and comfort are my priority.

~T

Her heart pounded at the beautiful, masculine script. No, he wasn't the beast they called him.

Biting her lip, she set the card aside and opened the box to find a beautiful thick bathrobe and slippers. Along with a stuffed lorina.

A lorina with a diamond bracelet attached to its neck. Gasping, she could tell by the workmanship that it was real. And *very* costly.

Her breath caught in her throat. Before she could stop herself, she picked up the link and called Talyn.

"Major Batur."

She savored the rich, deep baritone of his voice. "Talyn?"

There was a brief pause. "Is something wrong?"

She sniffed back her tears at his honest concern for her. "No. I found the presents you left. . . . Thank you."

"My pleasure. I hope you like them."

"They're wonderful. I just wish you were here for me to thank you in person."

"You don't have to do that. I only want you to enjoy them, not feel obligated because of them. They are freely given. . . . Beautiful females deserve beautiful things."

Felicia closed her eyes as she savored those precious words. "You're very sweet."

He snorted. "Don't say that out loud. You'll ruin my ferocious reputation."

Laughing, she shook her head. "Ferocious, huh?"

"Absolutely. How you think I got my rank at this age?"

"Your sexy sweetness?"

His warm laughter filled her ear. "Yeah, sure," he said drily. "That always works for rank advancement. You sweet-talk the enemy. They fall over, laughing at you."

"See. I knew it." She switched on the video feed and waited for him to accept it or deny her request. To her delight, he turned it on. From the looks of it, he was riding an airbike through traffic. All she could see was his helmeted head and the sky over his shoulders, until he lightened the shield on his helmet so that his handsome face was showing through it. "Is there really no way for me to see you sooner than five days?"

"Between training and work, no. They keep a really tight leash on me."

Funny how that was what she'd wanted in a patron, especially after her friends had told her what a beast he was. Now . . . "Can I come visit you at work?"

"This is my normal lunch time. I have an hour and a half for it."

"What about dinner?"

"I only have fifteen to thirty minutes for that."

She pouted at him. "That's not long." Barely enough time to eat anything at all.

"It comes at shift change when I'm on duty, and the married soldiers take precedence over those of us without. The rest of the time, I have to catch something fast at the gym before practice."

"Oh." She tried to imagine what his life was like. To protect his privacy, there hadn't been much on his profile sheet. While the agency saw the full family, psychological, and financial forms he'd submitted, they only gave companions part of the personality portion to evaluate.

She hadn't even known his family name until they signed the contract. "Do you have any brothers or sisters?"

"No. You?"

She bit her lip. "I had three half brothers and two half sisters, but we're not close. It's mostly me and my mother."

"Same here."

That made sense then as to why he was so concerned for her

safety. He must look after his mom like she did hers. "So what does your mother do?" she asked.

"She's a deputy commander for the armada."

Wow, that was impressive. "Your CO?"

"No. I'm a fighter pilot. She works at the palace. Protective detail. I've been trying to get into a command or palace assignment for the last two years, but they keep turning me down."

"Why?"

"I'm a bastard, Felicia," he said simply. "In more ways than one. They don't think I'm worth much, except as Tavali fodder."

"They would be very wrong."

Talyn swallowed hard as those words touched him in a place he hadn't known he had. Kind of felt like a kick to his stomach. Only it hurt worse.

Weird.

He offered her a smile. "I appreciate the vote of confidence." He traced the line of her jaw over the screen on his bike, wishing he could have stayed longer with her. "So what does your mother do?"

"She's a companion trainer."

"Hey," he chided her. "Don't do that."

"Do what?"

"Look ashamed. Ever. You're a beautiful female, Felicia. The most beautiful one I've ever seen. More than that, you have a soul. I don't ever want to see you hold your head down again. You don't apologize to anyone for who and what you are."

Felicia smiled as his words touched her much deeper than they should have. The one thing they'd drilled into her during training was not to fall for her patron. To keep everything professional and on a business level. But it was hard to do that with a male who made her feel like an Andarion princess. "You're not as bashful as you pretend to be, are you?"

"Just around you."

"Why?"

He shrugged. "Not used to conversing with others. Especially young females, unless they're in uniform. Then, we only speak when relaying or issuing orders. I'm not sure what to say to you, really."

She looked away as the doorbell rang.

"That's the manager, I'm sure."

"Oh." She hated to leave him so soon. "Can I have lunch with you tomorrow?"

"Sure. I'd like that. I'll e-mail you the address."

"Okay. I'll see you then." She turned the link off and kissed it, wishing it was him.

Stop it, Felicia! Keep this professional.

He wasn't her boyfriend. Talyn was a patron. He could and would never be anything more than the male who paid for her services. That was it.

Her gaze fell to his card.

Your happiness, safety, and comfort are my priority.

Professional. Always. His happiness and comfort were *her* priority. That was what he was paying her for. And she would keep her heart out of this. No matter what.

• • •

Felicia wasn't sure what she'd been thinking when she'd asked to meet with Talyn for lunch. The fortified Anatole military base was extremely off-putting and a little scary. The guards at the gate had all but strip-searched her before she was admitted here.

And they'd interrogated her like a prisoner of war.

Worse were the number of curious stares she collected as she stood surrounded by three giant guards in the humongous hangar bay of fighters and military transports. She couldn't stand being the center of anyone's attention.

There were pilots and ground crew bustling all around. It wasn't until a red and black fighter landed and she saw Talyn's name on it, above his call sign, Pit Viper, that she realized he'd been out on maneuvers.

Her heart pounded as she watched him climb down from the cockpit of his fighter. His red and black flightsuit and jacket clung to his muscled body. He paused to sign an e-ledger from one of the ground crew before he pulled his helmet off and approached her with an adorably bashful half grin that seemed completely out of character with his lethal persona.

A half grin that turned into a stern countenance as he stopped in front of the soldiers with her. "I'll take it from here."

They saluted him, then left.

"Do I salute you, too?"

He leaned down to press his cheek to hers. "Only if you want to." Pulling back from her, he called one of the crew over to him and handed his helmet to the male. "Could you put that in my locker?"

"Yes, sir." The crewman saluted him.

Talyn returned the salute before he tucked her hand into the crook of his elbow and led her toward the base's entrance. "There's a small deli and Andarion, Ritadarion, and Kirovarian restaurants close by. What would you like?"

She tried not to focus on how taut and large the muscle of his arm was. Dang, he looked simply edible in that flight suit.

Her face flushed as she realized he was waiting for her to answer his question. But what she really wanted to snack on wasn't one of her choices.

She glanced down at his backside. Yeah, major rump roast would definitely be more appealing to her than anything he'd named.

Felicia! Stop!

"Um, I've never tried Ritadarion before. Is it good?"

"Yes, but spicy."

"I love spicy."

"Then Rit it is. However, it's not quite walking distance." He led her into a transport locker.

Which she was fine with until he stopped beside a sleek, expensive airbike. That must have been what he was riding when she last spoke to him. "You're kidding, right?"

He glanced about with an adorable baffled expression. "I don't think so." Then his look turned playful. "Don't tell me you're scared."

Felicia swallowed hard. "I have *never* ridden one of those before, and I've been quite happy and healthy that way. Maybe we should go someplace we can walk to?"

Now that was the most charming smile any male had ever given a female in the entire history of Andaria. No doubt that had gotten him out of many punishments with his mother. "C'mon. Try it. You know you want to. I won't let you get hurt, I promise. If I go too fast or you get scared even a little bit, squeeze my stomach and I'll slow down instantly."

Biting her lip, she debated the sanity of this.

"I'm a fighter pilot, Felicia. Almost three years now. Thousands of hours logged. Countless dogfights with the Tavali and Gourans."

"How many times have you crashed?"

"Never."

That made her feel better. "Okay, but remember, you have to pay for all medical treatments that result from any injury I sustain as a direct result of your actions."

Laughing, he shrugged his flight jacket off and wrapped it around her.

She staggered from the weight of the "light" armor. Not to mention, it swallowed her completely, and gave her a whole new appreciation for how strong he had to be to move so effortlessly in it. Grinning like a child who'd won a game, he pulled two helmets out of the seat and handed her one before he put his on.

Still not sure she should do this, she watched as he slung one incredibly long leg over the bike and pressed his hand to the bio sensor to start the engine.

With a deep breath for courage, she straddled the bike and took her seat. The way it was cut, it intimately pressed her body against his, and her legs were tucked beneath his buttocks. Wicked, warm fantasies tormented her at their close proximity and the wall of hard muscle that made up his luscious body.

Yeah, okay, this was nice. Smiling in pleasure, she slid her arms around his lean waist and sucked her breath in sharply at how solid he was. How good it felt to hold him.

He looked at her over his shoulder. "I'm about to lift us. Remember, if you get scared at all, just tighten your arms or tell me and I'll slow down to a crawl."

"Okay. I'm ready."

He gently rubbed her hands with his before he leaned forward and hit the lifters.

Her stomach sank at the sensation, but his skill was superb as he navigated them from the locker, into traffic.

"You all right back there?"

"I am. It is kind of fun, isn't it?"

He turned right. "Absolutely. I'll make a pilot of you yet."

She wasn't so sure about that. Unlike him, she didn't thrive on danger.

Boring . . . that was her sweet spot. And she rather liked it that way.

A few minutes later, he landed in a parking space outside a small café and helped her dismount. While his features held their usual stern expression, there was a childlike gleam in his eyes that made him even more adorable.

"You like to live on the edge, don't you?"

He secured their helmets and the airbike. "Extreme sports appeal to me."

And that made her nervous again. Did that include bedroom activities, too? He was so strong and massive, he could easily snap her bones without any effort. One hit from him, and she'd be dead. . . .

Violent and merciless, the Iron Hammer dominates the Ring like no other fighter in history. He's the one fighter the others unanimously fear facing. We have it on good authority that several have even gone into seizures after their managers told them they'd been contracted to fight him.

He paused as he looked at her. "You okay?"

"Yeah."

Talyn hesitated. In spite of her response, she was obviously upset. "Did I say something wrong?"

"No. It's all good."

But it wasn't. And that made him ache deep inside. Was it his birth standing?

That made sense. It was the most common thing held against him by the world. And it was why he refused to give interviews. First question was invariably about lineage, then next how his parents felt about his fighting record. Whenever he answered that he had no father, it made them gasp and step back like he was a disease carrier. The second evoked pity, and he hated that most of all.

So he'd learned to keep himself isolated and avoid or deflect awkward questions like a crotch plague. He'd hoped a companion wouldn't make him have to tiptoe through land mines and guard every word he spoke.

Obviously, he'd been wrong. *You know better than to speak to others, dumbass. How stupid are you that you can't ever be taught?*

Why had he thought anything could change? That she, a paid companion, wouldn't be bothered by his social standing? If he'd learned anything in life it should be that his sheer force of will didn't matter for Andarion shite. In the eyes of his race, he was garbage and that was all he'd ever be.

Feeling daunted, he withdrew into himself and put more space between them. Fuck it. He couldn't change their culture.

Or her mind or morals.

Lesson learned. He'd just get through this meal in as much silence as he could manage, and return to base. Let her live out the next six months in his condo, and then he could go back to what he knew.

What he was used to.

She took his jacket off and handed it to him. No doubt, she didn't want it touching her skin and contaminating her. Heartsick, he shrugged it on, and gestured toward the café door.

Felicia hesitated, wondering about his suddenly withdrawn mood. He was very reserved and stern now. Quiet. Even more so than when he'd been waiting for her at the agency. Did he have a chemical imbalance?

A little frightened by his unwarranted somber mood, she entered the small café first, and immediately noticed how many Andarions cut Talyn a wide berth. He paid them no attention as he sat her toward the back.

"Major," the waiter said as he brought menus for them. "Tara."

"Thank you." Felicia opened the menu while Talyn set his down on the table. She peeked over the top of hers to find him staring at the floor. "Is something wrong?"

He shrugged nonchalantly. "Not used to having lunch with someone."

"You don't normally eat with your friends?"

"Don't have any."

She scowled at his emotionless tone. "None?"

"I'm a bastard," he said simply.

"Yeah? So am I." Yet she had a ton of friends. Well . . . depending on the time of the month.

"Your father isn't an Outcast, Felicia. I have no paternal lineage. At all. My caste class is Ӿ-12-6."

"Oh." Yeah, that would be a problem in a society that placed high importance and *all* personal value on dual family lineages. The only thing lower than his standing was an Outcast male.

Something *no* Andarion wanted to be.

While her parents had never married, both her mother and father came from elite noble families with very prestigious standings. Her caste was miles above his, which was even more rare on Andaria. Females always took care to tie themselves to males who were either equal to or above them in standing. The only exception being the royal eton Anatoles, who, as the ruling family, were the highest caste in their empire.

His eyes filled with remorse, Talyn shifted in his seat. When he spoke, there was no emotion in his tone at all. "If you want to terminate your contract with me before I taint you, I'll understand. You won't have to worry. I'll pay the severance fees and you can go back to your agency."

"Talyn," she breathed, touching his hand. "I don't care about your father or his standing. I'm more than happy to be here with you."

Before he could respond, the waiter returned with water. "Are you ready to order?"

Talyn inclined his head to her. "What would you like, *mu tara*?"

You on a platter.

Unfortunately, Talyn tartare wasn't one of her options. "I'm not sure. What do you recommend?"

"I'm in training, so all I'm eating is lean white meat with nothing on it and whatever plain grain they have. I don't recommend that."

She screwed her face up. "Seriously?"

He nodded.

She looked to the waiter. "What do *you* recommend?"

"The sunset steak is exceptional. As is the summer salad."

"I think I'll have the steak, well done."

"And to drink?"

"Wine."

He took the menus without asking Talyn for his order.

As she opened her mouth to speak, a human male hesitantly approached their table.

"Hammer," he said to Talyn, whose face turned even more rigid. "You ready for tomorrow night?"

"I am."

"Good. I've got a month's credit riding on you. I'm looking forward to the payout." He held a small link and stylus out to Talyn. "Would you mind signing this for my grandson? He's a huge fan of yours."

Only then did Talyn relax a degree. "Sure. What's his name?"

"Gelun. G-e-l-u-n."

Talyn signed it and handed it back to the man, who smiled happily.

He clutched the autograph to his chest. "I won't keep you from your female. Good luck tomorrow night."

"Thanks."

Felicia arched a brow at the strange occurrence.

"I'm a Ring fighter." Talyn took a drink of water.

"One of my friends told me that after I'd signed our contract. I had no idea before then. What made you want to be one?"

He sighed heavily. "They wouldn't let me into OT, otherwise."

"OT?"

"Officer training."

Felicia felt sick at what he was telling her. Ring fighting was a *brutal* blood sport where opponents tried to kill each other for entertainment. Many times, they succeeded. Honestly, the entire sport and those who participated in it repulsed her. "How long have you been fighting?"

"Nine years."

That shocked her even more. Who in their right mind would

allow their child to participate in something so horrific as a baby? "You were an infant when you started."

"Almost eleven. Normal age for most boys who seriously go into it. I was big for my age back then. They thought I was fifteen and I didn't bother to correct them." He let out a bitter laugh. "Besides, Open doesn't ask for ID—which is why it's called Open. So long as you have the entry fee, they'll let you fight."

Felicia barely caught herself before she contradicted him about the beginning age for fighters. For Vested fighters with lineage, seventeen was the normal age to start—after years of private training, with carefully selected instructors, and very specific rules and limitations for those who weren't ranked as pros. As a bastard without lineage, Talyn would have been in the Open league, which was even more brutal, as they were treated like, and viewed as, cockfighting animals. They had no rules whatsoever, or personal trainers, and she had no idea how old those boys were when they began. Obviously, they started in infancy.

"How often do you fight?"

"Two or three times a month, during prime season."

She was aghast at the amount.

"Iron Hammer! Holy shite!" This time it was an Andarion male in business clothes who came up to them. "I didn't know you ate here! Would you mind taking a photo with me?"

"Sure."

The male handed his link to his friend as Talyn rose to stand beside him. After his friend took the picture, he held his hand out to Talyn. "I'm a huge fan. It's so awesome to meet you."

"You, too." Talyn retook his seat after they left.

Frowning, she was confused by all the attention he garnered. "Are you famous?" Since they were considered the mongrel dogs of the Ring sporting world, it was rare for any Open league fighter to be known to the general public.

His cheeks mottled with color before he answered. "I just won the Zoftiq title for Vested a few months back. And I'm the former Open league Zof champ. I had to surrender that title when I won Vested."

She gaped at something that was as impressive as it was rare. Fresca had definitely *not* told her that. Nor had she found it on her cursory search.

Strange.

"Really?" she gasped.

Sheepishly, he glanced away. "I'm also undefeated in both leagues."

Her head spun at what he was saying. "Talyn . . . that's incredible! Why didn't you tell me?"

"You said on your profile that you hated Ring fighting and wanted no part of it."

"Well, yeah, but—"

"I didn't think you'd talk to me if you knew."

He was right. She probably wouldn't have. She'd always thought of fighters as brain-addled morons who pummeled each other because they were too dumb to know better. But that wasn't true of Talyn. He was definitely not what came to her mind when she thought of the lunatics who made their glory in violence and entrails.

"How long do you intend to fight?"

"Just until I make a commander's rank. If I don't fight, I have no other way to get promoted."

That didn't make sense to her. "You're Zoftiq champion of both leagues. Why *aren't* you a commander?"

"I'm the bastard son of a disowned male, Felicia," he repeated. "X-12-6. A slave or criminal has more standing than I do. Even in the military."

In that moment, her heart broke for him. He was right, and it wasn't fair. Any Vested Andarion would be adjutant to the prime commander of their military if they'd achieved so much, especially at *his* age. They'd have their pick of posts and ranks.

Yet he was merely a major. Not even one with a command position.

In that moment, *she,* a diehard pacifist, wanted to beat someone.

"Why has no one in your father's family adopted you?" That was normally what the family did to protect the children of sons who, for whatever crime, had been cast out of their lineages. Almost always, the grandmother, great-grandmother, or a sister stepped in and reclaimed the innocent children. "Do they not know about you?"

There was no missing the anguish her question caused him. "They know. They just don't care."

The waiter returned with their food. Felicia had to force herself not to curl her lip at what Talyn was forced to eat. Water, and a giant portion of plain white meat, brown rice, cut-up raw fruit, and three hard-boiled eggs. They weren't even salted.

"Is that really what you're eating?"

He nodded. "I have a very restricted diet whenever I'm in training."

"Out of curiosity, champ, when *aren't* you training?"

He snorted before he spoke again. "I have a very restricted diet, all the time."

She shook her head. "When was the last time you had cake?"

"My tenth birthday."

"Is that a joke?"

"I don't think so."

Feeling guilty, she sampled her delicious-looking food. Which was quite tasty. "So what exactly is your daily schedule like?"

He swallowed his bite of egg. "I get up at five, run ten miles. Shower. Have to make check-in by seven. The armada owns my worthless ass until nineteen hundred. Sometimes later. Grab a quick bite. Then I spend three to four hours in the gym at night, training. I usually have two evenings off from double-duty and practice, but the weekends are full training days or matches or maneuvers."

Gah, she couldn't imagine such a grueling, unforgiving schedule. How did he stay sane? "What do you do for fun?"

"Climb."

"And when do you get to climb?"

He ate a bite of rice. "Ground maneuvers, rescue and survival training, every couple of months. Then, once a year, during my liberty week."

"And?" she prompted.

"And what?"

"What else do you enjoy?"

"Sleep."

"Talyn, I'm serious."

"As am I. Why do you think I want a command position so badly? They'd drop my hours down to only ten hours a day, four days a week. And I'd get two weeks of liberty a year. Best of all, I'd have a later curfew. And I'd get one night a week without one."

Never had she been happier that her own half-Vest status had kept her out of the military.

"Have you ever thought about a career outside of the armada?"

He swallowed the fruit and reached for more. "I wanted to be a surgeon."

"Why didn't you go to med school?"

"Couldn't get in with my classification. Without a paternal lineage, no Andarion school would even accept my application."

"No one?"

He shook his head. "Believe me, I tried. I even applied to The League medical corps. They turned me down, too. Since they have so few Andarions in their service and the humans don't like for us to treat them, they said they didn't have any open slots for our kind. I applied three times, and with the third one, they sent notice that I wasn't going to get in, so I shouldn't waste time or money applying again."

That had to be hard for him. "I'm sorry, Talyn."

He shrugged with a nonchalance she was sure he didn't really feel. How could he? Anyone who'd kept trying after being turned down that many times must have really wanted it.

"I got over it."

His tone said he was being honest, but she saw the regret in his eyes. The quiet, tormented resignation.

Her heart breaking for him, she watched as he finished off his bland lunch that was forced on him by his limited career options. Options he didn't bitch about, but he had every right to.

"So what about you?" he asked, leaning back in his chair.

She wiped her lips. "What about me?"

"What are you studying?"

"Ironically, I'm in med school. Entering my second year. I just passed my PT licensing exams a month ago."

"Congratulations."

She was stunned by his sincerity. Especially since it was something he'd wanted to do and had been denied the opportunity. "Thank you. And by the way, I really appreciate your understanding about my class schedule." He could have been a real pain over it. All the others had been. Some were even blatantly rude—wanting to know why a whore had to go to school with decent Andarions.

Instead, Talyn had been more than accommodating, which was one of the primary reasons she'd considered him as her patron.

"I respect anyone who goes to university. My mom had a hard time going with me when I was a kid. It took her twice as long to graduate as it should have. If you need anything extra for class, just let me know. I don't want you to have to struggle like my mother did." He paid for their food while she finished eating.

His armband went off.

Silencing it, he rose to his feet. "I have to get back for check-in."

"I thought you had an hour and a half for lunch?"

"My CO shortens it sometimes." Now, she heard the defiant anger underlying his words.

Yeah, there was no missing the furious tic in his jaw or the flashing bloodlust in his white eyes. He wanted his CO's throat. But he didn't say a word about it as he led her back to his air-bike.

She returned to base with him. "Would you mind if I went to your match tomorrow?"

His expression was a mask of shocked incredulity. "Really?"

She nodded. "Your mom won't mind, will she?"

He scowled as if her question baffled him. "My mom?"

"That you have your companion at a fight with her?"

"Oh . . . No, my mother never attends my fights."

Again, she was shocked by his answer. How could a champion fighter's mother not attend his events? "Never?"

He shook his head as if it was totally normal. "She doesn't like to see me bleed." His mood lightened a bit as he winked at her. "What kind of selfish mom is she, right?"

She laughed at his warped humor. "So who goes for you?"

"My trainer and manager."

"And?" she asked.

"My trainer and manager." He said that so emotionlessly that she knew he didn't expect anyone else. The loneliness of his life made her ache. He truly had no one. No wonder he didn't treat her like other patrons treated their companions. He had no real understanding of Andarion relationships.

Or even family, it seemed.

Felicia pulled his head down until his forehead touched hers. "I will be there for you, Talyn."

He inclined his head respectfully to her. "I shall leave a family pass for you at the box office. It'll get you in the back with me, before and after the fight." He cupped her face in his hand. "May I kiss you?"

"Of course."

He brushed his hand through her curls before he slowly lowered his lips to hers.

Felicia trembled at the gentleness of his kiss. She shivered as his tongue swept against hers. When he pulled back, she smiled up at him. "I'm glad you're my first kiss."

"And I'm glad you're mine."

It wasn't until he'd walked away that she realized he meant that she was his first kiss, too. Not that she was his mistress. Warmth spread through her, even though a part of her was still a little scared of him. He was so much more than she'd ever hoped to find.

Like him, because of her parents' actions, she had limited options for a spouse and career. The only reason she'd been allowed into med school was because her mother was a distant cousin to the former tadar, and her father was a very high-ranking advisor to the current tadara, and while her parents were unmarried, her father did acknowledge her as his.

At least on occasion.

That allowed her many more options for careers, but it put her at an extreme disadvantage when negotiating marriage. It was why she'd followed her mother into companionship. At least as a companion, she had some control over her future.

Normally, companions were sought by older males whose wives had died or were injured, and they didn't want to damage or complicate the lineages of their existing children with a new marriage.

Or they wanted companions for things, usually perverse, their wives refused to do for them. Sadly, those males treated their companions like paid whores. Expected them to be at their beck and call, and completely subservient and submissive.

Physical and verbal abuse had been her worst fear. She'd grown up with horror stories from her mother and her mother's friends.

But as the cost for school had risen, and the reality set in that no decent male her age would ever do right by her, she'd finally accepted the inevitable.

And almost made the worst mistake imaginable. She still shivered as she remembered the male she'd interviewed with right before Talyn. On paper, Arux had appeared the most perfect patron imaginable. She'd thought him a dream come true.

But he'd been so demanding and rude to her when they met that she'd started to pass on Talyn's proposal without even reviewing it. If an elder male was so condescending and repulsive, she'd imagined that a younger male, who had options for a wife, would be twice as bad.

She couldn't have been more wrong.

And for the first time in her life, she was actually looking forward to losing her virginity.

"Batur! Point twelve! Now!"

Talyn bit back an insult at his CO's sharp bark as he ran to fall in line. He really hated the bastard. As an Anatole, his CO was the grandnephew of their tadara, and he thought he owned the entire armada.

"Sir, yes sir." He saluted Anatole and took position in front of him.

The colonel glanced to where Felicia had just vanished. "So who's the trim?"

Talyn ground his teeth at the derogatory term that reduced Felicia to nothing more than mindless arm candy. "My female, sir."

He moved to stand right in Talyn's face. "Bullshit. No self-respecting female would be seen in public with a mongrel dog like you. Did you bring a whore on base, Batur?"

"No, sir."

The colonel sneered at him. "You did, didn't you? What? Did you have her suck you off for lunch?"

His breathing ragged, Talyn had to force himself not to strike the bastard. It wouldn't just be a court-martial. Anatole was a direct member of the royal house . . . fifth in line to the throne.

Death sentence.

But it was *so* tempting right now. He could actually taste Anatole's blood on his face as he ripped out the bastard's carotid. He physically ached to do it.

Ferrick would be so happy to know that he really did have these fantasies.

"Why don't you call your female back for me and let me show her what it's like to screw a real male? One with lineage."

Talyn clenched his fists at his side. No other officer would have to tolerate this from the colonel. But he had no one to appeal to. If he tried to report Anatole, it would only get worse for him.

Or, worst case scenario, it might rebound and harm his mother and her rank.

"What? Does that make you angry, mongrel? You dare look at me with rage in your eyes?"

Talyn quickly averted his gaze.

"Go on, dog. Call your whore. I'll even let you watch her suck my dick."

When he didn't pull his link out, the colonel arched a brow. "Are you refusing a direct order?"

"I can't order a civ, sir. If you want your cock sucked, guess I'll have to do it."

The colonel backhanded him.

Talyn didn't budge. Honestly? His mother hit harder.

What it did do, though, was make him yearn for the day Anatole's testicles descended and the bastard found enough backbone to face him like a true Andarion.

In the Ring.

Warrior to warrior.

"You think you're something special? *Iron Hammer,*" he sneered. "I've got a year's salary riding on your opponent tomorrow night. What say we start your training early? Huh? Let's get you seasoned for your opponent. Report to the Ring. Immediately."

"Yes, sir. Looking forward to the day when you're Andarion enough to join me there."

That had the desired effect. Anatole's eyes flared with hatred. "Insubordination, Major?"

You think? But Talyn wasn't quite stupid enough to say that out loud. "No, sir. Just thinking that it might do the morale good to see one of our leaders in the Ring." Talyn saluted him and headed for the company gym. And with every step he took, he knew what would be waiting.

What forever waited for him there.

Because the odds were with Talyn winning, Anatole always bet against him, hoping for a bigger payout. But Talyn couldn't throw a fight. It would literally mean his life if he did.

So the colonel handicapped him. Or so he thought.

What the idiot couldn't figure out was that these meager little fights didn't hurt Talyn.

At all.

Andarion soldiers, while fierce, were not the same caliber as a pro Ring fighter. Vested brats, they'd never had to walk into an Open Ring and really fight for their lives. Never had to stand strong in a world determined to kill them.

Long ago, Talyn had learned to find pleasure in pain. And in true Andarion War Hauk fashion, fights invigorated him. Made him stronger. More determined. Nothing lit a fire in his ass quicker than someone trying to hold him back or beat him down.

Bring it with everything you have, bitch.

Nothing and no one would *ever* get the best of him.

As he went to dress out, his thoughts turned to Felicia and her gentle kindness during lunch.

She wanted to see him again. That thought warmed him in spite of his foul mood.

While he had a warrior's heart, she did bring an unfathomable peace to his soul. If he had to get his ass kicked, he couldn't think of a better reason than to protect her from bastards like his CO.

Best of all, she didn't appear to look at him like other Andarions did. Sometimes, she even seemed to enjoy his company. That was all he wanted in this life. Someone who could be with him and not resent or hate him for a birth he couldn't help.

But first he had to deal with Anatole and whatever Vested moron thought he could beat down the Iron Hammer.

Irritated by the bullshit, Talyn ground his teeth. Yes, he'd changed one thing in his life by bringing Felicia into it. But so far, everything else he'd tried had failed.

There has to be another way out of this.

Some way to get Anatole and the rest of them off his back. *Yeah, kill the bastard.*

Simple.

The trick was to get Anatole into that Ring and unleash all the hatred Talyn kept locked inside himself. Yet so far, Anatole had wisely refused.

One day, though . . .

He was going to find Anatole's weakness, and when he did, he planned to hand-deliver Anatole's soul to their gods.

CHAPTER 3

Reporters aren't allowed back here. You'll have—"

"It's okay, Erix. She's with me."

Felicia looked past the huge, fierce bald male in front of her to see Talyn sitting on a dilapidated bench in the run-down dressing room. This was so not what she'd envisioned for a champion's prefight area.

Her smile faded as she realized the other male with him was in the process of covering horrible bruises on Talyn's body. "Did I miss the fight? I thought it didn't start for another half hour."

A tic started in Erix's jaw as he returned to Talyn's side to wrap his hands so that Talyn couldn't use his claws in the fight to scar his opponent. "It doesn't. This is from his CO."

Felicia scowled. "I don't understand."

Talyn laughed wryly. "Anatole bets against me."

"And has his bastard goons beat the shit out of the boy whenever he has a fight coming, to handicap him."

She felt sick over the news.

Talyn brushed his wrapped hand lightly against her cheek and offered her a bashful smile. "It's all right. Pain's my best friend. Just makes me that much more determined to watch him cry like a bitch when he loses his pay." Dropping his hand, he sucked his breath in sharply as his manager touched a particularly nasty bruise on his back.

"Here," she said, pushing the male aside. "Let me."

Ferrick arched a brow.

She met his manager's sneer without flinching. "I'm a licensed physical therapist and med student. I can help him."

Talyn took her hand and placed it against his cheek. An Andarion gesture of extreme affection. "Ferrick and Erix, meet my Felicia."

Ferrick moved away so that she could take over. "He has limited mobility on his right arm. If you could loosen the muscles there, we'd all be grateful."

"Is there a table he can lie down on?"

Erix gestured past the lockers. "In back."

She gently tugged for Talyn to follow her to it. "Can't you delay the fight?"

He shook his head. "Only for death or military orders. Anything else is a forfeit." He hesitated at the table. "Face down?"

"Yes." She waited for him to lie down before she gently touched his back to evaluate what all had been done to him. It was even worse than it appeared. "Oh, Talyn." She wanted to weep at how badly he'd been beaten already. And he hadn't even stepped into the Ring yet.

"Really, it's okay, Felicia. Believe me, this isn't the worst ass-kicking I've had. And those were just from my mom for failure to put the toilet seat down at night."

She rolled her eyes at his offbeat humor. Given his immense size and muscle tone, she seriously doubted his mother had ever laid a finger to him. "No one should be used to this."

He lifted his head to look at her. "Would you think I'm a totally sick bastard if I said I'd gladly have the shit kicked out of me to feel your hands on my skin?"

She laid her palm against his cheek as those words brought tears to her eyes. "Yes."

He smiled at her. "Good. I don't want any pretense between us."

She kissed his cheek before she worked on his shoulder and back, where the worst damage seemed to have been done.

"Talyn! It's time." Ferrick joined them.

Felicia stepped back as Talyn sat up and took the ornate leather mask from Ferrick's hand. He slid it over his head so that all that showed of his features were his white eyes that held a tiny band of red around the outer edge of the iris.

"You look like an alien is eating your face."

Reaching for the hand wrap covers, he laughed at her comment. "Erix has a seat in front, reserved for you."

She screwed her face up at the thought of it. Okay, she totally understood now why his mother didn't come to these things, after all. "If you don't mind, I'd rather wait for you back here. I don't really want to watch you get beat on. But I am here for you, if you need me."

Her declination didn't seem to faze him at all as he shadowboxed to loosen his muscles. "Okay. I'll be back in a little while."

She walked slowly into his arms and hugged him. "Good luck."

Talyn savored the sensation of being held. No one had embraced him like this since he'd been a boy.

"Hammer! Let's go!"

Reluctantly, he released her and headed for the Ring. As he reached the door, he glanced back to see her watching him. Damn, she was beautiful. Like an ethereal vision. He still couldn't believe she'd agreed to accept him, given his lack of birth standing.

That she had yet to run screaming for the nearest door to escape his presence.

All he had to do was not get killed tonight. That would seriously screw up his future plans where she was concerned.

Clamping down on his fang guard, he smiled under his mask and winked at her. He hadn't been kidding. To have her with him, he'd gladly get the shit kicked out of him.

The gods knew, he'd been beaten for a whole lot less.

Unsure and terrified for Talyn, Felicia chewed her nails as she paced the back room while she listened to the sound of the crowd. She heard hisses and boos and cheers so loud, they shook the stained walls around her. None of it told her how Talyn was doing.

If he was winning or losing.

Part of her was dying to know, but she'd meant what she said. She couldn't stand the thought of watching him be pounded on by another fighter. Especially not with the savagery that went on in the name of entertainment. Ring fighting was the most popular sport in Andaria.

And it was the most brutal.

Every year, dozens of fighters died in the Ring. Dozens more after the match ended, from the injuries they'd sustained during the fight. While they wore masks and taped their clawed hands to keep from being scarred, there were no real rules. They fought until only one was left standing. However long that took.

A loud, thunderous roar went up. It was followed by an alarm of some sort.

Was it over?

Biting her lip, she went to the door. She held her breath until she saw Talyn coming down the hallway with a furious light in his eyes. Blood dripped from the mask over his face. More bruises and cuts covered him. But his injuries didn't seem to bother him at all.

As soon as he saw her, he pulled the mask off, spit out his fang guard, and gave her a grim smile. "Still undefeated."

Proud, and honestly, a bit terrified by this side of him that didn't seem to mind bleeding, she swallowed hard. There was an aura of death that clung to him now. "Are you okay?"

"Yeah. I'll feel the burn later. Right now . . ." He picked her up with a terrifying ease and hugged her close.

She started to wrap her arms around him, until she saw all

the bleeding welts on his back. They had to be killing him. "We need to get you something for your pain."

He shook his head as he set her back on her feet and led her into his dressing room. "I can't take anything."

"Talyn—"

He set his mask down and unwrapped his hands. "They'll test my blood as soon as I hit the barracks. If I have any drugs in my system, I'll be court-martialed and imprisoned for it."

"An aspirin?"

"I'll be court-martialed and imprisoned," he repeated. "I can't have anything in my system while I might be called to fly. It's an order my CO's dead serious about."

Aghast, she stared up at him and the horrific marks on his body. It looked as if his opponent had not only managed to get the covers off and claw him, but bitten him, too. There were definite fang marks all over his left arm. "How can you stand it?"

He shrugged nonchalantly. "I have no choice, Felicia. Without a paternal lineage, I can't even work as a janitor. The military's all I have open to me. And I'm damn lucky that I was able to fight well enough to be allowed into OTS, given my caste."

And the armada was the only solid income he could bank on. Ring fighting didn't pay for fighters.

While the promoters got rich, the fighters didn't. They were given a small stipend for each fight, and prestige, but no one could afford to live on a fighter's pay.

Not even a champion's.

Andarions fought for glory and military rank, not riches.

While humans paid their fighters exorbitant amounts, Andarions didn't. It was to be expected of their males that they could take a beating and not flinch. And because of their ferocity and size, Andarions were barred from human sports. Which kept Talyn trapped on Andaria, in this hellish existence.

She cursed the unfairness of it all as she helped him undress and enter the large shower so that they could wash the blood and sweat off.

Talyn winced as his adrenaline fled and left him in pain. He leaned with one arm against the wall while the water stung the various cuts on his body. In spite of the rancid physical agony, he hardened at the sensation of Felicia's hands sliding over his bare flesh as she soaped his skin for him. Her cheeks were bright pink, but she didn't say a word while she gently and carefully bathed him. In spite of the beating, his senses spun with bliss at being touched for the first time by a female's gentle hand.

Reaching out, he brushed his fingers along the line of her jaw and watched her pupils dilate in response to his touch. He still couldn't believe that she'd accept his caresses without flinching or insulting him.

Her nipples hardened through the fabric of her thin shirt. His breathing ragged, he was dying to know what she looked like naked. Because she was a virgin, her agency photos had been of her in skimpy panties and an exercise bra.

On the night they'd met, he could have forced her to disrobe so that he could inspect her body, but he'd refused to embarrass her in front of the others.

Now . . .

They were alone and all he wanted was to be inside her.

She hesitated as she neared the part of him that was most desperate for her touch. He was so hard, he could probably drive nails with his cock.

Feral with longing, he locked gazes with her and he held his breath, praying she wouldn't stop or pull back.

His hand trembling, he covered hers with his and slowly slid it against his hardness. The room spun even more as pleasure racked his entire body and drove the pain away.

Felicia couldn't breathe as she stared up at him and touched him for the first time. Dropping the cloth, she ran her fingers over his cock. Then down the length until she cupped him in her hand. He let out a feral growl. Biting his lip, he gently slid his hand beneath the hemline of her shirt until he could lightly touch and squeeze her breast through her bra.

A smile curved her lips as he slowly and gently rocked himself against her hand. He dipped his head down to kiss her with a tender passion that left her breathless.

Suddenly, his stupid band alarm sounded.

Cursing, he tore himself out of her grasp and turned the water off. He reached for a towel. "I have to go."

"Seriously?"

He nodded. "It's my CO. He always recalls me as soon as he gets the results of a fight. If I don't head right back, it'll be worse for me." His white eyes filled with regret, he cupped her cheek in his hand. "I probably won't be able to see you this week, after all."

"Why?"

Talyn grimaced as that ferocious fury returned to his gaze.

"He's going to be pissed that I cost him his bet. So he'll take it out of my ass. I'll call when I can, but if you don't hear from me for a few days, don't worry. It's normal." His jaw ticcing again, he stepped past her so that he could reach his uniform.

She helped him dress as Erix joined them.

He rolled his eyes. "Bastard recalled you already?"

Talyn nodded. "Can you see Felicia home for me?"

"Sure. You need anything else?"

Talyn shook his head. "I'll call as soon as I can make training again."

Erix clapped him on the back. "Take care, kid."

Talyn gave her a quick kiss before he left.

Her heart heavy, Felicia watched him go. "Will he be okay?"

"Yeah. He's a tough little bastard."

That description really didn't make her feel better.

She fingered the bloody mask Talyn had left behind before she handed it to Erix so that he could clean it. "How long have you known him?"

"Almost six years."

That was an impressive length from what she understood about fighters and trainers. "You've been training him that long?"

Erix nodded as he washed the mask off in a small sink. "Ironically, I'd never heard of him before that. I'm a Vested trainer so I never paid attention to the Open leaguers. I considered them rabid mongrels, not worth my time."

Because only those with prestigious lineages were allowed to fight in the Vested league, they, alone, could afford a coach's fees. Open was reserved for orphans, slaves, and bastards. Unlike Vested fighters, they had no equipment, protections, or reps. It was an all-out bare-fist-on-flesh brawl.

"So what made you take on Talyn?"

He sterilized the mask. "A good friend of mine had seen him fight and thought I should take a look at him. Talyn was going up against a much older, larger, and tougher opponent for the Mean Weight title. I thought it was a complete waste of time since I knew an Open leaguer couldn't afford me, but it was free ale and dinner with a friend so I agreed. Kid was only thirteen at the time. He came out alone and looked like a toy in comparison to his opponent. I figured he wouldn't last five minutes . . . three hours later, no breaks whatsoever, he was champion. In thirty-five years of coaching fighters, I'd never seen anything like it. He was fearless and determined. Skilled beyond his years. That giant bastard beat him half to death and still he stood strong and fierce—as if he was daring the gods themselves to try and break him. By the end, Talyn couldn't even open his eyes and yet there he stood. The youngest Mean Weight title champion in Andarion history. It took me two days to wrap my head around what I'd seen and to convince myself it'd been real. And then ten days to talk the kid into letting me train him." He dried off the mask.

"Really?"

He nodded as he picked up towels and placed them in a duffel. "Kid didn't want to spend the money on a trainer when they don't use us in the Open league. Plus, he was trying to save up to help his mom buy her rank commission."

Her jaw fell slack. "He paid for his mother's commission?"

"Yeah. He's always felt responsible for her. Told you, he's a good kid."

"And yet she never comes to his matches?"

Shrugging, he put the mask and Talyn's wrap-tape and covers in a smaller bag. "She can't stand them. He was already a title contender before she found out he was even a fighter."

Felicia gaped even more at what he was telling her. "How could she not know?"

"You've seen how the military treats its soldiers. She wasn't home much, and whenever she saw the bruises, she assumed they were from school fights. Talyn didn't tell her no different and she didn't ask."

Felicia shook her head as she had an image of Talyn as a bruised little boy, tending his injuries with no help. Never had she hated Andarion customs more.

But at least he'd found Erix to watch over him. "So how did you talk him into accepting you as his coach?"

"Told him if he'd give me five years, I could get him into the Vested league. I did it in three."

"Impressive." She helped him gather the rest of the damp towels and Talyn's shorts.

"Not on my part. While I never admit it to the media, I know the truth. I couldn't have done it for anyone else. It's a testament to his abilities and heart that I was able to get him in. At all. Believe me, the Vested league fought me every step of the way. They only agreed to it originally as a joke. Thought it'd be funny to trot out the mongrel freak, and show a Vested leaguer trouncing him. For that first fight, the kid was ridiculously paired with a fighter who outweighed him by over a hundred pounds."

"The Andarion Butcher?" Felicia asked, remembering what Fresca had said about her cousin.

He nodded. "He tried to break Talyn in half. Didn't work out so well for him. No one can deny that Talyn has a fire inside him no other Andarion can touch. You might get a shot or two in, but no one can take him down. He mangled the Butcher in under two hours."

And that was what scared her. What if he turned that level of ferocity on her one day?

He sealed the bags. "C'mon. Let me see you home like I promised. Last thing I want is for the kid to kick my ass because I let you get hurt."

She smiled at the tender note in his voice as he spoke of Talyn. "You love him."

"Like a son."

As they left, the media descended on them. Erix pushed his way through them, taking care to keep her safe through the crowd.

"Who's the female?"

"Is she the Hammer's girl?"

"She's my daughter," he snarled at the reporters. "Now get out of our way! I'll field interviews later!" He opened the door to a chauffeured transport and helped her inside. Then he joined her.

She shook her head incredulously at the spectacle. "Is it always like this?"

"Yeah. Talyn's a once-in-a-lifetime champion. No one's ever seen a fighter like him before. I doubt if they'll ever see another."

And Talyn had requested a contract with *her*.

She still couldn't believe she was tied to a famous athlete. "He should be celebrating his win. Not pulled back to duty before he could even finish his shower."

The look on Erix's face made her stomach shrink.

"What?"

He glanced away.

"Erix? What is it?" What was he not telling her?

"Nothing. Just agreeing with you."

There was more to it than that. She knew it. "Tell me why you look like that."

"Just thinking of what his CO will do to him for daring to win tonight. I hate that unreasonable bastard with a passion."

"Who's his CO?"

"Colonel Asshole Anatole. The tadara's grandnephew. A ne'er-do-well who bought his rank and hates every male who puts him to shame. Which is pretty much everyone. And, in particular, Talyn."

She knew the type well. "It's not Chrisen Anatole, is it?"

He frowned at her. "You know him?"

"Only by reputation." He was banned from her agency for almost killing one of the companions who'd been dumb enough to contract with him two years ago. Her agency used him as an example that though a patron might be highest caste, he might not be the best choice.

"Yeah, it really chaps my ass that my blood son died in battle to protect us, and that cowardly dog sits with a colonel's commission and uses it to bully and abuse those beneath him. There's just no justice in this universe."

"Is there no way to get Talyn out from under his command?"

"Yeah. Kill the bastard . . . and don't think the idea of taking that contract out with The League hasn't occurred to me."

She frowned at him. "Can't Talyn simply buy another commission?"

"It's not just a money thing. Officers have to bank training and service time for a promotion. Unfortunately, Talyn donated his to get his mother *her* last commission. And even if he had used it himself, it wouldn't have gotten him out from under his CO. He has to go up two ranks to bypass that asshole."

She cringed at the thought of him staying with such a beast. "So what do you think will happen when Talyn returns to base?"

"If experience holds, he'll be sent out on patrol as soon as he gets back and they check his blood to make sure it's clean. His leave for the next month will be revoked, and he'll be given every shit assignment that comes across Anatole's desk."

"And there's nothing we can do?"

Erix shook his head sadly. "Just be there for him when he resurfaces, and hope his CO doesn't kill him."

CHAPTER 4

"Hey, Felicia."

Felicia smiled as she heard Talyn's deep, sexy voice again. It'd been two weeks since she'd seen him at the fight. While she'd sent him several texts and had left messages, the most she'd gotten back was a word or two as a texted response.

"Hey, sweetie! How are you doing?"

Talyn hesitated before he answered. "I'm okay. I . . . um . . . where are you?"

"At home. Studying."

"Are you alone?"

She scowled at the strange note in his voice and the peculiar question. "Yeah. Why?"

There was a brief pause before he spoke again in the cutest little bashful tone. "I'm on my rec time, and I was wondering if you could talk dirty to me."

Her jaw dropped in shock. "Excuse me? Rec time?"

"It's private time we get twice a week for half an hour to, um . . . take care of our hormone levels."

His embarrassed tone made her cheeks heat up as she finally understood what he was talking about and why he was making such an odd request. Adult Andarion males had to have a fairly regular ejaculation schedule, or they became extremely aggressive and physically ill. It was the main reason why companions and prostitutes were acceptable roles for females in their society.

And her male needed help from her.

Smiling at the fact that he'd finally called her for something he was paying her for, she set her assignments aside. "Okay. What do you need me to do?"

He hesitated again before he spoke. "What are you wearing?"

"Shorts and a shirt."

Talyn laughed. "Not what I was going for, Felicia."

"Oh, sorry. I'm naked." She scowled as she looked at the really expensive brown sofa. "Though I should probably put down a blanket on the couch first. I'd hate to mess up this nice leather. Not to mention that's not exactly hygienic. Be kind of gross whenever someone comes over. Gods help us if they have a UV light."

Again, he laughed at her comments. "You've never done this before, have you?"

"No. Sorry. I didn't take the course on sex talk. . . . Um, I'm kissing your lips and breathing in your ear."

"How could you be kissing my lips *and* breathing in my ear?"

She bit her lip to keep from laughing. "I'm really limber?"

"Are you?"

"Yes. Does that help?"

"Not really." His tone said he was smiling at her.

"Well, if you're going to be literal, Major Picky . . . I'm rubbing your back."

"Not the part of me I want rubbed. I'm thinking of something lower."

Her face heated up even more. "Sorry. I'm rubbing your . . ." What word should she use? "Male hardness?"

"Ew," he said with a laugh.

"Turgid penis?"

He made sounds of extreme painful distress. "Gods, girl, you're killing me. Way too clinical. Put down your textbooks!"

"Sorry. I'll call my mom tomorrow and—"

"Uh, gah! No! Don't! Don't bring your mother into this! And for the love of the gods, don't discuss our sex life with her!"

It was her turn to laugh. "You sound like you're in pain."

"I am. Agony. I can't believe you just invoked the maternal image in my head. I don't think I'll ever purge that. You've scarred me for life." He sounded so miserable that she felt terrible for causing it.

She took a picture of herself pouting and sent it to him. "Did that help?"

"A little."

She snapped another picture of herself looking demure and sent it. "Better?"

Talyn grinned as his body hardened even more from the image. She was lying down, her face engulfed by the mess of curls that fell in every direction. All he wanted in life was to bury his face in that soft curly mass and breathe her in until he was drunk from her scent. "Much."

"Want me to try again to please you?" she asked.

He bit his bottom lip as he imagined her hands on his body. Closing his eyes, he hung on to the vision with everything he had, and elaborated on it with her sinking to her knees in front of him. His breathing turned ragged as he quickly reminded himself that she was waiting for an answer. "You already are. Just the sound of your voice saying my name is the sweetest thing I've ever known."

When she responded, he heard the tears in her sweet voice. That meant more to him than anything. "I miss you, Talyn. I really wish I could see you."

Not half as much as he wished he could see someone who didn't look at him with disdain and scorn. Someone who didn't treat him like the unwanted maggot that had somehow found its way into their favorite meal.

Only Felicia had ever welcomed him. Even if she was faking it, he was desperate enough to be grateful.

Felicia waited so long for a response that she was beginning to think they'd been disconnected. Finally, he sent over a picture of himself smiling bashfully. The dark red and black of his uniform caused his eyes to glow bright white in the dim light of the spartan room where he appeared to be lying on a small industrial cot. "Miss you, too."

She traced the lines of his face on the screen. "I'm so glad you finally had a chance to call. Have I told you how handsome you are?"

"Am I?"

"Yes, you are. Extremely gorgeous. Utterly lickable. Sexy. Hotter than any male I've ever seen, in the flesh or on-screen. I would love to be there to eat you up, from the tips of your toes, all the way to your delectable lips." She sighed happily. "I can't get the taste of you out of my mind. Or the feeling of you holding or touching me. Every night, I go to sleep imagining that I'm bathing you again. Only this time we get to finish what we started, and I get to nibble all of you while you lie in my bed."

"Mmm."

She arched her brow at the deep growl in his throat. "Are you okay, sweetie?"

"Mmm-hmmm." He sucked his breath in sharply, then let out an elongated groan.

Heat burned her face as she realized what was going on. "Did you just . . . ?"

"Yeah," he said breathlessly. "Sorry."

"Why are you apologizing?"

"Because you sound embarrassed and I didn't mean to do that to you. But I do appreciate your help. I really needed that." He sent her another photo.

"You look very relaxed now."

"I am. But I'd rather have done that with you actually participating."

"Me, too." She snapped another picture of herself pouting at him.

He sent over a video request.

Accepting it, she smiled as she saw his face in live time. "Hey, handsome."

"Gods, you're beautiful. Is everything okay with the condo?"

"Only one thing would make it better."

"What?"

"You being here."

His bashful smile made her heart race. "Did the school get their payment?"

"They did. Thank you."

"Any time." He grimaced as that familiar buzzing started. "My time in the locker's up. I have to go. I'll see you when I can."

"Miss you, Talyn!"

"Miss you, too, baby." He hung up.

Her lips quivered as she stared at the blank screen, hating it. How could she ache so much for someone she barely knew? Yet there was no denying what she felt. Or how deeply.

Holding the link to her heart, she drew a ragged breath as she glanced around the luxury Talyn provided for her. He spared no expense when it came to her needs and comfort. It wasn't fair that she was allowed to live here on his money, while he was forced to endure hell to pay for it all.

She'd never been one to suffer injustice, and this really pissed her off. All the assholes in the universe and a male so decent was punished for not being selfish. It was so wrong.

Felicia brushed her hand over her contact list and hesitated as she saw her half brother's name there. She never really spoke to that side of her family—they were too mocking for that, and she'd never asked a favor before.

Would it upset Talyn if she did?

There was no way of knowing. For everything she felt toward him, she didn't really know him well enough to guess how he'd react to her interference with his life.

Given his size and strength, the last thing she wanted to do was anger him.

Not willing to risk it, she turned the link off. For now, she'd leave it as it was. But if Talyn's CO didn't shape up and treat him right soon, she would call Lorens and see what she could do to help Talyn.

Talyn paused as he walked past the jewelry counter in the BX. After his call with Felicia, he'd come in on his way to the barracks to replace the flight boots that were starting to rub his heel, and to pick up a new brass kit and charges for his blasters.

While he'd known the jewelry section was here, he'd never paid attention to it before.

But in the small case in front of him was a collection of the hugging heart rings that were a popular gift pilots bought for their partners. A larger silver heart was wound around a smaller gold one, as if hugging or protecting it. One in particular was made of pale pink gold and encrusted with diamonds. For some reason, he thought Felicia might like it. It just looked soft and warm. Petite.

Like her.

"Major," the clerk greeted him as she approached from the other side of the counter. "May I be of service?"

Talyn started to walk on, but he couldn't quite do it. "I was just looking at the rings."

She smiled brightly. "Ah, yes. The Remember Me ring. You know, they're said to be good luck. It's why they're our biggest seller."

"How so?"

She reached into the case to pull out the display. "You give one to your special lady to keep, and so long as she wears it, it'll bring you safely home to her arms."

Talyn smiled at the thought as he reached for the one that had caught his attention. Up close, it appeared rather large. Felicia had tiny, graceful hands. "I don't know what her size is."

"I can give you a voucher and she can take it to any jeweler for sizing."

He held it out to her. "I should like this one, then."

"Very good. I just need to see your ID."

Pulling out his wallet, he flipped it open and held his badge toward her.

She gasped the moment her gaze fell to the black card that was bisected diagonally with a burgundy stripe. She recoiled from his badge as if it were poisonous. "I'm sorry, Major Batur. I can't sell this to you." She immediately returned the ring to the display and locked it in the case.

Confused, he scowled at her. "I don't understand."

She gestured toward his card. "You're a lack-Vest bastard. Your kind can't buy a ring, for anyone. If I sold that to you, we'd both be arrested."

Hurt and stunned, he stared at her in disbelief. "I have a legal contract with my lady."

Her jaw dropped as if she couldn't believe it. She quickly snapped her lips together. "It doesn't matter. It's against the law to allow a lack-Vest to buy a ring. For anyone," she repeated harshly.

Feeling slapped and humiliated, Talyn watched as she quickly sidled over to another counter to help a giddy male and female who were there to pick out pledge rings.

Something he'd never be able to legally do. That reality hit him like a kick in the crotch.

As he walked away, anger scalded every molecule of his being. He'd always hated showing his ID. Since they were color-coded, all anyone had to do was see that his was black and they instantly knew his caste. Now that same damn card kept him from buying Felicia a simple gift.

This is bullshit!

"Major?"

Talyn hesitated at the sound of an older male's call as he moved to cut off Talyn's path to the register. He just glared at the older male.

"I overheard you with Vyra, and I'm very sorry about the law."

Really don't want to fucking relive this. He was humiliated enough.

"Excuse me." Talyn started around the male.

He cut his path off again and gave him a fatherly smile. "I'm a big fan of yours, Major. And since we can't allow you to buy a ring, I wanted to show *this* to you. If you want it, I'll discount the price by half."

Still pissed, Talyn looked down to see a pretty hugging heart necklace that matched the ring he'd wanted to buy.

"I can even waive the courier fee for its delivery. If your lady lives here in Eris, I could get it to her tonight."

Pressing his lips together, Talyn picked the necklace up to see it better.

"It has the same legend of bringing good luck. A lot of pilots send these to their mothers and wives, instead of the rings."

Talyn wanted to throw it on the ground and stomp it. But the laws weren't this male's fault. And there was no need in depriving Felicia of something she'd like because his own feelings had been hurt.

If it made her smile, it would be worth it.

He returned the box to the clerk. "Thank you. I'll take it. Her condo is in Brooksyn, North Eris."

"Very good. I'll see it to her in less than two hours."

Talyn nodded before he went to pay for it. But still the burn was in his blood. A simmering heat that only increased once he returned to his barracks and saw that someone had placed a collar and leash on his locker with a black card attached to it. *Ha, ha. Real fucking funny.* You'd think by now the prank would have grown as old for them as it was for him. Even so, he knew better than to feed into their juvenile shit.

Grinding his teeth, he picked it up without comment and stored his purchases.

He grabbed a towel and started for the showers.

"It's not mongrel time, Batur. There's Vested in the latrine."

Biting back a nasty retort, Talyn returned to his bunk to wait while he listened to the others talking about their future plans.

With nothing else to do, he pulled out his link and started running stats on his next Ring opponent.

"You okay, Pinara?" one of the captains asked.

Talyn glanced over at the major who was a year older than him. The male was a cousin to the female pilot, Syndrome, who flew in Talyn's squad.

Fidgeting, Pinara kept shining his brass, and looking around as if waiting for something bad to happen. "Fine."

Yeah, he was lying his ass off. But like everyone else here, Talyn knew what that word meant. Something had gone down with the higher-ups and the major wasn't at liberty to talk about it.

Pinara looked over and caught Talyn's gaze. "What you staring at, mongrel?"

Without a word, Talyn returned his attention to his link. As he was logging on, five provosts came in and surrounded Pinara.

"Major, you are to be remanded into custody."

Pinara went pale. "For what?"

They didn't say as they cuffed him and hauled him out.

Silence echoed in the barracks as everyone tried to hide how disturbed they were over this. It could have been any of them, and they knew it.

Normally, it was Talyn who was singled out for trumped-up, bullshit infractions and punishment. Made him wonder what the high-caste Pinara had done to get on Anatole's bad side.

"WAR's right—"

"Bite it!"

Talyn scowled at the hushed exchange between two of his bunkmates. WAR was an antigovernment organization that had sprung up against the tadara and her family. For years now, they'd been trying to overthrow her.

Anyone found with their paraphernalia or with any ties to their group was summarily seized and executed. Without trial.

"Batur!"

Talyn grimaced at the sharp bark. Rising to his feet, he saluted the OOD. "Sir?"

"Cover Pinara's patrol. He was to fly in fifteen."

Talyn started to remind him that he was already seventeen hours over his patrol quota for the week, but then the OOD would know that even better than Talyn did.

"Yes, sir."

As he moved to reach for his flight suit, he heard Pinara's wingman, Mannan Xu, curse.

"Why am I being punished? I don't want to fly with a lack-Vest. Do you know who my parents are?"

The OOD glared at the major. "Insubordination?"

"No, sir."

"Then head out. *With* Batur."

Xu cut a glare at Talyn to let him know how much he hated being stuck with him.

No joy for me, either, punk.

As soon as he was changed, Talyn went to do preflight in their hangar. When he neared his fighter, Xu cornered him.

"You better remember your place, dog. Behind me, cleaning up after your superiors."

A tic started in Talyn's jaw. He wanted to punch the bastard so badly that it was all he could do to refrain. But he knew from experience that if he spoke a word, he'd lose what little free time he had, and this prick wasn't worth it.

Think of Felicia. He had a reason now to stay out of the brig and off reports. Not one of them was worth the additional patrol time.

Eye on the goal, Batur.

And that was a beautiful female who finally made him feel like something more than the dirt underneath their feet.

It'd been over a month since Felicia had last seen Talyn at his fight. As punishment for winning, he hadn't even been allowed to have visitors on base or to leave it for meals. His CO had kept him on total lockdown. He hadn't even been able to call her again during his rec time.

While she'd left voice notes for him every day, all she'd received as responses were very brief text messages back.

And random gifts that had come to the condo.

One of them was the beautiful double-heart necklace that he'd sent, which was around her neck. It'd come within a few hours of her hanging up the last time they'd spoken, and she hadn't taken it off since.

Kind of stupid, but it somehow made her feel closer to him. And she'd kept the small card that he'd sent with it.

Thank you for today, Gre Couranatara.

~T

The great lady of my heart. Every time she read that, it brought tears to her eyes.

Her link buzzed. Frowning, she picked it up and glanced at it, expecting a message from her mother.

It was Talyn.

Hey. What are you doing?

She typed back to him. *Studying.*

Are you at the condo?

Wow. This was the longest conversation they'd had since their failed attempt at sexting. *I am. Where are you?*

The elevator binged behind her. Turning on the couch, she was just about to call security when Talyn stepped out. Joy erupted through her as she let out a happy cry and shot off the couch toward the foyer.

"Talyn!" She launched herself into his arms.

Laughing, he held her against him. He buried his hand in her hair and pressed his cheek to hers. "Hi."

"I can't believe you're finally here! Why didn't you tell me you were coming?"

"I wasn't sure I'd be able to until an hour ago. Even then, I kept waiting for my TL to be canceled."

She squeezed him even tighter. "I almost went out tonight. I'm so glad I didn't."

Talyn savored those words and the sensation of her body

wrapped around his. He'd been dreaming of this every single night since he first saw her photo. "How have you been?"

"Fine. Everyone here's really nice. But I've missed you like crazy!" To his disappointment, she slid her legs down from around his waist to stand in front of him. Taking his hand, she led him into the condo. "Are you hungry?"

Yes, but not for food. "I ate earlier."

She narrowed her gaze on him. "How much earlier?"

"Lunch."

Rolling her eyes, she took him toward the kitchen. "This isn't how I wanted to greet you on our first night together."

"It works for me. I can't imagine any better reception." Except maybe her being naked when he came in.

Yeah, that would have been the only improvement.

As if she heard that thought, she glanced at him over her shoulder. "I was going to be in the red negligee I sent you a picture of."

"Yeah, okay, that *might* have been better. But the shorts and tee are nice, too. Much better in reality than what I had imagined when last we spoke."

Biting her lip, she shook her head at him. "I don't even have makeup on."

"You're still the most beautiful female I've ever seen."

She stepped toward him to kiss his lips. "You keep sweet-talking me like that and you're bound to get lucky tonight."

Talyn smiled bashfully at her teasing. "It's so good to see you, Felicia." Even better was being around someone who actually talked to him like a sentient being and didn't order him about like a dog.

She kissed him again. "Why don't you take a minute to get comfy and I'll heat you up something real fast? I bought some street clothes for you and put them in the closet and dresser. There's even sweatpants for you."

"Thanks."

"You're welcome."

He stole one more kiss before he went to change.

Felicia smiled at his hot, seductive lope. She couldn't wait to take a bite of that lush, ripped body. And tonight was finally the night. Her hands shook with anticipation.

Honestly, she wished she'd had a little warning. This wasn't how she wanted to seduce him the first time. But at least she wouldn't have to wait any longer.

As soon as she had a plate warmed, she went to find him. She had no idea why he hadn't returned.

Until she entered the bedroom.

Wearing only the pants to his uniform, he was sound asleep on the bed. She was slightly offended until she got close enough to see the deep welts and bruises on his arms and back. The marks on his chest. Tears blinded her as she realized just how badly he'd been mistreated.

She set the plate on the nightstand before she reached to cup his cheek. "Talyn?"

He sighed in his sleep, but didn't stir. If anything, he seemed to go deeper into his dreams.

The poor thing was exhausted. Wishing she could make it

better, she pulled out another blanket and used it to cover his body.

Feeling for him, she curled up at his back and held him close while he slept. How unfair that he was spending all this money for her and had yet to get the very thing he'd paid for. No wonder he told everyone she was his girlfriend. That was much more true of their relationship than companion and patron.

Brushing her hand through his braids, she wished she could give him the life he deserved.

Yet he never complained about anything.

Not once had he even hinted about how badly they treated him at work. Rather, he'd sent her little notes asking how she was doing. If she needed anything. Telling her that he was thinking of her. When she'd asked how he was doing, he'd responded with either *generic* or *missing you*.

Nothing else.

But then, he was a Ring fighter and had been one half of his life. Having someone routinely beat the utter hell out of him was normal. Yet for all that, he wasn't the beast others accused him of. There was a kindness in him that was unfathomable to her.

And the more she saw the real heart of the Hammer, the more she wanted to be with him.

"I think I'm in love with you, Talyn," she whispered, knowing she'd never dare say that to him if he could hear her. Honestly, she'd been infatuated with him the instant he'd gone from confident to bashful the night they met. And it'd turned to love the moment he'd refused to embarrass her with an inspection in front of her broker and guard. That amount of compassion and regard for her feelings . . . she'd known then just how rare a creature he was. How decent.

And as she held him in the dim light, she wanted more than to be his companion.

She wanted to be his lady. In every way. An impossible dream. Without a paternal lineage, he couldn't legally marry.

Ever.

If she stayed with him, she'd never be able to have children. They would arrest him for it, and it would be wrong to bring them into a world that would never hold them with any regard. His life showed her exactly the misery that would be theirs.

And still she wanted that dream of a family with a ferocity that scared her.

"*Stop with your useless dreaming, Felicia! The world is harsh and ugly. The sooner you accept it, the better off you'll be.*" Her mother's bitter words were implanted in her mind.

But she wasn't her mother. And she didn't want to be her. What she wanted was to be Ger Tarra Batur. Talyn's beloved and revered wife.

Most of all, she wanted Talyn to have what he deserved. A home he could go to every night and be held by her.

Talyn came awake to his wrist alarm buzzing. Thinking he was in the barracks, he cursed. Until he realized there was a warm body pressed against his bare back and a tiny hand tangled in his braids.

For one second, he was in heaven.

Turning over, he smiled as he met the sweetest gaze he'd ever imagined. Then he remembered that his alarm was still going off.

"Shit! I slept the whole time?" Gah! He wanted to kill himself for wasting his precious hours with her.

"I tried to wake you, but you were sleeping really soundly. Sorry, sweetie. I fell asleep, too."

Savoring the endearment, he turned off his alarm.

Felicia nibbled his jaw as she dropped her hand to stroke him through his pants. "Do you have five minutes?"

His breathing labored, he clutched her to him. "I would love nothing more, but I don't want our first time to be hurried like that." Since he was as virgin as she was, he wanted to have time to make sure he did it right and to savor it and her.

She nipped his chin before she unzipped his pants.

"Felicia—"

"Shh," she breathed as she kissed her way down his bare chest.

I really need to go. If he was late getting back, Anatole would bring down the wrath of—

Hello!

Talyn cried out as she slowly drew his cock into her mouth, with astounding skill. Oh to hell with his CO. Bastard could rot for all he cared. There was no way he could leave here while she was doing this to him. His senses reeling, he buried his hand in her soft curls while she gently tongued and teased him to a blinding ecstasy.

No wonder males killed for their females. He totally understood that now. Biting his lip, he'd never felt anything better than her mouth on his body. Unable to stand it, he came in a blinding wave of pleasure that was so fast it embarrassed the hell out of him and made him glad he wasn't inside her body.

That would have been useless for her.

Felicia smiled as he relaxed completely. Wiping her mouth, she met his gaze. "Better?"

He cupped her cheek in his hand and stroked her lips with his thumb. "No one's ever done that for me before."

"Really?"

He nodded. "You're the only female who's ever touched me, Felicia."

Felicia sat back. Her jaw went slack at his disclosure and she remembered him telling her that when they'd first kissed. Andarion males had very specific physical needs once they hit puberty. Within their first year of it, almost all males lost their virginity. None lasted more than two. To find a virgin as handsome and old as Talyn was unheard of.

"You've never been to a house of assignation?" It was what most unpledged males did until they were taken.

That adorable blush mottled his cheeks. "I went once."

"And you didn't do anything?"

He glanced away and blushed even more profusely. "It was so . . . uncomfortable. They had this system of four Ps."

"Four Ps?"

He nodded. "You picked a price, a . . . prostitute. A place and then a position. It was like ordering fast food. And they had things listed I wasn't even sure what they were. From the descriptions, some sounded downright dangerous. They even had some you had to sign a waiver to participate in."

Amused, but not wanting him to think she was laughing at him, she hid her face.

"Go ahead and laugh at me. I won't be angry. It was quite special and I'm pretty sure I left a vapor trail when I hit the door running. I think I might have even screamed on my way out." He rubbed at his face. "And then they banned me because of it."

Snickering, she climbed up his body. "I'm so sorry."

"It's all right. I had no intention of returning, anyway. Last thing I want is something so impersonal for something *that* personal. I figured at least with my hand, we have a committed relationship. I know exactly where it's been and who it's touched." He kissed her gently.

"I wish you could stay longer."

"Me, too. But I have to go." He held her tight before he rolled off the bed and dressed beside it.

She rose up on her knees on the mattress to fasten his uniform jacket and straighten it for him. "Next time, I won't let you sleep."

"Deal." He pressed her hand to his cheek. "I'll be in touch when I can."

Felicia wanted to cry as he left her alone again. His absence was like a part of her was being ripped away.

How stupid was that?

Angry over it all, she fell back on the bed and hated her

parents for what they'd done to her. But then it wouldn't have mattered. Had they been married, she wouldn't have been able to claim Talyn at all.

His father had screwed him over even worse than hers had. At least this way, he belonged to her. Maybe not formally, but she had a part of him no one else did.

A vital part of him. This was almost as good as having a stralen husband. Talyn wouldn't be able to break their contract, and he'd never leave her to marry another female. He would be hers for as long as she wanted.

Unless her agency canceled the contract. Though rare, it could happen if another, more prestigious male wanted to contract her. It was what had happened to her mother.

Her father had let her mother go without a single protest, mostly because his children had been angry over his relationship with her mother. It was what had made her mother so bitter toward the world in general and him in particular.

Even if Felicia said no to being switched to a new patron, if the male had enough power behind his lineage, her agency could break her contract and force her. And Talyn didn't have any social ability to fight it.

Suddenly terrified, she pulled up the agency site and made sure her profile was gone.

It was.

Breathing a small sigh of relief, she quickly e-mailed her broker and told him that she was no longer a virgin. A slight lie, but it would help to make sure they didn't offer her to someone else.

Once the probationary period was over, it would be harder to break their contract. She just had to make it four more months.

Four months.

Felicia refused to think about what could happen during that time. Talyn was a fighter and for him, she would be one, too. No one would take her male from her. Not without blood being shed. Her passivity did have its limits, and while she didn't like to fight, it didn't mean she didn't know how.

She froze as she caught a whiff of his scent on the pillow. Smiling, she buried her face against it and inhaled. She closed her eyes and tried to imagine the future she wanted. One spent with a sweet, thoughtful male who treasured her.

With her finger, she switched the screen on her link and texted him. *When will I see you again?*

It was several minutes before he responded. *Soon as I can. Promise.*

A highly unsatisfactory answer. *Fine. But we miss you already.*

We?

Biting her lip, she pulled her shirt off and snapped a quick photo of herself in her lacy bra before sending it to him. *The three of us.*

He sent back a picture of himself smiling so widely, she saw his fangs. *I have training tomorrow after my shift. I won't really have any free time, but if you swing by the gym, I can catch a quick bite with you.*

While it wasn't what she wanted, at least it would give her a few minutes with him. *I'll bring you something to eat. Just send me the time and place, and I'll see you then.*

He sent it over. *Remember, I need lean white meat with nothing on it. 175 grams of protein. Min.*

Wow, but then that made sense given that he was a fighter and a soldier with a large, muscled build. *Will do. Can't wait to see you. Oh, can I ask a favor?*

Anything.

Bring me your undershirt. Don't wash it.

Why?

She felt heat creep over her face and hoped he didn't think her weird for the request. *I want to sleep in it.*

Talyn's throat tightened as he read Felicia's response, and his body hardened even more. *Really?*

You don't think I'm gross for asking, do you?

He smiled at her question. *No. I think you're beautiful.* As soon as he hit Send, his link buzzed. He switched it over to answer. "Major Batur."

"Where are you?"

He checked the time as he heard the shift captain's agitated voice. "En route to base from my condo. You can check my tracker. I'm stuck in traffic, but I still should make check-in."

"Check-in was five minutes ago."

Talyn bit his temper back. "My curfew's ten. My band just went off fifteen minutes ago."

"According to the schedule, your curfew was nine. Your band must be malfunctioning."

You son of a whore. Yet again, Anatole must have changed the time after Talyn left base and then purposefully not updated the alarm on his band. "I'll have my band checked on arrival."

"I'll have to report you tardy."

Of course you will. Anyone else, they'd cover for. "I'll report to Provost on my return." Which would be a mark against him that would cause his current application for a command position and transfer to be kicked back again.

Beautiful.

"I'll notify them immediately to expect you." The captain hung up.

Talyn clenched his teeth as furious hatred tore through him. He was so tired of this shit. Just once, he wanted to be treated like a normal Andarion. His father was one of the famed and adored War Hauks. Theirs was a lineage that rivaled the tadara's for prestige. And in the military, it ranked above even the royal lineage. Hell, there was even a national holiday that celebrated his father's family.

By Andarion law, Anatole should be *his* bitch.

But because his father had turned his back on his Andarion family and married a human, it was a lineage Talyn could never lay legal claim to.

Thanks, Fain. Appreciate your kindness in humiliating my mother and abandoning her. His actions had been so egregious in the eyes of Andarion society that no member of the Warring Blood Clan of Hauk would acknowledge Talyn as one of them.

At all.

Neither of his grandmothers could look at him without sneering. And none of them had ever deigned to speak to him.

Only his Gre Yaya Hauk had ever made any kind of effort to acknowledge to him. But even she'd stopped once her husband learned what she was doing behind his back.

Since then, Talyn had been completely dead to all his Hauk relatives.

Which was fine by him. He didn't need any of those selfish assholes.

His link buzzed. Talyn glanced down to see another message from Felicia. In spite of his misery, he smiled. Just the sight of her playful kitten avatar made him feel better. How stupid was that?

I know you're probably back at base, but wanted to say goodnight. Miss you. She'd sent it with a picture of her lips pressed against the screen.

He held the link to his chest, wishing he'd stayed longer in her arms. In a life of hell, she was the only good thing he had. And it scared him when he thought about how close he'd come to not having her.

How easy it would be for him to lose her forever.

Don't think about it.

He had her now and that was all that mattered. For the first time in his life, he had a friend. At least that was how he liked to think of her.

It was so good to finally have something to look forward to. Better yet, someone who made him laugh when he felt like utter shit. She even sent him little things at the barracks. Fruit, and a stuffed bear with her perfume on it that had gotten him endlessly mocked.

And it'd been so worth it. Granted, he had to keep it in his locker. Still . . .

Someone, other than his mother, cared for him. He'd always wondered what that would feel like. This was so much better than any fantasy he'd ever had.

Don't be stupid, Talyn. She doesn't love you. You pay her for her kindness.

An arm and an effing leg, every month.

But it didn't feel that way. When he looked into her eyes, he saw . . .

What? Love?

You're an idiot.

He glanced out the window as painful reality racked him. Was he really that desperate to have a female care for him that he'd lie to himself so completely?

Yes.

Closing his eyes, he forced himself to face the harsh truth. She didn't care beyond what her contract stipulated. How could she? They didn't know each other. Not really. And unlike him, she could have *anyone* she wanted.

She could even marry one day. Have a family. But if she ever became pregnant from his seed, it'd mean at least ten years of his life would be spent in prison. It was why most agencies wouldn't accept a bastard's application for a companion, at all. Hers was one of the few without a huge banner warning his kind up front not to waste time applying. For that matter, most whorehouses wouldn't even allow a lack-Vest entry, and they were charged double for services, and only permitted to sleep with the older prostitutes who'd been sterilized.

What can you offer her?

Absolutely nothing. He'd be lucky if she renewed their contract at the end of his probation. Why should she? He barely saw her. Almost never spoke directly to her, except through sparse, sporadic texts. They'd been contracted for over six weeks and had yet to sleep together. What companion would want so little contact with her patron?

His throat tightened as he faced a bitter reality. He was shite and that's all he'd ever be. Wife, family, companionship? Those were only dreams for a mongrel dog who lacked lineage.

He swiped the screen to the last picture she'd sent over. Her long, curly hair was fanned out around her face as she lay in bed, looking up at her link. Her brows were perfectly arched over her silvery-white eyes. And her lips were slightly parted so that he could see just the tiniest bit of her fangs.

While her breasts were small, her bra pushed them up and made his mouth water for a taste. Something that wasn't helped by the sight of her taut nipples peeking through the lace.

Maybe one day he'd actually be able to see them.

Grinding his teeth, he squeezed his eyes shut and turned off the link. There was no need in thinking about what could be. About things he could never have. He had to think about the here and now.

And the miserable hell that was waiting for him once he returned to base.

Chapter 5

Felicia glanced around the gym that was filled with fighters who were training and talking. As soon as she spotted Erix by an open area, she headed toward him.

"Hi."

His fierce scowl melted into a friendly smile as he looked up from the screen of his link to see her. "Tara Felicia. What brings you here?"

She turned around to show him her white, flowered backpack. "I have Talyn's dinner and was going to watch him practice. Did I get the wrong time?"

He shook his head. "He must be running late from patrol. It happens sometimes. So how are you today?"

"Doing well. You?"

He looked past her shoulder and frowned again.

She turned to see Talyn, who was moving very stiffly. He wore that stern I'm-going-to-kill-you-and-hide-your-body-so-get-out-of-my-way expression that made everyone scurry at his approach. Worried, she closed the distance between them.

He offered her a bashful smile as soon as he saw her. She adored the way his entire face lit up whenever she was near. Every time he did that, he made her feel so incredibly special and welcome.

"Hey."

Worried about how he was moving, she frowned at him. "Are you all right?"

Talyn nodded before he placed a chaste kiss to her cheek. Pulling back, he met Erix's gaze. "Who am I sparring with tonight?"

"New kid I'm training. Try not to kill him."

He laughed, then grimaced.

"You okay?" Erix asked before she had the chance.

Talyn nodded again. "Can you double-check my curfew tonight?"

Erix cursed under his breath. "Did he change it on you again?"

"Yeah. Yesterday, after I left base."

"How late were you?"

Talyn sighed before he answered irritably. "I wasn't, but thirty-seven minutes went down on my record. I'm lucky they let me out to train tonight."

Felicia duplicated Erix's scowl. "That's not that bad, is it?"

Talyn didn't answer as he caressed her cheek with his hand. "I'll get changed and be back."

"Is it?" she asked Erix after Talyn left them.

"Yeah, it is." He pulled his link out and made a call to cancel the sparring for the night.

She set her backpack down and waited until Erix was finished with his call before she spoke again. "I don't understand what's going on. Why is this a big deal? It's just thirty minutes."

A tic started in Erix's jaw. "For every minute he's late checking in to post, he gets two lashes with a cane. Thirty-seven minutes equals seventy-four strikes."

The true horror of that wasn't apparent to her until Talyn returned and she saw the harsh, fresh bruises marring his back as he pulled on a T-shirt to cover them.

Tears choked her. She felt sick to her stomach. "Did I cause that?"

"No," Talyn breathed, pulling her into his arms. "It had nothing to do with you. I promise." He kissed her cheek again before he released her.

"His commander screws with his check-ins sometimes," Erix snarled.

"Why?"

Talyn snorted. "What can I say? I'm an abrasive asshole." He approached Erix and picked up his practice gloves. "Where's my opponent?"

He screwed his face up at the sight of Talyn's bruised back. "I canceled it. You don't need anyone else pounding on you until some of that heals. We can do cardio and weights tonight. Not to mention . . ." He held his link out to Talyn. "He changed your check-in again. You don't have that much time for training."

Talyn growled. "Thanks for looking it up."

"No problem."

Felicia opened her backpack and dug out the plastic containers. "I brought your dinner."

Talyn sat down on the mat next to where she stood. "Where'd you get it from?"

She handed him an airtight plate and cutlery. "I made it."

"You cook?" he asked incredulously.

She gave him a playful, menacing stare. "You don't have to sound so shocked. I love to cook, and your bland, unsavory meals are very easy to prepare."

With a sweet smile at her teasing, he opened his plate.

Erix gently clapped him on the arm. "Eat your dinner in peace, kid. You need it."

"Thanks."

Sitting down beside him, Felicia handed him some of the water she'd packed. "I feel so bad about what happened last night."

"Don't." He touched her hair and smiled at her. "I have no regrets. For what you did . . . they can skin me alive."

She looked at his back and scowled. "I find it hard to believe you feel that way."

He shrugged nonchalantly. "Beatings I can take. Trust me. My mother's given me harder kisses and hugs." He sampled the food, then flashed her an adorable expression of disbelief. "It's delicious."

"Thanks," she said sarcastically. "Appreciate your confidence in my abilities." She opened her own plate. Returning his smile, she fed him a bit of her cut-up fruit.

He nipped playfully at her fingers before he swallowed it. "How was school today?"

"Boring. How was patrol?"

"Not boring. Ran into a group of Tavali."

Her eyes widened at his casual mention of the bloodthirsty pirates who preyed on their corporate ships and freighters. "What happened?"

He swallowed and took a drink before he answered. "We fought. I struck a couple of blasts to one of their fighters, but they eluded capture."

"Did they blast you?"

"They tried. Luckily, I dodged. Ran them all the way back to their baseship, the *Storm Dancer.*"

"I'm glad. Please, don't get hurt."

"That's usually my game plan." He winked at her. "Especially now that I have a really good reason to stay out of traction." Wiping his hand off, he pulled the physiology book out of her backpack so that he could glance through it. "You have finals soon, don't you?"

She nodded.

"If you need any help, my mother's immediate family were all physicians and surgeons. In fact, I'm pretty sure this was written by one of her older brothers. And I passed the certs to get in. I've got a good handle on the subject."

"Be happy to have a gorgeous study partner. Not sure how

much studying I'll get done talking to you, but I'm willing to try."

Talyn pulled her against him and nuzzled her hair.

Closing her eyes, she savored the sensation of him holding her so sweetly. He took a deep breath in her hair before he got up and headed to the weight bag. While she packed away his empty plate, he shadowboxed. Until he started sweating, then he began punching the weight bag. Ferociously.

She cringed at the strength of his blows that hit it so hard it sounded like he was about to break the chains holding it in place.

"Impressive, isn't it?"

She nodded at Erix's question. "I would hate to be on the receiving end of that."

"Yes. You would." He wrinkled his nose playfully at her. "Luckily, he would never hit a female. And lucky for me, he'd never hit an old male." He glanced over at her. "Thank you, by the way."

"For what?"

"Taking care of him."

"I haven't really done anything."

"I disagree. There's an innate change in him. A peaceful calm he didn't have before. And I've never seen him smile and laugh like he does around you, never mind tease and play."

She wasn't so sure about that. Talyn was still very serious whenever they were together. "I find that hard to believe."

"You shouldn't. I swear. I didn't even know he *could* smile. At all. He's very different when you're not around. Deathly serious and stern. Silent, like he's sizing you up for a body bag. No one can get much more than noncommittal grunts or smart-ass retorts out of him."

She remembered glimpsing that part of his personality when he'd been in the room the first time they met. And again at the Ritadarion restaurant.

"You make him playful and happy, Felicia. I can almost see the kid in him whenever you're around."

She didn't believe that until Talyn ran at her and picked her up. Laughing, he swung her around and placed a quick kiss to her lips before he dodged to the double-end bag and started training with it.

He was so impressive that within a few minutes, everyone at the gym had stopped what they were doing to watch him train while Erix called out drills.

"Damn," one of the males next to her said to a friend. "I don't ever want to be in the Ring with *that*."

"That's the Iron Hammer. No one wants to be in the Ring with *that*."

"Did you see him when they were charting his PSI?" a third male asked the other two.

"No."

Felicia arched her brow at the conversation. "What was it?" she asked the males.

"Almost a ton of pressure. Just over nineteen hundred."

Her jaw dropped.

"Bullshit!" the male beside him said.

The male who'd spoken held his hand up in a sign of sincerity.

"No, I swear. It's why they call him the Iron Hammer. You can check it online, if you don't believe me. *Splatterdome* did it as part of a series where they charted the PSI for all the big-name fighters. And that was barehanded. He rated more than two hundred PSI over his closest rival, Death Warrant."

Wow! Her head spun at what they were telling her. But as she watched him, she didn't doubt it. He did hit like a sledgehammer.

The male closest to her raked an interested look over her body. "Who are you here with, love?"

His friend turned the male's face away from her. "Don't even. I saw her eating with the Hammer earlier. More to the point, hand-feeding him."

"Oh dear God." He passed an apologetic stare at her. "Sorry. It was nice speaking to you. Give your male my best." He quickly put space between them.

Laughing, Felicia returned to watching Talyn practice. There was a fierce beauty and grace to what he did. And like Erix had said, a deadly earnestness. But she still would hate to see him in the Ring being pummeled by another fighter. For that matter, she despised the bruises that marred his tawny skin.

Once he was done with the bag, he grabbed the towel from Erix and wiped his face. She walked over to him and pulled him against her.

He grimaced. "I stink and I'm sweaty."

She nipped his chin. "I like your smell. Have I grossed you out yet?"

"Are you trying?" He gave her a fierce squeeze.

His band started buzzing. It was a different alarm than normal.

"What's that?"

"Drill call. I have to leave immediately. Can you grab my stuff and take it back to the condo for me?"

"Absolutely."

Pulling his gloves off, he kissed her and handed them to her before he pulled on a clean, loose T-shirt and left.

Scared of what it meant, she took the gloves to Erix. "Should I be worried?"

"I don't know. It's a squadron alert. Could be an unexpected meeting or they're needed to fly."

She cringed as she remembered Talyn telling her about the Tavali. She hoped this wasn't them returning with a larger group. "I don't think I like this dangerous life he lives."

"Yeah, I feel your pain. And I hate that sound whenever I hear it. I was having dinner with my son when he got a call like that. It was the last time I saw him."

"I'm sorry, Erix."

His white eyes sad, he inclined his head to her. "Did you drive or take public transport?"

"Public."

"Then I'll take you home."

"You don't have to."

"Yeah, I do. Haven't you seen the news? Five females your age have gone missing this week. It's too late for a young one to be out alone."

His kindness warmed her heart. "Thank you. I'll grab Talyn's things and be right out." She went to the dressing room and found the small bag Talyn had carried in. Opening it, she paused. Folded neatly on top was the shirt she'd requested, along with a small red rose. Tears gathered in her eyes. He was always surprising her with such sweet, thoughtful gifts.

"Please be safe," she whispered. She didn't want to think about anything happening to him.

As soon as Talyn hit the base and realized they were scrambling for another Tavali attack, he rushed into the lockers to change his clothes. Emergency deployments like this were the only time he was allowed in here to change with the Vested.

Everyone's nerves were stretched taut as friends bantered and dressed as fast as they could manage, then ran to their fighters.

Talyn accidentally brushed his empty sleeve against a female's shoulder as he shrugged his flight suit on.

"Don't touch me!" she growled with unwarranted hostility.

Assuming it was because of his birth status, Talyn mumbled an apology and stepped away to finish dressing. But as he pulled out his boots, he glanced at her and noticed the way her hands shook as she struggled with the buckles on her suit. The fact that her eyes were swollen and red as if she'd been crying for a while.

More than that, there was a faint bruised handprint around the skin of her throat that was peeping out above her high collar. A slight crusting of blood around her nose.

Someone had attacked her, and by the way she was acting, he figured it wasn't in a legitimate fight.

Talyn knew better than to speak to a Vested officer, especially one with a higher rank, but she was obviously upset and shouldn't be battling like this. Though her name was Farina Pinara, he wasn't allowed to use it, so he defaulted to her call sign. "You okay, Syndrome?"

As expected, she glared ultimate hatred at him, then burst into tears.

Stunned, Talyn wasn't sure what to do. Before he could stop himself, he pulled her against his chest to comfort her. "Shh, it's okay."

She trembled in his arms. But to her credit, and in true Andarion fashion, she pulled herself together quickly and stepped back. "Sorry, Batur."

"No problem."

As Anatole and his two wingmen sauntered past, Talyn caught the way Anatole smirked at Farina. He mumbled something to the asshole on his right that caused the male to laugh before he raked a salacious stare over Farina's body. One that brought another wave of tears to her eyes.

And made her shake even more ferociously.

A bad feeling went through him. Sweeping his gaze around the room, he noted the way a number of the females reacted to Anatole and his high-caste wingmen. How fast they vacated the lockers.

Including Farina.

She went so fast, she left part of her uniform behind.

Don't get involved. This was none of his business and there wasn't a soldier here who would *ever* stand up for him. His current war record was proof of that. But he couldn't help it. His mother had taught him better than to turn away from an Andarion in need.

To fight for right, not for power.

Grabbing her gear, he went after her.

"Syndrome?" he called as he followed her into the hallway. "You forgot your helmet and gloves."

Tears swam in her eyes as she paused and turned back toward him. "Thank you."

Yeah, she was tore up. Normally, she'd be acerbic and pissy with him. When she reached for the helmet, he tightened his grip on it to keep her there for a minute longer.

"Did Anatole do that to you?" He dropped his gaze to her neck.

She trembled even more. "Nothing happened."

Bullshit, and he knew it with every instinct he possessed. Cursing, he started back for the lockers where Anatole was dressing.

Farina grabbed his arm. "Talyn, please. Don't."

He wasn't sure what shocked him most. The fact she deigned to touch him or that she'd used his name. From those actions alone, one thing was clear. Anatole had shattered her spirit. In the past, she'd have *never* touched the likes of him. For that matter, he was stunned she knew he had a given name, other than "mongrel." It was all any of them had ever called him. "Our females aren't his private harem."

Her grip tightened on his arm as her eyes widened. She lowered her gaze quickly and dropped her hand from his arm.

Talyn turned to find Anatole and his two friends drawing near.

"This isn't a practice drill! Do I need to put both of you on report?"

Defiant to the level of stupid, Talyn curled his lip at his CO. "I challenge you to the Ring, motherfucker!" he growled.

The colonel's friends and Farina sucked their breaths in.

Anatole laughed in his face. "You can't hit me, you stupid piece of shit. It'll mean your life if you do."

Talyn glared at him. Cowardly bastard had no right to sully an Andarion uniform. It was a disgrace to have something like him don it. "Are you not Andarion enough to face me?"

Anatole grabbed the front of Talyn's battlesuit and tried to shove him back. His eyes widened as he realized just how strong Talyn was and the fact that his limp touch had no effect on him. At all. "Watch yourself, mongrel. Be a shame to have such a regaled sports hero go up in flames." Snapping his fingers, he motioned his lap dogs to follow after him.

When Talyn started forward to finish their discussion, Farina cut off his path.

"It's not worth it, Batur. But thank you for being the male none of the rest have been."

Nightdice nodded as she stopped by his side. "Yeah. Everyone else has turned a blind eye."

A tic started in his jaw as he realized several other female pilots were also looking on with gratitude. Some of them were pledged, even married. That angered him even more. It wasn't just for them he fought. It was for his mother and Felicia. "I don't care what he does to me. This stops. Royal-blooded or not, he has no right to touch any of you. Ever!"

Farina offered him a grateful smile as she handed him his helmet. "I'll be your wingman, Viper."

He inclined his head to her.

For the first time in his career, Talyn walked into the bay with other Andarions. And that only saddened him more that he'd earned Farina's and the other females' friendship by simply doing the right thing. Something every male in their squad should be doing for them.

What had happened to the Andarion race that they would put up with this shit? That they'd allow their females to be threatened and abused by some royal-blooded asshole and his friends?

As he started to jog for his ship, a female stepped in front of him and struck her chest twice with an open palm—a friendly sign of good luck.

Stunned, he barely returned it before he went to his fighter. Even his female ground crew gestured at him.

Wanting to do more for them, Talyn pulled his mic into place. He had Tavali to fight right now. But once this was over, he had a much more pressing war he intended to battle. "Viper-Ichi ready for launch."

"Viper-Ichi clear to launch," the controller responded.

Talyn entered the clearance code in his con and was thrown back against his seat as the ship was ejected through its launch tube.

It shot him straight into hell. There were fighters everywhere.

"Damn, Viper," Farina said in his ear. "You seriously pissed off the Tavali earlier. What'd you do?"

"Apparently, they don't like being shot at. Who knew?" He banked right and narrowly missed an ion blast to his windshield.

He listened to their comm intel as he kept his eyes on the enemy. It was another group of Porturnum Tavali. Whether or not they were related to the earlier group he'd battled was unclear. While it was said the four branches of Tavali functioned like military governments, no one outside of their pirate world really knew what went on inside their organizations. They were as secretive as hermitic nuns.

The only thing Talyn knew for sure was that the western group of the pirate outlaws lived to prey on Andarion freighters. Most of all, they loved to take Andarions as slaves.

For some reason, the Porturnum leader hated the Andarion Empire and went out of his way to assault them as often as possible.

Talyn dove beneath the flaming remains of a Tavali fighter and came out in front of the *Storm Dancer.* He cursed under his breath as he recognized that ship. "Pit Viper to Command. This is the same Tavali group I engaged earlier. At least part of it."

No wonder they fought like they did. This was a vengeance run. Something proven as his fighter was ID'd and one of the Tavali peeled off the rest of the Andarions to chase him.

Laughing, Talyn did what he did best.

Made their mamas cry. Fortunately for his, he flew as well as he fought in the Ring. At least that was his thought until he came up on a black Tavali fighter with a pilot who was amazing. Slippery bastard cut through everything Talyn threw at him.

Worse, Talyn was having a hard time dodging the return volleys. Whoever had taught this one to fight had known what they were doing.

As he rolled to avoid another round of blasts, he caught the name of the pilot that was written in Universal on his wing.

Blister.

What kind of stupid call sign was that? He didn't even want to know what the Tavali had done to earn that moniker. Not that it mattered. This was a fiercely talented warrior, in spite of his name.

Talyn was actually worried.

"Viper! Point ten!"

Talyn hit his retro engines and pulled up and rolled. Brief blasts of color lit the silent darkness around him. Unfortunately, that move brought him into range for "Blister." The pirate opened fire with some kind of weapon Talyn had never seen before. It shredded his shields and burned through the outer layer of his fighter.

"Viper-Ichi hit." Talyn cursed as his controls shocked him. "My directionals are failing. Rear engine going dark."

Farina flew straight at him to engage the pirates who had a hard-on for him. "Syndrome covering Viper. Need a beam, Andarions. Hurry!"

"Nightdice sheltering Syndrome and Viper. We need help. Viper's taking massive fire and they're going for his throat."

Talyn jerked back as another shock went through his arm from the short-circuiting panels. He saw an Andarion fighter he assumed was Nightdice moving in to protect him.

Or so he thought.

One moment, he was opening the channel to warn Syndrome about two Tavali headed for her. In the next, the Andarion fired on him and his entire ship exploded.

Chapter 6

Felicia flipped through the news, looking for a report on Talyn and any possible battle he might have been involved with. There was nothing. Only stories about civilians who'd gone missing, and women who'd been attacked.

She forced herself not to pick up her link. She'd texted Talyn so much that she was afraid to do so again. At this point, he could have her arrested for stalking.

The link buzzed.

"Talyn?" she asked without even verifying the number.

"It's Erix. Is this Felicia?"

"It is. Is everything okay?"

When he didn't answer right away, it made her heart skip a beat. "I'm at the hospital."

Her breath caught as tears filled her eyes. "Talyn?"

"He's in surgery. They called me when they couldn't reach his mother. I knew you'd want to know. I've sent a transport for you. It should be there any minute."

"I'm on my way." Hanging up, she started for the lift, then remembered she was in her nightgown. Frustrated, she ran to the bedroom and threw on her clothes as fast as she could.

She didn't know how long it took her to get to the hospital. It was somewhere between a heartbeat and forever.

As soon as she entered the waiting room, she saw Erix, seated and looking sick to his stomach. Terrified and shaking, she rushed over to him. "Have you heard anything?"

He shook his head.

"Do you know what happened?"

Erix sighed wearily as he took her hand in his. "Tavali attack."

Felicia scowled at the look on his face. "What aren't you telling me?"

"I overheard the medics talking. They think it might have been friendly fire that brought him down."

"What do you mean?"

Anger snapped harshly in his white eyes. "They said that it was one of our own who fired on Talyn's ship."

"Anatole?"

"I don't know. They didn't say."

Rage darkened her sight as she craved blood. "Is there any way to prove it?"

"If there's footage from the battle . . . maybe."

But if it was Anatole, he'd make sure that footage was deleted. Bastard!

Never in her life had she wanted anyone's throat so badly.

Erix pulled her into a hug. "Why don't you sit down? I'll get us some coffee."

"Thank you."

As Felicia took her seat, a tall, gorgeous female who didn't appear much older than her came in wearing a commander's formal uniform. The commander swept her gaze around the occupants before she headed straight to the empty nurses' station. Impatiently, she pressed and held the buzzer.

The nurse glared at her as she came forward from a back room. "May I help you?"

"I'm Deputy Commander Batur. My son, Major Talyn Batur, was brought in and I need to know where he is and his condition. *Immediately.*"

Felicia held her breath as she waited for the update.

The nurse pulled up something on her monitor. "He's still in surgery, Commander. That's all I have. Sorry."

The anguished expression on his mother's face brought tears to Felicia's own eyes. "What was his condition when he was brought in? My parents are Doctors Garaint and Nila Batur." The nurse's eyes widened at those prestigious names that literally everyone in the medical profession knew. "Please, tell me what you have about my son. I have to know."

The nurse read from her screen. "Critical One. He took several direct hits that exploded his ship, and was ejected into space. It appears he slammed into shrapnel or debris and was coding when they hauled him into a medpod."

"No!" His mother fell to her knees and sobbed.

Felicia was grateful she was sitting because she had the same reaction. It felt as if all the air had been violently sucked out of her lungs.

But as she saw his mother's agonized grief, she went to her and pulled her into her arms.

The commander wept against her shoulder and shook so hard that Felicia feared she'd pass out. Her own tears blinded her as she prayed with everything she had.

A shadow fell over them. She looked up to see Erix's pale face.

"What happened?" he asked.

Patting Galene's back, Felicia forced herself to stop crying long enough to answer. "Talyn's still in surgery, but he was coding when they brought him in."

Only then did his mother pull back to frown at her. "Who are you?"

"Felicia."

Her brow furrowed by confusion, she looked up at Erix. "Who is she?"

"Talyn's female."

She blinked as she scowled even more. "Since when?"

Erix arched a brow. "For weeks now, that *I* know. Didn't he tell you?"

Shaking her head, the commander raked a less-than-flattering stare over Felicia. At least that was what she assumed until Galene lovingly cupped her face in her hand. "You take care of my baby?"

"As best I can."

Galene pulled her in for a crushing embrace and kissed her cheek. "Thank you."

Completely confounded, Felicia wasn't sure what to think.

With a ragged breath, Galene finally stood and allowed Erix to help her into a chair.

This wasn't the callous Andarion mother Felicia had expected. For one thing, the commander was really young. She couldn't be more than her mid-thirties, if that.

Since the commander refused to attend his matches, Felicia had assumed Galene would be uncaring and cold—something that wasn't unusual for their mothers. But as the hours went by, and his mother tearfully regaled her with hundreds of pictures, and story after story of Talyn's childhood antics, she learned exactly how much his mother loved and adored him.

Scarily so.

Galene even had copies of his elementary and primary school transcripts and grades on her link, as well as the stats for every fight he'd ever been in.

Most of all, Felicia learned that Talyn kept everything about himself bottled up. Felicia wasn't the only one he was reserved around. He really didn't talk about anything with anyone.

Not even his own mother.

In fact, he told Felicia more about himself than he did anyone else. And given how little that was, it was truly frightening.

When Felicia briefly mentioned med school to his mother, Galene had no idea that Talyn had ever applied. Never mind been turned down. Repeatedly. Felicia had barely caught herself before she outed something he must have kept from his mother for a reason.

Galene got up to pace again. Like her son, she was a fierce, intense beast. A force to be reckoned with. She checked the time and cursed.

"He'll be okay," Felicia reassured her.

"How can you be so sure?"

"Because if he's not, I'm going on a killing spree, and I'm sure the gods don't want me to do that."

His mother snorted. "I'll help."

"Good. I need someone to reload." Felicia stifled a yawn. It would be daybreak soon. They'd already changed out surgeons, which was a good and bad thing. Good that Talyn was doing well enough in surgery that they were willing to keep going. Bad that it was taking so long.

Erix had fallen asleep about an hour ago and was curled up in a chair, snoring.

"I'll get us more coffee." Felicia had just stood up and stretched when the surgeon came through the doors.

He approached them with practiced stoicism. "Is one of you Felicia?"

"I am."

With a grim nod, he acknowledged her. "Major Batur was calling for you when they brought him in. The first surgeon wanted me to tell you that and to make sure you were on hand whenever he wakes."

"How is he?" his mother asked.

"We won't know for at least twenty-four hours. If he makes it through, it's a good sign. But there was a lot of swelling in his brain and he had a number of broken bones that we fused back together. He'll probably have a permanent limp from the surgery on his left leg. Several internal organs were damaged when the dampners gave out, and it's probably what injured his head."

Felicia took Galene's hand into hers as she listened intently.

"Can we see him?" Galene asked.

"He's in recovery right now. But as soon as we move him to a room, I'll have a nurse come get you."

"Thank you."

He inclined his head to them before he vanished through the OR doors again.

Yawning, Erix joined them. "Is he all right?"

"He's out of surgery and in recovery." Galene patted his arm. "Why don't you go on home?"

He nodded. "Call me if you need anything."

"I will." She turned to Felicia. "You should probably go on, too."

"I'm not leaving," she said adamantly. "Not as long as he's here."

Galene pulled her against her and held her close. She placed a kiss to Felicia's head. "Thank you."

"You don't have to thank me. Not where Talyn's concerned. It's my highest honor to care for him." Felicia smiled at her. "I'll go get our coffee. You want it plain again?"

She nodded.

"I'll be right back."

As Felicia entered the break room, she heard two of the nurses talking.

"I'm telling you, it's *the* Talyn Batur. The Iron Hammer himself. If we call the media, we can make a fortune on this."

Felicia saw red over another group of Vested Andarions scheming to make money from Talyn's pain. Before she could think twice, she beelined to their table. "If you call the media—" She glanced at the female's name tag. "—Dorea, or if anyone else in this hospital, for that matter, calls them, I'll personally drag *you* down the hallway by your cheap hair extensions, and beat you every step of the way."

She sneered at Felicia. "Who *are* you?"

Normally, Felicia would have backed down from that scathing glare and condescension.

But not this time. She was tired of the way everyone treated Talyn when he didn't deserve it. Tired of the way their culture worked. Were he Vested, they wouldn't have dared breathe a word of his name out loud.

"Talyn's bloodthirsty female who holds his privacy sacred . . . *your* life? Not so much."

Her face went pale.

"Yeah, remember that. He is here to be treated and to heal, and not be disturbed by money-grubbing animals out to profit from the injuries he sustained while protecting his race from off-world pirates. He's a hero, not bonus pay for the likes of *you*."

Felicia returned to the pot to grab the commander's coffee. She cast one last threatening look at the females. "You better make sure no media shows, or I'll report you both. And before you ask, my father happens to be Satrapehs Saren ezul Terronova. I will have both your jobs *and* your putrid lives the minute you walk out the door." With that, she took the coffee back to the waiting room and handed a cup to Galene.

Her hands were shaking so badly from her anger that she was amazed she hadn't scalded herself. She'd never before made such a stand on anyone's behalf. And now she knew why. It was scary. They were a lot larger than her. But be damned if anyone was going to make a single credit off Talyn. The last thing he needed was a flock of vultures trying to interview him while he was fighting for his life.

While she didn't relish the thought of speaking to her father, she would make that call and bust the ass of every medical professional in this building. No one would harm Talyn. Not after everything he'd done for her, and asked for so little in return.

She forced her breathing to calm as she realized how much of Talyn was rubbing off on her.

"Are you all right?" Galene asked.

Felicia forced a smile. "Worried about Talyn." There was no need to upset his mother any worse. She had enough to deal with.

A tear slid down Galene's cheek. Brushing it away, she took a sip of coffee. "He's everything to me, Felicia. All I have in this universe. I couldn't live if something happened to my baby." She caught a sob. "Why didn't he go to med school like I wanted him to? Why?" She broke off into silent sobs again.

Felicia bit her lip to keep from speaking. She wanted to answer that question, but it wasn't her place. Talyn knew his mother much better than she did. If he'd kept the truth from her, he must have a really good reason.

She sat down beside her. "He'll be okay, Commander. I know it. He's too strong a fighter to go down. He won't do that to us."

Her lips trembling, she cupped Felicia's face in her hand. "You are precious. I can see why Talyn chose you."

"You only say that 'cause you haven't met me in the morning. I promise, I'm not nice. Rather ferocious."

Galene laughed. "Like a tiny *mia*."

Felicia smiled at the word for mouse. She flashed her fangs at his mother. "*Mia* with a vicious bite." At least she was finally discovering she had teeth.

Galene saluted her with the cup. "You'd have to be for my Talyn to love you."

Uncomfortable, Felicia glanced away. His mother didn't know she was a paid companion. Galene thought they were dating, and she didn't have the heart to tell her the truth. The last thing she wanted was for his mother to sneer at her like other Andarions did.

Especially given how much Felicia loved him.

She was just finishing her coffee when a nurse came to get them.

His mother took her hand before they followed the female to the private room where Talyn was hooked to monitors. At first, they scared her until she saw how strong his vitals were.

She tightened her hand on his mother's. "See! I told you he'd be all right. Look at that heart rate, and his oxygen and res levels."

"But his brain activity is low."

Felicia studied it. "He's still in a chemically induced coma. That's to be expected."

His mother frowned at her. "You're from a medical family?"

"I'm in med school. Second year."

A bright smile lit her beautiful face. "My mother is a leading cardiac specialist and my father's the royal physician who delivered the tizirani Jullien and Nykyrian. What's your primary focus?"

"It was pediatrics. But I'm now leaning toward sports medicine."

"Because of Talyn?"

Felicia nodded. "I've already passed my PT certs, and I know he'll have long-term concerns with what he does during his off-duty hours. I'd like to be able to help him later."

That seemed to please her.

Galene inclined her head to the small recliner in the corner. "Why don't you rest while I keep first watch?"

"You sure?"

She nodded. "I'm military and used to sleep dep. And you look like you're about to fall over."

Honestly? Felicia was. It'd been a long day, and with finals coming up, she hadn't been sleeping well. Yawning, she went to the chair.

Galene pulled a spare blanket from the medical supply cabinet and covered her with it.

"Thank you."

She patted Felicia's shoulder. "Good night, sweetling."

As Felicia closed her eyes, she saw Talyn's mother move to the bed to take his hand into hers. She pressed it against her lips to kiss his knuckles, then held it to her cheek as she whispered desperate prayers for his recovery.

I was so wrong about you. Now she understood why Talyn was devoted to his mother. Why he never spoke ill of her, and had given his hours for her promotion.

He was his mother's entire world.

Unlike Felicia's parents with her, Galene didn't see him as a burden or nuisance. He was her blessing and strength.

That was something Felicia not only understood, but related to. Tears brimmed in her eyes as she glanced back to his bruised face.

Don't leave us, Talyn.

They both needed him. All her life, she'd felt unwanted and alone. Subpar. But Talyn needed her as much as she needed him. For the first time, she felt like she had a place in this world. Someone who really cared about her. And yet in the back of her mind was the reality that any time in her life things had gone well, they'd derailed. Horribly.

Please don't die.

As she gazed at the monitors, she knew, in spite of what she'd told Galene, that the odds weren't with the Hammer in this. His chances of survival were so small, she couldn't bear to think about it or she'd scream.

CHAPTER 7

Talyn slowly blinked his eyes open and groaned as pain split his head in half. Gods, it hurt. His breathing harsh and labored, he felt pressure on both his hands. Scowling, he looked up into Felicia's bright gaze.

Then his mother's.

Confused, he started to speak, only to feel the tube in his throat that kept him from it.

His mother buzzed for the doctor while Felicia tightened her grip on his hand.

"Hey, baby." She lifted his hand to her lips and kissed it.

He tightened his grip on her fingers.

"You had us both terrified," his mother lovingly chided. "Don't you ever get hurt again. I mean it!"

He really hadn't meant to get hurt this time. To be truthful, he couldn't remember what had happened. One minute, he'd been dogfighting. The next . . .

Everything else was a blur in his memory. Even most of the day was missing. He really couldn't recall anything.

His mother and Felicia stepped back as the doctor and nurse came in to evaluate him.

"It's amazing," the doctor said at last. "He's still recovering, but his vitals are strong and he should be back to normal in a few weeks. He's definitely healing better than we'd hoped."

Gee, Doc, thanks for that happy prognosis. Nice to know he was still defying the odds that said he'd drop dead any second.

"If the two of you will give us the room, I'll remove his tube."

His mother left first. Felicia hesitated.

With a sweet little nose wrinkle, she smiled at him. "Don't bite the doctor."

He laughed, then choked.

The doctor, however, didn't appreciate her humor.

At first Talyn did fine as the tube slid out. Until it caught. Then he started throwing up immediately.

The nurse scrambled and barely caught it.

Shaking all over, Talyn leaned back as his stomach slowly settled down again.

"Breathe easy." The doctor retook his vitals. "You're doing fine."

Yeah, right. Talyn looked at the doctor as if the male was crazy. He didn't feel fine. He felt like total shit.

After a few minutes, the doctor let them in again. "Feed him ice chips. He's not ready to drink just yet, but he needs to stay hydrated."

Felicia went to get a cup as his mother returned to stand by his bed.

"You should have told me about Felicia. She was quite a shock to my system."

He swallowed hard before he tried to speak. "I haven't known her that long. Just a few weeks."

She narrowed her gaze at him. "She's a companion, isn't she?"

He glanced away.

"You don't have to answer. She has to be. But you should know that she hasn't left here since you were brought in four days ago. She's fetched for me and taken care of us like a daughter, and has been genuinely scared for you. I don't know which of us prayed harder for your recovery." She brushed her hand through his braids. "Paid or not, that girl adores you. No one could fake the heart I've seen in her, and definitely not for almost a week with no sleep."

He swallowed hard as those words choked him with emotions he couldn't even begin to fathom. But one, he could easily identify. "I love her, Matarra."

His mother tensed. "Talyn . . . you're too young to know what love is."

He emphatically disagreed with that. While he might be young, he knew what he felt. And he was a lot older than his parents had been when his mother "fell in love" with his father.

If what his mother felt for the dickhead who fathered him wasn't love, damned if he knew what that word meant.

"You've never had a female before, son. Don't make the mistake of thinking your hormone levels can sustain a difficult relationship. You know why you can *never* have a female or family of your own. What would happen if she ever saw the real you. The risks . . . you can't let anyone that close to you, and you know it."

Talyn glanced away as he bit back a sneer at her dismissal of his feelings. Unfortunately, he knew exactly what she meant. Love was hard for two *normal* Vested Andarions.

For someone like him . . .

He had nothing to offer Felicia, except profound risk and heartbreak.

"Please tell me you haven't said any of this to her."

He shook his head. "We're still on our probationary period."

"Then I wouldn't tell her. No good can come of it. You know that."

As much as he hated to admit it, she was right.

Licking his lips, he grimaced and changed the subject. "Is there something I can use to brush my teeth?"

His mother smiled. "My proper little soldier. Always so meticulously clean and well-kempt." She went to the sink to open his shaving kit.

"Yeah, well, I got tired of the ass-spankings and tirades whenever I let myself go."

Laughing, she returned to help him brush his teeth. "I don't know about that. I think you must have enjoyed the spankings. You went from letting me do it, to every Andarion stepping into a Ring with you."

He spit out the paste into the plastic container she held for him. "What can I say? Big and hairy as they are on their worst day, they're nowhere near as scary as you on your best."

His mother let out a tired *heh* sound at that.

As he finished brushing his teeth, Felicia returned with the ice chips. "Is he speaking yet?"

"I am."

She smiled warmly. "I've so missed the sound of that deep, rumbling voice." She dipped a spoon into the cup and held it for him to eat.

He dutifully opened his lips and allowed her to feed ice to him.

His mother cocked a brow as she watched them. "I feel like an outsider."

Felicia blushed. "I'm sorry, Commander." She held the cup out toward her. "Would you like to do this?"

She shook her head. "I have a feeling he'd much rather eat from your hand than mine."

Talyn ate another bite of ice. "Shouldn't you be in class?"

"I spoke to my professors. They understand, and I've been doing my assignments while we took turns watching over you."

He glanced over to his mother. "What about you?"

"I don't have class."

He rolled his eyes. "What about your post?"

"I spoke to my superiors and they understand. Sorry, champ. You're stuck with both of us."

"I wouldn't have it any other way. Well . . . maybe with a little less pain." He grimaced as he adjusted himself in the bed.

Felicia took a bite of his ice chips.

"Hey!" he said playfully.

"What?" She blinked innocently without the least hint of guilt in her eyes. "I'll get you more, you big old baby." She fed him another bite.

In spite of the pain, his body hardened at the intimacy of her feeding him with the same spoon that had just touched her lips and tongue. But it wasn't the spoon or ice he wanted to taste. It was those sassy, glossy lips that made him hunger.

Damn the hospital blanket for being so thin. He bent his knee to disguise the sudden bulge he was afraid was way too obvious.

The blush on both his mother's and Felicia's faces corroborated the fact that his erection was as apparent as he feared.

"Want a pillow, baby?" Felicia asked.

"Yes," he groaned, humiliated to the core of his soul.

Laughing, she pulled one from a small recliner and placed it over his groin.

"Thank you."

His mother cleared her throat. "I think I'll go call . . . somebody. I'll be back in a few."

As soon as she was gone, Felicia leaned in to give him the kiss he was dying for. When she started to pull away, he kept her there for a moment longer.

"Better?" she asked with a wicked grin.

"Not really." He pulled the pillow back to show her.

She tsked at him. "Poor baby. Want me to kiss it and make it better?"

"Don't tease me like that when you know the answer."

Biting her lip, she glanced out the door. "It's really public."

"I know. Damn it."

She nibbled his lips as she snuggled against him.

Closing his eyes, he savored the warmth of her body and scent of her curls that teased him even more. It was so difficult to not tell her what he felt. How glad he was that she appeared to care for him.

Even if she might be faking it, he'd take it. The only ones who'd ever been really kind to him were his mother, Aunt Jayne, her husband, and Erix. It was nice to have someone else watch his back.

Felicia gave him a light squeeze before she sat on the bed and continued feeding him ice. She glanced over to his monitors. "Your heart rate and BP are up. Are you in pain?"

"Yes, but I'm rather sure *you're* the reason for the elevation." He glanced to the pillow in his lap. "As well as other ones."

The blush returned to her cheeks. "I think you like embarrassing me."

He brushed his hand through her thick curls that he wanted to literally bathe in. "You are adorably beautiful when you blush. Have I really been out for four days?"

"Not counting the day you spent in surgery. Yes."

"Damn, they're right. I am a thoughtless bastard to be such boorish company for you."

Snorting, she rolled her eyes. "Do you remember the crash at all?"

Talyn shook his head. "I vaguely remember anything about that day. The last clear memory I have is you feeding me at the gym." Then he gave a short laugh as he remembered one innocuous detail. "Oh, wait . . .. there was a Tavali named Blister in the battle. How stupid is that?"

She wrinkled her nose. "Blister?"

"Yeah, we all get embarrassing call signs in the beginning, but they normally fade after a fight or two. Seldom do they make it onto our ships."

"So yours wasn't always Pit Viper?"

"No. It was Mongrel Ass until I got fed up with the giant, arrogant bastard who gave it to me. He was mocking me as usual and then made the mistake of speaking ill about my mother. I froze midstep and, without warning, took him down with one punch. Hence the name. When I go stock still, you need to run. Means I'm taking aim and about to strike . . . with fatal consequences."

She fed him more ice. "So *Blister* is the only thing you recall from the whole fight, huh? I think I need to do a psych eval on you about that."

Grinning at her playful teasing, he glanced away. Until he did recall something. "Now that you mention that, I think I was talking to Syndrome when my ship went up."

Felicia went cold at the name. "Syndrome?"

"A female in my squad . . . why are you so mad?"

She tried to suppress her anger, but it was impossible. A part of her wanted to beat him.

Most of all, she wanted to find this female and make sure she understood in no uncertain terms that Talyn had someone in his life.

With a jerk of her chin, she indicated the bouquets of flowers and balloons that lined the shelf in front of his window. "Syndrome sent those to you . . . a new one every day you've been here. She must really like you."

Talyn rubbed his head as he struggled to remember. "Not really. She usually growls out an insult if I so much as glance in her general direction." There was a ghost of something about Syndrome in the outer fringes of his mind, but he couldn't quite pull it. "I must have taken a blast for her. Or something slammed into me. Maybe."

"You were shot," his mother said as she rejoined them. "You really didn't hear the alarms to warn you you'd been sighted?"

He shook his head. "I would have taken evasive action had they done so."

"What does that mean?" Felicia asked his mother.

Talyn explained for her. "Whenever an enemy's targeting system locks on us, our alarms go off to warn us we're about to be fired on, so that we can get out of the way."

"Did they malfunction?"

"Possibly."

His mother crossed her arms over her chest. "I spoke to the ground crew who combed the wreckage of your ship yesterday. They were pretty sure and clear that you were hit by friendly fire."

Still, he couldn't believe it. "How? Our systems can't lock on each other, or fire. They're blocked from it."

His mother wasn't willing to let it go. "It's been known to happen, from time to time."

"Could the Tavali be using our armada system?" Felicia asked. "Maybe it really was them."

He shook his head again. "There's a special fight program we use. Even if they had one of our systems, it wouldn't provide the right code to silence the alarms on my fighter. Every battle has a new and unique code that isn't generated until we launch for that specific fight."

Fury darkened his mother's gaze. "When I find out who fired on you, there will be blood shed for it."

Talyn stared at the wall without responding. There was only one Andarion who'd have dared it. Only one who would have had access to the override codes.

Anatole.

He had no idea why that bastard had such a hard-on for him. But he did. And there was nothing his mother could do. She couldn't even get Talyn reassigned to another post. So he said nothing. All the truth would do was upset her. She'd never handled it well whenever something was out of her control. Especially when it involved him and his well-being. Then her guilt kicked in, and Talyn hated seeing that in her eyes.

It wasn't her fault that his father had abandoned her while she'd been pregnant. That was solely on Fain Hauk's shoulders. He was the irresponsible bastard who'd impregnated her and walked away without looking back.

The only thing she'd done wrong was give up her life and

prestige to keep Talyn. Though there were times he wished he'd never been born, he'd never regretted his mother staying with him. His life would have been infinitely worse had she given him up. While orphans with no paternal or maternal lineages were technically above his caste in their rigid society, they were completely ineligible for the military. His role would have been that of an opinionless servant, forced into the most menial of jobs.

Taking his mother's hand, he held it to his heart.

"I love you, Talyn," she whispered, kissing his temple.

Talyn tightened his grip on his mother's hand, but didn't speak. His gratitude to her was too great to be trivialized by words that couldn't convey the depth of what he really felt.

He reached for Felicia and took her hand, too. "My two *munataras*. I couldn't ask for better company."

"Well, look at this . . . and here I was feeling sorry for your rotten ass. Hell, for two such gorgeous females to dote on me, I'd set myself on fire, too."

Snorting, Talyn glanced to the door to see Erix joining them. "Sure you would. You cry over a hangnail."

With his arms crossed over his chest, Erix moved to stand at the foot of the bed so that he could scowl at Talyn. "How you feeling, kid?"

"Like I've gone a few too many rounds with *you*."

Erix tsked at him. "Flattery will only get you an extra hour of laps."

"You always threaten that, but you never do it."

"'Cause you're so pretty, you remind me of my daughter."

Erix glanced over to Talyn's mother. "Any word on when they might release him?"

"Once they ease him back on solid food for a full day without any complications, they'll let him go home."

He nodded. "I'll have Ferrick reschedule a few fights."

"Ferrick's going to kill me."

Erix scoffed. "Don't worry about that old buzzard. I'll take care of him. You focus on getting better."

Talyn nodded. "I'll get out of here as soon as possible." He had no intention of staying in this bed one minute longer than was absolutely necessary. But as he listened to his mother and Erix talk, his memory began to slowly fill in details of his mission.

More than that, he remembered why Syndrome had sent him flowers.

Anatole was seriously abusing his power and Talyn had challenged him. Apparently, this was how the royal prick answered a legitimate invitation.

With treachery.

Fine, bitch. If Anatole didn't want to face him in the Ring like a true Andarion, Talyn would go over his head and report him.

One way or another, he'd end this.

Alone in his room, Talyn sneered at the news report that covered the battle against the Tavali.

"Colonel Anatole emerged as the hero of the day. With seven kills, he single-handedly saved his unit and the lives of every Andarion who fought beside him. Andaria owes a tremendous debt to the royal family member. We're lucky to have one such as he on our side."

Talyn turned the news off before he threw up, just on principle. Ridiculous.

His link buzzed. Thinking it was his mother or Felicia checking in with him, he answered without reviewing the ID.

It was Command. "Major Batur, we have received your report and the prime commander has gone over it. We wanted to make sure that you are willing to stand by what you've written, as it seriously contradicts what Colonels Anatole and Pinara have reported."

He scowled. "What do you mean?"

A file popped up on his link. "They claim that you are the one who has been propositioning the females in your squad, and Colonel Anatole has sworn testimony from six different females who say that you have behaved inappropriately with them. The commander is currently reviewing the rest of your file to see if a demotion is in order. So again, I ask you, do you wish to submit your report and have it as part of your record?"

Talyn couldn't breathe as those words sank in and he realized Syndrome had thrown him to the wolves for daring to help her. "What exactly did Colonel Pinara say?"

"She claims you have accosted her on two separate occasions, and that she's seen you expose yourself to other females in your squad."

Talyn ground his teeth. So, he'd put his ass on the line for Syndrome and she'd sold him out. *Minsid* hell.

Why was he even surprised?

"Do you wish to proceed with your report, Major?"

The suicidal part of Talyn was ready to see it through, but the saner half of his brain knew better. He was a lack-Vest bastard. Without corroboration, no one would ever believe him. Not against a member of the royal family.

The nail that stands out gets hammered down. The old Andarion proverb went through his head. And he was tired of taking those blows.

Screw this shit.

"No. Please destroy the report."

"Very well. You should know that when you return to duty, the commander wants you to report to his office for disciplinary action."

Of course he did. "Duly noted." Talyn hung up and fought the urge to destroy his link.

This was bullshit.

He'd just put his link away when it rang with the armada's tone. *What fresh hell is this?* There was no way it could be good.

His gut knotted, he answered it to find Anatole on the other end.

"You think you're smart, mongrel? You're lucky I caught this. And I promise you that as bad as you think you've had it, it's nothing compared to what you're going to face when you're cleared for duty again. I swear you will regret the day you ever decided to don an Andarion uniform. End of the day, I own your sorry ass. And I intend to make you bow down to your betters and lick my boots. One way or another, you will learn your place." Anatole hung up.

Talyn growled low in his throat as reality kicked him hard. Why had he bothered to stand up for someone else? Anyone else?

Now . . .

He was going down in flames and no one would be there to help him through this. No one.

Ta-lyn No-kin

Born in sin.

No matter what, you'll never win. . . .

In that moment, he wanted the throat of every Andarion ever born. But none more so than his own father's.

And that of every member of the Anatole bloodline.

"Thank the gods, you're here."

Felicia frowned at the nurse as she left the lift and approached their station in the hallway. Her heart pounded in fear. She'd only left Talyn long enough to go to her final. Had he taken a turn for the worse during her absence?

I should have never left him.

"What's happened?"

Her face a mask of horror, the nurse gestured toward Talyn's room. "That . . . male is the most infuriating, surly, nasty beast to ever breathe! We're down to drawing straws to see who has to go in to check his vitals."

Felicia gaped at the female. "What?"

"You know he signed the orders yesterday that we couldn't give him anything without his express approval?"

"Yes."

"Well, now he's in extreme pain and he refuses to eat. He can't sleep. He takes the head off anyone who goes near him. And if we don't get food into him, we're going to have to reinsert a feeding tube. And none of us want to do that, for fear of what he'll do to us to retaliate. . . . The doctor's in a meeting right now, trying to overturn Batur's right to refuse treatment, or get him kicked out."

Felicia was aghast. "Where's his mother?"

"She had to leave not long after you did. He's been impossible ever since."

Felicia shook her head. "All right. I'll deal with him. Where's his food?"

The nurse went to her station and returned with a tray. She handed it to Felicia. "May the gods be with you."

Unsure of what he'd do to her, she headed to his room and gently pushed the door open to find Talyn with his arm bent over his eyes.

"I told you I didn't want to be disturbed," he snarled. "Get the fuck out!"

"Okay. If that's really what you want. I'll go."

He immediately uncovered his eyes. "Licia?" he breathed her name like a prayer.

She stood in the doorway with the tray. "You want me to stay or go?"

"Please, stay."

Nearing his bed, she glanced to his monitors and cringed at what she saw there. She set the tray aside. "Oh honey, you need to take something for the pain."

"I can't. Once they release me, I can't take anything. You know that. I need it out of my system as soon as possible."

"Tay . . ."

"Lis, you know I can't. Please, don't nag me. I'm in enough pain."

She placed her hand against his cheek. "Okay. Can I use pressure points with you?"

He nodded.

Swallowing hard at the sympathetic ache she felt for him, she sat on the bed and started rubbing his temples. A single tear slid from the corner of his eye. She kissed it away before she moved down to his neck so that she could massage him. He didn't speak a single word while she worked.

Within a few minutes, she had his blood pressure almost back to a normal range.

"Breathe with me," she whispered. "In deep. Hold. One. Two. Three. Now out." She kept doing that until his res and heart rate were back down, too. "Good Hammer."

He actually gave a half laugh at that.

She moved to rub his arm and shoulder while she continued to force him to breathe deeply. "Better?"

"No." He grimaced irritably. "How much can one body hurt and not kill you?"

"A lot. But then you know that better than I do."

He clenched his teeth.

"Breathe through it, baby." She used the pressure point in his hand to distract his brain from whatever was hurting him.

He followed her lead.

"Now, can you eat for me? If you don't, you'll have to go back and fight in the Mean Weight Division. Think of all the puny males you'll have to go through to get back to Zoftiq."

"You're not funny."

"I'm funny-looking. I have big ears. It's why I keep my hair long and never wear it up."

He lifted his hand to finger her lobe. "Your ears are perfect."

"You're delusional from your pain."

He laughed again.

Felicia pulled the tray stand over to the bed and uncovered his food. "Let's see what we have here. Hmm . . . it's got to be better than the shite you normally eat."

"I've never heard you swear before."

"I don't often." She picked up the small pudding cup and fed him a bite. "How's that?"

"Tastes like shit."

She narrowed her eyes at his surly tone before she took a bite of it.

"Hey!"

"I'm seeing for myself. And it's quite good. I think the crap you call food has destroyed your taste buds."

Talyn stroked her cheek with the backs of his fingers. Since Anatole's call, he'd felt like utter hell. But somehow, just her gentle presence made him feel better.

He'd give anything if he could just stay with her and forget everything else in his life.

But the gods had never been that merciful to him.

"How did your test go?"

"Pretty sure I aced it. Your mom is a great study partner. She really knows her stuff."

"Yeah, she grew up in a hospital, with her parents."

She fed him a bite of the soft sandwich before she ran her finger along the stubble on his chin. "They didn't shave you?"

"I wouldn't let them. I was such an ass that I feared they might slit my throat if I let them get that close to me with a razor."

She snorted. "You shouldn't be that way."

"I know. I was trying to be good. But it hurts so much . . . and I don't like them as much as I like you."

"Yes, but you need to be nice to Andarions who give you shots."

"If you say so."

"Dear gods! What did you do? Perform an exorcism?"

Laughing, Felicia looked to the door to see his gaping doctor. "No. I just beat him down. I might be smaller, but I'm meaner."

The doctor snorted as he came in to check Talyn's vitals while she continued to feed him. "It's a good thing your girlfriend came in when she did. I just went over your head to get permission to knock you unconscious if you get unmanageable again."

"Sorry."

The doctor gaped again. "He even apologizes. Holy Andaria." He looked incredulously at Felicia. "That's it. I'm calling your school and telling them to send a proctor over with your exams. You're not allowed to leave until we release him. I'm dead serious. What school do you attend?"

"North Eris."

"No wonder their tuition is so high." The doctor scowled at Talyn's vitals. "This is the best he's been since we admitted him. Incredible. What did you do?"

"Basic trigger points. A little PT massage."

"Keep it up. Can I get you anything else?"

She glanced to the tray. "He needs more protein than this and he likes citrus. Could you please put an order in for it?"

"Absolutely. If you need anything else, just let me know."

"Thank you."

Talyn pulled her hand to his lips so that he could nibble her fingertips. "Some privacy would be better."

"You're not well enough for *that*."

He lowered her hand to his erection. "My body totally disagrees with you." He let out a deep, pain-filled growl. "I'm in utter misery, Felicia."

She narrowed her gaze on him. "Have they bathed you today?"

He shook his head.

"Hold on." Felicia went to the nurses' station for a bathing kit.

The nurse handed her one. "I put the order in for more food. Do you want it when it arrives?"

"I'll be back for it after I finish his bath."

She nodded before she took Felicia's hand. "Thank you, by the way."

"For what?"

"Dealing with him. You are a saint!"

"Not really. He's actually very sweet."

The nurse snorted in denial. "You're insane if you think that."

Then she must be insane, because he was the kindest male she'd ever known.

Felicia took the kit back into his room. She shut the door and placed the tray stand in the way to give them some warning before she went to the sink and ran warm water into the small tub. Once it was half full, she carried it and the washing implements to his bed and set them next to him.

Talyn watched her peel the blanket and sheet away from his body. "What are you doing?"

She gave him an impish grin. "Bathing you."

His heart raced as she pushed his gown up and bared his body to her warm gaze. Her smile insidious, she wet the sponge and then carefully ran it over his skin, leaving chills in the wake of her touch.

He struggled to breathe as pleasure pushed away every bit of his pain. The only thing he felt was her delicate hands torturing him. And when she brushed against his cock, he had to bite back an ecstatic cry.

Burying his hand in her hair, he watched as she slowly bent down and took him into her sweet mouth. He arched his back and growled at how good she felt on him. Nothing was sweeter than her tongue and the gentle pressure of her lips.

And when he came a few minutes later, he saw stars from it.

With a satisfied smile, she finished bathing him and changed his gown.

"Thank you," he breathed before he pulled her lips against his.

"You're very welcome. And every day you're nice to your nurses and doctors, I'll make sure to put that very smile on your face."

"I will be an absolute angel."

"Good boy." She tucked the covers around him, then pulled the tray stand back to the bed, cracked open the door, and moved to shave his face.

Just as she was finishing, his mother joined them, carrying the other tray of food.

Setting the tray down, she gave him a chiding stare. "I hear you've been quite the pain today."

"Sorry."

"Umm-hmmm. Sure you are."

Felicia wiped the last bit of soap from his upper lip. "They won't be having any future problems with him. Will they, *keitling*?"

He shook his head. "I plan to be a model patient."

His mom arched a brow at them as Felicia moved the stand closer to the bed so that Talyn could reach his food.

"You need to eat more." Felicia uncovered the plate and handed him the peeled orange slices.

"The doctor told me that you're refusing pain meds?"

Talyn swallowed his bite before he answered his mother's question. "I don't know when they'll release me back to duty, and I can't afford to have a single trace of anything in my system when I report in."

His mother frowned. "I don't understand."

Felicia arched her brow. "Is that not a standard military thing?"

"What?" she asked.

"Talyn told me he can't even have an aspirin or they'll court-martial him."

Galene gaped. "What?" she repeated at Talyn.

Talyn took another orange slice. "Company policy."

She pulled out her link to look it up. "Each officer can set the limits for what he'll allow those on protective detail, but that's ridiculous." She held it out for Talyn. "Your policy manual says that mild painkillers are—"

"Mom, *I* can't have anything in my system."

She scowled at him, then looked back at her link. "Explain this to me."

"My CO forbids it, okay? There's nothing to explain. I don't care what the manual says. I'm under orders. If I have anything in my system at check-in, I'll be arrested for it."

She slid her link back into her pocket. "Why?"

"It's orders and I'm a soldier. I'm not allowed to ask why."

"His CO's a jackass."

"Lis, don't."

Seething over it, Felicia glanced away.

His mother glared at him. "You, Major," she said to Talyn, "silence. Felicia, explain."

She met Talyn's pleading gaze. "It's not my place."

"Fine," Galene snapped. She turned back toward her son. "I'll pull your reports and file, and start interviewing until I find out what's going on."

Talyn let out a frustrated growl. "I have a personality conflict with my CO, Mum. Okay?"

"What kind of conflict? What's he been doing?"

"Any time he gets a wild hair, he cancels my leave or resets my check-in times. I pull a lot of double shifts and get every fun assignment he has. He keeps restricting me to my barracks. If I sneeze wrong, it goes to Provost."

"Have you reported him?"

He gave her a sullen stare. "And have him retaliate? No thanks."

"Have you put in for a post transfer?"

"No, Ma, it *never* once occurred to me."

"Don't get smart with me, boy!"

Talyn glared at her. "Of course I've put in for transfers, promotions, you name it. Everything comes back either filled or denied."

Felicia's eyes watered at the frustrated pain she heard in Talyn's voice. At the obvious anguish in his eyes. In that moment, she really wanted Anatole's heart in her fist.

"I don't understand," Galene breathed. "Perte always speaks so highly of you."

Talyn set his orange aside. “Perte was reassigned eight months ago.”

“Then who’s your CO?”

“Colonel Anatole.”

“Chrisen or Merrell?”

“Chrisen.”

Her face went pale at the name. “Oh.”

“Oh, what?” Talyn asked. “What’s that look mean?”

Now it was her turn to be evasive. “Why didn’t you tell me about this?”

Talyn sighed. “What could you do?”

“I’m a commander.”

“Yeah. In a separate division that won’t touch me. If you say *anything,* Anatole will come at me, no holds barred. No offense, Mum, but if I want that kind of punishment, I’d rather walk into the Ring and have it taken out of my ass where I can fight back. The last thing I want is to be known as the company cry-baby.”

Felicia felt for his mother as she saw the same hopeless despair on her face that she had.

“I will get you transferred, Talyn. I swear it.”

“Mum, please don’t interfere. I can handle this. Okay?”

The tone of his voice made Felicia sick. For him to sound like that, it had to be an even bigger nightmare than she could possibly imagine.

Galene nodded. “I’m so sorry, Talyn.”

“It’s okay. Really. Conflicts happen. Ain’t no big thing. I rub most Andarions the wrong way. It’s a personal choice.”

Tears glistened in her eyes as she brushed her hand through his braids. "Ever my brave soldier." She kissed his cheek.

As she started to leave, Talyn caught her hand.

"Don't blame yourself for this. It's not your fault. I'm the one with a severe asshole allergy that causes me to lip off when I should remain silent. I'm old enough to know better."

Smiling sadly, she patted his hand. "Love you."

"You, too."

As Galene left the room, Felicia sat down on the bed and frowned. "What happened?"

"What are you talking about?"

She narrowed his gaze on him. "You're hiding something from your mother."

"You don't know that."

"Yes, I do. I'm learning you, my friend. And by that look in your eyes, I'm guessing that you made the mistake of reporting your CO?"

"I tried to appeal the first time my band *malfunctioned*—"

"You mean he screwed with your reporting time?"

He nodded. "The higher-ups don't give a shit about lack-Vest bastard whiners with no pull. I was told not to waste their time with another appeal. To soldier up and make sure that I'm back to post at least an hour prior to check-in. That would solve my problem. So I did that, and he began resetting my times to two or three hours prior to check-in, which meant I was sometimes AWOL even before I left my barracks."

She could only imagine how many lashes that was. "God, Talyn. That's awful. And there's no way to get transferred?"

"Let me reiterate that I'm a bastard without lineage who now has a long list of check-in violations, and a lengthy record of disciplinary actions against him for insubordination and failure to follow orders."

In that moment, she wanted to personally beat his CO. "Do you think he's the one who shot you down?"

"I'm not at liberty to speculate."

"But let's say, for argument's sake . . ."

"It wouldn't matter. He's a decorated war hero, who is the grandnephew to the tadara, and I'm a mongrel dog who isn't even allowed into the officers' or enlisted clubs to clean them. I can't even use the company washrooms or lockers with the rest of my unit or squad."

Felicia winced at the cruelty.

Talyn tightened his grip on her hand. "Don't look so sad, Felicia. I'm glad the bastard shot me down."

She looked at the bandages on him. "How so?"

"It gives me time with you I wouldn't have had otherwise." He pressed her hand to his cheek. "Trust me, you're worth it."

"You are one sick Andarion, Talyn Batur."

"And you are one sexy *tara*."

Felicia kissed him. In that moment, she knew she was going to make the last call she'd ever thought to make. Yes, it would be painful and degrading, but she couldn't stand by and let Talyn be hurt. Not if she could help it.

Her pride was a small price to pay for his safety.

• • •

Felicia frowned as she saw Talyn's mother sitting alone in the waiting room. She'd only left his side to take the tray back to the nurses' station while the doctor evaluated him.

"Commander?"

His mother dabbed at her eyes before she looked up. "Is he okay?"

She nodded. "The doctor's with him. Are you all right?"

Galene drew a ragged breath. "I was trying to get ahold of myself before I went back in."

Felicia sat down beside her. "What is it?"

"Can I tell you a secret?"

"Sure."

Galene bit her lip. "I'm the reason his CO is attacking him."

Felicia went cold. "I don't understand."

"Years ago, when I was in school, Chrisen's older brother wanted to pledge with me. But I was pledged at the time to Talyn's father."

Oh . . . that explained why his mother was so incredibly young.

"After his father left me and was disinherited for it, Merrell still wanted me . . . but only if I agreed to abort my baby."

"You chose to keep him."

Galene nodded. "I wanted to hang on to that bit of his father that only I had. Stupid and selfish, I know, but I loved his father, Felicia. More than you can imagine. Sadly, I still do. Don't get me wrong . . . I'd give anything to gut the bastard for what he did to us. But deep inside . . ."

"I know. Feelings are so frustrating. I hate my father with

a vengeance for things he's done, and yet I still love him terribly."

Galene sighed and folded up her tissue. "It pains me that Chrisen was transferred to Talyn's base. He was always vindictive and cold. Like his brother, he truly hates Talyn's entire paternal family. I wouldn't have pledged with Merrell even if I hadn't been pregnant. He always made my flesh crawl."

"Is there any way we can get Talyn away from him?"

She handed her link to Felicia. "That's why I was crying. Chrisen's set Talyn's career back by a decade with what he's done to him. On paper, Talyn is nothing but a disciplinary nightmare. No commander will touch him with that file. He's lucky his rank hasn't been busted because of it all." More tears fell. "What am I going to do?" She pointed to the screen. "Look how they treat my baby. And there's nothing I can do to stop it. I had no idea all that was going on. He's never said anything to me about it. Whenever I ask about his welfare, all I get out of him is that he's fine. Not to worry so much."

Felicia choked on her own tears as she read all the times he'd been punished for Anatole's vendetta. It sickened her to see it. Especially what had been done to him since they met.

Like his mother had said, he never once breathed a word of it. To anyone.

She held Galene against her. "It'll be okay."

"How?"

"My half brother is a commander and my father is one of the advisors to the tadara."

Galene pulled back with a gasp. "What?"

Felicia nodded. "We're not really close and they're both obnoxious snots, but I'm going to call in a favor."

Her jaw slack, Galene stared at her. "Are you sure?"

"I don't know if they'll do anything, if they *can* do anything, but I'm going to try my best. I'll start with my brother and if that gets me nowhere, I'll call my father. Surely, between the two of them, we can get Talyn transferred away from Anatole."

"You would do that for him?"

Felicia touched the heart necklace Talyn had sent to her. "Absolutely."

Galene pulled her in for another tight hug. "I would be forever in your debt."

"Think nothing of it. Just promise me that you'll never tell Talyn what I've done. I don't want him to be angry at me or to feel obligated in any way."

"But—"

"I'm serious, Commander. You gave me your secret. I'm giving you mine. Win, lose, or draw, I never want him to know."

"Okay. I'll take it to my grave." Galene pulled back as the doctor left Talyn's room and came over to them.

He inclined his head to them. "Good news. Barring infection or fever, I'll release him day after tomorrow."

"For home or duty?" his mother asked before Felicia had a chance.

"Home. He still needs to recuperate before he's ready to return to active duty. I trust he won't be left alone?"

Felicia smiled. "I'll stay with him."

"In a week, he'll need to start therapy. I have the number for a therapist—"

"I'm a licensed therapist. Can I do it?"

He glanced back toward Talyn's room. "Given what I've seen here, I think you're an excellent choice. The best we could have. I'll write everything up and e-mail you with the instructions on what I want him to do."

As he walked away, Galene laughed. "Talyn was always a *very* stubborn beast. Hardheaded like his father . . . ah! The stories I could tell you about that aggravating male! The more you try to tell him what to do, the more he digs his heels in."

That was definitely the truth.

"Who's his father?"

Deep agonized pain descended over Galene's face. "It doesn't matter. But if you ever see his father, you'll know. He looks and acts just like him." And with that, she headed back toward Talyn's room.

Felicia frowned at what Galene had just said. If his father was just like Talyn in actions as well as looks, then there was a lot to the story of why his father had left them. As protective and loving as Talyn was, he'd never abandon his family.

Not without a damn good reason. And not without one hell of a battle.

CHAPTER 8

At their condo, Felicia helped Talyn into bed. It was his first day out of the hospital and the ride home had taken its toll on him. His features pale, he struggled to breathe against the pain as she peeled his uniform off while he lay on the mattress.

She covered him with the blanket.

"What's that look for?" Talyn asked as she tucked him in.

"What look?"

"That little pouty face you just made. I know this kind of care isn't part of our contract. If you want, I can return to the barracks to recoup, instead of here."

"Oh, *keramon*, don't you dare! I doubt you'd make it to the lobby before you collapsed. And that's not why I pouted, anyway." She grinned at him. "I was just thinking that my plan had been to rip your uniform off you the next time I had you alone in my bed, and ravish you until you were senseless from it. Unfortunately, I don't want to hurt you."

Relaxing, he laughed. "Ravish me, then. At least I'd die happy and sated."

"Ummm-hmmm. You say that now, but I'm pretty sure you'd be crying like a baby if I tried."

He winked at her. "I'm willing to go for it, if you are."

She kissed the tip of his nose. "I just got you home. Last thing I want to do right now is break you, again."

"You're a cruel female, Felicia. Heartless!"

She snuggled against his back and spooned him. "Am I?"

Talyn closed his eyes as he savored the warmth of her body pressed against his. "Maybe?"

Kissing his shoulder, she buried her hand in his braids. "I'm so glad to have you here, finally." She draped her arm over his waist and cuddled him, taking care to not put any pressure on any of his healing wounds. "At night, I go to sleep while trying to figure out which of the rooms is your favorite."

"How do you mean?"

She gently caressed his muscled arm. "Before I moved in. Where did you spend the most time?"

"Oh . . . I didn't. I only saw the condo once before you got here. And then, only long enough to make sure it was safe and furnished before I bought it for you."

Felicia froze at what he was saying. Now that she thought about it, she vaguely remembered them mentioning that, but once she was here, she'd assumed her agency had to be wrong. That Talyn wouldn't have done such a thing. "This really wasn't your home before you contracted me?"

He turned to look at her over his shoulder. "No. Your terms

stipulated that you wanted a place within walking distance of your school."

"I thought it was just luck that your place was so close to it."

Snorting, he shook his head. "Since I'm required to live in the barracks, I didn't need another place. This is the first property I've ever owned."

"Well, that explains why there aren't any personal items of yours here. I'd wondered about that. . . . You really bought this just for me?"

He nodded.

"Why would you spend so much on a companion?"

Rolling over to face her, he caressed her cheek in his hand. The sincerity in his gaze scorched her. "I know you had your choice of males, Felicia. I didn't want you to regret picking me."

Yeah, right. They hadn't exactly lined up for her. She'd only had two other interviews. Not to mention . . . "Talyn, *keramon*, why would you think *that*? I wasn't even *your* first choice."

He scowled at her. "That's not true. You were the only reason I went to your agency. Any agency, for that matter. I saw your profile online and when I contacted them about applying to adopt you, they said I was too late. That you were in negotiations with someone else. It devastated me that I'd missed out."

Felicia wanted to believe that, but she knew better. "My friend Rynara told me that you'd tried to contract with her before me."

"No, I didn't. When you weren't available, they submitted

my application to her without my consent or knowledge and pissed me off to no end."

"Really?"

"How else would I know you were in negotiations with another male?"

She narrowed her gaze at him. "You really didn't ask for Nara?"

"God, no. Check with the agency. I had a fit that they did that without consulting me. Hell, I'll show you the e-mails. Even if she'd said yes, I would have turned her down. I didn't like the way *any* of the others looked, and I was highly offended they pitched me to her without asking first. You were the *only* female I was interested in."

"Oh, honey!" Tears filled her eyes as she hugged him close and laughed. "I'm so glad I was a bitch to Rynara."

He arched his brow. "What'd you do?"

"She kept being a snot. Telling me how the only reason I had you was because *she* found you completely unacceptable. To get back at her, I showed off condo photos and rubbed her nose in what she'd said no to. Told her that I was eternally grateful she was an idiot."

Talyn laughed. "So what happened to your other contract, anyway?"

"He wasn't you."

Rolling his eyes, he gave her a droll stare. "You didn't know me then."

"True. But he was a beast when we met. I didn't like him at all. You, on the other hand, looked at me and I melted on the spot. Best of all, you seemed to respect me even though I'm a—"

"Don't you dare insult yourself."

She smiled at him. "That right there is why I chose you. And one day, I hope we can actually have sex."

He laughed again. "It would be nice. . . ." He glanced down, then wagged his brows at her. "I'm up for it if you are."

She tsked at him. "Not today. I can tell by the jagged way you're breathing how much pain you're in. I wasn't kidding. I don't want you back in the hospital. But if you're a good boy . . ."

He dutifully closed his eyes and feigned a soft snore. She kissed his forehead.

There was a light knock on the bedroom door. Dimming the lights, Felicia went to answer it.

Galene peeped around her to look at the bed. "How's he doing?"

She opened the door to admit her. "He's in bed, but resisting sleep."

"He's always been that way. I used to get so frustrated at him when he was a boy. There were times I thought I'd have to stunblast him to get him to settle down."

"And she would threaten my pudding if I didn't obey," he said sullenly.

"That's because spanking never mattered to you. I should have known then you'd grow up to be a fighter."

"Only because you numbed my ass from all the beatings I got as a kid." He grinned at her.

Galene scoffed at him. She met Felicia's curious gaze. "The lies my boy tells. I rarely ever got onto him. Honestly, he was an angel and a joy . . . when he wasn't literally climbing up walls, furniture, and countertops. He took much better care of me than I ever did of him."

"Now who's lying?"

His mother ruffled his hair. "Can I get you anything?"

"I'm good. I've got my pillow. My bed. And best of all, my two *taras*. Life couldn't be better."

His mother kissed his cheek. "Good night, baby. Love you."

"You, too."

She paused in front of Felicia. "I'll head back and leave the two of you alone."

Felicia stopped her. "If you want, please feel free to stay. Not like we don't have plenty of room here for you."

She glanced back at Talyn.

"I really don't mind," Felicia said sincerely. "You're his mother. I get it."

"Talyn? What do you want me to do?"

Talyn pressed his lips together. "The Andarion symbol for war is two females under one roof. My mother didn't raise no fool. Honestly, it makes no difference to me, but I don't want either of you to feel weird or uncomfortable."

"I really, truly don't mind," Felicia reiterated. "If you want to be close by in case something happens, I'd rather have you down the hall than across town. You can even sleep in here and I'll take one of the other bedrooms, if you want."

Galene smiled. "Now *that* I'm sure he'd object to." She

patted Felicia's arm. "I'll take the room at the end of the hall. And I'll make dinner tonight for both of you."

"Thank you."

"Thanks, Mum."

Inclining her head, she left them.

Talyn bent his arm under his head. "I'm glad you get along with my mother."

"I adore her. She's very sweet."

"Don't know if *sweet*'s the word *I'd* go with. She can be scary when stirred. But while I might doubt her sanity at times, I've never doubted her love for me."

Felicia laughed. "You know she can probably hear you."

"Yeah, but she raised me. It's not like she doesn't know I'm an irritable ass. Contrary to what she claims, I haven't exactly hidden it."

"I don't think you're irritable."

"What can I say? You bring out the best in me."

Felicia felt weepy over that. "You need to rest."

"Fine." He stuck his tongue out at her before he rolled over.

Laughing again, she closed the door and went to help his mother in the kitchen.

Galene was washing vegetables as Felicia entered the room. "What can I do to help?"

The commander shook her head. "Chop an onion?"

"Sure." She grabbed a chopping block and knife. As she started, the hair on the back of her neck raised. She looked up to catch Galene staring at her. "Is something wrong?"

"If I asked you something very personal, would you be offended?"

"Depends. Is it offensive?"

"It might be. But I don't mean it that way. It's more nosy than anything else."

"Then ask."

"Why are you a companion?"

Felicia's face heated up at the extremely personal question. Not to mention the fact that it was coming from the mother of her patron, which only made it worse. "I needed the money for school."

"Didn't your mother try to talk you out of it?"

"A little, but she quickly came around, once I pointed out my reasons and the benefits of it. Ultimately, she's the one who trained me."

"Why would she agree to such a thing?"

"Well . . . given my options for a husband and the terms I'd have been forced to agree to for marriage, it seemed the better choice. And I didn't want to put either her or myself through the embarrassment of another female acting like she was doing a magnanimous favor by allowing her son to mix blood with us. Both my parents are very high-lineaged. My mother only became a companion because she met and fell in love with my father after he was already married. Granted, she was young and stupid, but it was the only way she could legally be with him. She'd have never done it otherwise."

"Really?"

Felicia nodded. "Besides, I wasn't planning to do it forever.

Just until I got through school and passed my physician's license."

"What if you get pregnant?"

"Then I will have a beautiful baby to love." She returned to chopping. "You've done well on your own."

Galene snorted as she returned to prepping the meat. "I wouldn't wish my life on anyone. Talyn deserved much better than what I was able to give him, and I hate myself for what I've done to him by being so selfish."

"You shouldn't. He seems much happier and better adjusted than my siblings who come from a married couple. A very high-ranking married couple, no less. I've never met a kinder or more decent male in my life. You did an incredible job with him."

"Thank you. Now that you mention it, he is a much better individual than any of my siblings. Still, I hate how much time he spent alone when he was young . . . how isolated he is as an adult."

"Friends are overrated."

Galene arched a brow at Felicia's comment. "What makes you say that?"

"Just that I've had a few stab me pretty hard over the years. I'm a little skittish now."

"You're too young to be so jaded."

Felicia held the knife up. "You haven't seen how many of these I have embedded in my spine and heart."

Galene nodded in sympathy. "I'm sorry. I've had more than my share of them, too."

Felicia gave her a grim, determined smile. "Here's to better days for all of us."

"Here, here."

As she finished chopping the onion, Talyn's link buzzed. Felicia picked it up from the counter to check the ID. "It's his base. Should I take it to him?"

"Answer it. It should be nothing."

Switching on the speaker, she did. "Major Batur."

"Funny, you don't sound like the major. Did they cut off your dick while you were in the hospital?"

Felicia screwed her face up at the male's condescending tone. "Major Batur is resting. Can I take a message?"

"Yes. This is his CO, Colonel Anatole. You can tell that mongrel bastard that he failed to check in on his release, and I shall be reporting him for this. That is, unless you wish to discuss the matter with me? You and I might be able to come to an arrangement on his behalf."

Her eyes snapping fire, Galene snatched the link up. "Colonel, this is Deputy Commander Batur. And I will be expecting you to forward to me the company manual that dictates your policy, as it is one I'm unfamiliar with. Especially the one that allows a civ to discuss military procedure and discipline with a senior officer."

He sputtered in response.

"Have you something you wish to say to me, Chrisen?"

"Major Batur is well aware that, given his record, he is to report his location in, any time he's away from base or post."

"I do believe that that is the primary function of his locator bracelet and tracking device that's embedded in his body. Or do you wish to go on record by claiming both are malfunctioning, simultaneously?"

"With all due respect, Commander, you're not the one he reports to. Nor do you work in this division. Fighter pilots have their own procedures. Protocols the major is more than familiar with and has chosen to blatantly disregard. Again. I have no choice but to write him up for it." And with that, he hung up.

Galene slammed the link down as frustrated tears gathered in her eyes. "It's not fair that I protect the tizirahie and heir, while no one protects *my* son."

"This stops!" Felicia pulled her link out and dialed for her brother before she could rethink it.

Or chicken out again.

"Lieutenant Commander ezul Terronova."

Galene gasped at the name.

Felicia cringed over the fact that she'd forgotten the speaker was on. Switching to video, she waited for him to accept. "Lorens? It's Felicia."

His handsome face appeared instantly. He was the spitting image of their father, except for his hair. While their father wore the short style of his political station, Lorens, like Talyn, had warrior braids that he pulled back from his face with a red band. "Felicia? Really? Who died?"

Rolling her eyes at his droll tone, she blinked away her tears. "Are you still a giant Ring fan?"

"Always. Why?"

"Do you know who the Iron Hammer is?"

"Oh hell, yeah. Of course." Now he sounded a little more normal and not the snot he was around her. "Am I breathing? Everyone knows who he is. The fact *you* know his name says it all. Why do you ask?"

"How would you like to have dinner with him?"

Her brother gaped. Then he turned deadly serious. "Who do you want me to kill?"

She laughed, even though she actually considered it. "Colonel Chrisen Anatole."

"Done. Spill-kill. Quick-kill. What are we talking? You want his head as a trophy? Penis? Just tell me what body part you want delivered, how many pieces to cut him into, and it's done."

Snorting, she wiped at her eyes. "Talyn is a fighter pilot stationed at Anatole Base with a major's rank and Anatole is his CO. Can you get Talyn transferred to another post, out from under the beast?"

Lorens arched a brow. "I don't have to really kill Anatole?"

"Not unless you can't get Talyn transferred. Then I want his head on a platter or pike . . . I'm not that picky."

Lorens nodded thoughtfully. "Transfer's easy. I don't have to risk jail time or court-martial for that. Where do you want me to assign Batur?"

Felicia hesitated. This was entirely too easy and way out of character for her eldest half brother. "Why are you being so cooperative? You're scaring me."

"You're offering me dinner with *the* Hammer, Felicia. There's really nothing I *wouldn't* do for that. Are you kidding? That male is my one true hero. I'd sacrifice my young to meet him. Even a testicle. Maybe both."

Still, it seemed so weird to her. "He's an Andarion soldier. You could just order him to eat with you."

"Not the same. Besides, I didn't know *that* until you told me. Had no idea he was a fighter pilot. But I can easily get him transferred to the Tadara's Guard or any place else. Hell, the Guard's where he *should* be with his skill set. I don't understand why he's not. And why are you crying, anyway?"

Wow, he only just now noticed that. Typical.

She sniffed. "Anatole propositioned me. He's threatening to hurt Talyn unless I meet with him."

Lorens screwed his face up as if he couldn't fathom what she was telling him. "Can I ask why he's threatening *you* about the Hammer?" Now there was the condescending tone she was used to.

She glanced over to Galene before she cleared her throat. "I'm Talyn's female."

"Ah, hell, no, you're not . . ." He gaped. "Are you really?"

The doubt in that one word offended her. "Yes, I am."

"And you're just now calling me? You. Suck. So hard."

"Well, you've never been this nice to me before. Why would I have told you?"

"Yeah, well, you weren't sleeping with the greatest fighter to ever step into the Ring. This changes things."

Offended, she growled at him. "Thanks, Lorens."

"What? You want me to lie?"

She narrowed her eyes at him. His honesty was the *only* good thing she could say about him, sadly. "I would call you an obnoxious ass, but I don't want to insult obnoxious asses or for you to reconsider transferring Talyn."

Lorens laughed good-naturedly. "Not going to happen. I'll put him wherever you tell me." He signed something before he glanced back to his monitor. "Can I bring my oldest boy to dinner, too?"

"You get my baby transferred away from Anatole's control and you can bring both boys."

He flashed a fang-tinged smile at her. "Have I told you how much I love you, Felicia?"

"Never."

"Bad oversight on my part. I'll put in for an immediate transfer. And I'll do you one better. The Hammer wins his next fight, I'll personally give your male a promotion in rank."

And for that, she would kiss her obnoxious brother's cheek, and those of his evil spawn, too. "There is one condition to all of this."

"I still have to kill Anatole?"

She laughed, even though she wanted to say yes. "No. Don't tell Talyn I requested this from you. Ever."

"Then how are you getting him to dinner?"

"I'll worry about that. You get the transfer and I'll get you your dinner with Talyn."

"Deal. I'll put it through today."

"Thank you, Lo. I won't forget this."

"Hey, I'm just glad you called me and not Paka. He wouldn't

have invited me along. He's selfish that way." Lorens inclined his head to her. "I'll see you soon."

"Bye." She hung up and met Galene's stunned expression.

"Your paka is Satrapehs Saren ezul Terronova? *The* male head advisor for Tadara Eriadne? And your brother is Lieutenant Commander ezul Terronova, the second-in-command of the *entire* Andarion armada?"

"Yes," she said sheepishly. "I told you my father was high-lineaged."

"You did, but you left out those vital details at the hospital when we talked about this."

Nervous over the nondisclosure, Felicia twisted a strand of her hair around her index finger. "I didn't know if Lo would do it. He really is a big jerk. Normally."

"Yes, I know. I've dealt with him on several unpleasant occasions. And he's *never* sounded that nice before."

"I know, right? But he's been a huge Ring fan all his life. It's the only thing our paka ever did with him, growing up. Lorens fought some, but he sucked at it so he quit within his first year of primary school."

Galene shook her head. "Do you really think he'll do it?"

"He usually has good follow-through. Especially when it's something he wants. And he definitely seems to want this."

An evil glint appeared in Galene's eyes. "I would love to see Chrisen's face when those orders come through. He'll be livid."

"You think he'll fight them?"

That stole the happiness from the commander's face. "Sadly, I do. He's a spiteful bastard."

Felicia released her hair as a new fear went through her. "What are the odds that he might be successful?"

"I don't know. Your father is the head male advisor for the tadara. Chrisen's mother is the tadara's head female advisor and niece. If it comes down to it, the tadara will side with her blood relations. That I know for a fact. And God help Talyn if it comes to that."

Felicia's stomach tightened. *Please, don't let me have made it worse for him by trying to make it better.* She'd never be able to live with herself if she hurt him.

CHAPTER 9

What are you doing?"

Talyn froze instantly at Felicia's peeved tone, wondering what he'd done to piss her off. "The most obvious answer seems to be getting into trouble with my girl. But against my better judgment and common sense, I'm going with the typical male response to female ire, and answer with . . . nothing."

She stood up from the couch and put her hands on her hips. "Nothing? Really? Then why are you up?"

He frowned, even more confused than before. "I was thirsty."

She cursed under her breath. "What did the doctors tell you, Talyn? You're not supposed to be out of bed! What were you thinking?"

"That I was thirsty, and unless I wanted to drink out of the toilet, I needed to come to the kitchen to get water."

He could tell by her expression that she was struggling not to laugh at him. "Did it not occur to you to ask someone to get it *for* you?"

Talyn snorted at her sarcasm. "I dare you to try that in the barracks. When I get my ass kicked, I expect to get paid and be applauded for it."

"You are a sick male . . . in more ways than one. Now get back in bed where you belong, and I'll get the water for you."

"Yes, ma'am." He trod back toward the bedroom, then paused. "Would I be pushing my luck to ask for a snack, too?"

"Yes, and yes, I'll bring you something to eat. Now go!"

"Gah, bossy thing. You should work for Command."

"I heard that!"

"I should hope so, given that I didn't whisper it," he groused as he returned to bed.

Felicia joined him there a few minutes later, with a small tray that she set on the bed beside him. Frowning, she tested his temperature with the back of her hand. "How are you feeling?"

"Good."

"Just good?"

"I felt better till I got yelled at for trying not to disturb you while you were studying for your exams."

"Sorry, *mi keramon*. I'm just worried about you. You've slept for almost thirty straight hours."

His jaw went slack. "What?"

She nodded. "Your mom was about ready to call an ambulance for you."

"How'd you keep her from it?"

"Your vitals were good. I told her that your body must need it, and that you were better off here than in the hospital where they annoy you, and you bark at them constantly." She fed him a bite of chicken.

Raking his hand through his hair, he frowned as he chewed and considered that. "I need to call my CO. I'm sure they've notified him that I'm at home, and—"

"We took care of it for you. All you need to do is focus on getting better."

Fear lacerated him. What had he missed? "Took care of it, how?"

"Your mother and I talked to Anatole."

Fear turned to a sick feeling of dread. "Shit. I'm screwed, aren't I?"

"No." She handed him the water. "Have a little faith."

Yeah, right. Faith was a heartless bitch who hated him worse than Anatole did.

"I know nothing of this faith you speak of." He took a drink and sighed at the inevitable. There was no way to fix it until he faced the wretched bastard.

What's done is done.

Instead of focusing on it and being mad, he changed the topic to something much more pleasant.

Felicia.

"So how are your tests coming?"

"I have one more tomorrow. Your mom has graciously volunteered to babysit you while I take it."

He rolled his eyes as he reached for bread. "Is she going to change my nappies, too?"

"If you need it." She fed him a bite of fruit.

The lift buzzed.

Talyn frowned at the sound.

"It's your mom returning."

"Oh."

Felicia went to the door to let his mother know that he was finally awake.

Grimacing, Talyn leaned back and pulled the tray closer so he could reach the food easier.

His mom swept into the room with a huge smile on her face. "Guess what I have?"

"I can't imagine, and that look on your face kind of scares me."

Scoffing at his irritable tone, she moved to his side and duplicated Felicia's gesture of checking him for a fever.

"Satisfied I'll live?"

"Very." She smiled at his sarcasm, then handed him the files she held. "I have a present for you."

He glanced at the Andarion military badge on the folder and bit back a snarl. Just the mere glimmer of a thought of returning to Anatole's "tender" care put him in a shitty mood. "Work!" he said in an exaggerated, sarcastically happy tone. "Just what I wanted! Thank you, Mum. How thoughtful!"

She jerked at his braids. "When you open that, you're going to feel like the ass you're being."

He doubted that. With a grimace, he licked the grease from his fingers, then opened the file to see what order he'd violated now that would be on his record forever.

The moment his gaze fell to the words, he gasped. "Is this for real?"

"It is."

He started to get up, then remembered why he was in bed as pain ripped through him. He cursed and grimaced.

"Talyn!" Both his mother and Felicia started toward him.

"I'm okay. I just wanted to hug you. How'd you get me transferred?"

She glanced to Felicia. "I know people."

Grateful beyond belief, he took his mother's hand, led it to his cheek, and held it there. "You're right. I feel like a total asshole. Oh gah, Mum, I can't thank you enough for this."

Felicia smiled at his heartfelt happiness and gratitude. That tone of voice told her just how bad Anatole had treated him. Her eyes tearing, she met Galene's grateful gaze.

Until guilt for taking credit for the transfer darkened Galene's eyes. By her expression, she knew his mother was about to tell him the truth.

Felicia shook her head to let her know it was all right to keep this secret. They'd decided that this would be best. While she was still learning about him, one thing Felicia knew for a fact was that Talyn didn't like to feel beholden to anyone. He hated being in debt, even in favors.

"What is it?" she asked Talyn, feigning ignorance.

Opening his eyes, he grinned at her. "I'm being transferred to the Royal Guard Corps as soon as I'm cleared for active duty again."

Now that was something she hadn't known for sure. Lorens had been frustratingly short on the exact details of what he was doing for Talyn. "You'll be at the palace?"

He nodded. "I don't know my CO, though. Commander ezul Nykyrian?"

"He's a cousin of the former sýzygos," Galene explained. "Stern, but fair. I think you'll like him. I know he'll adore you . . . you'll be guarding the tahrs and his court."

Talyn bit back a curse and steeled himself not to show his revulsion at the thought. Part of the tahrs's court included Colonel Asswipe. If an enemy ever came after Anatole while Talyn was on duty, he'd have a hard time protecting the douche.

But he didn't want to dampen his mother's happiness, so he held it in and hoped an assassin made a move on the bastard. Soon.

"Will you two be seeing each other?" Felicia asked hopefully.

Galene stepped away from the bed. "Not too much. My duties are with Tizirah Cairistiona. She's mostly . . . bedridden. She doesn't really leave her quarters in the palace. Tahrs Jullien, on the other hand, travels quite a bit. So I'm sad to say that we probably won't see Talyn much, as he'll be required to travel with Tahrs Jullien and his entourage."

That was another big concern for him. "What about my fight and training schedule?"

"There are special accommodations for that. It's all in there for you to look over. I think you'll be more than pleased."

Happiness returned as he pulled his mother against him for

another tight hug. "You are *the* best, Matar! I don't know how you did this, but I am forever in your debt."

Felicia's eyes teared at his exuberant gratitude.

Patting his head, his mother bit her lip as she met Felicia's gaze over his shoulder. The guilt there was so sweet, but there was nothing to feel guilty over. This was for the best.

Don't, Felicia mouthed to her. "Your mum is wonderful, Talyn. We're both in her debt." She scooted across the bed to pick up his folder. "Can I read it?"

"Sure."

Felicia smiled as she saw what her brother had done for them. She felt awful about every nasty thought she'd ever had regarding Lorens. "I'm so jealous! Your new barracks are at the palace. Near their guardhouse. Are those as nice as they sound?"

Galene snorted. "They're not *this*." She gestured at their bedroom. "But they're not as miserable as gen-barr, which is what he had. He'll finally have a private room and his own bathroom."

"Really?" Talyn gasped with wide eyes.

She nodded. "It's very small. Just a bed, chest of drawers, monitor, and tiny shower stall. Really a closet, but you don't have to share it."

The look of sincere joy made Felicia sick. What she'd learned was that Talyn had been relegated to using public washrooms at his old duty station. And he'd been allowed to use their showers only during certain hours, and never when there was a Vested soldier in them.

"It sounds great," he said with a grin.

Not to her. It sounded miserable. But she didn't want to dampen his happiness, so she returned his smile.

Galene headed for the door. "I'm meeting with my CO tonight for a status report so I'll leave you two alone for a bit."

"Be careful." Felicia ate a piece of fruit from the tray.

"Hey, Mum!"

She paused in the doorway. "Yes?"

"Love you."

Smiling, she blew him a kiss. "You too, baby."

As soon as she was gone, Talyn picked the folder up and flipped through it. "This is the best present in the universe. I've got to do something really nice for my mom. But there's no gift that's equivalent to it."

"I think the look on your face was gift enough."

He grimaced. "I don't."

"Trust me. I do." She kissed him. "Did you get enough to eat?"

"Mmm." He nibbled her chin. "It didn't quite fill me."

She shivered as his fangs gently scraped her skin. "Are you up to this?"

He let out an evil laugh as he brushed her hand against his hard erection. "Oh, I'm definitely *up* for it."

Sucking her breath in sharply, she pulled back. "Hold that thought. Let me get the tray out of here first. I don't want to roll around in your food."

Talyn pouted as he watched her leave. She was right, but he

didn't want to stop. Not when he was so happy and ready. Since the moment he'd first seen her photo, all he'd dreamed of was making love to her.

Now . . .

Trying to distract himself in the short interim, he pulled the file toward him and flipped through his orders while he waited for her to return.

He still couldn't believe his mom had pulled this off. Anatole would have a stroke and he might protest it. But there wasn't anything the bastard could do to stop it.

At least, he hoped not.

Then again, Anatole was the son of the tadara's niece. There was no telling what kind of reach he could pull.

Don't think about it. He had other things that were on his mind tonight. A beautiful angel to hold on to for a while.

More than eager for Felicia, he slid his pajama bottoms off and dimmed the lights.

"Felicia?" he called, wondering what was taking her so long. Had she run for the exit?

"Just a second."

Talyn was about to go after her when the door opened and his stomach hit the floor. Probably his tongue, too.

Dressed in a sheer red negligee, she walked toward him so seductively that he was pretty sure he was drooling.

With the most salacious smile he'd ever seen, she pulled the blankets off and straddled him. "Hi, gorgeous."

His breathing ragged, he couldn't respond. All the blood had left his brain. Honestly, he was afraid to touch her. To move. If he did, he might ruin this by doing or saying something really stupid.

Tsking at him, she led his hand to the ribbon bow at her hip. "Whenever you're ready, my panties are tied on. Just pull."

"It's like opening a present."

She nodded with the sweetest smile he'd ever known.

His senses reeling, he rubbed himself against the scratchy lace. "Are you ready for this?"

She leaned forward, her long, curly hair brushing against his chest as she moved. "I've been ready since the first time I met you."

He hoped she couldn't see how unsteady his hands were as he pulled the ribbon between her breasts and uncovered her. Aching for a taste of her body, he slowly ran his hands over her breasts, reveling in the softness of them. He brushed his thumbs over the nipples, amazed at the way they hardened instantly. While he'd seen photos and films of naked females, he'd never seen one in the flesh.

Her body was amazing to him. So incredibly supple and beautiful.

Felicia bit her lip at the tender expression on his face as he gently and very slowly explored her. It was so obvious that he'd never been with a naked female before. He took his time and savored every inch of her flesh, inspecting it with great care and curiosity, which made her burn all the more.

He was such a large, fierce beast and yet so incredibly gentle. She had a hard time reconciling this side of his personality with the Iron Hammer who fought so ferociously in the Ring. There, he was terrifying.

Here, he was all hers and gentle. Something that was all the more precious because it didn't come naturally to him. He had to make an effort to be kind and sweet.

With an adorable half smile, he untied her panties and slid his hand over her hip and through the small curls until he touched her where she ached most for him. She hissed as he lightly teased her with his thumb.

Talyn swallowed hard as he stared into her eyes. The wetness of her body amazed him. The velvety skin, even more so. He'd had no idea how incredible a female's flesh would feel. How very different her body was from his. Unlike him, she was so soft and supple. Smooth. Licking her lips, she held his gaze as she slowly rode his fingers.

His throat dry, he brushed the red lace from her, until she was fully exposed to his starving gaze. "You're so beautiful," he breathed as he returned to stroking her taut nipple.

She covered his hand with hers and pressed it flat against her breast. "I'm so glad you saw my profile. I can't imagine doing this with anyone else."

Before he could speak another word, she lifted herself up and slid onto his cock, taking him in all the way to the hilt. He growled at the unexpected ecstasy of being inside her.

Felicia couldn't breathe for a second as he filled her completely. He was huge and her body wasn't used to this. It took a full minute to catch her breath as her maidenhead tore to accommodate him. But once the pain receded, she was left with an incredible full sensation of holding him deep within, in the most intimate of embraces.

Worry lined his brow. “Are you all right?”

Smiling, she leaned down to kiss him. “All good.”

As she started to move against him the way she’d been trained, he locked his hands on her hips and held her in place.

She froze instantly. “Am I hurting you?”

Biting his lip until it bled, he shook his head. “I’m trying not to come just yet. Slap me.”

She gaped at his earnest request. Slap him? Was he insane? “I’m not going to slap you, Talyn.”

Talyn fought his body with everything he had, but he was quickly losing himself to the pleasure he felt. “Don’t move. Don’t even breathe.”

She didn’t listen.

Before he could speak again, she reached out and pinched his nipple.

“Ow! Hey! That hurt!”

She pinched his other one.

Scowling at her, he rubbed the offended area.

“Better?” she asked impishly.

He laughed as he realized it’d worked. And it was better than her slapping him. Kind of. While he was still hard inside her, he wasn’t quite on the verge anymore. “Thank you.”

With an adorable expression, she slowly rocked her hips against his. “No problem. But if you return that favor, I will get up and leave.”

Laughing, he ran his hands over her breasts as she rode him, slow and easy. "I would *never* do that to you."

"Good."

Felicia lifted his hand to her lips so that she could nibble his knuckle as she savored the feeling of him deep inside her. In all her dreams, she'd never imagined just how good he would feel there. Even with the pain of her virginity, she welcomed the sensation of his thick fullness. He was so gorgeous and sweet.

So adorably innocent and worldly.

The bruises and cuts on his body still made her want to hunt his commander down and skin the rotten beast. But the smile on his face as he watched her kept her focused on this one precious moment with him.

She shivered as he rose up to capture her lips. He sank his hand in her hair as he lifted his hips under her.

"Don't hurt yourself," she breathed. "I'll do all the work."

His gaze adoring, he dipped his head so that he could lave her breast. "You taste like heaven."

She cradled his head to her breast as a wave of love for him tore through her. "I love—" She barely caught herself before she confessed her feelings to him. "How you feel."

He sucked his breath in sharply an instant before he came. Groaning, he leaned back to look up at her. "Sorry."

She leaned down over him to kiss his lips. "It's okay, sweetie. I'm amazed you made it as long as you did."

"Yeah, but I'm not done with you." He flipped with her.

"Talyn! Don't get hurt."

Lifting himself up on his elbows, he grinned. "No worries." Then slowly he began nibbling a blazing trail from her throat to her breasts.

"What are you doing?"

"I'm devouring you. It's what I've been dying to do to you since the first time I saw your picture. I'm going to taste every single inch of your body tonight . . . until you're begging me to stop."

It was a promise he more than delivered on. And when he got to the part of her that ached for his touch, she thought she'd die on the spot.

Lifting her hips, she buried her hand in his braids as his tongue and fingers teased and delighted her.

He growled, using his chin and fangs to heighten her pleasure. Within minutes, he had her body humming with heat.

She threw her head back and cried out as unimaginable pleasure ripped her apart. "Oh my God! Talyn!"

Still he continued until he'd wrung every last bit of tremor from her. And still he stroked her with his fingers as he kissed his way over her stomach and back to her breasts.

Her entire body quivering, she kept waiting for him to stop, but he didn't. Not until she came over and over again.

The moment she cried out, he slid himself back inside her. She bit her lip at the sensation of him hard once more.

He held her close as he rocked himself against her hips. "I'm not hurting you, am I?"

"No. Not even a little."

He kissed her cheek then pressed his cheek against hers as he quickened his strokes. "Say my name, Felicia."

"Talyn."

Lifting himself up to look down at her, he smiled. Then he kissed her and came again with a soft growl.

She felt his heart pounding as he slowly lowered himself over her. "Am I too heavy?"

"No. You feel wonderful." Wrapping her legs around his waist, she ran her hands over his muscled back.

He let out a happy sigh. "I can't believe I finally got to do this. I was beginning to think I was going to die a virgin."

She laughed at his angst-ridden tone. "It did seem like the very gods were against us."

Rolling over, he pulled her to rest on top of him. "I never want to leave this bed again."

She ran her fingernail over his nipple. "I'm game if you are. But you'll have to surrender your Ring title."

"Done, even though Erix will kill me. Probably Ferrick, too."

"You'd die happy."

"That I would." He pulled her hand to his lips so that he could place a kiss in her palm. "Thank you, Felicia."

"For what?"

"For agreeing to be part of my life. The best part of it."

Tears choked her at the sincerity she heard. "I don't know. You are such an onerous burden. Quite unmanageable."

He laughed. "Now you sound like my nurses." Letting out an irritated breath, he kissed her cheek before he rolled out from under her. "I'll be right back."

"Nature calling?"

"Like a beast." Talyn picked her panties up from the floor and placed them on the bed, then headed for the bathroom.

With an inexplicable peace, he quickly tended his needs and washed himself. But as he went to turn the water off, he glanced into the mirror and froze.

Oh shit.

Instead of the white eyes he'd had since birth, they were now glowing a sharp, deep red.

Minsid hell.

He was stralen.

Chapter 10

Talyn returned to the bedroom with two cool cloths. Making sure to keep his eyes hidden, he slid into bed and handed one to Felicia.

"You okay?"

"Headache." He covered his eyes with the other one.

"Poor baby. Can I do anything to help?" She draped herself over him.

"Keep the lights off . . . please."

"Sure." She snuggled close.

Talyn hated lying to her, but no good could come of her learning he was stralen. It was a rare, rare genetic defect that ran through the males of certain lineages. Because of the legend of the thirteen War Hauks who'd once defended their homeworld from invaders, he'd long known that the trait ran through his father's DNA—it was almost as big a curse as the one that ran through his mother's. But given his father's abandonment, Talyn had assumed the trait had missed the two of them.

Could I have been more wrong?

No. He was the lucky bastard who got to carry not one, but *two* of the most recessive traits in all of Andaria.

Woohoo!

At least it explained his fierce feelings toward Felicia and the foreign serenity inside him whenever she was near. Why he was so protective of her. The overproduction of oxytocin and vasopressin in the brain that caused the stralen made the males with it extremely protective and possessive of the female who'd caused it. For some reason, the first onset of the condition always appeared during, or within an hour after sex. Usually, it receded within a few hours after climax, once oxytocin and vasopressin levels returned to a certain level. In even more rare and extreme cases, it was permanent and caused the eyes to remain red forever. Lucky him—that, too, ran in his father's family.

Either way, he was screwed. In a married male, stralen was the most desired trait in their culture.

For an unmarried male . . .

Ridicule. Humiliation. It would make all his previous abuse seem mild. And he didn't know Felicia well enough to even begin to guess how she'd react to it. She might welcome it, fear it, or use it against him.

The first was the best-case scenario. The other two were horrifying to contemplate. If it scared her, she'd leave, and he'd be royally screwed since she was the one he needed in his life. Worst case, she'd manipulate him with it, knowing he would do anything for her.

Even die.

Why, gods?

His life sucked enough. He really didn't need anything else added to the misery. Especially stralen.

You can fix this.

With luck, it'd recede by morning and he could buy colored contacts to cover it. No one would ever know.

He hoped.

Please be normal by morning. Surely the gods would grant him that one small mercy.

Yeah, right . . .

Talyn got up slowly. He slit open his eyes to make sure he was alone in the room.

Thankfully, he was. Breathing a deep sigh in relief, he rolled out of bed and went to the bathroom to check his eyes.

They were white again.

Thank you, gods! Grateful beyond measure, he quickly bathed and dressed. He wouldn't dare touch Felicia again until he had a way of concealing it. At this point, even a small kiss could bring the stralen right back.

Now he just needed to get to an optometrist without his mother or Felicia grilling him. *C'mon. You can do this.* Biting his lip, he left the bedroom to find his mother in the kitchen.

Crap.

"Where's Felicia?" he asked.

"She went to take her test."

"Ah, okay."

"Are you hungry?"

"Sure." He sat down on the barstool while his mother made him a bowl of hot cereal.

"Why don't you go back to bed? I'll bring it to you."

If only he could. "I really need to run an errand before Felicia gets back."

"Honey—"

"I'm . . ." He tried to search for some reasonable lie. But the truth came out before he could stop it. "I'm stralen."

She dropped the bowl in her hand. It went straight to the floor and shattered, sending cereal and porcelain in every direction.

Cursing, she quickly picked up the pieces. "What?"

Talyn nodded. "Felicia doesn't know. And I've got to keep it covered. From everyone."

Eyes wide, she cleaned up the mess and fixed him more cereal. "Are you thinking contacts?"

"Yeah. Will it work?"

"I don't know. But it's worth a shot. I'll get you a set immediately."

"Thank you."

She set the bowl on the counter, then cupped his cheek in her hand. "My poor baby." Wincing, she buried her hand in his hair. "I just wish you were married."

"Me, too. It would make things much easier."

His mother nodded. "How did you conceal it from her?"

"I lied to her last night, and I feel like crap. I hate to do that."

"You had no choice."

"It doesn't make it any easier."

She patted his shoulder. "And that's what makes you a good male. What makes me proud to be your mother." She kissed his cheek. "Now eat your cereal and go back to bed. I'll get the contacts and return as soon as I can."

"Thank you."

She pressed her cheek to his. "Stay away from Felicia until I get back."

"Don't worry. I'm way ahead of you on that."

His mom grabbed her purse and left him.

Talyn finished eating. He rinsed out the bowl and headed toward the bedroom to review his new orders.

He'd just finished reading through the whole packet when his mother entered the room.

She handed him a small bag. "I bought two pair for you to try. If they work, we can easily get more."

"Thank you." Getting up, he went to try them on.

His mom followed him into the bathroom to talk while he tried to figure out how to insert the contacts. "What do you think about your new orders and post?"

"It looks pretty sweet. Extremely cushy. I might get fat and lazy from it."

She laughed. "You could use some weight."

He carefully washed off the contact and gently placed it over his eye. "Yeah, right. I weigh as much as a transport." He grimaced at the strange feeling of the lens. Blinking, he turned toward his mother. "How's that?"

"Great. I can't even tell they're contacts."

"Yeah, but my eyes aren't red under them . . . yet." He put the other one in. "So is there anything I need to know about working at the palace?"

"Just remember that you're not to meet the gaze of any royal family member. And you can't strike them. It's an automatic death sentence."

He forced himself not to rub at his eyes. "Why do you think I'd hit one?"

"Honestly? Jullien can be an arrogant ass. I've been tempted to sock him a few times. He's very condescending toward his staff. I've heard from highly reliable sources that his valet spits in his food before he takes it to the tahrs. And you don't want to know what some of the others do. So never touch anything brought to him."

Talyn was aghast at that audacity. "Are you serious?"

"Yes, but I'm told Jullien wisely leaves his guards alone. Since they protect him, they tend to be immune from his *charming* personality. They mostly complain about how much noise he makes while having sex. But everyone else is fair game for his abuse."

"Great."

She nodded. "You will also have to sign nondisclosures and take an oath of loyalty."

"I've already done that."

"These are different from your initial service intakes. They're not about national security as much as they are about royal secrets."

"Such as?"

"The two biggest ones you'll find out your first day there is that Tizirah Tylie is a lesbian and Tizirah Cairistiona is bat-crap crazy."

He gaped at her as he made his way back to bed. "What?"

Nodding, she sighed heavily. "That being said, I adore Cairistiona. Unlike her mother and Jullien, she has a good heart. She just can't accept the fact that her son's dead. You'll see her wandering the halls, from time to time, looking for Nykyrian. Invariably, she makes her way to Jullien's wing that the boys shared when they were young. And she'll probably ask you a few thousand times if you've seen her Nykyrian, or know where he is. Just tell her that it'll be all right and help her back to her rooms. Whatever you do, don't go into his nursery or bedroom for anything. No one's allowed to touch his personal items. She'll have you executed if you do."

Wow, that was extreme.

"What happened to him?"

"He died in a school fire when he was a boy. She was the prime commander of the armada at the time it happened. In a heartbeat, she lost her mind and has never recovered."

"That sucks."

His mother tucked the covers around him. "It does, indeed. But I understand her pain. I would be the same if something ever happened to you. In fact, I think I'd make her look sane in comparison."

He heard Felicia returning.

Felicia pulled up short as she came into the room and saw them together. "Am I interrupting?"

"Nope." He yawned.

"Is your head better?" Felicia asked as she moved to check him for a fever.

"His head?"

"He had a headache when he went to bed last night."

"It's what I was telling you about, Mum. I'm better now, though."

His mother nodded. "Good."

He turned his attention to Felicia as she placed her backpack on the floor. "How was your test?"

"I think I did okay on it."

His mom picked up the shopping bag before Felicia saw it and held it out of sight. "Well, I'm going to put my things away. I'll see you two in a bit."

Looking upset and concerned, Felicia turned back to him. "Can I ask you a huge, giant favor? I swear that I'll never ask you again."

Not quite certain why she was so skittish and afraid, he nodded. "Sure. What?"

"I know how much you hate company and being with strangers, but . . ." She clenched her eyes shut as if really dreading his reaction.

"But?"

She twisted her hands together in the cutest, most adorable way. Little did she know, when she looked at him like that, there was nothing he wouldn't do to make her happy. "Is there any way I could talk you into having dinner with my brother and his two sons?"

Talyn cringed at the mere thought of it. To say he hated company was tantamount to saying the core temperature of a star was slightly warm. "Can I ask why?"

She sat down beside him on the bed. "It's my nephew's birthday and they're huge fans of yours. I screwed up and told my brother that I knew you. I swear I'll never ask another favor. Ever. Ever. Ever . . . ever."

He brushed her hair back from her face. "Only if you do something for me."

"What?"

"Kiss me."

"That's it?"

"That's it . . . well, and smile. Don't look so scared, Licia. I'd *never* hurt you."

Laughing, she kissed him. "Thank you!"

Talyn held her against his chest. "No problem." For her, there was nothing he wouldn't do. He just couldn't afford to let her know that. He'd already seen what happened when one partner loved another and the other one left.

It was devastating. Even decades later.

The last thing he wanted was to have the same heartache his mother dealt with every day. He had no idea how she could still love his father, but she did.

Talyn swallowed as he tried not to think of the picture his mother kept hidden in her nightstand. The photo he'd found years ago while hunting for clues on what to get her for a birthday gift. It was of his parents in school. His mother had been staring up at his father with an adoring look he'd never seen on her face. One of complete, untainted happiness. To this day, even when she was ecstatic, there was always a twinge of sadness in her eyes that nothing ever erased.

For that alone, he hated his father. And he hated how much he looked like him. It had to have been excruciating for his mother to watch him grow into an exact duplicate of the male who'd fucked her over and ruined her life. Yet to her credit, she'd never once said anything about it. At least not negatively. Nor would she allow him to say anything against his father. That, too, told him how much she'd loved Fain Hauk.

Bastard. Too bad *he* hadn't been stralen.

"You okay?"

He blinked at Felicia's worried frown. Smiling, he fisted his hands in her beautiful curls. "Fine."

"You sure you're not mad at me?"

"For this? No, baby. Not even a little."

Her eyes widened. "Are you mad at me for something else?"

"Gods, no!"

Letting out a relieved breath, she gave him a light squeeze before she pulled away. "Good. I'll go call my brother and make his day."

Talyn bit back a groan at the reminder. He really wasn't a social creature. Too many years of being rebuffed at best, ridiculed at worst had made him extremely skittish around anyone else. Though, to be honest, he'd had a friend once.

For five minutes.

It'd been his first day of military training. When he'd moved into the barracks, his bunkmate had been nice and welcoming.

Until his CO had walked in and announced Talyn's lack-Vest status to everyone there.

So had ended any semblance of normality.

Although, once he'd entered the Vested league and had begun winning titles, Andarions would come up to talk to him. But only because of his fame. He was well aware of the fact that they didn't know him or care to befriend him. He was like a zoo animal in a cage. They wanted to pet his fur and take a photo, then beat a hasty retreat from his presence.

At least Felicia would be with him for the ordeal. That alone made this bearable.

She stuck her head back in the door. "Do you think you'll feel up to dinner next week?"

"Sure."

With a dazzling smile, she returned to her call. "He says that's fine. No, Lo, I'm not telling him that." She paused for a second to roll her eyes. "Fine, I'll tell him. My brother says that your last fight paid off his transport. He loves you for that. He's hoping with your next fight that he can top off his son's university tuition."

"Tell him thanks. I'll do my best for him."

She laughed at whatever her brother said. "Yeah, okay. I'll see you then. Bye." She hung up. "You made his day. I've never heard him so happy."

"I'd much rather make his sister's day."

Pressing her lips together, she closed the distance between them. "And I'd rather make yours."

"You did that the minute you came home."

Felicia hated the weepy feeling she had every time he said something so sweet to her. She'd always prided herself on being pragmatic. Always on keeping a level head, no matter what, but all that went out the window whenever he was around. He made her want to believe in fairy tales and lies. In males who were decent and loving.

Things she knew didn't really exist. She was living proof of what happened after a few years of marriage, once the new wore off. Her father had contracted with her mother, saying he loved her and would never love another, and abandoned his wife's bed.

And since Felicia's birth, her mother had cycled through patrons routinely. They were all married. They all claimed to love her mother for a year or two, or sometimes as long as five, which seemed to be the magic number. And then they were taken with someone who was shiny and new.

Love, unlike bills, never lasted. Hearts were made to wander. Unless a male was stralen, there was no hope of a lasting relationship with one. A stralen male was one in a billion.

Maybe even more rare.

She kissed Talyn's hand, wishing for impossible things. She was his mistress and that was all she'd ever be. Females like her didn't marry and they didn't stay in committed relationships with any male.

Never mind the Andarion laws that would never allow Talyn to marry at all. Or have children. She had no idea who his father was, but he must have been extremely important and high-ranking to have been pledged to a Winged Blood Clan Batur.

Out of curiosity, she'd investigated Galene's lineage and seen the prestige on her side that went back for generations. They weren't just doctors, warriors, politicians, and lawyers. They were nobility. Talyn's maternal great-grandfather had been the Andarion her father had replaced as the queen's advisor.

Most likely, his father had been even more connected and well-lineaged than Galene. It was how unifications usually worked. Unless the female was royal-blooded, the male in most marriages held a higher lineage. Talyn's father might have even been royal. It would make sense given how tight-lipped they were about the male's identity.

It would also explain Chrisen's hatred for Talyn. And if that was true, then what had been done to Talyn was the greatest travesty of all. How could he stand the injustice of it?

That, too, said a lot about him—that he never ranted against his lot. He went on courageously, and with an honor and dignity that amazed her.

Talyn brushed his thumb over her brow. "You okay?"

"Just worried about you."

"Don't be. I'm a cockroach. Even after nuclear-level devastation, I'll survive."

She snorted. "While I believe that might be true, I don't want to find out." She snuggled up against him and held him close as a bad feeling went through her. "You're not going to get caught up in royal politics at the palace, are you?"

Talyn frowned at her strange question. "Not intentionally. Why?"

"I watch the news. I see how bloody the royal family can be. Especially now with this whole new group that's been working against them."

"You mean WAR?"

She nodded.

Talyn could understand her fear. Warriors Against Royalty was the latest group to try and overthrow a monarchy that was drunk on its own power. And given what his mother had told him about the eton Anatoles and what he'd experienced with Chrisen, he could understand why. The gods knew he was no fan of the current reigning order that held him down with a crushing foot on his throat. He sure wouldn't weep to see the royal house overthrown and a new system of government put in place.

But that being said . . .

"I'm not a terrorist, Felicia. I have no intention of committing treason, especially not after I've taken oaths to uphold the monarchy and laws of Andaria. My mind doesn't work that way. Besides, I wouldn't be the only one who'd pay for it. Given my mother's rank, any military action I might take against the crown could blow back on her, and I'm not about to risk that. As you've seen, I'm a male of simple needs. All I want is to keep you and my mother safe and happy. That's it."

"Okay. Just remember that when you're at the palace and all those gorgeous, scantily clad females are throwing themselves at you."

He laughed bitterly. "Trust me. They won't, and even if they did, I'd have no interest in them. At all. The only female I want in my bed is currently in my bed."

Felicia's breath caught as she felt him hardening against her hip. As she saw the hooded expression on his face, and his breathing changed. Gone was her playful male and in his place was the fierce predator that truthfully scared her a little. It was too easy to forget just how large and dangerous her male was while he was being playful and sweet with her. But at the end of the day, Talyn was a trained killer. In the Ring and outside it. Every part of him was honed by battle and hardened by life.

His gaze holding hers, he pushed her skirt up and pulled her panties down her legs. With an astounding gentleness, he fingered her until she was slick and panting. Only then did he slide himself inside her and thrust against her hips. This time, he was almost feral as he made love to her. Yet even so, he took care not to hurt her and to make sure that she came first.

Talyn growled as he felt her release and saw the ecstasy on her face. He loved the way she said his name whenever he was inside her. Loved how she clutched at him and gently clawed his back with her nails.

Best of all, he adored the scent of her skin and hair. It was as if she'd been made solely for him. He could forgive the gods everything they'd done to him if they allowed her to stay in his life.

And yet as he came in her arms, he couldn't shake the feeling that something was going to happen. Something that would tear her out of his world and leave him coldly solo again.

He buried his face in her hair and tried to tell himself it was an unfounded fear. But the past wouldn't leave him alone. It tormented him with memories he didn't want.

Tay-lyn No-kin,
Born in sin,
No matter what, you'll never win!

Grinding his teeth, he tried to blot out the memory of the rhyme other kids had used to torment him when he'd been a child in school. He'd hated his mother for giving him a name that was so easy for Hyshians to mispronounce and rhyme with his bastard status.

While Felicia didn't seem to mind the fact that he wasn't Vested right now, sooner or later, that would change. She wouldn't be in med school unless she wanted to better her caste for unification. One day, she'd want children—she'd said as much on her agency questionnaire. Something he could never legally give her.

They couldn't even adopt.

And here he was stralen for a female he knew he couldn't keep. Ever.

Damn them. His classmates had been right, after all. He couldn't win. Even though thirteen members of his father's family had once held back an invading alien army and saved this planet from the Oksanans, they hadn't done it single-handedly.

They'd had each other to rely on.

Someone at their back.

One single Andarion couldn't change anything. He'd stood strong his whole life against storm after storm. Vowing with each one that he would not be broken.

That was never supposed to change.

But as he looked down at the female in his arms, he knew that it had. And Felicia was the one thing that would ultimately break him. He was sure of it. In a life he'd carefully, meticulously carved in blood and stone, she was his only vulnerable spot.

The gods had never shown him mercy. Not once. There was no way they'd have sent her to him and turned him stralen for her unless they were planning to use her against him somehow.

That made sense.

Like some mindless pawn, he'd allowed her inside his heart. Now it was too late.

He *was* damned.

And he had no doubt she would be the angel of death that delivered the killing blow to his worthless heart.

Chapter 11

Felicia smoothed the collar of Talyn's black shirt down. His mother had returned to her post yesterday, and it'd been the two of them alone ever since. Something she'd enjoyed a lot more than she should have.

"Remember, I'm having the dinner here, so that as soon as you're sick of my brother, all you have to do is say you don't feel well and I'll eject him from the condo."

Talyn laughed at her. "The way you say that tells me you want me to feel sick before dinner is even served."

She wrinkled her nose at his perceptiveness. "He's always been a bit of a booger with me. I'm hoping he'll be on good behavior. If he's not, I might be the one who starts feeling ill."

He kissed her brow. "One frown and I'll toss him out my-self."

The building intercom buzzed. Felicia stepped away to tell security that it was fine for her brother and nephews to come up.

Talyn took a minute to finish dressing. In all honesty, he dreaded this. He'd seldom had a decent encounter with other Andarions. And he'd meant what he told Felicia—if her brother said one thoughtless or mean thing to her, he would toss him out on his ass faster than the male could blink.

Taking a deep breath for courage, he pulled his jacket on and went to join them.

Her brother and his two teenage sons were stepping out of the lift.

Felicia gasped at the sight of the kids. One was average Andarion height . . . which reached Talyn's shoulder. His younger brother was an inch or two shorter. Handsome and lean, both had black braided hair that told Talyn the teens were considered adults in their world, and eligible for marriage.

The fact that Felicia didn't hug or touch them was a big clue as to how they normally treated her—like she wasn't family or friend. And that seriously pissed him off. How dare they disregard her so. She was worth more than the rest of the Andarion race combined.

With an apprehension that didn't help his mood, she stopped in front of them with her hands primly folded in front of her. "Wow! You two have really grown. Look at you, Brach. I think you've grown a foot since I last saw you. And you, Gavarian. You look like you're about ready to join the armada with your paka."

His hands folded behind his back, Gavarian blushed. "I start my service next fall."

Talyn froze as he realized why her brother was so familiar

to him. And why he had the bearing of a staunch military official.

Minsid *hell* . . .

Yes, his usual bad luck was holding fast. No wonder Felicia hadn't bothered telling him her brother's full name. Talyn would have balked over this disaster.

"Commander ezul Terronova." Talyn gave her brother a sharp salute. "It's a pleasure to meet you, sir. Welcome to my home."

With a bright smile, he waved Talyn's salute off. "None of that. We're not in uniform here, Major. Just having a nice dinner with family." He held his hand out to him. "Call me Lorens."

Talyn hesitated before he reached out and shook it. "Pleased to meet you, sir."

Laughing as he stepped back, Lorens passed an amused look to Felicia. "He can't help it, can he?"

Her face lighting into a beautiful smile, she shook her head. "He's always very proper."

Talyn fell into a relaxed military pose similar to Gavarian's. "Sorry. My mother beat me down when I was young over my manners." He turned toward her nephews, who were eyeing him with a mixture of fear and awe. "Which of you is the birthday boy?"

The older one, Gavarian, stepped forward. "That would be me. I'm turning eighteen."

"Happy birthday."

"Thanks."

Brach smiled so wide, he exposed his fangs. "Mine was last

month. My paka took me on my Endurance. Did your paka take you for yours?"

Talyn cringed at the most natural assumption. "I went with my matarra."

Brach made a face at the mere thought. "For real? What did you do with your mom?"

"Got grounded for a year over my actions during the climb, ate more vegetables than the gods ever intended Andarions to eat, and had to do all the dishes. Definitely a lesson in Endurance . . . in more ways than one."

They all laughed.

Felicia gestured toward the dining room. "And speaking of vegetables, everything is ready. I'm sure you boys are hungry."

"We're always hungry, Felicia," Brach said as he skipped toward the table.

Lorens snorted. "We're going broke on the food bill. Either of you know someone willing to pay a fair price for a healthy Andarion teen?"

Laughing, Felicia led them into the formal dining room that overlooked the city, where the catering company had already set everything up.

Talyn was grateful that she put her brother at the opposite end of the table and took a seat to his right. Times like this, he was acutely aware of just how socially awkward and reclusive he was. He seriously hated interacting with others.

The only thing that made this bearable was the sexy red dress Felicia wore. One that made him curse their company and wish for five minutes alone to take care of the heavy need in his groin.

"I still can't believe that I'm actually sitting here with *the* Iron Hammer. This is just . . ." Lorens swept his gaze over his sons before he chose what must be a more appropriate word. "Incredible. So Hammer, how's it looking for your next match? I was reading that it's with Death Warrant?"

A caterer brought out the first course. Talyn thanked the female server before he answered. "It is. While I respect Dalun's abilities, and in particular his right hook, I expect to mop the floor with him in three to four rounds."

"Aren't you scared he might kill you?" Gavarian asked.

Talyn shook his head. "I couldn't do what I do, if I was."

Brach's eyes widened. "How is it that you've never been defeated?"

Talyn passed an amused glance to Felicia. "Want to know the secret?"

He nodded eagerly.

Talyn sat back in all earnestness. "Every morning before a fight, I sacrifice two goats to the gods."

"For real?"

He laughed. "No. I just train hard, study my opponents, and eat right."

"I want to Ring fight." Gavarian glared at his father. "But I'm not allowed to."

"I keep telling him how dangerous it is. He equates it to schoolyard fights and his wrestling matches."

Talyn choked at that. "Listen to your paka, Gavarian. It's not like any fight you've ever had. I promise you."

Gavarian snorted. "How can it be different?"

Talyn bit back a snort of derision. How he wished he could have been that arrogant and foolish at that age. But the gods had never allowed him such naivete. "When we step into that Ring, it's not over a girl or hurt feelings, or with school referees who want to protect us from harm, and make sure we follow game rules. It's for honor and glory. With only one law. Two warriors walk in. Only one walks out. You're not facing a bully or former friend who's ticked off. It's cold-blooded ruthlessness. All-out war. Every punch or kick is one from someone who is trained to put every ounce of their strength and weight behind the blow. You've never been really hit until you take a punch with a ton of weight behind it. The first time you receive a pro hit, you have this moment where you think, did I just lose a kidney? Or control of my bladder? No, wait, it's my mind. Definitely every brain cell I possess . . . I have to be crazy to be in here. What the heck was I thinking? Where's the exit? Medic! Help!"

They laughed.

"I don't believe that for an instant. Not the way you fight." Gavarian reached for his drink.

"It's the truth. I swear. It's not as glamorous as you think it is. There's a big difference between sitting in the stands, watching the fight, and being the idiot in the Ring looking out at the crowd with blood streaming into your eyes. Take my word for it, you'd much rather be tasting snack foods and soda than your own blood, sweat, and bile."

"Yeah, but the cheers from the crowd—"

"Don't register through the roar in your ears from your heartbeat and the sound of blood rushing through your body."

"Really?"

"Really. The only thing I hear in a Ring is the sound of my trainer calling drill moves from practice. That and the voice in my head saying I'm an absolute moron for being there, and telling me to run while I still have all my body parts attached."

Her nephews looked at him suspiciously.

"You don't believe me?" Talyn asked. "After dinner, we'll go to the gym in back and I'll show you."

Brach's eyes widened with joy. "Seriously?"

"Seriously."

"That's going to be awesome!" Gavarian dug into his food. "So how do you prepare for a fight, Hammer?"

Talyn shrugged. "It's no different than what your paka does. You drill, every day. Study your enemy. Carefully. You have to know what you're getting into before you accept the challenge. And recognize that some fights aren't worth it. The real skill lies in deciding which fights to take, and which to walk away from."

Lorens reached for his wine. "How do you mean?"

Talyn gently declined the wine when the server tried to pour some for him. "There are a lot of fighters who are out for blood. Like Death Warrant. I know going in that he's there to kill me if he can. Normally, I'd have passed on the fight."

"Then why did you take it?" Brach asked eagerly.

"End of the day, fighting is a business. While I know he's after my throat, the payout on the fight is substantial compared to most. Plus, he's only lost two fights. I take him down, and it'll be a while before I have to defend my title again. A match like this keeps the posers at bay. And makes them think twice about calling me names in public."

Gavarian wiped his lips. "You have a lot of those?"

Talyn nodded. "There's always a new kid out to prove himself. Comes in cocky and ill-trained. They're actually more dangerous in a fight than someone like Death Warrant."

Lorens cocked his head as he tried to understand that. "How so?"

Felicia passed the bread to Brach, knowing Talyn wouldn't eat it.

Talyn took a drink of water. "Death Warrant is a calculated, cold-blooded killer. You can study his moves and know where and how he'll react to every blow. How he's going to strike. He's practically choreographed. There will be a new move or two that he hasn't used before, but he's reliant on his previous fights where he picks those up. So again, you study his last few fights and you can still predict what he's going to do with pretty good accuracy. But the new fighters are wild cards, usually emotional and highly volatile . . . They get angry or they can't handle the pressure and adrenaline, and just start pounding their opponent. They're the ones who are going to break your back and leave you crippled, if you're not careful. So before you step into that Ring with one of them, you have to know beyond a doubt that you're willing to kill them if you have to."

The boys sucked their breath in.

"Have you ever killed anyone in the Ring?" Lorens asked.

"Not that I know of . . . That's not why I fight."

Gavarian frowned. "But isn't that the point of serious Ring fighting? To kill the enemy?"

Talyn shook his head. "That's the point of war. Not sport. And it's not easy to kill someone, especially when they're so close to you that you can feel their breath on your skin. Andarions respect strength and we are natural-born fighters. But we are sentient creatures, and we have a conscience. In battle, you know that you're protecting your family and our homeworld. In that Ring, you're fighting only for personal glory. In my opinion, that's not worth my opponent's life. No matter how much I might want to close his mouth forever."

"Here, here," Lorens said, raising his glass. "Truly, there are some battles not worth fighting. And not every insult is worth a broken jaw. We're not Phrixians. As I often tell my boys, sometimes you just need to shrug it off and let it go."

Talyn lifted his glass of water to return the salute. "Very true."

"Even if they insult your mother?" Brach asked.

Talyn flashed a grin. "That's different. A mother's reputation is a sacred thing. Notice, that's one public insult no fighter ever hurls to another. We know better." He took Felicia's hand into his and held it tight. "Nor any of their females. For we are Andarion. Family honor and lineage, the honor of our females and children . . . that we *will* all take a life over. You never threaten or assault, even verbally, those we hold in our hearts."

Smiling, she pressed his hand to her cheek. "I would still rather you walk away from all fights than ever be harmed." She looked to her nephews as she kissed Talyn's hand and released it. "And your mother would agree with me about the two of you."

"As would your paka." Lorens took a deep drink. "So Talyn, what got you into fighting?"

"Honestly? Got tired of having my butt handed to me in school. Figured if I was going to get that bloody, that often, I should be paid for it. As my mother often says, don't ever bring a fight, just make sure you finish it."

Her brother scowled at the food Talyn was given. "Is that really your dinner?"

Talyn shrugged nonchalantly at his plain meal. "Told you, a fighter's life isn't glamorous. My diet is very specific. Especially when I have a big fight coming up."

Gavarian stuck his tongue out. "All right, Paka. You win. I'll *never* fight! Not if that's what I have to live on. Thank you for forbidding it."

Brach nodded in agreement. "How often do you have to eat that . ." He cut a sideways stare to his father. "Crap?"

Talyn glanced to Felicia and laughed. "Always. I have to stay in shape, and can't afford to cheat."

Eyes wide, she duplicated Brach's nodding. "He's not joking. First time I saw him eat, I wanted to weep. Especially at the quantity. You don't *ever* want to know how much food he goes through in a day. It's insane."

Lorens laughed. "Judging by what's on that plate, for one meal . . . yeah. Glad I don't have *your* grocery bill."

"There's a reason they time us in the mess hall, and why we eat really fast." Talyn took a bite of his *vorna* breast.

"That explains the mad rush at dinnertime that made me so glad I got a command position early in my career."

Talyn snorted. "What? You don't miss getting shoved aside by the giant gunners?"

Gavarian laughed at his words. "Yeah, I'd like to see one of them try to shove *you* aside."

"Believe me, they've tried." Talyn flashed a devilish grin at her nephews. "Food is another thing you're allowed to shed blood for. Especially when you've just come back from maneuvers and are starving. There's always the one moron who wants to be cute. But remember, the more time you waste pounding on him, the less time for eating. So drop him with one punch, grab your food, and go."

Felicia winked. "And now you know why his call sign is Pit Viper."

Lorens snickered. "Yeah, we've all done that. Nothing like a herd of hungry Andarions."

"The real reason humans fear us." Talyn thanked his server for the plain, steamed vegetables she set down by him.

Felicia didn't miss the hot look the female passed to him before she went back toward the kitchen. Lucky for the server, Talyn *did* miss that look.

She glanced to Gavarian.

"Planning her funeral?" he asked her with a wicked gleam in his eyes.

"No. Just a new hairstyle."

"Hairstyle?" Lorens asked, scowling. "What?"

Felicia jerked her chin toward the kitchen. "If she gives Talyn another beckoning look that says she wants him on her platter, I'm going to snatch her bald."

Talyn choked. Reaching for his water, he swallowed before he spoke. "What?"

She patted his hand. "It's okay, Major Oblivious. I'm extremely happy and proud that you took no notice of her overt ogling."

"Yeah," Gavarian chimed in. "She's been pretty obvious about it every time she comes out here."

Lorens snorted. "How long have I been married that I didn't even realize our server was female?"

"Given the fact that Felicia handles my food out of my eyesight, glad I didn't either. Spit sauce is not something I enjoy." Talyn kissed her hand.

Lorens eyed them for several minutes before he spoke again. "Talyn, you really study every fighter you go up against?"

"Yes, sir. When you're going to battle, you have to know your enemy. I have extensive dossiers on everyone I've ever fought against."

"So what's Death Warrant's biggest handicap?"

Talyn wiped at his mouth. "He took a bad blow to his right eye two years ago that dug his mask into it. It left him with limited peripheral on that side. He also has a bad tendency to kick instead of punch. When he does that, he throws his balance off and is easy to plant. That being said, his stinger is that vicious right hook. He hits with approximately fifteen hundred PSIs, provided he's properly grounded, weight evenly distributed. No one can survive that kind of hammering for long. But if you keep him off both legs, and kicking, his punch PSI is halved. Still not fun. However, you can survive and win against that. Just don't let him hit your chin or kidney."

"Wow . . . you really do know your opponent."

Talyn shrugged. "I don't want to lose. And I *definitely* don't want to die or end up maimed. They didn't name him Death Warrant because he sings in a band."

Chuckling, Lorens sat forward in his chair. "Out of curiosity, Major, why the hell are you a pilot? Why didn't you ever go into command?"

Talyn cocked his jaw and let out a tired sigh as he toyed with his water glass. "It was never from lack of trying on my part, sir. I put in for a Command position every year, as soon as I'm eligible, but it always gets kicked back with a rejection."

Her brother's face was a mask of disbelief. "Why? Do they ever say?"

Talyn glanced away sheepishly. "I didn't go to the right schools."

"From where did you graduate?"

"Brunelle Academy."

"Is that in Eris?"

"No, sir. It's a Hyshian school."

Lorens passed a shocked stare to Felicia before he returned his attention to Talyn. "Hyshian? Why in the name of the gods were you in a Hyshian academy?"

Talyn cringed inwardly as he saw this disaster coming and couldn't avert it. He hated answering this question more than anything. "It was the only one that would take me."

"I don't understand. What's your lineage?"

Heat suffused his cheeks as he cringed over that inevitable question. "My mother's the third daughter of the Winged Blood Clan Batur."

"Impressive. And your father?"

Here it comes. . . .

"He's an Outcast, sir."

"Oh." Yeah, there it was. That sound of horror and condescension.

Talyn glanced to Lorens's sons. "I can understand if you need to leave now."

Lorens hesitated. "If either one of you breathes a word of this to your mother or grandmothers, I'll beat you till you bleed."

They held their hands up in quick surrender.

"To the grave, Paka," Brach breathed.

Gavarian reached for more bread. "I don't know what you're talking about. We're all good here. I didn't hear nothing."

Lorens grinned. "That's right. Just having dinner with my baby sister. Don't know of the harm in that."

But an awkward silence hung in the room while they finished eating.

"Is your father why you don't give interviews?" Lorens finally asked.

Talyn nodded. "It's not something others need to know about me."

"Where's your father now?"

"Don't know, sir. I've never met him."

Her brother paused to consider that. "He was disinherited before you were born?"

"Yes, sir."

"Lorens, is it okay if we change the subject?" Felicia asked graciously. "Talyn is an Andarion of high honor and an extremely capable fighter pilot. I would run him up against anyone on Andaria."

Reaching out, Talyn squeezed her hand in gratitude.

"I'm sorry I was nosy. You're right. It's none of my business. And I hope I didn't offend you, Talyn."

"No offense taken, sir. I'm used to being judged for my father's shortcomings."

Lorens looked ill as he must have realized how inconsiderate he was being to his host. "Talyn? Would you be adverse to my seeing what I can do to move you into a command position?"

Talyn's eyes lit up with a hopeful joy that tightened her throat for him. "I would love nothing more, sir. Honestly. Just don't ask me to throw a fight for it."

He laughed. "No. I won't do that. And I don't expect anything for it. We could use an Andarion like you. The gods know I'm sick of the subsentient creatures they keep sending me. You wouldn't believe what passes in the academies today. I had this one officer, a colonel no less, actually asked me where Arundel was located."

Talyn's jaw dropped. "Our northernmost outpost?"

"See! You know right where it is. Oh, and there's a commander I met who still thought Huwin Quiakides was the prime commander for The League."

Talyn winced at *that* stupidity. Huwin had been assassinated by his own son a decade ago. "Ouch."

"Yeah. You see what I have to deal with? And here's my quiz for you. Who's Nemesis?"

"Rogue assassin wanted dead by The League, who, along with four others, leads The Sentella."

He looked at his sons. "And that, my boys, is why you pay attention not only in school, but watch the news." He held his glass out for more wine. "Seriously, I have got to get you into command. I can't take the idiots there anymore. I'm over it."

Felicia laughed. "You sound so much like Paka that it's frightening."

"I know, right? The very thing I swore I'd never be is what I morphed into the minute I had kids and took a command position. What was I thinking?"

Felicia shook her head playfully at his feigned angst.

As soon as they finished eating, Talyn led the boys to his gym. They stripped down to their pants while he showed them how to strap on the gloves and padded head protection. When he stripped down to his pants, their jaws dropped.

Gavarian laughed nervously as he scanned Talyn's body with

an envious stare. “I thought they doctored those pictures of you in the magazines. Shit, you’re ripped.”

“Gavarian!” Lorens snapped. “Watch your language!”

“But Paka . . . look at his body. How do you get *that* kind of definition?”

Talyn snorted as he finished putting his gloves on with his fangs. “I work out a lot, and you see what I eat. You willing?”

He looked down at his much smaller frame. Screwing his face up, he glanced to his brother. “We have noble titles for female magnets. We don’t need muscles. Marshmallow pecs and high lineage are the new ripped.”

Talyn rolled his eyes before he walked them to one of his training mannequins. “All right. Pointers. You don’t just start swinging. It’s not about power. It’s all control. Power without control is absolutely worthless. You don’t just throw a punch or kick. You have to know when to pull them, too.” He demonstrated by stopping his powerful blows just short of striking the dummy.

“How you do that?” Brach gasped.

“Like I said. Control. You have to be aware of every muscle in your body, every second you’re in a fight.” Talyn punched the dummy so hard, he lifted it up and rattled the chain. “Now, you try.” He stepped back for Gavarian to punch it.

Smirking, he did, and then cursed again. With a fierce frown, he cradled his hand to his chest. “Mommy! I think I broke my hand. How heavy is that thing?”

“Three hundred and twenty-five pounds. It’s what an average Zoftiq fighter weighs.”

They gaped again.

"Seriously? How did you move it?"

Talyn kicked it and lifted it up again. "I weigh three hundred and twenty pounds. As of his last weigh-in, Death Warrant is four hundred and eight pounds. And I practice a lot. As I said, you haven't been punched until you stand toe-to-toe with a pro."

They both tried to kick the bag and neither could move it at all. It just hung there, taunting them with its rude inertia.

Felicia moved to stand by Lorens while Talyn coached the boys on how to hit and kick so that they could actually move the bag.

"You all right?"

Her brother glanced down at her. "Having a weird moment while I reevaluate my way of thinking about things I once held sacred and true."

"What do you mean?"

"Talyn's not what I expected. At all."

"He's amazing, isn't he?"

Lorens nodded. "Thank you so much for this. You have made Gavarian's life."

"Thank you for saving Talyn's with that transfer to the palace."

"Yeah," he breathed. "Now that I've spent an evening with him, I know how doctored his report files have been. Anatole must really hate him. I just can't figure out why."

"His mother went to school with Anatole. She thinks it's a personal grudge from back then."

"That actually makes a lot of sense. The gods know Talyn isn't the disrespectful, reactionary moron his evaluations claim. Believe me, I'm around those idiots daily. Damn, I hate that I gave him over to the palace after I read his file. I really meant what I said earlier. We could use someone like him in my division."

"Can't you transfer him again?"

"It's not that easy. If he was above an O-4 in rank or X-12-6 in lineage, yes. There wouldn't be a problem. But he's just high enough in rank to stay in protective detail and not rise to command level."

"Can he not buy a promotion?"

"Again, it's not that easy, Felicia. Anatole's bullshit has really done a number on the kid's advancement potential. And while I can pull strings for Talyn, Anatole can pull just as many, if not more, against him."

"That's what his mother said. I was hoping she was wrong."

"She wasn't. You wouldn't believe the favors I had to call in to get him transferred to the palace. No one wanted to touch him because of his negative reports and disciplinary strikes."

"Hey, Paka! Did you hear that?"

Lorens arched a brow at Gavarian's shout. "Hear what?"

"Talyn said that we can come to his fights anytime we want. Ringside!"

Lorens smiled. "That's really nice to offer, but I know those seats are limited and I don't want to shove his family out."

"It's no problem," Talyn said as he handed water bottles to the boys. "We always have seats to spare. My mother and Felicia refuse to watch me get punched—no idea what's up with that. You'd think after putting up with me, they'd be paying my rivals to kick it for them. And my trainer rarely has his friends come—he's afraid one of them might poach me from him. As for his daughter, she hates Ring fights. So just let me know at least two hours in advance, and I can get you added to the list for the seats any time you want them."

Lorens gaped at her. "You really never go?"

"I'm there. I just stay in the locker room. Like Talyn said, I don't want to watch him get hurt. It pains me to see him get hit. Even in old video clips." She shivered at the memory of when she'd mistakenly thought she could watch a former match of his from years ago. Unable to deal with what he took without flinching, she'd turned it off forty seconds in.

Lorens grinned. "Then I have to say that I'd love to come see your fight with Death Warrant."

Talyn looked over at the boys. "How many seats? We have six allotted in total."

"You don't have friends who want them?" Lorens asked in disbelief.

"Yeah," Talyn said with a laugh. "They're clubbing each other in the head for them. All none of them . . . You want all six?"

Lorens smiled so wide, his fangs showed. "Hell, yeah. You'll make me the most popular Andarion on my shift. Thank you."

"No problem. Just don't forget your ID. You'll need it to pick up the tickets." He went back to coaching the boys.

Felicia froze as Lorens hugged her. It was the first time in her life he'd ever done that.

"Thank you, Felicia."

"Don't thank me. He obviously likes you and the kids or he wouldn't have offered. Trust me. He's not social or insincere. And he doesn't expect anything in return."

He tightened his arms around her. "I know I've been a giant asshole to you all your life. I'm really sorry about that. I should have had dinner with you a long time ago. For no reason."

She patted his back. "It's okay. I'm the bastard child who wasn't supposed to be born. You and your family aren't the only ones who get pissed off about it."

He scowled at that. "What do you mean?"

"My mother wasn't and isn't exactly thrilled by the complication of having me as a bonus from your father." But unlike Talyn, her father wasn't a bastard himself, so he'd been immune from prosecution. Felicia was merely an inconvenience for him. Not jail time.

"Well, I am glad that I finally got a chance to know you tonight. I hope we can have more talks and meals, and not always with Talyn in tow."

His words warmed her. Did he mean them? She wasn't sure, but it was a nice gesture for him to make. "Really?"

He winked playfully. "Don't get me wrong. The boyfriend is a sweet bonus, but I'm not doing this to have access to him. I meant what I said. I've been doing some soul searching lately, and have learned a valuable lesson here tonight about judging people, and assigning them categories based on their births and parents." He kissed her head. "I have spent many, many nights at dinners with the ranked and privileged, and never have I had more fun or seen my kids laugh more than we've done tonight." His eyes glowed as he watched his sons sparring with Talyn, who had all the patience in the universe with them. "He's really good with kids, isn't he?"

"It's actually the first time I've seen him with them. But yes, he is." Her eyes widened as Gavarian hit the bag and finally lifted it.

"Ha!" he shouted in triumph. "I did it! Take *that,* bag!"

Talyn tapped gloves with him. "Impressive hit. You're a quick learner. Good job!"

Felicia laughed as her nephew did a goofy walk of pride.

"Nah, nah," Talyn teased. "You do this."

She laughed even harder at his ridiculous strut that reminded her of a wounded chicken. "Please don't teach him that! I'm sure his parents want grandkids one day, and no female will *ever* find that attractive."

Talyn pouted. "Not even when *I* do it? C'mon, Licia, you know I make *this* look sexy."

"Um . . . no. You don't." She gestured toward the dining room. "But will you do that in front of the server? I'll never have to worry about her looking at you again."

Laughing, Talyn grinned. "If it'll make you happy, be glad to embarrass myself publicly. The gods know that I've done it for a lot less than your gorgeous smile." He returned to coaching the kids.

Lorens shook his head. "You two have a lot of chemistry together. How long have you been with him?"

"Not very, actually."

"Yet you love him."

She froze at something she thought she'd been hiding pretty well. "How do you know?"

"The same way I know he loves you. It oozes from both of you whenever you look at each other. I've never seen a couple hold more regard for one another. It's really very sweet. I hope the two of you have a long life together."

Her heart broke at those words. "Talyn can never legally marry."

Lorens turned his back so that he could whisper to her and his sons wouldn't overhear him. "Marriage isn't always what it's cracked up to be, Felicia. Just look at my parents."

And by his tone, they weren't the only ones who were unhappy in their union.

"Yes, but I'd like to have children one day."

Lorens nodded sadly. "*That*, I'll give you. There is nothing I wouldn't do for those boys or my daughters. And there's nothing like holding your baby in your arms and watching them grow and learn."

She could imagine. But she wasn't selfish enough to bring a child into their world when Talyn had no paternal lineage to offer it. That would be beyond cruel. Their child would grow up with the same limitations and stigma that Talyn had known the whole of his life. Not to mention, Talyn would be instantly arrested for impregnating her and damaging *her* lineage.

Lorens sighed. "You know that's why I hated your mother, don't you?"

She frowned at him. "What do you mean?"

"My father was never happier than when he was with her, and I hated her for that. I blamed her for my parents' never-ending fights. Now I lie awake sometimes, angry at myself for the way I treated them both when they were together. I was just so young and stupid. I thought that if he gave up your mother, he'd feel the same way toward mine. As a boy, I didn't understand how feelings really worked. How awkward and harsh an arranged union could be."

She patted his arm. "We're all stupid when we're young."

He turned back to watch his sons. "Yes, we are . . . except Talyn seems remarkably astute."

"Adversity makes you grow up fast and hard. He was never allowed to be a child."

Lorens took her hand into his, and led it to his cheek. "And neither were you. I'm sorry I was never there for you, Felicia. But I promise that's going to change."

Felicia wanted to believe that. She did. However, she had a suspicion that a lot of what he was feeling tonight had to do with his younger brother, who'd died a few months ago. Even so, she was willing to give him a chance. Everyone deserved one.

And the longer she watched Talyn patiently instruct her nephews, the more her heart broke. A male like him deserved to have children of his own that he could laugh and play with.

Life had royally screwed Talyn, and still he got up every day and relentlessly shouldered the scorn and hatred he couldn't stop. Scorn and hatred he couldn't help.

She'd never known anyone more courageous or honorable. While she knew it bothered him—she could see it in his eyes—he never spoke of it. Never blamed his mother, his father, or anyone else for the circumstances of his birth.

For that alone, she would love him. But there was so much more to him than that. Honor. Respect.

Tenderness.

She still couldn't believe how fortunate she'd been to find him. How close she'd come to choosing someone else.

Now she couldn't imagine not having him in her life.

You're going to have to let him go. Companions never stayed with their patrons. That just wasn't how it worked. And they definitely didn't stay with patrons who lacked lineage. It was a miracle her agency had even allowed Talyn in the door. Most wouldn't have.

Yet she dreamed of things she knew could never be. A long, happy life with a male so wonderful.

It was useless. Dreams didn't come true. And life took its jollies by ruining everyone's plans.

CHAPTER 12

Peeking into the small window on the dance studio's door where Felicia was teaching a class of twenty little girls, Talyn froze. Before their contract, she'd worked as a dance instructor in this school, but the small salary hadn't been enough to cover her tuition and living expenses. After their arrangement, she'd been designated as a floating substitute, which was why she was here for a few hours.

His breath caught in his throat while he watched her laughing and twirling and swaying with the children. From these past few weeks, he'd known she possessed a beautiful heart and soul, but never was it more evident than here and now. She gently corrected and encouraged them, all the while maintaining a dazzling smile and more patience than he could fathom. No wonder she was able to tolerate his assholishness so well.

And the grace she held . . .

Damn, he was instantly rock hard and in pain. All he wanted

was to barge in, sweep her into his arms, and make love to her in the nearest closet he could find.

One little girl fell during a twirl and skinned her knee. Felicia rushed to her and spoke words that had the child laughing through her tears. And it wrung his heart. No wonder Felicia had said on her questionnaire that she wanted children. Like his mother, she was loving and giving. Inspiring.

How could I deprive her of this?

She was born to be someone's mother.

Feeling like shit, he started to leave, but the moment he did, Felicia looked up and saw him in the window. A beautiful, welcoming smile lit her entire face.

She motioned him in.

Unable to resist her lure, Talyn entered, and would have gone quietly to the corner, but the moment he opened the door, the girls let out a terrified squeal and ran for cover.

Felicia laughed playfully. "He's not an evil beastie, girls. He's my male." She came over to place a chaste kiss to his cheek to show them how "harmless" he was. At least where they were concerned.

Suddenly, they swarmed him like buzzing, giggling bees. For the first time in his life, he panicked.

Felicia laughed out loud as she saw the expression on his face. "Oh my God, Talyn! You're not seriously afraid of a bunch of little girls, are you?"

"I've never seen so many. And they're so breakably frail. I don't remember them being this small when I was in school."

She laughed even harder before she pulled them away. "All

right, class, our time's up and your mothers will be waiting. Good job all!"

They scurried away to gather their things.

Felicia sauntered over to him. "So what brings you here, Major?"

"I thought I'd pick you up and take you out to dinner so that you wouldn't have to cook when you got home. I mean, I would have cooked *for* you, but I'm not particularly good at it. I once set my mom's flat on fire, trying to boil water."

She pressed her cheek to his. "Thank you. You're so thoughtful."

As Felicia pulled back, one of the little girls came running back to Talyn with a piece of paper in her hands.

She handed it to him. "They had us draw this in school for our pakas, but I don't have a paka now. Mama says the evil tahrs had him killed and we can't talk about it. But since I don't have a paka no more, I thought I should give it to Tara Felicia's male 'cause I really like Tara Felicia. She used to be my teacher all the time, but she had to quit and I miss her a lot, but she says she'll come back to teach when she's not at school anymore. Here!"

Talyn gaped at the sweet gift of a stick girl holding on to the hand of what must have been her father. Her name was in the corner. "Xarah, I can't take this."

She nodded eagerly. "Yes, you can. I don't got no one else to give it to, and it'll make my mama sad to remember my paka. I was going to throw it away, but I want it to go to you instead of the garbage can."

He knelt in front of her and brushed her hair back from her face before he inclined his head to her. "I will treasure it, always."

She beamed a happy smile and threw herself into his arms. "You're really, really big. You know that?"

He laughed. "I know, sweetling."

She patted his shoulder before she withdrew and ran off.

Choked by the innocent gift, Talyn stared down at it. "Do you know what happened to her father?"

"Not really. He used to pick her up while her mother worked late. Then one day, he didn't. Her mother has never said a word about it to me."

Rising to his feet, Talyn carefully folded the picture and tucked it into his pocket. "I see why you like teaching."

Felicia smiled. "They *are* precious. If you'll give me a minute, I'll see them to their parents and get my things."

He watched her return to help them dress and remember their belongings. And in that minute, he knew that when their contract ended, he needed to let her go.

To deprive her of the children she wanted . . .

It would be all kinds of selfish.

And as he watched Xarah, he wanted blood from whatever asshole had taken her father from her. Having been raised without one, he knew how much it sucked. How much he dreaded school assignments like the one she'd given him. And how many times he'd tossed them on his way home to keep his own mother from feeling bad over the fact that his father had been a total dick. Teachers never thought about it when they assigned such. They believed they were being thoughtful, but it burned in a way unimaginable.

Closing his eyes, he fought against the bitterness that wanted to swallow him whole. Especially since he knew his father's actions and their society kept him from what he wanted most.

A family of his own.

Unshed tears stung his throat as he remembered trying to buy a simple ring for the female he loved. The humiliation it had caused him.

You have to let her go.

But it hurt him so deep inside that he couldn't imagine going back to his empty life. To not hearing her voice or feeling her hand on his flesh. She was what saw him through this hell known as life.

Yet as he watched her herd the kids out to their waiting parents, he knew that one day she'd look at him with resentment over the fact that staying with him would curtail everything she'd wanted to do with her future. It would limit her opportunities and taint the way others looked at her. He was nothing but a liability to her, and he knew it. And to see hatred in *her* eyes for him . . .

That would destroy him.

No, he would never taint her smile the way his father had tainted his mother's. The last thing he would ever be was Felicia's regret.

• • •

Two days later, Felicia wanted to cry as she saw Talyn in his uniform. She'd had him at home for so long that she'd grown accustomed to his being here. Worse, she'd enjoyed every second of the time they'd been together.

They hadn't fought once. Not really.

"Oh, Licia, don't." Biting his lip, he cupped her cheek in his hand. "If you cry, I'm going to cry, too."

That succeeded in making her laugh. As if. "I don't think anything could make you cry."

"That's not true. I just cry on the inside."

She pulled him into her arms and held him flush against her. "I don't want you to go."

"I wish I could stay. But I have to report in."

She tightened her grip on his sleeve—where his rank patch was stitched. She fought the urge to rip it off and spit on it. "I know."

Sinking his hand in her hair, he gave her a sizzling kiss. "I'll call as soon as I can."

She fisted her hands in his braids. "I won't breathe until I hear from you."

He smiled sadly at the old Andarion saying. "I could just throw you over my shoulder and take you with me. Think they'd notice?"

"I'm willing if you are."

Talyn grinned at the serious light in her eyes. She was so incredibly precious to him. He'd never once thought anyone could mean so much to his well-being. Especially not in such a short amount of time. But every day he was with her made him crave her more. It actually hurt him to see her in pain. He felt her sadness even more deeply than he felt his own.

Dipping his head, he kissed her one last time. "Look on the bright side . . . I won't be hogging your covers anymore."

"I would give them all to you for your cocoon if you'd stay."

"*Now* you say that. You didn't feel that way last night while you were cursing me for it." He kissed her forehead as his band went off. "I have to go, baby."

"I know. Be careful. Stay safe."

"You, too." He kissed her hand before he went to the lift. He turned around to watch her until the doors closed.

Silent tears slid down her beautiful cheeks as she waved at him.

With a heavy heart and tight throat, Talyn left their building and made his way to the palace across town. At least he'd be able to see his mother more often. She'd been assigned to the palace guard for half his life. Though he didn't know her exact duties, they weren't particularly dangerous or taxing. She actually had a lot of liberty to come and go. Something he was looking forward to after the heavy restrictiveness of flight patrol.

Flight patrol . . .

Talyn ground his teeth at the memory of what Anatole and his friends had done to the females in his squad.

Against his common sense, he'd reported Anatole to Lorens for disciplinary action. They were supposed to meet for lunch so that Talyn could review and sign his statement to continue the investigation that would allow Lorens to take steps to remove Anatole from his position and rank.

If anyone ever did that to Felicia . . .

Screw the Ring. He'd murder them on the street.

One punch.

Bitterness stung his throat. He still couldn't believe Anatole had all the males so cowed. It went against everything Talyn's mother and Aunt Jayne had drilled into him. You stood up for others, especially those who couldn't defend themselves.

And one way or another, Talyn was going to stop it.

Pulling out his link, he scrolled through his pilot contact list until he found Farina's information. He tried to call her again to tell her what he was doing, only to have it roll to her voice mail.

Talyn had left half a dozen messages, but for whatever reason, probably fear over the lies she'd told against him, she never returned his calls. Not that it mattered. He wouldn't rest until he took care of this and made sure the females under Anatole's command were safe.

Determined, he entered the main gate guardhouse. Pulling out his orders, he handed them to the daytime duty officer's adjutant.

Bored by it all, the female signed him in and summoned a lieutenant to escort him to his new CO's office. Like his mother's office in the tizirah's wings, it was massive and impressive. Elegant.

The older male had graying hair and the royal bearing of an emperor. As soon as Commander ezul Nykyrian saw Talyn, an odd smile toyed at the edges of his lips. Rising to his feet, he returned Talyn's salute. "So you're Galene's boy." Then he scowled and tilted his head to study him. "You remind me of someone."

His father, most likely. Before Fain Hauk had been disinherited, he'd answered to Commander ezul Nykyrian at one of their embassies. But Talyn withheld that information.

"We might have met when I came to work with my mother. Years ago."

The commander nodded slowly. "Tizirah Tylie said that you used to calm her sister when you were a child. She also made it clear that you were to be treated with regard, in spite of your caste and what your record says about you."

Talyn went cold. "Sir?"

The commander sat down and pulled up Talyn's file. "I want you to know that while I respect my dear cousin, Tizirah Tylie, I'm not one to put up with insubordination. Unlike my nephew and regardless of what my cousin wants, I will have you whipped for *any* infraction. You *will* stow your attitude and toe the line. Understood?"

Nephew? Cousin?

Minsid fuck. He should have known he'd be reporting to one of Chrisen's relatives.

"Yes, sir."

"Nor will I tolerate dereliction of duty or late check-ins. I have no idea what favors your mother was forced to call in for you, or perform on your behalf, but your past behavior stops now. I run a tight crew. The safety of my family relies on the skills of our guard corps. You step out of line, Batur, just once, and you'll learn why they refer to me as the Bloody Axe. Understood?"

"Yes, sir."

The commander buzzed for his adjutant. As soon as the door opened to admit him, Talyn felt his world tilt even more.

Merrell Anatole. Chrisen's older brother.

Shit.

Talyn saluted him.

With eyes lit by malice, Anatole returned his salute. "I shall take it from here, uncle."

"You sure you can handle this?"

An insidious smile curled his lips. "Absolutely. It'll be my pleasure to show the major around and finish his orientation."

"You're dismissed."

His stomach knotted tight, Talyn followed Anatole from the room.

Merrell didn't speak until they were in the hallway. Then he turned on Talyn with a sneer. "My brother told me what a tattletale little bitch you are, Batur. You should know that if you try that here, it won't be just your rank we'll take." He moved to invade Talyn's personal space. "My blood family rules this planet, never mistake that. This is *our* empire. You live in it only because we allow you to live. Got it?"

"Understood." None of the Anatoles could stand on their own. They bullied and intimidated, and expected everyone to bow down to them.

If only that was in the nature of the Baturs and Hauks.

Merrell arched a brow. “Do I hear treason in your voice?”

Talyn shook his head slowly, reminding himself all the kinds of stupid it would be to punch that look off Merrell’s face. “No, sir. I understand your terms.”

And just like at his previous post, there was no one to appeal to. No justice left in this empire. WAR was right. The Anatoles were rotten, through and through. They had become a disease that needed to be carved out of their gene pool.

What sickened Talyn most was that all but one member of his father’s family had been slaughtered in war to put these bastards and their forefathers on the Andarion throne. His mother’s lineage had been persecuted to the brink of extinction by the Anatoles—hence the real reason the commander was called the Bloody Axe. His mother’s direct family were the last of the once-great Baturs, who had rivaled the Hauks for their military strength and expertise.

Until the current tadara herself had gone after the Baturs and driven them into exile or graves. Only his mother’s grandfather had survived the “Purging” to remain in Andarion territory.

“Is that defiance I see in your gaze, Major?”

Yes, it was. But he wasn’t *completely* stupid enough to confirm it. “I can’t comment on your delusions, Commander.” Talyn cringed at the fact that he hadn’t quite managed to get the sarcasm out of his tone.

Merrell tried to intimidate him, but since the moron only came up to Talyn’s armpit, it was a less-than-impressive ploy.

"Wipe the smirk off your face, Batur. It's time you met your royal charge." Merrell raked him with a sneer. "Follow me."

A bad feeling went through him. But he had no choice except to obey his orders. Yet every instinct he possessed told him to cut Merrell's throat while he could.

And when he entered Jullien's office, he knew why. The prince sat with Chrisen standing smugly at his side.

His stomach cramping in angry trepidation, Talyn saluted them.

They didn't return it.

Corpulent and pompous, Jullien leaned back in his chair. Unlike a pure-blooded Andarion, his eyes weren't white. They were a strange greenish-brown, rimmed in red. His long black hair was pulled back into a ponytail that really didn't enhance his looks. Even with the Andarion title of tahrs, Jullien would have a hard time getting laid.

"Damn, Chris," Jullien snarled. "You weren't kidding. He looks just like the slimy bastard. How did you stand looking at him every day?"

"Now you know why I shot him down. It was a moral imperative."

Merrell curled his lip. "Remember that time when we were playing with that serving bitch and Fain reported us?"

"I wasn't there for that," Jullien said, his eerie humanesque eyes glowing with fury. "What I remember is that hybrid piece of shit we went to school with. We'd just found the way to get rid of him. Permanently. And then, that little whore,

Dancer Hauk, showed up with my class ring. 'Look what I found,' " he mocked. " 'His Highness must have misplaced it. The hybrid didn't steal it, after all.' " He sneered at Talyn. "You've no idea how much we hate Hauks here."

Probably as much as the Hauks hated Anatoles, would be his guess.

"No, shit," Chrisen agreed. "I still have the scar from when Dancer crashed our pod because of his bleeding heart. Not even plastic surgery could remove it."

Jullien snorted. "Never met a Hauk yet who wasn't a bitch."

Talyn kept his jaw locked. To strike Jullien would be a death sentence. To hit a CO was a court-martial. He kept repeating that over and over again in his head as he held his salute.

"Hauks and Baturs have always thought they were so superior to the Anatoles," Jullien continued. "Too good to mix their blood with ours."

Chrisen and Merrell closed rank around Talyn.

Merrell had to stand up on his toes to meet Talyn's gaze. "Your worthless father and pussy uncle were smart. They jumped planet to save their little bitch asses. You should have followed their cowardly example."

"Instead of threatening *me,*" Chrisen snarled in his ear. "Reporting me to Commander ezul Terronova. You little bitch!"

Jullien moved to stand in his face. "Are you a quim, too, Iron Hammer?" He glanced at his cousins as if seeking courage from them. "You must be."

"Yeah," Chrisen said with a laugh. "He's a puss. Tattletale

little bastard. Just think, boy. Had your whore of a mother sucked my cock instead of your father's, you'd be a commander now."

Talyn's gaze darkened.

"Aw now," Jullien taunted. "Does that hurt your little feelings?"

Chrisen slapped his brother on the arm. "Wait until you see the whore he has sucking his cock now. Nicest piece of ass I've ever seen on a female. We're going to have fun with her."

Talyn smiled evilly at them as his temper broke. He'd never been all that smart. And this was more than he was going to take. No one insulted his mother or threatened Felicia.

It was time for them to meet his two best friends.

Right and left fist.

Before he could stop himself, he punched Chrisen in the throat. Merrell reached for him. Talyn caught his arm and flipped him to the ground before he slammed his fist into Merrell's chest.

Screaming, Jullien ran for cover as his guards attacked and called for reinforcements. Talyn lost count of how many he went through, trying to reach the only real bitch in the room.

Jullien eton Anatole.

But all too soon, they began stunning and shooting him. Not that it mattered at first. Too used to physical pain to care about the blasts, he powered through until his nervous system gave out.

Even then, he fell to his knees for several heartbeats before he finally collapsed and the darkness took him under.

Jullien scowled at Chrisen, who was unconscious on the floor. He met Merrell's stunned gaze as he stood on trembling legs. "What the hell is he?"

Shaking his head, Merrell put more distance between Batur and them. "He's an effing War Hauk and the last of the Winged Baturs. Crazy lineages."

"Have you ever seen anyone take that much with a stun blast?"

The guards hesitantly nudged Batur's body with their booted feet. "I unloaded three full charges into him, dead on."

With fear in his eyes, Merrell swallowed hard. "Don't stand there! Get him out of here before he wakes up."

"Yes, sir. Where do you want us to take him?"

Merrell locked gazes with Jullien. "You're the tahrs. What's your command?"

"He's assaulted two members of the royal family and would have hit me had he been able to. Smacks of treason. Throw him in with the lifers and make sure you tell them they have a celebrity in their midst."

Laughing, Merrell wiped the blood from his lips. "I can't wait to see which one of them makes the Iron Hammer his bitch first."

Talyn came awake to the worst feeling of his life. And given how many times he'd had the crap beaten out of him inside a Ring, that said a lot. His head throbbing, he opened his eyes to find himself inside a pit, surrounded by males who didn't appear to be friendly.

They were, however, huge bastards.

Awesome.

He suddenly felt like a kid again, attending temple on holy days of obligation. An unwanted specimen of vermin that had found its way onto the top of their shiny new shoes. In spite of his pain and nausea, Talyn rose to his feet to face them. While he'd been unconscious, someone had removed his uniform jacket and boots, and left him with his pants and undershirt only.

A massively muscled male approached him with that familiar smirk that said the two of them were about to dance.

Name the tune. . . .

Without flinching, Talyn met his gaze.

"You really Iron Hammer?"

"I am."

Another male approached at his back and spat on the ground. "Vested piece of shit." He moved to shove Talyn's shoulder.

Talyn caught him and knocked him unconscious with one blow. He caught his next attacker, then two more, and quickly dispatched them.

Not even breathing heavy yet, he faced the first one who'd approached him. "I might fight in the Vested league now, but I held the title in all three Open league divisions first, and longer than anyone before *or* after me. Anyone else want to find out why?"

The male in front of him laughed. "Gutter rat?"

Talyn nodded. "My father's an Outcast."

A loud whoop went through them at that.

"Batur's one of *us*!"

Talyn stepped back, even more trepidatious now than he'd been before they attacked him. What was going on?

The male in front of him inclined his head. "I'm Maren. When they dumped you in, we assumed you were one of *them*." Maren jerked Talyn's jacket off a much smaller male who must have stolen it. He handed it back. "Whichever one of you assholes took the Hammer's shoes, return them. Now!"

They came flying out of the crowd to land near Talyn.

"Thanks," he said, reaching for them.

The males laughed as they befriended him.

"So why were you arrested?" Maren asked while Talyn pulled his boots back on.

"I was unconscious at the time of my arrest, so I don't know the exact charges."

Maren scowled. "Were you drunk?"

"No. I was, however, beating the shit out of two tizirani and their guards when I was stunned."

A laughing roar of approval went through the other prisoners.

"What about you?" Talyn stood and pulled on his jacket.

"I accidentally met Merrell Anatole's gaze while I was fixing his bathroom sink."

Before Talyn could say anything else, the monitor over their heads came on to show the face of a palace guard. His stare went straight to Talyn.

"I just received word from Commander ezul Nykyrian himself. Any prisoner or prisoners who defeat or kill Talyn Batur will be instantly released."

Talyn's stomach hit the dirt as he heard those words. Words that sucked out every bit of camaraderie from his fellow inmates. He looked to Maren, who gave him a sad smile.

"Sorry, champ. We'd kill our own mothers to get out of here."

Talyn cursed as he mentally calculated the number of males around him.

It was bad. But not as bad as the number of males he knew were here beyond them that he couldn't see.

So this is how I die.

Just like he'd lived every day since he'd been forced out of his mother's womb.

Fighting with everything he had.

CHAPTER 13

"Lena? Is something wrong?"

Galene blinked at the tizirah's unexpected question. She'd thought Cairistiona was still sleeping. But she was awake in bed and frowning at her.

"Forgive me, Highness. I didn't hear what you asked."

"You look upset and worried. Is something wrong?"

She smiled at the tizirah and shook her head as she slid her link back into her uniform pocket. "I'm fine."

"Don't lie to me. We're alone, and you're the only friend I have. The only one who believes that my baby is still alive." Cairistiona held her hand out toward Galene.

Taking it, Galene allowed Cairie to pull her down beside her. The tizirah laced fingers with her and sighed before she closed her eyes.

Unsure if the tizirah was lucid or not, Galene bit her lip as she saw her future. Cairistiona had been one of the most capable military commanders in Andarion history. Fierce. Confident.

Against tradition, Cairistiona had boldly and defiantly taken a human tiziran as her lover. Because Aros was an heir to an empire every bit as powerful and vast as theirs, Cairie had known from the beginning that they could never marry. Even so, she'd birthed twins for the man she loved.

Two boys.

Ironically, the twin who was named for his human father—Jullien—had looked the most Andarion, and her son who'd appeared the most human had been named for Cairie's father's paternal lineage, Nykyrian. Pictures of both boys hung all over the walls of her bedroom. But it was Nykyrian's photo the princess slept with. His stuffed toy that she kept in her bed with her at all times.

Against every reason, Cairie swore he was still alive. Even though his body had been identified and buried. She refused to believe it.

Maybe it was easier that way.

"Aros called last night," Cairie whispered. "Did I tell you that?"

"No, Highness."

Aros Jullien Triosan was the human father of Cairie's sons. He'd tried to marry her many times over the years, but neither Cairie's mother nor his government would approve the alliance. His government out of fear of an insane Andarion female sitting on one of their thrones, and the Andarion tadara out of fear that Cairie would wake from her stupor and take the throne that was her birthright.

The tizirah clutched Galene's hand tighter. "He's being

pressed by his senate to name another heir. The humans don't trust my Jullien." She opened her eyes to look up at Galene. "Do you trust him?"

"He's a fine boy, Highness."

She laughed. "You're lying. I'm not asking the military commander for her opinion. I want to hear from my friend who played with him when he was a boy."

Galene glanced around the room. In truth, she hated Jullien and always had. Obnoxious and cruel, he had relentlessly picked on her when she'd been a girl. It was why she'd spent her time at the palace with Tahrs Nykyrian. He'd been a sweet, quiet boy who reminded her a lot of Talyn.

But that was something she could never tell the tizirah who'd birthed them. "Your friend is afraid that we're not alone here and she doesn't want to see you drugged more."

Cairie nodded and blinked slowly. "They're afraid of me."

"Who?"

"My mother. She's afraid I'll depose her. It's why she drugs me. But I don't want the throne that makes my family so vicious. It killed all my brothers and sisters. Except for Tylie, who doesn't want it either." Cairie pulled Nykyrian's toy to her chest. "Why are you so sad, Lena?"

"I haven't heard from my son."

Cairie gasped. "Where is he?"

"With yours."

She relaxed instantly. "Then he's fine. Jullien knows to take care of what I love, and I love you. I always have. Therefore I love your son, too."

"And I love you, Highness."

Smiling, Cairie snuggled closer to the toy. "I shall call Jullien tonight and tell him to have your Talyn contact you."

"Thank you, Highness. I would be forever grateful."

Cairie lifted her head and listened. "Nykyrian?" she called. "Is that you, *keramon*?" She started to leave the bed, but Galene caught her.

"Highness, you're too sick to walk." Actually, she was too drugged for it. The nurse had only left a short time ago. Every four hours, Cairie was given a shot "for her health."

It was sickening what the tadara did to her own daughter to keep her complacent. But there was nothing Galene could do to stop it.

She'd tried once and had lost her rank as a result. She would have lost her post and life as well, but Tylie had stepped in and prevented it. Because Galene had once been Nykyrian's playmate, she was the only one who could manage Cairistiona. The tizirah thought of her as a strange cross between cherished daughter and beloved friend.

Galene hummed to her while she tucked the covers around Cairie's body. She still remembered the first time she'd seen the tizirah. It was one of her earliest memories. Cairie had been pregnant. Dressed in her sharp military uniform, the tizirah had been breathtakingly beautiful.

Because her immediate family was mostly medical, Galene had never seen a female officer before. She'd been completely awestruck.

"Can I touch your blaster?"

Galene's father, the royal physician who'd been overseeing Cairie's pregnancy, had been horrified. "Forgive my daughter, Highness. She's never seen a royal family member out of imperial robes before. She doesn't realize who you are."

Placing her hand against her stomach that was just beginning to round out, Cairie had smiled and knelt down by Galene's side. "Would you like to touch it?"

Galene had looked nervously to her father, then nodded.

Cairie unholstered her blaster and ejected the blast cartridge before she handed it over to Galene to hold. "Be careful, little one. The moving parts can still pinch your skin. And as small as your fingers are, they might eat one."

"Really?"

The tizirah had nodded.

And still Galene had carefully examined the blaster.

"Aren't you afraid of it?"

Galene had shaken her head. "It's very lovely, Highness. Like you."

"How old are you, Galene?"

"Three and almost a little more."

She'd smiled warmly. "After my babies are born, you'll have to come back with your father and help me watch over them."

It was a promise Cairistiona had kept. Those days had been some of the happiest of Galene's life.

Even after her boys had been born, Cairistiona had spoiled Galene. Until the day Nykyrian had died. The tizirah's descent into madness had come fast and furious. She'd refused to listen to anyone.

To keep Cairie from searching for her dead son, the tadara had ordered her sedated immediately.

She'd been sedated ever since.

Because Galene had been close to Nykyrian, her father had feared what the tizirah might do to her in her grief, and so she'd been banned from visiting the palace. Years had gone by before she'd been allowed back. And in a strange twist, she'd been the one in the uniform and Cairistiona had been the one dependent on Galene's kindness.

On Galene's visit to the palace for an assembly, Cairie had seen her among the Royal Guard. Even drugged, Cairie had recognized her immediately and grabbed her for a hug.

Arm in arm, she'd pulled Galene aside and asked her how Nykyrian was. When they'd tried to separate them, Cairie had become so uncontrollable that she'd been shot with a stunner and Galene had been sent back to her base.

Terrified of being reassigned and stripped of her rank, Galene had been shocked when, hours later, Tylie had shown up and told her that she would be Cairie's personal guard. That her sister had demanded it and refused to let another guard near her.

They'd been inseparable friends ever since.

Cairie reached into her nightstand and pulled out a drawing that she handed to Galene. "Do you remember when your Talyn gave that to me?"

Tears gathered in her eyes as she saw the drawing of her and Talyn together, waving at the tizirah and her boys. He'd been barely seven when he'd brought it to Cairie, the first time he met her. "I do. I'm surprised you kept it."

Cairie took her hand and held it in both of hers. "You have a good boy, Lena. I will make sure you keep your baby with you. Mothers should never be away from their children."

Stunned and infuriated, Merrell showed Jullien and Chrisen the footage from the pit where they'd dumped Batur. Bodies were strewn about like the killing fields left behind after a vicious battle.

His breathing ragged, Talyn, alone, stood.

Barely.

Though he was wobbly, he was on his feet while the rest were either dead, unconscious, or begging for help as they tried to crawl away from Talyn's reach. In all the years of military service, Merrell had never seen anything like this. It terrified him just how easily Batur had plowed through dozens of ruthless killers and predators. The most vicious criminals Andaria had.

Batur wiped at the blood on his face as he moved to stand in front of the camera to glare at them. When he spoke, it was a raw, feral growl that was even more terrifying than his reckless stance that dared them to come after him. It was also the words that had been spoken by the male who had founded Batur's paternal lineage almost four thousand years ago at the beginning of Andarion civilization. "A Hauk is not a politician. There is no room in our hearts to sit in peace with those who would do any Andarion harm. We are, and will forever be, protectors of our brethren, family, and homeworld. So long as a single War Hauk lives, no nation will defeat us. No race will dare to invade our air, lands, or sea. We will stand and we will defend. For we are not bred of mercy and we are not bred for peace.

"We are born of fury.

"Forever fear the Warring Blood Clan of Hauk." Talyn spat blood on the ground. "But most of all, you better fear *me,* you quivering quims! For every drop of War Hauk blood flowing in my veins, I am of the Winged Blood Clan of Batur and we are born of defiance. When I get out of here, and I will, I'm coming for *you*. And no one will be able to save any of your putrid lives from my vengeance."

Chrisen gasped. "We are in deep Andarion shite."

Jullien rolled his eyes. "You think? Saint Zaran, why didn't you tell us what he was capable of?"

Chrisen choked as he watched Talyn sit down to tend his wounds. "I had no idea he could do *this*. He's always been subservient."

"No," Merrell said between clenched teeth. "He was a conscientious soldier, taking orders from his CO. And a vicious Ring champion. Our mistake was to forget all that in our arrogance." He looked from his brother to Jullien. "We can't control him. He is the only fucking War Hauk of his generation, with all the insane skill and strength that goes with that untainted bloodline."

Jullien lifted his chin. "We're still tizirani. And I *am* tahrs."

Merrell gestured at the bodies scattered around Talyn, who sat with a terrifying calmness. "Yeah, that so stopped him. You're lucky he didn't make it to you before your guards stunned him unconscious."

Chrisen let out a heavy sigh. "As much as it pains me to say this, should we offer him a deal?"

Shaking his head, Merrell stared at the fallen bodies surrounding Talyn. "It's too late for that. He'll be gunning for us from now on . . . like Fain and Keris, back in the day. We have to get rid of him the same way we got rid of them."

"It's not that easy." Jullien curled his lip. "Galene Batur hates me—she always has, and my mother loves and adores that *minsid* bitch for some reason. While my mom might be bat-shit crazy, she is the favored daughter of our tadara and Tylie pets her like a psychotic child. Even nuts, she still holds a lot of pull." Jullien kicked the chair he'd been sitting in across the room. "Not to mention, if my mother *ever* comes to her senses, she's going to ask questions none of us want to answer."

"We could kill her, too."

Jullien backhanded Chrisen. "She's my mother! I'd kill *yours* first."

"Stop it!" Merrell snarled. "We have a problem here. How do we fix it?"

"I can buy us time with Galene." Chrisen narrowed his gaze on Jullien. "If you're off-planet, she'll assume her son is with you. Can't you stay with your paka for a while?"

"Yeah. Why? What are you thinking?"

Merrell licked his lips as he caught his brother's line of reasoning. "We dump him where no one can find him."

Jullien wasn't sure about that. "Where?"

"Onoria."

That would do it. The magnetic fields there rendered all

tracking and comm devices worthless. A slow smile spread across Jullien's face. "You're right. No one will ever find him there."

Chrisen shook his head. "I still think we ought to kill him."

Merrell pulled Chrisen's blaster from his hip and handed it to him. "Good luck with that."

Chrisen glared at him drolly.

"Your brother's right," Jullien growled. "Batur's too well known. If we order him killed, someone will rat us out. If we bring him up on charges publicly, his mother will defend him and my mother will have him pardoned and released. But, if we accuse him of treason and dump him before anyone knows what we've done, we won't be punished. No proof. No crime. Galene can scream all she wants. But he did attack us. That's not a lie and we can prove it with the guards who stunned him and video surveillance. We have every legal right to remove him to Onoria, based on that."

"And what if he comes back?" Chrisen asked.

Merrell snorted. "We'll break his legs before we dump him. No one, not even a Hauk bastard, can survive an environment that hostile with no working legs. He'll be dead in less than a week."

Talyn came awake with a fierce groan.

"Shh . . . take deep breaths."

He was in so much pain his teeth chattered. Someone lifted his head and held water to his lips.

"Drink slowly."

He obeyed as the dimly lit cave and the eight Andarions around him came into focus. Confused and hazy, he tried to make sense of this. "Where am I?"

"Hell," the female who was holding the water murmured as she lowered his head back to the dirty pallet where he lay.

A male came forward to check Talyn's bandages. "We found you on the Dying Plains after you were dumped." He tapped the tattoo on his neck that was given to every prisoner, to permanently mark them with their crimes. Like Talyn, he was designated as a traitor. "Everyone in the colony has been falsely accused of treason and dumped on this shithole by the royals. We assume, especially given what was done to you, that you're one of us."

"Done to me?"

"They broke your legs," the female whispered. "They only do that to the prisoners they're afraid might make it home with proof of royal corruption."

"Viper was always getting himself into shit with the royals."

Talyn scowled at the familiar voice as another female approached from the shadows. "Nightdice?"

She came forward with a grim nod. "After Anatole shot you down, Syndrome and I tried to report him for what he did to you and to us."

Sure they did. "I was told you recanted your statements."

Impudent rage darkened her eyes. "You would have recanted, too, had they tortured you the way they did us. I promise you."

He dropped his gaze to the vicious scars on her neck that corroborated her story. In that moment, he felt like an ass for accusing her. "Sorry."

Self-conscious, Nightdice rubbed at the scars. "Yeah. Me, too. At least you tried to help us. That's more than most did"

Fat lot of good it'd done any of them. Trying not to think about that, he narrowed his gaze on their small group. "Where's Farina?"

Nightdice winced before she answered. "After we signed the papers to stop our torture, Anatole shot her in the head and then dumped me here before I could tell anyone about it. By your presence, I'm assuming you filed a report, too?"

Talyn nodded as anger went through him. Lorens would have been the only one who'd seen it, which meant he'd gone straight to Anatole with it. So much for thinking he had an in with command. He should have known better than to trust anyone. Even Felicia's brother. "I never meant to get either of you into trouble. Or hurt. I didn't even list your names in my final report. Just mine."

"Relax. You didn't cause this. You're the only one who ever tried to help us, and you got blown apart for your troubles." She glanced around. "And banished here, to boot." Nightdice, whose real name was Berra Altaan, knelt beside him and held her hand out in friendship. "Sorry we dragged you into this."

Talyn laughed bitterly as he shook it. "My mouth is what dragged me into this."

She snorted. "Pretty sure our mouths are what dragged us *all* into this."

Talyn slowly sat up and looked around. Counting himself, there were seven males and three females. "Are we all accused of the same crime?"

Nightdice nodded. "You and I are the only two who were active duty when dumped. They usually kill AD, but my father's a satrapehs to the tadara. They couldn't afford for my body to be found. Too many unfortunate questions would have been asked. I'm guessing with you being the Iron Hammer, they were afraid of an investigation."

Not really. "My mother's a personal friend to the tizirahie."

"Ah. That would do it, too."

The other female handed him a small bowl of porridge. "I'm Terisa. We call this place the colony. It's a hole, but it's relatively safe from the drones and others."

"Others?"

Nightdice clenched her teeth. "The real criminals. They roam in heavily armed gangs. There are too few of us to fight them or make a stand."

"It's why there are too few of us," the male broke in. "We've tried. They obliterate us or throw us in their pits to cockfight. The females, they take, but they never last long."

Talyn winced at what that meant. And all it did was fire his determination. "There has to be a way to get out of here."

The oldest of the males laughed. "We were all like you once, boy. Full of piss and vinegar. But in time, you'll adjust and accept it. Just like we all have."

Nightdice sighed. "He's right. It's easier to just roll with it and know that this is our lot." That attitude was what had led to her call sign. She rolled with everything, especially invitations to sleep with Vested males. "We'll never see home again."

Talyn refused to blithely accept that. "Bullshit. We've got to get home and let the others know what the Anatoles are doing. We owe it to our race to stop this."

She jerked her chin toward the older male. "Do you know who Rhys is?"

"No."

"I'm the founder of WAR," he growled out. "And you see what telling others about royal corruption got me. They slaughtered my son in front of my eyes. All I wanted was to make Andaria better for him and his children. Instead, my grandsons were taken by gangs the first week we were here and killed in the pit. My granddaughter . . ." He broke off into tears. "I'm sorry I ever started this shit. It's not worth it. No one wants to listen or care. So long as their status quo is maintained, they don't give a shite about anyone else. And nothing has changed. It never does."

Talyn refused to believe that. "Thirteen War Hauks drove back an entire invading army."

"And were slaughtered in the process," Rhys snarled. "Only one of them survived that battle and what did it get them? Nothing. Not a damn thing. There's not even a single young War Hauk left on Andaria today. And there's definitely not one *here,* with us. No offense, but I've buried enough. I just want to live out whatever amount of time I have left, in peace. I'm through fighting for a race that doesn't care about me."

Talyn scoffed. "I'd rather be a memory than a coward."

Rhys rose up to stare down at Talyn. "This isn't the Ring, Iron Hammer. There are no rules here. No refs to call your enemies off when you go down."

And that right there told him what a Vested piece of shit Rhys was. He'd started a rebellion, but didn't have the temerity to see it through.

In spite of the pain and the broken bones, Talyn rose to stand in front of him. He glared at him with every bit of defiant fury he possessed. "And I didn't earn my name in the Vested Ring, old man." He used the worst insult he could for an Andarion. It equated them to the weaker human race. "I earned it in the Open league. Fighting with everything I had. . . . I didn't start this *minsid* fight. But by every god of Andaria, I am going to finish it."

CHAPTER 14

Limping and in pain, Talyn threw the *vorna* carcass down for Nightdice and Terisa to clean and cook. After his last attempt at preparing a meal, he'd been banned for everyone's safety. His job was to make the kill. The others cooked it.

While they started prepping, he moved to check his legs. The pain was still excruciating, but it was slowly getting better. Between homemade braces and the handful of illegal drugs Nightdice had given him that could speed-heal his injuries, he was making good progress.

Satisfied, he headed outside the cave to where an old fighter had crashed years ago. For the last three weeks, he'd been working on the engines, trying to repair them. Rhys thought it was a complete waste of time, but Talyn was determined to prove him wrong.

In all things. Besides, it wasn't like he had anything better to do. And it just wasn't in him to give up.

As Talyn scraped at the rust and oiled the pieces as best he could, his thoughts turned to Felicia. She was what he fought for most. All that saw him through these shitty days of hell.

Right now, she was alone. With no one to protect her. No matter what, he had to get home and make sure nothing happened to her. Especially not because of him.

Closing his eyes, he summoned an image of her bright, sweet smile. For the merest moment, he was warm.

Until fear drove the peace away and left him terrified for what Anatole and the others might be doing to her in retaliation for his actions. What they might be doing to his mother.

Rhys's stories spurred him on with a vengeance. He had to get back and make sure they were okay. Without him, they had no one to defend them.

Please, please be okay.

"Talyn?"

He glanced over to see Terisa with a small, chipped cup in her hand. She held it out to him.

He declined it. "I can't take your rations."

She climbed up to stand by his side on the ship's wing. "You need them. We can't afford for you to go down."

"I'm fine." He returned to the rusted engine.

Terisa reached out and cupped his cheek. She turned his face toward hers. "I believe in you, Talyn. I know you're going to get us out of here." She moved in to kiss him.

Talyn pulled back immediately.

"Is something wrong?"

"I have a female."

Terisa scoffed. "She's not here."

"No, but she's here." He tapped his heart. "And I would never dishonor her."

"And if you don't survive to return to her arms?"

"I will die trying."

Licking her lips, Terisa closed the distance between them and brushed her hand along his jaw before she reached to stroke him through his pants. "You have to maintain your hormone levels. She'll never know you had help."

Catching her hand, Talyn stepped back. "*I'll* know." And he wasn't his father. He'd seen firsthand the hurt his father's infidelity had caused his mother. He would *never* harm Felicia like that.

"You're bastard-born, Talyn. You can't even marry her. Do you really think she's being loyal to you in your absence?"

Instead of weakening him, those words only solidified his resolve. If they were at home, Terisa would have no use for him. At all. She wouldn't have even looked at him in Eris.

But his caste had never mattered to Felicia. She'd welcomed him regardless. And he would not repay her love with cruelty. Not take it for granted when he knew she could have given it to anyone else in the universe, and had chosen to give her love and heart to his sorry ass.

"I am forever Felicia's male."

"You speak as if you're stralen."

"Stralen or not, I would never bring hurt to my Felicia. She only deserves my best, and that's what I intend to give her."

"Then I hope you make it back to her and that she appreciates what an incredibly rare male you are."

"Incoming!"

Talyn sucked his breath in at Rhys's shout as he moved for a weapon. It was either scavengers or another drone. Not that it mattered. Both groups would be after their blood. And they would kill them if they could.

Felicia bit her lip as she called her brother. She'd been debating for days whether or not to do so, but as each one passed with no word from Talyn, she became more worried.

"Commander ezul Terronova."

"Lorens, it's Felicia."

"Hey. What's wrong? You sound really stressed."

"I . . . um. I'm sorry to disturb you. I haven't heard from Talyn since he reported for duty at the palace over three weeks ago, and I didn't want to scare his mother needlessly. He hasn't called or e-mailed or texted. And that's not like him. He doesn't do this. I haven't seen hide nor hair of him, and his inboxes are full. He hasn't even called his trainer about missing practice. When I go to the palace, they won't admit me past the gate. They say he's off-world and for me to go home. No one's heard anything, and Erix and I are extremely worried. But when I call his DO, they keep saying it's normal. That he's off on assignment and can't be contacted for security reasons. They promise they'll tell him I called and came by, and yet I never hear back. I wanted to check with you and see if this really is normal."

"Maybe. I know the *tahrs* has been off-world, and it is SOP to keep the exact details of his whereabouts classified, at all times. But hold on and let me check Talyn's reports and assignments. As you know, he has check-ins he has to make, regardless of his post or AD."

Biting her lip, Felicia waited impatiently while he checked on it. "How are the kids?"

"They're fine. Gavarian and Brach have gone on and on about how much fun they had with you. We're all excited about Talyn's . . . son of a bitch!"

"What?"

"You need to call his mother. Fast."

Her heart stopped. "What's going on?"

"They arrested Talyn for treason. He's not off on assignment. He's been exiled and deported."

Felicia paced the small palace office with her heart in her throat as she waited for Galene to arrive. The soldier kept eyeing Lorens, who'd driven her over. For something this traumatic, the last thing she'd wanted to do was call Talyn's mother and dump it on her.

She still couldn't believe what Lorens had told her. There was no way Talyn had committed treason. It wasn't possible. He was too much in control of himself at all times.

Galene drew up short as she saw Lorens.

"Commander ezul Terronova." Galene saluted him sharply.

He returned the salute. "Commander Batur."

Looking from him to Felicia, Galene scowled. “What’s going on?”

“Have you heard from Talyn?” Felicia asked.

“No. I was told he was off-world and under secure assignment protocols. Why?”

Unsure of how to break the news to her, Felicia glanced to Lorens.

He sighed heavily. “You need to check his duty roster with my pass code.”

Galene’s frown deepened at Loren’s serious tone. “Okay.” She moved to the soldier’s desk and bumped her off her computer before she allowed Lorens to log in.

Felicia knew the moment Galene saw the report. All the blood faded from her face. Eyes wide, she met their gazes.

“Is this for real?”

Lorens folded his arms over his chest. “It appears to be. I tried to get more information, but I was told—by my own CO, in no uncertain terms—that it wasn’t a military matter. It’s civil and criminal, and that I should keep my nose out of it if I wanted to maintain my rank.”

“When did this happen?” Galene breathed. “Why wasn’t I notified?”

“I have no idea.”

Tears stung Felicia’s eyes. “Because I’m not family, they wouldn’t tell me anything. I was hoping you could learn more.”

Galene blinked back her own tears as she stared in horror at the report. “Who did you call?” she asked Felicia.

"Talyn's CO. I didn't know who else to try, except you and my brother. Commander ezul Nykyrian refused to discuss it with me."

Her hand shaking, Galene picked up the intercom. "I'm calling the tahrs." She dialed, and waited until his secretary answered. "This is Commander Batur. I would like to talk to Tahrs Jullien about Major Batur. Immediately."

Waiting with bated breath, Felicia toyed with her necklace Talyn had given her.

Galene's face turned bright red. "I see. Is that his last word on the matter?" Her grip tightened on the link. "Thank you." She set the link down and, without a word to them, headed out.

Glancing to Lorens, Felicia followed after her. "What did he say?"

"That it doesn't concern me." She walked with a hurried purpose.

Tears started falling as hopeless despair ripped through her heart. "What do we do, Commander?"

"We go to someone the royal prick can't brush aside so easily."

Felicia sucked her breath in sharply at Galene's brazen words. That, too, could be construed as treason, should the wrong ears hear it.

Galene stopped outside a door and knocked. A moment later, a young servant opened it. "I need to speak with Tizirah Tylie immediately."

"Please come in, Commander." She opened the door and

showed them into an elegant sitting room. "I'll notify Her Highness." She vanished through another door.

Felicia wiped at her tears. "Do you think the tizirah will help?"

"I don't know. I can only ask."

Eternity seemed to have passed before Tylie came through the door with the bearing of the royal tadara herself. Her long black hair was braided and coiled elaborately around her head. She wore a sheer red dress that showed her exquisite body off to perfection.

She frowned at the sight of all three of them in her receiving room. "Galene? Is there a problem?"

This time, it was the commander who teared up. "They've arrested my baby, Highness."

Gasping, Tylie reached for Galene's hand. "What? Who?"

"Tahrs Jullien." She sniffed back her tears. "They won't tell me anything. They say he committed treason. But I know my baby and so do you. You know Talyn would *never* do such a thing. He's always been fiercely loyal to the crown."

Tylie cupped Galene's cheek in her hand. "Breathe, sweetie. Just breathe. We'll get this taken care of immediately. I promise you." The tizirah rubbed Galene's back. "Kelsei!" she called. "I need you to locate Major Batur. Now!"

A secretary appeared instantly from the same room Tylie had been in on their arrival. "Yes, Highness." She quickly typed into the pad she was carrying. "There's nothing anywhere about a Major Batur."

"He was arrested."

The secretary shook her head. "Nothing's showing, Highness. I'm searching everything . . . with your codes, even. We have no records for him."

Tylie scowled. "Are you sure about this, Lena?"

She nodded. "I even talked to His Highness's secretary and was told that I should stay out of it."

"Highness," Lorens said, stepping forward. "I've spoken with the tahrs's staff and Commander ezul Nykyrian myself. I know they took Major Batur into custody. But they wouldn't tell me anything more."

Tylie broke off into a list of profanity under her breath. "Come with me." She walked with the same determined stride Galene had used as she crossed the palace and entered another wing.

Without preamble, she threw open a set of doors.

Indignant over her entrance, Tahrs Jullien, who was supposed to be off-world, rose to his feet. The moment he saw the commander, rage darkened his gaze. "What is the meaning of this?"

"You tell me," Tylie demanded. "Where's Major Batur?"

"He's of no concern to you."

"And there you would be wrong, Julie. Where is he?"

"He's part of my staff."

"Really?" Tylie's voice dripped with sarcasm. "You employ felons now? So much for those mandatory background checks, eh?"

Jullien curled his lip. "Batur is my—"

"Enough!" Tylie growled. "You will produce him for me,

right now, or I'll go to my mother, and you won't like that, I promise you. While you think she loves you, I *am* her daughter she nurtured at her breast. And if that doesn't scare you as much as it should, I'll put a bug up *your* mother's ass. Cairie will get him or take it out on *you*."

Jullien lifted his chin defiantly. "He attacked me."

"Show me the evidence."

"You would defend a felon?"

"You have a history of lying, Jules. Let's not go there. Now I'm sure if the Iron Hammer hit you, you'd have one hell of a bruise. In fact, knowing you, you'd have a medical record for it. So show me the bruise or the write-up from your doctor. Now!"

"Why do you hate me so?"

Tylie glared at him. "I am not playing this with you. You have three seconds to produce the major, or I will rain down a hell-wrath so fierce that the gods themselves will weep for your remains."

His expression sullen, he crossed his arms over his chest. "I can't do that. He was banished by Commander Anatole for assaulting him and Chrisen. And for your information, he was leading a revolt against *our* family. I have a vid of him threatening us all."

Felicia gasped.

Tylie cursed again under her breath. "What did you do, Jullien?"

"I merely allowed my cousin to punish a traitor. That is my right as tahrs!"

Tylie ignored his outburst. "Where is Talyn?"

"He's on Onoria."

Felicia had never heard of the place, but the look on her brother's, Galene's, and the princess's faces said that it was deplorable.

Tylie winced as she turned back toward Galene. "I'm so sorry, Lena."

Galene appeared to be one wrong word away from assaulting Jullien herself. She faced Tylie. "Highness? If I get him back, will you pardon him?"

"Lena—"

"Please. I know someone who can track him, even there."

"They'll die trying to find him. You know that. It's impossible to retrieve someone from that hellhole. If he's even still alive."

Galene shook her head. "He's alive . . . I know it. Will you allow me to send them in?"

Finally, Tylie nodded. "Get him back, and I'll make sure he has a full pardon waiting."

"You can't do that!"

Galene spun on Jullien. "You really need to visit your father for a while, Highness."

Jullien started to speak until Tylie cut him off. "She's right, Jules. Run. Run to Aros."

Terrified and frantic, Felicia sat in Galene's elegant palace office while the commander spoke to her friends in The Sentella.

Felicia had wanted to go after Talyn herself, but the planet they'd sent him to was so dangerous, and she lacked the training needed to navigate it. Unlike Talyn, climbing wasn't her hobby. And the last thing Felicia wanted was for her inexperience to get in the way of Talyn's rescue or to delay it in any way.

They had to get him home as quickly as possible.

Lorens had been recalled to his post shortly after their arrival here, but had promised to return as soon as he could.

Galene finally rejoined her in the posh sitting area. "They're already en route to his location. We should know something by midday tomorrow."

"Do you think they'll find him?"

Galene bent over to whisper in Felicia's ear, making sure to keep her lips covered so that no one would be able to read them through a monitor. "One of my best friends is a member of The Sentella High Command. She's like a mother to Talyn. Trust me, she'll find him."

No wonder Galene was so cautious with that nugget. While The Sentella was technically a legal military organization, they skimmed the laws of The League and had a lot of enemies in high places.

Including the tadara of Andaria.

Eriadne had issued a death warrant for any member of their High Command. It said a lot for Talyn that he'd never betrayed them. With one word about The Sentella to his CO or Lorens, he could have had any command position he wanted.

Galene patted her arm. "I have full faith that if anyone can find him, Hadrian can."

"Hadrian?" she whispered between clenched teeth.

She lowered her tone again to the faintest of whispers and spoke behind her hand. "He views Talyn as a son. He won't rest until he finds him and returns him to us."

Felicia nodded. She prayed Galene was right. But then Galene loved her son enough that if Hadrian and the others weren't more than competent, she'd never trust them with Talyn's safety.

"What can we do, Commander?"

Galene wrapped her arms around her chest. "Wait for them to do their job." Tears glistened in her eyes. "If Talyn's still alive, they'll find him for us." A single tear slid down her cheek. "Either way, they'll bring him home."

As she whispered a prayer for them all, Felicia's biggest fear was what condition he'd be in when they did.

CHAPTER 15

Jayne Erixour paused as they neared one of the most inhospitable places she'd ever seen—and given some of the shitholes she'd been forced to live in growing up while her father hid from various authorities, criminals, and governments, that said a lot. The more she skimmed from their readings, the more she wanted Jullien eton Anatole's testicles in her fist. This was ridiculous.

What kind of sentient creature would place a boy on a planet like this, alone? Yes, Talyn was a soldier and he was a fierce fighter, but he was barely old enough to shave.

No one should be relegated to *this.*

Over and over, she saw Talyn as the painfully shy boy he'd been when she first met him. And that did nothing to settle the bloodlust in her heart. Payback for Anatole was coming, and she planned to be the brutal harbinger who shoved it up his arrogant ass.

"Hon?"

She glanced over to her husband. At six foot nine, Hadrian was one of the few men she looked up to, and was the only one she'd ever dated she could actually wear heels with. A warrior of fierce skills, he kept his brown hair cut short around his gorgeous face. And those silvery-blue eyes betrayed his birth race that had been hunted to the brink of extinction. It was why he was more than happy to stay home and voraciously protect their babies from the assholes of the universe, while she risked her life fighting against the very tyrants who'd slaughtered most of Hadrian's family and left him an orphan in hiding. "What is it?"

"Nero wants us to buckle in. We're about to break atmosphere."

Nodding, she pulled at the straps and secured herself. Her thoughts wandered as she glanced between her husband and his older brother, Nero. At first glance, they bore little resemblance to each other—something that had served them both well while Hadrian, unlike Nero, had grown up alone and in relative safety.

With blond hair, Nero was supposedly the spitting image of their father. Hadrian with his darker hair color took after their mother. Because they were two of the last of their hunted species and the sole survivors of their royal house, they were rarely seen together. The risk to each of them was too great.

No one outside of this ship knew Hadrian had lived through the massacre of his family. He'd been barely eighteen months old when they'd been executed. Narrowly escaping that so-called *cleansing* himself, Nero had hidden Hadrian among loyalists and surrendered himself to his enemies to make sure that his baby brother lived and grew to manhood in total safety.

For that alone, Jayne would have loved and adored Nero. But he was a decent male, with a loyal heart and humorous, dry wit. When Hadrian had called his brother about Talyn, Nero had instantly appeared to help them find him. No questions asked.

But that was how Nero was.

And as a professional tracker, Nero was the best in the Nine Worlds. Not to mention, he and her husband were full-blooded Trisani—some of the last of the full-bloods. A psychic race with skills of unfathomable psionic abilities. It was why their race had been extinguished. Fear and greed. People either wanted to control the Trisani and use their powers for their own petty purposes, or they were too terrified of them to let them live in peace.

Hadrian took her hand into his. "We'll find him, Jaynie. Have no fear."

"I know, baby. I just hope he's still alive."

Hadrian and Nero exchanged a quick glance. "He's alive," Hadrian assured her. "I can feel his life force. But he's . . . angry."

She smiled at the one truth of Talyn's character. "Ever full of fight."

Hadrian nodded before he buckled himself in beside her.

Her heart aching, Jayne turned her link on and pulled up the old photo she kept of Talyn from back in the day when he'd been in her class and she'd first met him and Galene. It'd been her first year as a student teacher at Brunelle Academy. Nervous and unsure, she'd kept waiting for someone to recognize her as the daughter of her nefarious father, and throw her out.

Or have her arrested.

But no one had. And as the class had filled with students on that first day, she'd just begun to relax.

Until Talyn had walked in. The moment he did, a fissure of friction permeated the air so thickly that she could have sliced it with a dull spoon.

Only eight years old, he'd held his chin high and walked in alone, unlike the others whose parents had brought them in and helped them to find their seats. Without a word, and acting like a full-grown adult, Talyn had ignored the sneers of the Hyshian students and parents who didn't want an Andarion male in the mix, and had gone to his desk. He'd been so adorable with his caramel skin and bright white eyes. Since his black hair was longer, per Andarion fashion, than the rest of the males in his class, Talyn had worn it under a dark-colored religious Azukarian cap, which he continually tugged at to make sure it didn't expose his hair.

"Gah, why am I stuck with *that* in my room?"

Jayne had arched her brow at her senior teacher's derision. "Is there a problem?"

She'd jerked her chin in Talyn's direction. "I can't believe the administration allows *him* to go here. He's no business in this room with our kind. Imagine a universe where they mix freely with us."

By the sudden tenseness of Talyn's jaw and hurt look in his young eyes, she knew he'd heard the older teacher. But rather than call her out, he'd unpacked his bag and kept his gaze on the floor in front of his desk.

Little had the stupid bitch known, Jayne's own grandmother was a full-blooded Andarion. It was why her hair was black and she was so tall. And it'd been just such prejudice that had forced her grandmother from her homeworld and made Jayne's father the angry criminal he was.

Feeling for Talyn and knowing he had to be even more nervous on his first day than the others, Jayne had gone over to him.

"Hi."

He'd glanced up at her with a frown that said he wasn't sure why she was talking to him.

"I need your name so I can mark you as present."

Instead of speaking and exposing his tiny fangs, he'd pulled his name tag from his shirt and handed it to her.

"Talon Batter?" She'd intentionally mispronounced it to force him to speak.

His eyes full of patience, he'd shaken his head. "Tah-lean BAH-tour." His little high-pitched voice had barely been a purred whisper as he rolled his *l* and *r* like only a native Andarion speaker could.

Jayne had held her hand out to him. "I'm Miss Erixour. It's a pleasure to meet you, Talyn."

Cocking his head in an adorable fashion, he'd stared at her hand as if he wasn't sure what to do with it. Which made sense, since Andarions didn't greet each other that way.

Jayne had dropped her arm as she was called away to assist with other students. But over the next few weeks, her heart had broken more and more for the boy who was ignored at best and mocked at worst.

Talyn never spoke. To anyone. He just glared out at the world with a procacious gaze and tolerated the meanness so that no one at their school would call Galene about his behavior and get his mother into trouble at work.

Months had gone by with Jayne wondering about his parents, and why they'd so cruelly put him in a Hyshian school, until the day when word had come that Talyn's mother had been severely injured in an attack on the Andarion tizirah. As Jayne helped him pack his bag to go home, she'd finally seen real vulnerability inside him. He'd been so afraid, his little hands had trembled.

"She'll be fine, Talyn."

Still, stark terror and grief had glowed deep in his white eyes. It had stunned her how well he'd managed emotions that had to be tearing him up inside.

When the office had called to say his great-grandmother was there to take him home with her, Jayne had thought nothing more as she sent him to the front.

Hours later, she'd been on her way to her transport when she happened to glance to the side doors, out of habit to double check their room entrance. Talyn was there, huddled behind a set of bushes, with his books spread around him as he did his homework.

Scowling, she'd gone over to him. "Talyn? What are you still doing here? I thought your great-grandmother picked you up hours ago."

When he met her gaze, his young eyes had betrayed the bitter agony inside his heart. "My gre paran came while I was getting in her transport, and said that he doesn't want a mongrel dog tainting his home and making it smell. He pulled me out and made my gre yaya leave me here."

Jayne was aghast at the cruelty. "She just left you in the parking lot?"

He nodded without emotion.

"Why didn't you come back to class?"

He'd sighed heavily. "I tried, but there was no one to check me in again. The office secretary said that I couldn't do it without an adult and that I wasn't supposed to be on campus without being checked in. She told me if I didn't go, she'd call security. And I didn't want to get into trouble, so I hid here."

Tears had scalded her throat as she imagined how the poor boy must feel after being so cruelly abandoned. So much for Hyshians being a compassionate race. Bastards. "Who else can I call to come get you?"

Swallowing hard, he looked up with tears in his eyes. "I'll just wait for my mama. She'll come for me when she can."

Jayne had knelt down beside him. "Baby, your mother's in surgery. She can't come."

"She'll come. She will. I'll wait here for her so she can find me and won't be worried."

Cupping his cheek, she did her best to understand his situation. As crazy as her family had been, she'd always had someone she could rely on. Someone who would come for her. Even in jail. "Talyn, I can't leave you here alone, overnight. It's not safe. You'll freeze. Don't you have anyone else to call?"

He'd shaken his head. "It's just me and my mama. We don't need anyone else."

In that moment, she'd decided to take him home with her. She knew better than to call the authorities. There was no telling what Hyshians might do to a lone Andarion male. Even a boy. While they'd been currently at peace, they'd fought enough in the past that some Hyshians harbored a profound hatred of his species. In spite of his Andarion heritage, Talyn was a gentle soul, and the last thing she'd wanted was for anyone to hurt him.

And over the next three weeks while she'd cared for him, she and Hadrian had fallen in love with the quiet, reserved boy who quickly became an extended member of their family.

Several times, they'd taken him to the hospital to visit Galene, who'd finally explained that Talyn's father had never been in the picture and knew nothing about Talyn's birth. Over and over, Galene had cried and thanked Jayne for a kindness that really shouldn't be so unusual.

They'd been best friends ever since.

"Jaynie?"

She looked up at Hadrian's voice that pulled her away from the past, and realized they'd landed and that both he and Nero were dressed in protective gear. "Yes?"

He cupped her face in his hand. "We're heading out. You joining us or do you want to stay with the ship?"

"I'm coming."

Hadrian handed her a mask and helped to secure it to her suit as Nero opened the door to the inhospitable landscape.

As soon as she was on the ramp, Jayne cursed Jullien for his cruelty. This planet, like so many others, had been bombed to oblivion by The League. What remained of the native life forms were mutated aberrations that preyed on anything they could find. But what sickened her most was how long Talyn had been here.

Even if they found him, he'd never be the same again.

Jayne cursed in utter frustration. After hours of finding no trace whatsoever through the heavily charged atmosphere that rendered their tracking equipment worthless, it was about to be too dark to keep going.

Hadrian caught her arm. "You go back and we'll continue searching."

"I'm not going to rest while you risk your life. Are you nuts? You stay. I stay."

Hadrian cupped her cheek. "Think of the babies. They need their mother. You're much more fierce than I am. Go back and we'll keep looking."

She hated it whenever he pulled the children card on her. It was the one and only thing he knew she wouldn't argue against. "You're a rank bastard, Hadrian Scalera!"

Instead of getting angry, he flashed that charming grin

that always melted her heart. "Hadrian Erixour." He pressed his helmet to hers and turned her around to head back without him.

Just as she took a step toward the ship, she saw Nero's hand go up in a gesture that told her to hold position.

She pulled her blaster out and gripped it tight, looking for the threat.

Hadrian grabbed her as something went rushing past. She barely saw the blur of the twisted animal that appeared to have three malformed heads. Howling, it left a bright trail of blood in its wake.

She screwed her face up in distaste. As she straightened, she noticed the peculiar light in Hadrian's eyes that said he was using his Trisani powers. "What?"

He ignored her. "Nero?"

The way Nero acted said that he was talking to his brother telepathically.

"I hate it when you two do that. It's so rude. Now, what is it?" she whispered to her husband. "Talyn?"

"Not sure." Hadrian stepped back from her to cover his brother as they moved forward, toward a hole in the cavern wall where the beast had come from.

There was even more blood here.

A *lot* more blood.

As they went farther in, they heard echoing voices.

"Did you see what he did with his bare hands?"

"Shoot the fucking bastard!"

"Are you crazy? Last time we did that, it only pissed him off more."

"He's going to get out of there and kill us. Throw something at him!"

"Fight! Fight! Fight!"

Jayne froze as she finally saw what was going on. At least three dozen men and women stood at the top of a large, steep pit where someone had thrown Talyn. They were in the process of dragging another huge male in chains from a cage toward the hole, as if intending to throw him in on top of Talyn so that they could fight.

"Enough!" Nero shouted.

They froze until they realized they outnumbered Jayne's small group.

"Get them!"

Those words had barely left the man's lips before Hadrian threw his arm out and sent a shock wave through the place that blasted them into the walls so hard, it knocked them instantly unconscious.

Nero turned toward his brother with an arch stare. "It seriously pains me that you can do that and not get a migraine."

Hadrian laughed. "I have a migraine. It's a big motherfucker, too. Stands about six four . . ."

Nero shoved at him. "Don't rub it in, half-bit. Hatred stunted my growth."

Ignoring them, Jayne ran to the pit. Bile rose in her throat as she took in the brutal sight of where Talyn was imprisoned. Steel spikes lined the pit, pointing downward so that he couldn't climb out without being impaled or mangled. There were several bodies in the pit with him, and the ground was soaked with things best not thought about. "Talyn?"

His breathing ragged, he glared up at her and bared his fangs as if daring her to come for him.

She pulled her helmet off to show him her face. "Sexy baby T?"

He blinked twice then rubbed at his eyes as if unable to believe what he saw. Tilting his head, he frowned as if he couldn't place her face.

Tears choked her. "It's me, precious. I'm here to take you home."

Instead of moving toward her, he drew back and collapsed into the filth, near one of the smaller bodies.

Using his powers, Hadrian jumped straight into the pit so that he could reach Talyn first. "Nero! Keep Jayne out of here. Toss me a rope and we'll lift him out."

Talyn turned on him with a fierce growl, as if he was about to attack.

Hadrian removed his helmet and held his hands out. "Hey, little buddy. Remember me?"

Talyn blinked slowly before he finally calmed down. "Uncle Rian."

"That's right. Just hang on. We'll . . ." His voice trailed off as he looked at the walls around him and saw what Talyn had clawed into the stone with his bare hands. "Nero! Hurry with the rope." He used his powers to rip down the spikes so that they wouldn't accidentally harm Talyn on the way out.

Jayne cursed every being who'd had a hand in doing this to her little T. Before Nero could obey Hadrian, Jayne did something she was *never* supposed to do. She unfurled her wings and flew into the pit to retrieve them both.

Be damned if she was going to leave them in that mess for one heartbeat longer than she had to. Screw the rope. Her baby and husband were all that mattered.

As she went for Talyn, he pulled back and shook his head. "Get Berra first."

"Berra?"

Talyn's senses dulled so fast, he feared he'd pass out. Everything was so blurry around him. Like walking in a thick dream. But the one thing he'd promised was that he'd keep Nightdice safe and see her home again.

He licked his chapped lips as he knelt in the filth by her side. "Berra?"

She didn't move.

"Nightdice?"

Her eyes slowly fluttered open as blood ran from the corner of her lips. She reached up to touch his face before she went limp in his arms.

"No!" he growled, trying to shake her awake. "Berra!"

"She's dead, T."

Roaring in pain, Talyn glared at Jayne. "I'm going to kill them! So help me gods!" He rose, intending to climb out with his bare hands, but the moment he stood, everything went dark.

• • •

Hadrian caught Talyn before he hit the ground. Her heart breaking for Talyn's pain and injuries, Jayne quickly flew Talyn out, handed him off to Nero, then returned for her husband.

She made one more trip for the female's body.

"Who is she?" Hadrian asked as Jayne flew up and handed off the female to him.

"I don't know. But I don't think we should leave her behind. She's obviously important to Talyn."

Hadrian took the female's body from her.

Tucking her wings in, Jayne swept her gaze around the unconscious males, littering the ground, who had abused her Talyn. He was so hurt, and bleeding. Filthy. It was all she could do not to retch at the sight and smell of him. Before she could reconsider her actions, she headed for his captors.

Hadrian caught her arm in a gentle grip. "Forget them. We need to get Talyn out of here as fast as we can before he dies, too."

"I want to kill them!"

"So do I, but Talyn's more important. Focus, Jayne. He's barely holding on right now. We have to get him medical help."

Nodding, she pulled Talyn into her arms and flew him back to the ship while Hadrian and Nero teleported with the female's body—something they couldn't do with Talyn because of his special anatomy. His breed of Andarion didn't play well with Trisani teleportation powers.

Tears blinded her. Talyn was so beaten, malnourished, and dehydrated that she wasn't sure if he'd really understood who they were. That he was finally going home.

As gently as she could, she laid him down on the floor of the ship while Nero went to do preflight checks. Hadrian placed the female a few feet away and respectfully covered her with his jacket.

Jayne pulled their first-aid kit out and started rudimentary care. At least as much as she dared. Since Andarions were very different from humans and Hyshians, she couldn't do much for fear of harming him more.

"Who's Felicia? Is she the female we recovered?"

She paused at Hadrian's question. "How do you mean?"

He lifted Talyn's hand up so that she could see his worn-down claws. "Talyn scratched her name into the walls, over and over again."

"I don't know." Tears choked Jayne as she noted the number of fresh scars and wounds on Talyn's body. The traitor's mark that had been tattooed on his neck, below his left ear. Andarions were fiercely vain creatures, and any scar or physical mark was viewed as hideous and undesirable.

It was obvious Jullien and his friends had gleefully "deformed" Talyn's beauty. Worse, they'd shaved his head. While older Andarion males might do that later in life, for a male Talyn's age, it was a mark of dishonor or military cowardice. Desertion of post.

Rage burning inside her, she met Hadrian's stern frown. "Why did they do this to him?"

"Punishment."

She duplicated his scowl. "I don't understand."

"You know my powers are limited when it comes to this sort of thing, but . . . this was done for no other purpose than to cripple Galene. There's dissension in the royal house. If they can get Galene to resign, there won't be anyone protecting Cairistiona."

"What does that matter? She hasn't been in line for the throne in well over a decade."

"So long as she lives, they see her as a threat. All of them. She and Tylie are the only two beings left of the queen's immediate family. All the others have been murdered, including the queen's husband. So long as Cairie lives, she's a threat to those who might want to take the throne."

Jayne growled at Hadrian.

He held his hands up in surrender. "I'm not saying it isn't bat-shit crazy. You're talking to someone whose entire family was slaughtered. Brutally. Over a *minsid* throne. There's a reason why neither Nero nor I have ever tried to reclaim our titles or land. We're done with the bloody politics."

"Yeah," Nero breathed as he began firing their engines. "I've had my fill of burying family members because of senseless greed. It's a harsh universe we live in, and if they want the fucking throne, let them have it." He glanced at them over his shoulder. "Every sentient creature should have the right to lay their head down in peace, and not fear having their throat cut while they dream of better days."

Jayne hated to admit how right Nero was. It was why she

and her friends had founded The Sentella to fight against The League and any corrupt government that abused its powers.

Nero turned back toward the controls. "Fasten up. Let's get Talyn home."

They secured him to the floor with a loose harness before they took their seats for the launch. Even so, Jayne kept her attention on Talyn's unconscious body. She hadn't seen anyone beaten this badly since Darling had gone after his uncle in retaliation for Arturo putting Darling's younger brother in ICU.

Her heart broken, she met Hadrian's pensive stare. "Will he heal?"

"You want the truth or what you want to hear?"

"Truth."

Hadrian glanced to Nero. The sad light in his eyes was haunting. "He might come to terms with this, but he won't ever be the same."

That was what she was most afraid of.

CHAPTER 16

Felicia paced the ER hallway as she waited for Talyn to arrive. Galene had called her and told her they'd located him and were bringing him in. She'd rushed here as fast as she could.

His mother and her brother were still en route.

Every time the doors opened, she ran forward, only to be disappointed that it wasn't Talyn arriving. It was a cruel, cruel game.

The doors opened again.

Felicia started toward them, then stopped. Two human males came in with a bald Andarion between them. As she turned away in more aggravation, recognition hit her.

No . . .

Gasping, she snapped around to see Talyn, bald, bleeding, and unconscious. Horrified for him, she rushed to the gurney they were laying him on while the shorter, older human called for help.

"Talyn?" she breathed, taking his hand into hers. His claws had been virtually sheared off. *My poor baby.*

The taller man tensed as if he was going to chastise her, but then he blinked. "You're his Felicia?"

"I am." She sniffed back her tears while she brushed her hand over the nastiest wound in Talyn's cheek. "What did they do to him?"

Before he could answer, the doctor approached them with the shorter human. But as soon as the doctor's gaze fell to Talyn, he hissed and stepped back.

"We don't tend his kind here. You need to take him somewhere else for care."

Felicia gaped at the doctor and his unwarranted prejudice. "His mother's fully Vested!"

The doctor curled his lip. "And she's disowned him. He's a traitor and an Outcast. You know the law! We can all be arrested for aiding him."

It was only then that Felicia saw the marks of dislineage on Talyn's chest and arms. Claw scars that said his own mother had cast him out of his family. "His mother didn't do this," she insisted.

The doctor didn't hear her. He was too busy calling to have Talyn arrested again.

In that moment, Felicia lost every semblance of sanity. All she felt was the hatred and anger inside her over the injustice of what had been done to the one being she loved above all others.

Reacting on pure instinct and defaulting to the defense classes that had been a mandatory part of her primary education, she grabbed the blaster from the human closest to her and angled it at the doctor's head. "You will treat him. Now! And you will save him, or I will paint the walls with your brain matter, so help me, gods."

One of the security guards ran at her.

She shot him without flinching, then returned her sights to the doctor's head. "That is the only warning I'm giving." With her thumb, she switched the blaster setting from stun to kill. "Tend him or you'll be the one needing a doctor *and* a mortician."

"Felicia?"

She glanced sideways to see Galene coming through the doors. "They won't tend him, Commander. They're trying to throw him out of here and have him arrested. I will burn this place to the ground before I let that happen!"

Galene's face went white before her own anger ignited. "What?"

"I can't legally tend an Outcast!"

Galene growled at the doctor. "He's not an Outcast! I didn't do that to him."

"He's marked as one, and as a convicted traitor!"

"And he's an Andarion hero." A tense ripple went through the room at the sound of Tylie's regal voice. Everyone except Felicia, the doctor she held at blaster point, and the humans bowed to the tizirah.

Tylie came forward to stand by Felicia's side. "Put the blaster down, child. I promise you, no one's going to turn your Talyn out."

Only then did Felicia hand the weapon back to the human she'd taken it from. "Sorry."

Laughing, he holstered it. "I get it. My wife would do the same . . . only I doubt she'd warn them before shooting. I'm Hadrian, by the way." He jerked his chin at the shorter male. "He's Nero."

Tylie glared at the doctor. "What are you waiting for? A grave injustice has been done to one of our soldiers. A hero. Snap to, or you'll face a far worse sentence than what was unjustly given to the major."

Finally, the doctor and staff began treating Talyn.

Still shaken and horrified, Felicia went to Galene. "How could they do that to him?"

Tears glistened in her eyes as she choked on her sobs. "He was supposed to be safe at the palace. I was right there when they dragged him out under my nose. How could I let this happen to my baby?"

Felicia pulled Galene into her arms. "I'm the one who got the orders to put him there. I'm so sorry, Commander. I just wanted to protect him. I never meant for him to be hurt like *this*." Guilt and remorse shredded her. If Talyn ever learned the truth, he'd hate her for the part she'd play in his arrest. And she couldn't blame him for it.

She hated herself.

There was no such thing as safety in their world, and honestly, Felicia was sick of it. Somehow, she was going to get back at the prince. Even if it meant her life . . .

No one would do this to Talyn and get away with it. No one!

Talyn came awake with a start. For a full minute, he was still in the pit, mired in entrails and blood. Only this smelled very different.

It smelled clean.

Best of all, it smelled like a delicate female whose face had haunted him, night and day.

Blinking in disbelief, he focused his gaze on the most beautiful thing imaginable. A curly head of hair that was only a few inches from his face. Unable to believe it was real, he reached to bury his hand in the silken strands.

The moment he touched them, Felicia looked up with a gasp. "Talyn?"

Still, he couldn't speak. All he could do was marvel at the sensation of something that didn't hurt him. In all the time he'd been gone, this was what had seen him through. The hope that he'd be back here.

With her.

His hand shaking, he lifted her hair so that he could brush a lock of it against his lips and inhale her precious scent.

Felicia couldn't breathe as she saw the agony in Talyn's eyes while he savored her hair as if it were the most sacred relic in existence. Tears choked her as she took his chapped and calloused hand into hers and held it tight.

He pulled her against him and buried his face in the crook of her neck.

An instant later, she felt his silent tears on her skin. Tightening her grip, she held him against her. "It's okay. I've got you."

But in truth, he had her captured in an iron grip that was absolutely terrifying in its strength. His breathing ragged, he locked both arms around her as if she was his lifeline, and without her, he'd drown.

"Talyn?"

Instead of pulling away at his mother's voice, he held on even more tightly to Felicia.

Unsure of what to do, she met his mother's gaze over the bed. The hurt in Galene's eyes made her ache in sympathetic pain. "Your mom's been terrified for you, Talyn. If not for her, we'd have never found you."

That didn't seem to placate him in the least. Instead, he picked Felicia up with a frightening ease and put her in the bed with him. Without a word, he spooned against her back and held her with his face buried in her hair.

Eyes wide, she stared at Galene. *What do I do?* she mouthed to his mother.

"Talyn?" Galene tried again. She reached over Felicia to touch him.

"Please, leave me alone," he whispered in a ragged tone.

If Felicia lived for a thousand years, she'd never forget the anguished look on his mother's face. She wanted to take him to task, but how could she? He'd been through a nightmare.

Besides, Nero had warned them both about how much psychological damage Talyn might have when he awoke.

"Can I do anything to help?" Felicia breathed.

Talyn tightened his grip. "Stay with me."

"I've no intention of leaving you, *keramon*." Not that she could, given the way he was wrapped around her entirely.

Talyn closed his eyes and let the warmth of her body ease the fury inside his heart. He kept waiting to wake up and find this a dream. To be back in that hole, covered in blood, fighting for his life, and what little sanity he had left. But as minutes passed and Felicia remained warm and soft against him, he began to realize the horror was over.

Somehow, he'd made it back.

And with that knowledge came a whole new terror. The Anatoles had ripped him out of his life without any effort at all. He, the strongest Andarion of his generation, had been erased in a matter of minutes. If not for Jayne and her Trisani husband, no one would have ever been able to find him.

No one.

His head spun with the new reality. Nothing was as it seemed. At any time, the tahrs could do anything he wanted.

To anyone.

"Talyn? Where are you?"

He allowed Felicia's voice to pull him away from the darkness that was quickly swallowing him whole. "I'm with you."

"Stay with me. Don't return to wherever you were."

Nodding, he forced himself to relax and calm his breathing. He didn't want to be there, either. "I love you, Felicia."

"I love you, too." She started to roll over.

Talyn held her in place. "Don't look at me. I'm hideous."

She tugged at his arms until he was forced to loosen his hold or hurt her. Then she did the last thing he wanted . . . she rolled in the bed to face him. "You are gorgeous."

But he knew the truth. They'd maliciously scarred him. Marked him as an Outcast. Shaved his head and dumped him like garbage. What little honor and standing he'd had was stripped from him along with his flesh and braids.

He was nothing now.

Just a piece of Outcast shit.

She cupped his face in her hands. "Your hair will grow back. And your mother has already contacted a plastic surgeon to remove the scars."

"They'll always be there." They had cut him deep enough to ensure it.

"And I don't care. Would you cease to love me if I were hurt?"

"Never."

"Then how can you doubt me?"

Tears choked him as he stared into her silvery-white eyes and saw the sincerity. But with it came a fear so profound that it shoved him into madness.

Jullien, Chrisen, and Merrell had suppressed him with almost no effort. He was a trained warrior. A Ring champion. And they'd broken him. He'd had no way to protect himself.

The thought of them doing that to Felicia to get back at him . . .

"Talyn?"

He couldn't breathe. He couldn't focus. Rage surged so violently in his veins that it made a mockery of what he felt in the Ring. Afraid he might hurt Felicia, he got out of bed, only to realize he was tethered to the equipment by monitoring devices and hoses. He snatched frantically at the lines.

Felicia shot of the bed to take Talyn's hand. "Baby, you're going to hurt yourself."

Honestly, he didn't care. He just needed to be free of restraint. He couldn't be tied down. Not again. Panic set in even more.

Nurses ran in to sedate him.

That only riled him more.

Felicia motioned them back. "Talyn! Look at me!" She cupped his face in her hands. When that didn't work, she rose up on her tiptoes to kiss him.

Talyn calmed the moment her lips touched his. She was the only thing in this life he would *never* hurt. Holding her against him, he reveled in the scent and taste that was his Felicia.

Until a nurse neared them. Tearing away with a growl, he was ready to kill her.

"Stop!" Felicia motioned the nurse away. "He's all right. Can we get the monitors off him?"

"He needs the IV."

"I'll keep him hydrated. I promise." Felicia slowly and carefully began removing the monitoring devices and IV, and handing them to the nurses, until he was free.

She smiled up at him. "Better?"

He nodded.

With a tender hand, she led him back to bed and placed him in it while the nurses withdrew from the room. Felicia tucked the covers around him. "You're safe, Talyn. Do you remember Nero?"

"Yes."

"He's right outside the door, along with six royal guards and your mother. Tizirah Tylie has an order signed by Tadara Eriadne that you're to be protected at all times. No one's going to remove you from this room without a brutal fight from all of us." She kissed his cheek. "Do you want me to get your mother for you?"

Tears gathered in his eyes. "I can't."

She sat down next to him. "Why? What is it?"

He hesitated before he answered in a whisper. "I don't want to hear her tears. And I don't want to see the guilt in her eyes that will make me feel like an asshole for having caused it. Just one time in my *minsid* life, I want to be selfish. I'm tired of eating my pain and hiding it to protect *her* feelings. I'm sorry she feels guilty for my life. But just once, I want to feel sorry for myself, and fuck everyone else!"

She stroked his cheek. "Okay. You're allowed. The gods know you've earned it after what you've been through."

His breathing ragged, he looked away from her. "I ran away

once, Felicia. Right after I graduated. I had this stupid idea that I could find peace, somewhere else."

Felicia's jaw went slack at a secret she was sure he'd never shared with anyone else. "What happened?"

"I learned that as much as the Andarions hate me for my birth, the rest of the universe hates us even more. For a month, I tried to find work. I went system to system, looking. Everywhere it was the same. Humans hate us. Phrixians don't trust us. I couldn't even find housing. No one would rent to me. Not even for a night. I had to sleep on the street, in alleyways. Had to travel in cargoholds." He swallowed hard. "I came back home and my mom didn't even know I'd been gone. She was at a summit meeting with the tadara. That's how irrelevant I am."

"You're not irrelevant, Talyn. Have you any idea how important you are to me?"

He scoffed. "I've ruined you by having you in my life. Tainted you. Forever."

"No. You've given me a life and home the likes of which I never thought I could have. Until you, *I* felt worthless and irrelevant. Unwanted. But every time I hear your voice, my heart sings."

Talyn brushed the back of his index finger down her cheek. "I don't ever want you to regret me, Felicia."

"How could I?"

Talyn started to smile until a dark shadow appeared in the doorway. He expected it to be his mother.

It wasn't.

Tadara Eriadne of the Most Sovereign Blood Clan of eton Anatole stood there with a royal contingency of guards. Well over six feet, she was the epitome of a bloodthirsty queen, who'd murdered half her family to take her throne. And she eyed him as if he was the next to join them in their graves.

Felicia jumped up with a small squeak before she bowed to her queen.

"Leave us," Eriadne said without even looking at her.

That pissed Talyn off. And the way Felicia hurried from the room didn't help his mood even a little.

How dare the bitch treat Felicia that way. Even if she was queen. In his world, *tadara* meant nothing.

She *was* nothing.

Once the guards had withdrawn, the tadara approached his bed. "You're not afraid of me?"

He curled his lip. "Should I be?"

"I could have you killed."

Good luck with that, bitch.

Even though it was illegal, he met her gaze without flinching. "Death doesn't scare me. And neither do you."

"You are a bold one, aren't you? Full of that great War Hauk spirit. It must be hard-coded into your DNA."

Just as ruthlessness must be coded into hers.

"To what do I owe this pleasure, Tadara?"

The tic in her jaw said that she noted that his delivery of her title was more insult than obsequiousness. "You should watch your tone, boy. You have assaulted members of my direct family. You're lucky you're still alive."

Actually, they were lucky he wasn't dead. Had he not survived, he had no doubt his mother would have gone on a royal killing spree.

Starting with Eriadne.

But he refused to be intimidated by her. "Why are you here, Majesty?"

She swept a withering glare over him. "When I leave, my secretary will enter with forms for you to fill out. The pardon your mother and my daughter lobbied for comes with certain conditions."

He quirked a brow.

"You are never to speak of anything that happened to you. Should anyone ask, you were off on an official assignment."

Yeah . . .

"And my hair?"

"You were disciplined for your behavior."

For *his* behavior. Priceless.

"Failure to fall in line, *Captain*, will have most dire consequences for you."

"I'm a major, Majesty."

A sinister half smile curled her lips. "*Were*. Again, let me reiterate how lucky you are to be let off so easily." She slid her gaze toward the door. "Next time you assault a member of my family, it won't be *you* we throw into a pit on Onoria."

And with that, she walked out.

Talyn sat in bed, barely controlling the rage inside him. And when the secretary handed him the nondisclosure and he read through it, the lies and injustice scalded his throat and branded his soul even worse than the abuse he'd survived.

"Is there a problem, Captain?"

Talyn gripped the stylus and reminded himself that it wasn't the secretary's fault she served a whore queen. But really? He wanted to stab her with it. "No problem."

He signed his name to the document and saved it. They thought they had him.

They were wrong.

Yes, he was a Batur, but more than that, he was a mighty War Hauk. So named for their willingness to bleed in battle and take the life of those who threatened their family.

This wasn't over. He would have sucked up what they did to him and taken it.

Their mistake? Threatening his mother and Felicia. For he was a stralen War Hauk. No one, not even the fucking tadara of Andaria, threatened his family and got away with it.

That bitch was going down, and by all the gods, he was going to be the one to bind her in chains.

Or personally send her to her grave.

CHAPTER 17

Lorens ground his teeth as he read over Talyn's medical report and saw what Jullien and the others had done to the poor kid. It disgusted him.

Talyn was *barely* older than Gavarian. At that age, Lorens had just been entering the military under his father's direct tutelage and fierce protection.

He hadn't been tortured for the pleasure of a demented tahrs and his court. Sadly, he hadn't realized just how young Talyn was when they'd had dinner together. The warrior had seemed a lot older and far more worldly than he should be. That, too, said a lot about Talyn's upbringing and past treatment.

"You summoned me, Commander?"

Lorens looked up from his files to see Colonel Anatole. In that moment, he wanted to put his fist through the bastard's smug face. "A disturbing report has come to my attention. I want you to explain to me what happened to Major Batur."

"Pardon?"

"Major Talyn Batur. Don't play stupid with me, Colonel."

More calm than anyone had a right to be, Chrisen met his gaze fearlessly. "As you know, *Lieutenant* Batur was transferred from my command. I know nothing about him beyond that."

Bullshit.

"Fascinating. Your log reports show that you've spent weeks at the palace and not at your duty station."

He shrugged nonchalantly. And why shouldn't he? Chrisen thought himself above reproach and discipline. "The palace is a big place and the tahrs, my cousin, wanted extra security. Seems he feared an assassination plot from someone close to him."

"So you know nothing about Batur's arrest?"

"I didn't know he was arrested at all."

Lying sack of shit. But then, Talyn hadn't technically been arrested. He'd been seized and tortured.

"Get out of my sight."

Anatole paused. "You might want to rethink your tone with me, Commander. While you do outrank me in the military, you'd do well to remember that socially, I outrank *you*. It is my blood family that has ruled us all for thousands of years. Be a shame for your children to grow up fatherless."

"Is that a threat?"

Anatole smirked. "Just a friendly reminder."

Lorens ground his teeth as he watched the bastard glide out of his office. Honestly, he was sick of the Anatoles. Sick of the fact that none of them respected Andarion life or the values their civilization had been founded on. He'd suffered it for years, but as his children came into their own, new fears haunted him.

He couldn't allow them to meet Talyn's fate. Nor that of his brother or sister. Never mind what had been done to the two females Talyn had tried to protect and had been banished over. Not if he could stop it.

Picking up his link, he called his best friend.

As soon as Kerell answered, Lorens spoke without preamble. "I have a new member for us to consider for our club. Talyn Batur."

"The Ring fighter?"

"Yeah. Meet me for lunch. You're not going to believe what I'm about to tell you. I don't believe it, and I'm looking at it."

Lorens hung up and sat back in his chair while he copied Talyn's file before it mysteriously vanished like all evidence of the Anatoles' egregious actions always did. And why not? The tadara had made her own grandson disappear. What was the medical file of an insignificant bastard in comparison to the Andarion royal heir?

And it was time for the Anatoles to start answering for their actions. Time for them to learn that the Andarions weren't weak-willed ants to be trod upon.

For the one truth about Andarions, they were all fierce creatures.

Even their ants and mice were fanged and poisonous.

• • •

Grimacing, Talyn pulled himself up in bed. He'd just been released from the hospital that morning and was still in enough pain that he wanted to kill the tahrs himself.

And forget what he wanted to do to Chrisen and Merrell. He'd sell his soul to have them alone for five minutes. While they wouldn't enjoy it, he'd get his jollies and then some.

Pain sliced him as his thoughts turned to Berra and Farina. Two more innocent lives lost over their cruelty.

Payback was coming. . . .

And he intended to shove it down their throats with both fists.

"How you doing?"

He looked to the door to see Lorens hesitating. Anger splintered him at the sight. He still wasn't sure Lorens hadn't ratted him out about the report he'd made on Chrisen. The timing had been extremely suspicious.

"Fine. I had worse beatings in grade school . . . from Hyshian girls."

At least externally that was true.

Emotionally was another story. Talyn was still having a hard time coping with the degradations they'd heaped on him. He wasn't sure if he'd ever come to terms with that aspect of it all. And the fear he held for his mother and Felicia was tangible.

Lorens came in and gestured toward the padded chair in the far corner. "Mind if I join you for a bit?"

He frowned at the male. "Where's Felicia?"

"I asked her to give us some time. There's something I wanted to discuss with you in private."

Every instinct in his body went off at that. "About?"

"What you've been through."

Talyn curled his lip. He had no intention of talking about it with anyone. Least of all his commander and his female's older brother *and* someone he suspected of having betrayed him. "I've already signed the nondisclosures, Commander. I'm well aware that if I speak about any of what was done to me that I'll be put to death for it." And he didn't want to think about what they'd do to his mother and Felicia.

"That's not what I'm here about."

Talyn arched a brow.

"Well, it is, but it isn't."

"I don't understand."

Lorens moved the chair until he was so close that he could whisper. But first, he scanned the room for a bug and put up a static jammer.

Talyn arched a brow at his actions. "What are you doing?"

"I'm not the one who told the Anatoles about your report, Talyn. I stupidly trusted that information to the prime commander and asked for his assistance on how best to proceed. That was my stupid, naive mistake, and I can't apologize enough to you for it. The gods know, I never meant for you to have that blowback."

Lorens clenched his teeth before he continued. "He's the one who went to Merrell, and Paers ezul Nykyrian, without my knowledge, and deleted the report I'd prepared against them. Had I known what he was about, I would have protected you and warned you. I swear on the lives of my children. I never meant to bring you harm, in any way."

Either he was a damn good liar or he was speaking the truth. Even though trust didn't come easy, Talyn nodded. "I'm glad to know you're not a rat bastard, after all."

"Contrary to popular belief, and what my younger sister would normally say, I really try not to be." His gaze haunted, Lorens swallowed hard. "You should also know that I'm here on behalf of another organization," he whispered in a tone so low, Talyn had to strain to hear him. "Ever heard of WAR?"

"Yeah, it's my stock and trade."

Lorens gave him a droll stare. "Warriors Against Royalty."

His blood ran cold as he thought back to Rhys, who'd been killed when their colony was overrun by the last group of scavengers—the old male had died protecting Terisa while Talyn had protected Berra. "I know of them."

Lorens dropped his tone even more. "They're not the traitors in this regime. They're patriots who are sick of what's being done to innocent Andarions on the whims of the royals. Andarions like you, who are minding their own business and are ripped from their homes and tortured for no reason whatsoever."

Talyn shook his head. "We shouldn't—"

"Listen to me, Talyn. My youngest brother was assassinated before his wife and children so that Merrell Anatole could marry into the lineage of his widow. My sister was taken and raped by Nyran Anatole. Like you, she was forced to sign a nondisclosure saying that if she ever mentioned it to a living soul, she'd be executed. Every day, Andarions are killed, brutalized, threatened, and taken for no reason whatsoever. The royal family is out of control and has never been smaller than it is, right now. They've virtually murdered each other into extinction, and now is the time to finally stop their bloodthirsty reign. The entire history of the Anatole lineage is written in the bloody feuds of their children. As soldiers, we are the ones who have sworn to protect our fellow Andarions from all enemies. Enemies that include a royal family drunk on its own power. Imagine an Andaria where males and females, like you, can live their lives without fear."

Yeah, right.

He'd still be bastard-born and hated by all. Even if they brought down the entire royal family, nothing in this empire would change for him.

"It's treason," Talyn repeated in a whisper, even though he agreed that changes should be made. He still wasn't sure this wasn't some kind of setup.

While he fully intended to personally slaughter Eriadne and Chrisen, he wasn't stupid enough to let *anyone* know his plans.

"Did you know the tadara had her own grandson killed . . . Why? Because he looked human. Tahrs Nykyrian was slaughtered in cold blood. He was just a child when he was ripped from his mother's arms, and sent to his grave. You've seen the tizirah. You know she's not right in the head, because she knows her own mother killed her son and can't handle the truth of it.

I have it on tape where Tahrs Jullien himself brags about it, and the fact that his grandmother intentionally keeps his mother, her own daughter, in a drugged stupor so that she won't have to answer for her actions."

Talyn hesitated. If this was a setup, Lorens would be in even more trouble than Talyn for speaking those kinds of accusations. "Then why haven't you taken it to the media?"

"Because the station we gave a copy to was bombed before they could air it. Everyone in the building was killed instantly, and the Phrixians were blamed for the attack. Just like what happened with you. Before I could make the report against an Anatole, it *and* you were erased. The royal house has spies everywhere."

"Yes, they do. And if they find out about—"

"They won't. We are very careful who we recruit."

Sure they were. "Then why are you recruiting me?"

"Because of your record and history with them. And what they did to you. You had no reason to stand up for the females in your squad who had never stood up for you, and yet you did the right thing, knowing it could cost you your career." His eyes burned into him. "I know the truth of your character, Talyn. But have you seen your military file lately?"

Talyn shook his head. "It's above my clearance level."

"Yeah, well . . . here." Lorens handed him a thick folder. "I've made a copy for you. And by the way, you're not a captain as you were told. After your interview with the tadara . . . more disciplinary action was added to your history. You've been demoted back to a lieutenant's rank and pay."

Sick to his stomach, Talyn stared at him in complete disbelief. "What?"

Lorens nodded. "As further discipline against you, you won't be eligible for a promotion again for three years, provided you keep your mouth shut over what was done to you."

Talyn felt like he'd just been punched by Death Warrant. "I didn't do anything!"

"That's our point. My brother didn't do anything, either. He just happened to have married into the wrong lineage. And don't get me started on Tahrs Nykyrian eton Anatole. His biggest crime was that his mother slept with a human and he happened to look more like his father than his mother. For that matter, Jullien, Merrell, and Chrisen single-handedly drove the entire War Hauk male lineage from Andarion soil because the last thing they want is for any of our beloved heroes to be here to stop them."

Talyn went silent as old memories stirred.

Lorens sat back. "I knew Keris Hauk—he was one of my best friends from childhood. He rose too fast through the Andarion military ranks for their taste, and they couldn't stand it. Merrell hooked him on drugs and saw to his execution through the hands of Keris's wife. It's a fact I know, but have never been able to prove. Likewise, I know they're the ones who drove Fain out of his family. And don't you find it odd that it was Jullien and Chrisen who were in the pod with Dancer Hauk when it crashed? You think that was a coincidence? They escaped unscathed, but he damn near died . . . and because of that, Dancer was barred from Andarion military service.

Forever. They deprived him of his birthright. It's why he's working for The Sentella now."

Talyn's head swam as he tried to digest all of that. He would call Lorens out, but it strangely made sense. Especially given the insane hatred Jullien, Chrisen, and Merrell bore him personally when he'd done nothing to them, other than try to stay out of their way. And it corroborated a lot of what they'd said to him about his father's family. "How do you know all that?"

"We've been gathering evidence on the royals for a long time. But every time we try to come forward, we're put down like rabid lorinas."

Like Rhys, Farina, and Berra.

"Then what's your agenda?"

"To remove the royal family from power and institute a governing body that the people control. A republic of officials who are reasonable, responsible, and honorable. A governing council that won't dare abduct our race, and beat, exile, and rape them at their leisure."

Talyn couldn't agree more. He wanted blood. Royal blood. Lorens must have smelled it on him.

But if he joined ranks with them, he'd be committing treason. With witnesses. He wasn't sure if he trusted anyone that much.

One snitch in their group, and everything he loved would be brutalized and lost.

If he didn't . . .

They were out to get him, and that wasn't paranoia. It was fact. His new rank showed that.

Either way, his mother and Felicia were targets. And he had no idea how to protect them from harm on his own. Not with his bastard status and low caste.

Strong alone. Stronger together. That was the motto for The Sentella group his aunt Jayne had helped to found.

One Andarion, alone, couldn't make much difference. But thirteen War Hauks had saved their entire race from enslavement and extinction.

Lorens rose to his feet. "Look, I know I've given you a lot to think about and I blindsided you with it. Just consider what I've said. If you decide to join us, call and invite me to a party at your house. I'll know by that phrase that you're in. If you decide not to, just leave a message saying the party's canceled. Since you live with my sister, no one will think anything about either comment. And I know what I'm asking from you. Believe me, I know. It wasn't an easy decision for me to make either. It goes against everything I was raised to believe. Everything I thought I was. But when I stood over my brother's closed casket—because of what they'd done to him—and saw my children there . . . *his* children, I knew I couldn't stand by and let them die next. Not when I had the ability to stop it. Andarions don't live in fear. We fight back." Lorens placed the file on the bed and left.

Sick to his stomach, Talyn opened the file and read his demotion letter first.

Rage burned through him. He'd worked and fought his ass off to get the rank of major. Honestly, after four years, and given his training, lineage, record, and education, he should have been a colonel or commander by now.

But no . . .

A *minsid* lieutenant. Beginner's rank for the next three effing years.

For *disciplinary* reasons.

Bellowing in rage, he threw the file across the bed as the injustice tore him apart. Of them torturing him and laughing about it.

"Talyn?"

He didn't respond to Felicia. He couldn't. Not while he hurt like this. He wanted their blood so badly, he could taste it.

She stooped to pick up the pages that were strewn across the bed and floor. Without reading them, she returned them to the folder and set it on the nightstand. "Did my brother upset you? I'll bar him from the condo if he did."

"No," he breathed. "The commander didn't do anything other than tell me that I've lost my rank."

"What?" she asked in a shocked tone.

He drew a ragged breath. "I'm now *Lieutenant* Batur."

"Oh honey, I'm so sorry." Sitting down beside him, Felicia rubbed his back. "Did he say why?"

"Because of my history of write-ups and disciplinary problems. The fact that I've been disrespectful to my superiors and my blatant disregard for check-ins and military protocol."

"Can't you appeal it?"

"To whom, Felicia? Eriadne herself busted my rank. Who's

going to believe the word of a worthless bastard against the tadara? I can't even apply to regain a captain's rank for three years."

"I'm so sorry, Talyn."

"I should have just let them kill me."

"Don't say that!"

"Why not? It's true. What am I fighting for? Really? No matter what I do, it all comes down to the fact that I have no paternal lineage. Even when I'm ten times better than anyone else, I'm seen as only half as good." He touched his bald head and cursed at the reminder of what they'd done to him. "A lieutenant, a fucking lieutenant. Do you know what kind of shit assignments they're going to stick me with? I can't even fly with a rank that low. It relegates me back to flight deck prep. Cleaning toilets." He could hear the mockery already. Gah, he was so sick of the abuse.

"Tizirah Tylie said that your mother would be your CO. She won't—"

"I'm a lieutenant, Felicia. I'm no longer qualified for palace duty. I have to go back to reg-staff." Disgusted, he stared at the wall as bitter resentment and hatred filled him.

Felicia swallowed against the wave of tears she felt for him. There was so much raw agony in his eyes that it made her ache. "Did Anatole say why they did this to you?"

He let out an acrimonious snort. "Because they hate my parents."

"What?"

He nodded. "My father pissed them off in school and I look

enough like him that it chafes the tahrs's ass." He met her gaze. "But most of it is because my mother refused to pledge with Anatole when she was younger. They can't attack her. She's a high-lineaged female, and as such, she has rights through the courts."

Rights that were denied to him.

"Is there nothing your mother can do?"

"No. And you can't breathe a word of this to her. It would kill her to know they attacked me because of her past with them."

No wonder he'd refused to look at his mother in the hospital. It made total sense now.

"Why hasn't he used you to blackmail her?"

"Anatole can't. Her family is equal in status to your father's. For that threat, she could have him arrested. He's hoping if he abuses me enough, I'll say something to my mother and her guilt will force her to negotiate with him."

"He doesn't know you very well, does he?"

Talyn shook his head. "They spanked my ass the moment I was brought into this world. Why the hell should anything change after that? I'm not his pampered, pansy ass. Beatings I can take. Even being a lieutenant. I survived it once. I can survive it again."

But there was more to it than that. He was sugarcoating it for her and she knew it. She'd heard her half brothers laughing about the hazing that was done to low-ranking officers. Hazing that was mitigated depending on the families the officer was tied to. She could only imagine how horrific it would be for someone like Talyn, who had no lineage protection at all.

"Who is your father, Talyn?"

"What difference does it make?"

He was right. But . . .

"Can't you go to his family? His mother could adopt you as hers."

"She won't. My mother tried that when I was an infant, and she threw my mother out of her house, insulting her the entire time. The only one who was willing to do it was his grandmother, but his grandfather refused to allow me their name. He said I wasn't worthy of carrying their lineage. If my father was such a disappointing son, he could only imagine how much worse *I'd* be."

"Your mother told you that?"

He shook his head. "She would never hurt me that way. I was in school when my mother was wounded and couldn't come get me. My gre yaya showed up, and just as I got into her transport, my gre paran arrived, yanked me out of my seat, and threw me to the ground with my things. He told her to leave me in the gutter where I belonged. The rest, he sneered in my direction while they screamed at each other in the parking lot."

She was aghast at the horror he emotionlessly described. "He did that at your school? How old were you?"

"Eight."

Appalled, she stared at him. "Your great-grandfather told your great-grandmother to leave you at school, alone, with no one to care for you, while your mother was in the hospital?"

He nodded.

"Please tell me your great-grandmother didn't do that."

"She had no choice."

Oh dear gods . . . "What happened to you?"

"My teacher took me home with her and kept me until my mother was released."

Felicia ground her teeth as fury seethed deep inside. How could anyone do that to a child? How? It made her feel selfish and bitchy for everything mean she'd ever said to her father for his actions that were nowhere near on par with this.

"So, no, Felicia. My father's family despises him for shaming them, and me because I come from him. As far as they're concerned, whatever happens to me is no concern of theirs. All I have in this entire universe is you and my mother."

And Galene had no idea how bad things were for her son. For the love of his mother, he said nothing to hurt Galene's feelings.

Never had she loved Talyn more than she did right now. Rising up on her knees, Felicia pulled him against her and held him tight. "I think you're wonderful, Talyn. You're more Andarion than anyone I've ever known or met. Or even heard of. You have the heart of a mighty War Hauk."

Talyn flinched at her choice of words. In her mind, she thought she was complimenting him. After all, his father's bloodline went straight back to the most heroic legend of their people. What it really did was slap him in the face and remind him of the heritage that should have been his.

But right now, none of that mattered while Felicia held him. She didn't see a worthless bastard. She didn't see a victim or a mongrel. The one they'd all thrown away.

In her beautiful eyes, he was still honorable.

Taking her hand, he led it to his cheek and closed his eyes so that he could savor the softness of her flesh on his. "You are and will always be *munatara a la frah*."

Felicia choked on a sob as he called her the most precious lady of his life. In Andarion, it was the highest avowal of love. Something no male said lightly.

Tears filled her eyes as fear tore through her. As much as she loved him, she couldn't tell him the news she'd been given earlier that day from her agency, that they were refusing to allow her to contract with Talyn when their probationary period ended. Even though she was no longer a virgin, they had a new patron for her.

One with more money and a much stronger lineage that Talyn wouldn't be able to fight against. Because of her contract with the agency, she was going to have to leave Talyn forever.

But how could she tell him that after this blow? It would devastate him. He had no way of fighting their decision. No way of keeping her contracted to him.

You could buy out your contract and live with Talyn without one.

If she were human, it would be easy. On Andaria, that would make her a whore. Lower than even a prostitute. No male would ever consider her fit for dating or pledging, and marriage would be out of the question. Forever.

All relationships on Andaria were done through legal contract negotiations, with a third party overseeing them. With all parties, and their families, signing off on it.

While the life of a companion wasn't the most perfect way

to exist, it was legally acceptable. Socially acceptable. But with it, she was forced to bend to agency rules.

What do I do?

She couldn't decide right now. There was no way. And whatever decision she made, she wasn't going to discuss it with him. Especially not while he was hurting like this.

Talyn kissed her hand. "It's okay if you don't love me, Felicia. I'm just glad I have you with me. And now that I've lost my rank, I fully expect you to leave when our contract expires. You're too decent a female to stay with someone you know has no future of any kind. You should be with a male who can give you a lineage and children you can be proud of. Someone who can protect you."

"Tay—"

"Shh," he said, cutting her off. "There's nothing more to say. Just because I get hit in the head a lot doesn't mean I'm stupid or delusional. You're planning to be a great doctor one day, and while your parents aren't married, you have both lineages. Once you have your degree, you'll have your choice of husbands. That's how it should be."

"And you should have your choice of females."

Talyn sighed. She had no idea how right she was. His paternal grandfather had been pledged to Tizirah Cairistiona at one time. The Baturs had practically beaten down the door of his grandparents to pledge their daughter to his father. Had his parents married, he would have been Talyn of the Warring Blood Clan of Hauk—the only male of his entire generation who could legally use that prestigious name. To the Andarion race, that was even more impressive than Jullien of the Most Sovereign Blood Clan of eton Anatole.

But that was a title that would never be his.

Not as long as the royal family was in power, and not as long as the old traditions stood.

You could change that.

All he had to do was call her brother and help WAR overthrow their government.

Closing his eyes, Talyn wanted to play by the rules. He wanted to believe that hard work was rewarded. Yet the one thing he'd learned in the Ring was that sometimes you had to take that cheap shot. Even when it was repugnant. Even when you didn't want to. Sometimes, just sometimes, you had no choice. No one could win a fair fight when your opponent didn't respect the rules.

Fight fire with fire.

He'd spent his entire life doing what he was supposed to. And they'd figuratively gelded him for it. It was time to leave the gloves in the dressing room. Time to meet them on the terms they'd set when they bound his hands behind his back.

Degradation was a bitch and it was time he acquainted her with Jullien and the entire Anatole family.

CHAPTER 18

Felicia sat outside her broker's office with a sick lump in her stomach. For three days, she'd wrestled with what to do about leaving Talyn.

She still had no answer.

The last thing she wanted to do was hurt him. That alone told her what she *needed* to do. But it was much easier said than done. Especially since he seemed to want her out of his life.

"Felicia? The director will see you now."

Swallowing hard, she got up and went into the elegant office where her broker, the director of her agency, sat behind his ebony wood desk. He smiled as he saw her.

"Come in, Felicia." He gestured to the padded chair in front of his desk. "Have a seat."

Her limbs trembling, she obeyed.

"I'm assuming you want to talk about the new contract?"

"Yes. Very much so. I don't understand how I ended up being offered to someone."

"Actually, you weren't. They called and asked for you by name. Apparently, the secretary who contacted us had been calling all the agencies, looking for you, but all they had was your first name and your patron's name. The female I spoke to was elated to have finally located the right agency that held your contract."

"Female?"

"Mmmm, yes." He pulled up a file on his computer. "The terms are incredible. While your condo won't be so grandiose or that close to your school, your new patron is willing to buy out the current contract, plus pay a staggering fee to the agency to convert you before your probation ends."

Felicia gaped. One of the items she'd been firm on was the location of her condo. While Talyn had graciously provided her with a transport, most patrons didn't, and Eris was too congested to rely strictly on public transportation for her classes.

"I know!" her broker said, mistaking her stunned facial expression for approval. "It's incredible that he'd be so generous. But he said that he wants your services immediately . . . within a standard Andarion week."

"May I ask who this patron is?"

He pushed a folder toward her. "Commander Merrell Anatole."

Bile rose in her throat as anger ripped through her. She gently pushed the folder back toward her broker. "The answer's no."

He arched a brow. "You don't have a say in this. Especially given the amount he's offering to pay."

Aghast, she stared at him. "I believe I do."

Now anger darkened his eyes as he glared at her. "If you turn this down, we won't offer a contract to your current patron. Period. You'll have to start the process over again. Only this time, you're no longer a virgin and you won't have the same bargaining power you had before."

Rising to her feet, she tapped the folder with her fingertip. "This isn't about me. This is the commander trying to hurt Talyn, and I refuse to be a part of that. The only reason *he's* doing it is because we have a ban on his brother contracting with the agency after he killed a companion. No offense, I'd sooner walk the streets as a prostitute. If you force me to do this, I will leave this agency."

He scoffed at her bold words. "You can't. You owe us ten years of fees at your current contracted rate. That's what you agreed to when we took you on and trained you."

"Fine. I'll buy my contract back."

"And do you have a half million credits? Those are the buy-out terms and fees."

Her vision dimmed at the amount. Dear gods, if she had that kind of money, she'd never have had to sell her virginity. "That wasn't what I signed on for."

"Those are the fees that are currently being paid by your patron and the fees Anatole has agreed to continue for the next ten years."

Talyn was paying fifty thousand credits a year to her agency to have her? Holy gods! That was more than five times the normal agency fee! Was he insane? And that was in addition to paying for her living expenses, university fees, and monthly spending stipend and salary.

"You're the only one I wanted, Felicia." He seriously hadn't been joking when he'd said that. Virtually every credit he made as an officer was going to *her*. Probably more, given his caste. What the hell was *he* living on?

And never once had he told her to go easy on his money. *"Your comfort and safety are my priority."*

If she hadn't loved him before, she would now.

Tears choked her. "I will not break Talyn's contract. I'll get you your buyout fee."

"With what? You're not *that* attractive."

She ached to slap the arrogant, insulting expression from his face. But she couldn't afford the lawsuit. She needed every credit she had to fight this. "You'll get your credits."

"Then I'll e-mail you the bill. You have fifteen days to pay it or we will accept Anatole's contract on your behalf." He hit the *Send* button on his computer screen.

Her link buzzed immediately, letting her know that the bill was already in her inbox.

"Now, if you don't mind, I have work to do."

Dizzy and shocked, she pushed herself away from his desk and headed to the street. As soon as she reached the lift, she took out her link and wanted to die as she saw the full amount she owed her agency. ᒣ) 524,050.

Her mind reeled. Not even her brother had *that* kind of

money. No one she knew did. Except *maybe* her father. But he'd laugh her out of his home if she dared ask him for that amount.

What am I going to do?

She'd kill herself before she let a monster like Anatole touch her.

Climbing into a transport, she set her home address, then used her link to access her bank account. She didn't even have three thousand credits to her name, and that was *with* the savings account she'd had since she was fourteen.

Her heart breaking, she erased the condo address and typed in her mother's. The transport turned and headed in the opposite direction. Choking on a sob, she called Talyn, who was alone at the condo.

"Maj . . ." his voice trailed off as he caught himself. "Lieutenant Batur."

Even though she wasn't running the video feed, she brushed the tears from her cheek. "Hey, sweetie. Is it okay if I see my mom while I'm out? Would you mind?"

"Not at all. Is everything all right?"

"Fine. Why do you ask?"

"You sound weird. Like you're upset. Did something happen at the agency?"

More tears fell as she ached to tell him. But he didn't need to hear it right now. "Just regular crap." She cringed as he requested a video chat. Wiping her cheeks again and taking a deep breath to calm herself, she accepted it. "Hey, handsome."

He frowned at her. "Do you need me to come get you?"

His thoughtfulness choked her. No matter what, he always put her first. "I need you to rest. You're not supposed to leave the bed. You know that."

His scowl deepened. "I will come get you if you need me to. Just say the word."

She traced the lines of his face on her small screen. "Thank you. But I haven't seen my mom in a few weeks. Do you want me to pick something up for you while I'm out?"

"Nah. I'm good. Just be safe."

"I will. Now lie back down and rest."

"Yes, ma'am." He kissed his fingers, then held them out to her.

Smiling, she duplicated the gesture before she hung up and sat in silence while she ran over every possible legal way to get that amount of money.

I can always rob a bank. Prison was an acceptable alternative to being Anatole's companion.

The transport stopped outside her mother's condo building. Felicia paid the fee, then headed for the door. She ran up the stairs and waited for her mother to buzz her in to the complex.

As soon as she reached the hallway, her mother was at the door, waiting.

"What's wrong?"

Felicia started crying again as she threw herself into her mother's arms and told her everything. Ever tall, elegant and graceful, her mother led her into her the kitchen and made them tea. She didn't speak as Felicia unloaded her entire predicament.

"What do I do, Mommy?"

Her mother handed her a box of cookies. "What did I tell you about being a companion?"

"Not to fall in love."

"And what's the first thing you do?"

"I can't help it." Felicia held her link up to show her mother the lock screen photo of Talyn in his uniform. "Could you say no to this face?"

"He is pretty. But—"

"You don't know him, Mama. He's not like other males. He takes care of me like I'm his beloved wife. Talyn's precious and kind. Funny. Warm."

"And your father once took care of me, too. Until his wife forced him to leave us. Even though I'd given up everything to be with him, including my family's support and a staggering trust fund, he didn't look back."

That was true. But Talyn wasn't her father. "Talyn can't legally marry."

"You think that makes this better, Felicia? You stay with him and you'll never have children of your own."

She shook her head. "I can't be the mistress to Anatole. Not for five minutes, never mind ten years. He's a beast like his brother . . . who he'll probably share me with. I'd sooner kill myself."

"Don't be melodramatic."

"I'm dead serious. The thought of it makes my skin crawl."

Her mother sighed wearily. "I have fifty thousand I can loan you, but it has to be a loan. I don't have that kind of money and it's every bit of what I have in savings. Maybe we can work out a payment plan with your agency?"

She gave her mother a droll stare.

"I said *maybe*." With a heavy sigh, her mother sipped at her tea. "Since the day you were born backwards, you've been impossible, child. You've never, ever done anything the easy way."

"I know. I'm working on shaving more years off your life."

Her mother snorted. "Yes. You are." She took Felicia's hand into hers. "But you are ever my beautiful baby girl. And I will do everything I can to help you. You know that. Give me a few days to talk to your father, and see if I can work something out with that old goat."

Felicia choked on another sob as the uselessness of that cut her to the bone. "He didn't pay for my school. Why would he do *this*?"

"You didn't ask him to pay. You didn't want to."

"Fine. Assault me with the truth. But he doesn't love me. Not the way he loves his legal children. You know that."

"Still . . . you are his flesh and blood. I'll ask him for a personal loan. If he doesn't have it, maybe he'll cosign a loan with me for it from a bank or one of his investor friends."

"You would do that?"

Her mother gaped at her astonishment. "I'm not a total heartless bitch, Felicia. You are my daughter and I don't want to see you become the pawn of a male like Anatole. He obviously intends to use you to strike back at Talyn. The gods only know what he'll do to *you* in the process. I will kill him myself before I allow him to hurt you like I fear he might."

"Thank you, Mommy."

Her mother hugged her tight and kissed her head. "Smile for me, daughter. Trust in the gods as I've taught you. We will find a way to get you out of this. I promise."

They spent the rest of the afternoon catching up. By dinnertime, Felicia felt a lot better. She still had no real solution, but it helped to know that her mother was on her side.

On her way home, she stopped at her favorite restaurant and picked up dinner for them. She texted Talyn to let him know, and headed back to the condo.

As she neared the front door, a shadow fell over her.

"Excuse me," she said, stepping around the male without looking up from her link.

An iron grip fastened onto her biceps.

Gasping, she looked up into the face of Chrisen Anatole. "Let me go!"

He shoved her against the wall of her building. "No *minsid* whore turns down my contract. Who do you think you are?"

Felicia shoved her dinner at him and tried to run.

He caught her wrist and backhanded her so hard, she feared she might black out. He grabbed her dress, ripping it, and dragged her toward his transport. "I'm going to show you what happens to whores who don't mind their place."

CHAPTER 19

Major Batur!"

Talyn shot out of bed as he heard Aaron's shout. A shout that was punctuated by Felicia's gut-wrenching sobs. His heart pounding, he ran to the living room to find Aaron carrying her. He set her down on the couch and stepped back. Her face was red as if someone had struck her, and her dress was torn.

In that moment, a horrifying rage the likes of which he'd never known descended on him. Worse, it started that forgotten sensation of burning skin on his back.

He had to get control. Fast.

"Felicia?" Talyn pulled her gently against him.

Trembling and sobbing, she latched on to him and held him as if terrified.

Aaron swallowed hard. "I saw a male trying to pull her into a transport on the street. I only got part of the transport's markings. Sorry."

His back still burning, Talyn fought down his fury before

he let loose something he couldn't take back. "You saved her. That's the most important thing."

Aaron nodded. "I just wish I'd seen her sooner. One second more . . ." He met Talyn's gaze. "I'm so sorry. I swear to the gods, it won't ever happen again."

"Could you call a medic for us?"

"Absolutely."

"No," Felicia said. "It's okay. I'm not really hurt. Just scared."

Talyn dipped his head to make sure she wasn't being brave as he slowly got his body under control. "You sure?"

Nodding, she sniffed back her tears. "I lost our dinner, though. I beat him with it."

Talyn rolled his eyes. "I don't care about dinner."

"I'll make sure you have food delivered from the restaurant downstairs. Free of charge."

He inclined his head in gratitude. "Thank you, Aaron. For everything."

Felicia reached out to touch his hand. "Yes, thank you!"

Aaron bowed slightly. "Any time, *mu tara*. I'll see to your food."

As he left them alone, Talyn cupped her cheek in his hand. "What happened, baby?"

Felicia bit her lip, unsure of what to tell him. But the one thing she knew above all was that if he ever learned it was Anatole, he'd kill him. No questions asked. As much as she hated to lie, she could *never* let Talyn learn the truth. Not if she wanted to keep him from execution. "I don't know. It happened too fast to see anything."

"Lish . . ."

"I mean it, Talyn."

"If it was Anatole, I will fucking kill him!" he snarled.

As he started to rise, she latched on to his arm to keep him by her side. "No! You don't know it was him! You can't go after him. They'll kill you if you do."

His gaze burned with a fury so raw, it singed her.

"Talyn . . . please! I can't live if they take you again! We don't know, okay?"

Tears filled his eyes as he pressed his forehead to hers and held her in a way that told her exactly how much he loved her. His hands shook as angst darkened his gaze. "Is that why you're pulling your contract from me?"

"What?" she breathed.

He nodded grimly. "Your agency called yesterday to tell me. They wanted me to pick another companion." If she lived a thousand years, she'd never forget the deep-seated hurt in his handsome features.

Never in her life had she wanted blood the way she did right then. After what Anatole had told her about Talyn and this . . . "I'm not breaking the contract, Talyn. I went to them to ask about buying it back."

He flinched and nodded. "It's for the best. I understand."

As he started to withdraw, she cupped his face in her hands and forced him to look at her. "I wanted to buy it back so that I can stay with you. Forever. I love you, Talyn. *Only* you. They told me a few days ago that they had accepted another contract for me, and that they were the ones breaking this one. I told them that I refused to do it. And I only went there today to find out how much I'd need to buy my contract out." She pulled her link from her pocket and handed it to him. "You can see the e-mails for yourself, and the timestamps on them."

He scowled at her. "What are you saying?"

"What I started with. I. Love. *You*. Talyn. I don't want another male. Ever."

He winced. "Felicia, I can't give you anything."

Biting her lip, she searched for the words to make him understand that in this universe that hated him for things he couldn't help, she loved him for what he was. "I don't need things, Talyn. In spite of who my father is, I grew up with very little. For the most part, I was raised in one-room efficiencies. It's why I know how to cook and take care of myself. Material objects don't matter to me. They never have. But *you* do. You're *all* that matters to me."

Still, he shook his head as if he couldn't fathom her words. Or her loyalty. He brushed his hand over her bruised cheek. "I can't put you at this kind of risk. I can't."

"Talyn—"

"I'm stralen, Felicia."

Her breath caught in her throat. "What?"

He reached up and pulled a contact out of his left eye and then his right. There underneath, the entire iris was bloodred. "It was temporary at first. I only had it for a few hours whenever we had sex. But after I came back from Onoria and you touched me again, it became permanent. It's why I told you I had a headache the first time we slept together. I didn't want you to feel obligated to me because of it. Now you understand . . . I *have* to keep you safe."

Horror and happiness mixed inside her. It was what every Andarion female dreamed of having in her life. A stralen male who was hers, alone. One who would never stray.

That was the fairy tale.

But the reality was that he would die for her. Without hesitation. That he would be driven to protect her, no matter the cost to himself. He would never have a sense of self-preservation when she was threatened.

"Talyn—"

The intercom buzzed. She started to ignore it until she heard Aaron's voice.

"I have an enforcer here to take Tara Felicia's statement."

Talyn cursed. "Show him up." He rose to his feet. "I have to put the contacts back in. I'll return in a second."

No sooner had he gone than she covered her mouth with her hand as she remembered finding contact solution in her bathroom after he'd reported to the palace. She'd stupidly assumed it was his mother's, and had even wondered why it was in *their* bathroom instead of the guest room.

Now she knew.

Stralen.

Everything had just become more complicated and at the same time clearer.

Like muddy water.

The lift pinged. Aaron led the enforcer off. Rising, she realized that she was still in her torn dress. Just as she started to excuse herself, Talyn returned with her bathrobe. He draped it around her and met her gaze.

Weird. With those contacts in place, there was no sign of his condition at all. It was shocking really that they concealed it so completely. Had he not told her, she'd have never known.

"Tara Orfanos," the enforcer said with a slight bow. "I'm sorry to have to disturb you, but I'm sure you'd rather file your report here than come down to the station and do it."

She nodded.

Aaron cleared his throat. "I'll put your food in the kitchen until you're ready."

"Thank you." She gestured to the armchair. "Would you like a seat, officer?"

The male nodded and sat down before he pulled his ledger out and navigated through it. But he kept glancing up at Talyn in a strange way that said he knew exactly who Talyn was.

"Are you a Ring fan?" she asked him.

The enforcer actually blushed. "Yes, *mu tara*. A huge one."

She took Talyn's hand in hers and led it to her cheek. "Then to answer your unspoken question, yes. He's the Iron Hammer. You're not crazy."

A wide grin broke across his face as he shot back to his feet. "Ah, I knew it!" Biting his lip, he slid his stylus into his pocket. "This is so inappropriate of me, but could I please shake your hand?"

Talyn held his arm out to him. "Sure, Officer . . ." He glanced to the male's name tag. "Hawas."

The enforcer shook his hand quickly, then returned to work.

"I'm so sorry for what happened to you, *mu tara*. I promise, we'll make finding the male who did this a priority. No one attacks the Hammer's female!"

Talyn didn't speak as he sat down next to Felicia.

"I have most of the details and a description from your security guard. What I need are the specifics from you. Do you know him? Have you seen him before? Did he say anything during the attack?"

"Honestly, it all happened so fast that I'm really fuzzy on the details right now. All I remember is him grabbing me and shoving and shouting. And thinking that I just needed to escape him." Tears welled in her eyes, but she quickly blinked them away. "Is there any way I can call you if I remember something more?"

The enforcer finished typing it in with his stylus. "Absolutely." He pulled a card from his pocket and wrote a number on the back. "My office link is on the front. The back is my personal one. You call, day or night. If you feel threatened at all, we'll gladly send someone over. And if anything comes to you, no matter how insignificant you think it is, give me a call." He handed her the card. "And I hate to ask, but I assume the bruises on your face and arm are from the attack?"

She nodded.

"Would you mind if I took a photo of them for the evidence log? And your dress?"

"Sure."

He held his ledger up and had her pull her hair back from her face and neck so that he could document it. Likewise, she removed the robe.

Talyn ground his teeth as he saw the tears starting to flow down her cheeks. He pulled her against his chest and held her close. "Shh, *munatara*. It'll be all right."

Her legs buckled.

Talyn caught her up into his arms. He met the enforcer's concerned gaze. "If you'll wait here for a moment, I'll be right back. I just want to put her to bed."

"Yes, sir."

He carried her into the bedroom and covered her with the blankets.

"I'm sorry, Talyn."

"Don't you dare apologize. I know how hard it is. I'll be right back." He kissed her cheek and grabbed a magazine from the nightstand before he returned to the living room where Officer Hawas was chatting with Aaron.

"Thank you," Talyn said to the enforcer. "I really appreciate your compassion with her."

"No problem. I have a wife and daughter, and I know how furious I'd be if something like this happened to them."

"Yeah. He better be glad Aaron was there and not me. Otherwise, this would be a homicide report."

The enforcer nodded. "Thank you for your time, Major Batur. I'll have a patrol in the area for the next few days. Just in case."

"Thanks." Talyn held up the *Splatterdome* magazine in his hand. "Would you like me to sign this for you?"

"Really! Gah, I'd be so honored. Could you make it out to Theris?"

"Absolutely." Talyn signed it to him and handed it over. "Again, thank you both." He walked them to the lift, then went to get dinner for Felicia.

Felicia came out of the bathroom to find Talyn in the bedroom with a large tray of food and wine. Love for him spread through her. No one had ever made her feel the way he did.

Beautiful. Cherished.

"I wasn't sure what you'd like or what goes with the food since I can't drink, so I brought both red and white."

"Thank you, *keramon*." Dressed in her nightgown, she slid back into bed. "But I'm supposed to be taking care of you."

"It's all right. I'm pissed now. Feel no pain past the fury that makes me want to go hunt down whatever animal did this to you and skin him alive while he screams." He handed her a glass of wine. "I swear I'm going to find the bastard and—"

"We need to be productive with this, Talyn."

"I am being productive. His mutilation would be a service to all Androkyn."

"But it would get *you* a death sentence."

He took a bite of her salad. "I could die happy with that."

Rolling her eyes, she took a sip of wine.

Swallowing, he cupped her bruised cheek in his warm palm. "I'm sorry you were hurt and I'm sorry about your agency. I should have known better than to contract with you and drag you into my fucked-up life." A tic started in his jaw. "I was so lonely that night I first saw your photo. Just looking up fighting stats on Steel Jaw when the ad for your agency popped up. I never click on them, but you were so beautiful and you looked so kind and sweet. Innocent."

He stroked her cheekbone with his thumb. "It was the photo where you had your left hand up, pulling your hair back from your face. Your eyes sucked me in and I lost my heart to you in that instant."

She snorted at him. "Yeah, right . . . *that's* what you noticed. Not that I'm in my tiny bra and panties in that picture."

He laughed at her surly tone. "Your bra and panties were more circumspect in that photo than the bikinis the others wore in theirs."

"I thought you didn't look at anyone else."

He laughed. "I wasn't stralen then, nor dead. I did look." The humor died on his face as he locked gazes with her. "But I wasn't interested in them."

She wrinkled her nose. "Yeah, okay. It was a sports bra and briefs, not a thong. The agency cameraman had a stroke when he saw what I'd brought to be photographed in. They were all horrified over my choice . . . and the fact that I had more muscle mass than both of the males combined."

He ran his fingers down her arm, raising chills in his wake. "I loved that you weren't skinny, but muscled. The one where you were flexing your arms . . . that was the one that really got me."

"Muscle? Please. Compared to you, I'm a flabby old female. I'm pretty sure your left biceps are bigger than my waist."

Laughing, he sank his hand in her hair. "And these curls . . .

they haunted me. All I wanted was to bury my hand in them and have you whip your hair over my chest."

"So it was the curls and muscles that sold you, huh?"

"No. What sold me was the fact that when I logged in, there were no photos of you naked. Unlike the others, you were a real *tara*." He traced her lips with his fingertip. "In all my life, I've never wanted anything as much as I wanted to talk to you. To see if you were as sweet and soft as you appeared."

"Big letdown, eh?"

He shook his head. "You were so much more than I'd ever expected to find. I still can't believe you're here with me."

She wanted to cry at the sincerity in his eyes. "Is that why you agreed to pay me your entire officer's salary?"

He pulled back with a shocked gasp. "What?"

She narrowed her gaze on him. "I have to buy out the value of my contract with you from the agency. They sent me the bill for it. Fifty thousand a year, just to the agency? Are you insane?"

He looked away sheepishly.

Felicia wanted to choke him for throwing his money away like that. "That is what you're paying, isn't it?"

He cringed even more before he answered. "Actually, I'm paying seventy-five. The fifty thousand buyout was negotiated before the contract was drafted."

For a full minute, she couldn't breathe as those words fell against ears that didn't want to believe them. "What?"

He nodded. "I had to pay thirty-five up front. And agree to seventy-five for the probationary period and first five years. And fifty for the next ten years, after that, provided you agreed to extend the contract with me."

She slapped him with a pillow. "Are you mental? That's over a million dollars for me! Oh my God. Talyn, you're an idiot!"

He gaped at her.

"Well, you are! Who does that? Oh my God!" she repeated. But in her heart, she knew the real answer. A male who had no choice. One who was being gouged by those who could demand anything they wanted and his only choice was to pay or be alone. "I can't believe you agreed to *that*."

"I would gladly pay that and more for you, Felicia."

She snorted at his sweet words. "That's the stralen in you talking."

"I wasn't stralen when I signed the agreement." He tucked the pillow behind her. "So how much do you need to buy out your contract?"

"A little over half a million."

He sucked his breath in sharply. "How soon do you need it?"

"Fifteen days."

Cursing, he winced. "I have three hundred and fifty left in a savings account."

She gaped at that amount. "How? Officers don't make *that* kind of money."

"I had to prove to the agency that I could afford you and their fees. So I contracted for fights I'd have normally passed on, and put the up-front prepayments into savings, investments, and this condo."

She felt sick as she realized what he'd been willing to do for her. "That's the real reason you're going against Death Warrant?"

He nodded. "And Iceman. Steel Jaw. The Mountain. Slayer."

"Five fights?"

"Six, counting the one I already fought."

"Talyn!"

"What? It's what I had to do to get that kind of cred. For death-styled title matches, I get eighty-five thousand a fight, plus another twenty if I win. Normally I only get fifteen with a five-thousand win bonus."

She fell silent as she did the math in her head. "So what you're telling me is that in a death match, out of every two-hundred credit ticket they sell, you barely make four credits?"

"Three and two bits, after locker and cleaning fees. Then after I pay Erix and Ferrick, I clear just under a single credit. After taxes, I make half a cred."

For putting his life and health on the line.

She couldn't believe it. Shelf-stockers earned more. "Yet you're *the* reason they sell out every fight?"

He nibbled at her salad with a nonchalance that made her want to beat him. "I used to make only three percent of that in the Open league. And I made fifty thousand less a fight before I won the Vested Championship. I'm very happy with what they pay me now. Trust me. I'm the highest-paid fighter in Ring history."

Great. Not what she wanted to hear.

"It's still not fair."

Talyn didn't comment on that as he swallowed a bite of food. "If I agree to four more title fights in the next six months, we'd have what you need to buy back the contract."

She gaped at him and what he was willing to do.

For her. But she wasn't so sure she wanted him to make that sacrifice. "Talyn, I can't do that to you. I'm sick over what you've already agreed to. I don't want to be the reason you're beaten to a senseless pulp."

"I'm senseless without the beatings," he said teasingly. "Besides, I'm the reason they're doing this to *you*. I can get an up-front loan from Ferrick until we contract the other fights. You can pay off your contract at the first of the week. Then you're a total civ and your agency can't touch you."

That was all well and good, except for one thing. "*You'll* be broke."

"I don't need anything, Felicia. My uniforms and military room and board come out of my pay already. I bought my air-bike free and clear. Because I'm a champion, the gym supplies me with training equipment and time for free. The only thing I ever spend credit on is lunch, and I can eat in the mess hall. I don't have to go out. And since my rank's busted, I don't have to carry flight insurance anymore to cover the cost of my ship in case I crash it. That's an extra three hundred creds a month I get to keep now."

He made it all sound so feasible and easy. Yet she knew it wasn't. "I can't ask you to do this for me."

"Felicia, I'd have had to pay it anyway, if you'd contracted with me after our probation period."

"But *I* didn't know that before this."

He took her hand and led it to his heart. "*Munatara a la frah.* If I had one wish, it would be to have a name and lineage to give you. But the gods didn't grant me that. All I have to offer you is my heart and loyalty. Besides, if we were married, all I have would be yours, anyway. So take it all. I don't want any of it without you."

She pulled his lips to hers so that she could kiss him. "I hate you, you bastard!"

Aghast, he pulled his head back as if she'd slapped him. "Excuse me?"

"You have ripped out my heart and made me cry more than anyone ever has. You are everything in this life to me. I don't care about laws or names or anything else. I just want you safe, Talyn."

"And that's how I feel about *you*."

Yet they were the greatest threat to each other. Felicia picked at her food. Honestly, she had no appetite for it.

He placed his cheek to hers. "Finish your dinner. I'm going to call Ferrick and get him started on transferring funds."

She held him to her. "I don't need a contract to be yours, Talyn. Screw Andarion custom and laws."

"Love you, too." He kissed her, then left.

Alone, she touched her throbbing cheek and winced at how much it burned and ached. Like it was on fire. Her eye was still watering from the blow. Anatole had barely struck her. She couldn't imagine what it would feel like to take the blows that Talyn did in a single fight.

Worse were the hints of the horror stories Anatole had sneered at her about Talyn while he'd tried to drag her into his transport. Covering her ears, she closed her eyes and did her best to blot it all out.

She still couldn't believe what Talyn was willing to do to bail her out from this. It was more than any male should have to do for a female who wasn't his blood or wife.

"I will pay you back," she whispered. "Every last bit of credit."

And somehow, she was going to find her own way to permanently remove Anatole from their lives. Even if she had to kill him herself.

Chapter 20

"Where is she?" Galene pulled up short in the foyer as she eyed Talyn leaving the kitchen to head back to their bedroom.

She'd made remarkable time, crossing town. He'd only called her a short time ago to ask her what he should do to help Felicia. He'd barely finished saying Felicia had been attacked before his mother beelined to them.

She hugged him close. "Are *you* okay?"

He shook his head as another wave of fury scalded his throat. "I want to kill the bastard who's responsible, Matarra. It's all I can think about."

She cupped his face in her hands. "I know, baby. I know."

Guilt, fear, and impudent rage suffused every molecule of his body. "If Aaron hadn't been paying attention, she'd be in his hands. Right now." He ground his teeth. "I came so close to losing her . . ."

Nodding, she blinked back her tears. "Don't you worry, precious. I'll stay tonight and make sure she's not left alone for anything. And I already put a call in to Jayne. She's going to handle security for Felicia. No one will get near her again. I promise you."

"Tell her to bill me."

His mother gave him an irritated glare. "You know better than that." She kissed his cheek and went to the bedroom. As soon as she saw Felicia, she cursed.

Felicia's eyes widened as she met Galene's gaze. "Commander? What are you doing here?"

"I came as soon as I heard. How are you doing?"

"Wondering how Talyn can stand up after a fight. I never realized how much it hurt to be hit."

Nodding, Galene sat down on the bed beside her to inspect her cheek and lip. "I know. I was struck once in training and my eye watered for days." She cupped Felicia's chin in her hand and tilted her head back very gently. "I'm so sorry about this."

"It wasn't your fault."

"I somehow feel like it is."

"Don't, Commander. I'll be much more vigilant in the future. No more texting while I walk."

Galene patted her hand. "Have you told your brother?"

"Not yet." She cut her gaze toward Talyn. "I figured one highly irate male filled with bloodlust was all I could handle tonight. Like you, Lorens would head straight over, and then I have a bad feeling the two of *them* would team up and go looking for a head to bust."

Galene laughed.

Talyn, not so much. "He needs to be found and taken out of the gene pool."

Felicia gestured at him. "See."

Completely unrepentant, he crossed his arms over his chest. "My job is to protect the females who are important to me. I'm not my father. I don't walk away from my responsibilities."

"You shouldn't blame your father for that, Talyn. He didn't know I was pregnant when he left me. That is solely on me for bad judgment. Had he known, he wouldn't have left."

Talyn let out a derisive scoff.

"Why didn't you tell him?" Felicia asked Galene.

"I didn't want him to stay out of obligation. That would have been wrong. As stupid as it sounds, I wanted him with me because he loved me. That is where *I* was selfish. If I could go back, if I'd only known then how hard that decision would make Talyn's life, I'd have told him and just dealt with it. But I was a stupid kid who thought that things would work out differently. That somehow magic fairies would swoop in and make it all wonderful and fun. I had no idea just how mean-spirited and cruel Andarions could be. Never mind my own family."

Talyn touched his mother's shoulder. "You did what you thought was best."

"For me." Closing her eyes, Galene moved his hand to her cheek. "I'm so sorry for what I've done to you. I wish I could change that day and my reaction."

"Matarra, don't. It's been my honor to be your son. Regardless of assholes."

Felicia wasn't sure which of them was crying harder. Her or his mother. Galene pulled Talyn into her arms. "No mother has ever borne a better son." She kissed his cheek.

As Talyn pulled back, the intercom buzzed. Excusing himself, he went to answer it.

No sooner had he left the room than Galene's link buzzed, too.

Suddenly afraid, Felicia swallowed. "Is there something wrong? Are we under attack?"

Galene scowled even more deeply as she met her gaze. "Talyn's signed up for four blood title matches? Is he out of his mind?"

Felicia sputtered, unsure of what to say.

"I'll kill him!" Furious, Galene got up to go after him.

Suddenly terrified for Talyn should his mother get her hands on him, Felicia followed and drew up short as an older couple entered the foyer to meet Talyn, who was waiting for them.

She exchanged a confused frown with Galene as she belted her robe over her nightgown.

Solemn and respectful, Talyn inclined his head to the couple.

The elder male appeared as baffled as they were. His disbelieving gaze danced over Talyn. "Major Batur?"

"Was. I'm now Lieutenant Batur."

The fury in the older male's eyes was tangible. "Because of what you did for our daughter?"

"For many reasons."

The female looked past his shoulder. "Your mother and female?"

Talyn stepped back. "Yes. Deputy Commander Galene of the Winged Blood Clan of Batur and Ger Tarra Felicia . . . this is Pyra and Selahan of the Fighting Blood Clan of Altaan."

Felicia choked up as he gave her the highest honor by claiming her as his true lady.

Pyra smiled as tears filled her eyes. Covering her heart, she bowed her head to them. "It is my greatest honor to meet you both, and especially you, Commander. I commend you on your noble and honorable son. He is a light to our race."

"Indeed," Selahan agreed. "He is a credit to you both."

Her hand shaking, Pyra pulled out a set of prayer beads that held a small Asukarian emblem on the end of them. "I don't know if you're Yllam Orthodox or not—"

"I am," Talyn breathed.

She smiled as a tear slid down her cheek. "These were my Berra's. They belonged to her grandmother who gave them to her as a Confirmation gift. It would be our eternal honor to hand them over for your child, one day."

"Ger Tarra, I can't take a piece of your family history."

She pressed them into his hand. "Please. I know what you did for my precious daughter. How hard you fought to keep her safe. Had it not been for you and your friends, we would have never known what happened to her. Never had her body to send her on her way to eternity. She would want you to have these so that she can always watch over and protect what you love."

In true Andarion fashion, Talyn cupped her hands with his

and inclined his head to her—a gesture of supreme respect and appreciation. "I shall treasure them always."

She rose up and placed her cheek to his. "Thank you."

When Talyn went to salute her father, he pulled Talyn into a tight hug. "May the gods watch over and protect you, son. Always." Then he pressed his cheek against Talyn's as well. "Thank you for doing what you could." Pulling back, he saluted Galene, who returned it with tears in her eyes.

"I'm very sorry for your loss," Felicia breathed. "I know the gods and saints are welcoming her home."

"Thank you." They bowed respectfully before they left.

Felicia moved to rub Talyn's back while he ran the beads through his fingers. "Berra?"

"Nightdice. I tried to keep Anatole from attacking her and Syndrome. They were both punished for it, and she died on Onoria right as I was rescued."

"I'm so sorry."

He turned and wrapped her in a hold so tight, she could barely breathe. "I won't let that happen to you, Felicia. Whatever it takes, I *will* keep you safe. To my dying breath."

"And what about you?" Galene asked angrily. "You are *my* baby, Talyn. But right now . . . it's taking everything I have not to shoot you where you stand."

Releasing Felicia, Talyn went pale. "What? What did I do?"

She held the link out to him. "I'm on the Ring newswire. Ferrick just released to the media that you've accepted blood matches with the Mortician, Widowmaker, Soulless, and

Slaughter House? What the hell is this? Why would you do something so stupid? Have you lost your mind?"

He clenched his teeth before he answered. "I had a reduction in pay and rank."

Shaking her head, she moved to confront him. "I forbid this! Do you hear me? They are four of the most *ruthless* killers in the business. They make Death Warrant look like a petulant schoolboy. All of them pride themselves on killing anyone dumb enough to step into the Ring to fight them. You've *always* refused their invitations. Why would you accept now? For a title blood match, no less!" She turned to Felicia. "Talk to him! Tell him no!"

Felicia swallowed hard as she met Talyn's sullen gaze. "What's a blood match? Is that different from normal somehow?"

"Oh yeah," Galene said, breathlessly. "Blood matches are fought with Warswords."

For a moment, Felicia couldn't breathe. Talyn had left one *extremely* important detail out of their discussion. At no time had he told her he'd be fighting to the death . . . with swords! Good thing he outweighed her by about ten times over. Otherwise, she'd start a blood match with the Hammer early.

Like here and now.

Dizzy with fear, she gaped at him. "Why *them*? With *that*?"

He glanced to his mother before he responded. "Bloodier the match, the higher the purse. We needed a full house. It's what I told Ferrick to do. I handpicked them as my opponents."

Felicia felt sick to her stomach. "I'm with your mother. I

don't want you up against anyone with those names. Definitely not with swords. Are you crazy?"

"I have *no* choice." He looked from her to his mother. "I can't even put in for a promotion for *three* full years. Walking into the Ring with them isn't as dangerous as what I do every time I report to post. Especially *now*." He flicked his claws against the scars on his shoulders that marked him as an Outcast. "So long as I bear these marks, any Andarion who sees them is honor bound to attack me. At least they pay me in the Ring. And I can legally fight back there."

Galene shook her head in denial. "Tylie promised that she'd get you transferred to the palace again. And that wasn't to me. She made that promise to her sister, who wants you under my command."

"And Tylie isn't the tadara," he growled. "She doesn't run the military. She's never even worn a uniform. I'm a fighter, Mum. It's all I know to do. The tadara herself reduced my rank. You think for one minute that bitch is going to let me into her personal guard and that close to her family members I want to tear the throats out of? Unfortunately, she's not quite *that* stupid."

Growling, Galene flicked her claws at him. "I'd throw dirt at you if I had some." Furious, she left them, cursing him and his father under her breath as she headed to her guest room in back.

Talyn met Felicia's arched brow. "She needs to calm down. I can't talk to her when she's like this. She's completely unreasonable. My luck, she'll shoot me, just to keep me out of the Ring."

"Maybe she should. The gods know, I'm tempted."

"We talked about this, Licia."

"No. You talked about fighting. Not . . ." She gestured after his mother. "Walking into a killing match with Andarions out for your throat and wielding Warswords."

"It's why they call the Ring the Splatterdome and not the Land of the Pink Fluffy Bunnies." He bit his lip before he spoke again. "What do you want me to do, Felicia? Pull guard duty in Anatole's bedroom and watch while he violates you? 'Cause I promise you, that's what he's planning to do."

She reached to touch him, then quickly pulled away. "I can't do this, Talyn. I can't risk your life for my freedom. My God, what if something happens to you in one of those fights?"

He turned on her with his eyes blazing. "I'd rather die than have that animal lay his hands on you. Sooner or later, death comes for us all. None of us can stop that. But I'm not going quietly to my grave. Whether it's tomorrow or a hundred years from now, I'm checking out with blood on my fists. Fighting every step of the way into eternity."

Wanting to kill him herself, she pulled his head down so that she could press her forehead to his. "I want to beat you so badly I can taste it. You are so infuriating!"

"And you love me for it."

She bit his chin.

Hissing, he pulled back. "Ow!"

"You're lucky that's all I can bring myself to do to you. Because what I really want is to take a paddle to your butt like an angry priestess catching your hand in the temple collection bin."

"Now you're just trying to turn me on."

As his mother had done, she flicked her nails at him. "Don't even try to make this a sexual thing. You're sleeping in another room tonight."

"Felicia—"

"I mean it, Talyn. I'm so mad at you that I don't trust myself to be in the same bed with you right now while you're defenseless."

A tic started in his jaw. He was far from defenseless. At least against anyone other than Felicia.

"Fine," he snapped, heading for the bedroom. He grabbed his pillow from the bed. "Sleep alone. I'm a big boy. I can take it. The gods know I've taken worse." He headed for a room farther down the hall.

Felicia started after him.

Don't you dare!

You let him stew until he comes to his senses!

She forced herself to go to the bedroom and lock the door. This wasn't about his hurt feelings. It was about saving his life. Honestly, she wanted to vomit at the mere thought of his going up against those monsters to buy her from her agency. She wished she'd never found out that was what he'd done to get her this condo and to buy her contract in the first place.

Patrons were supposed to be old males whose wives were tired of servicing them. Or widowers who wanted companions to take care of them until they could find a respectable family to pledge with. Seventy-five . . . that was the average age for a patron. Seventy-five. Not twenty! Her own father had been well into his fifties when he contracted with her mother.

She'd never heard of a patron as young as Talyn before. Which had been part of the reason she'd agreed to meet him.

Utter curiosity.

Unless they were pledged or married, males Talyn's age went to prostitutes. That was how their society worked.

His mother was right, he'd never done anything in his life like other Andarions did. Ugh! She could kick his—

Talyn's link went off.

She looked over to answer it and froze as she saw the name Jayne and the picture of an incredibly beautiful female blowing a kiss.

What the hell was *that*?

Before she could recover from the shock, it rolled to the speaker voice mail he used whenever he was home.

"Hey, sexy baby. It's Jaynie calling about your girl problems. As always, I'm more than happy to take care of your needs, and will be there as soon as I can. Just hold tight and stay precious, my beautiful sweet cheeks. Don't want to see no frownie baby when I get there. I promise, I'm going to put a giant smile on that gorgeous face of yours. Love you, sexy T! See you soon."

Her jaw slack, Felicia wasn't sure what pissed her off the most. The woman's looks. Her words. Or that exaggerated high-pitched sopping, sweet, sultry voice. Maybe it was all three that came together to light a fury in her so foul, she could taste the Talyn-blood she intended to let.

Oh, forget the Ring. The Splatterdome was here. Tonight. This condo. And she was going to get her pound of Iron Hammer flesh.

• • •

Snarling in aggravation, Talyn slammed his fist into the pillow as he tried to get comfortable on the bed. He still couldn't believe Felicia had thrown him out of his room, given everything he'd done to make her happy.

Did she think he *wanted* to fight those animals? Did his mom? Who did his females think they were to be pissed off at *him*?

Everything he did, he did for his mother and Felicia.

Face it, you can't please anyone! Andarions suck! Females most of all.

The door opened. For a second, his heart lightened at Felicia's appearance.

Until she furiously hurled his link at him so hard that had it made contact with his body, it would have hurt.

"You rank, two-timing bastard!" Felicia seized his pillow, snatched it from under his head, and started beating him with it. "Stralen, my ass!"

Talyn lifted his arm to protect himself. Damn, for a pillow, it hurt more than it should have. "What is wrong with you?"

"Besides you? Nothing! Not a damn thing. I hate you!"

Talyn jerked the pillow out of her hands. She moved to actually bite him.

With fangs.

Talyn caught her and rolled with her so that he could pin her on the bed. Gently, he held her hands by her face.

Shrieking, she tried to buck him off.

If he wasn't afraid of being gelded, he'd laugh at her useless efforts. His thigh bone weighed more than she did.

"Felicia, what is wrong with you?"

"Who the fuck is Jayne, Talyn? Huh? You should have taken your link with you, you faithless bastard!"

Instead of clearing things up, that only confused him more. "What?"

" 'Sweet cheeks'? 'Stay sexy'? You bastard! I hate you!"

It was a stupid thing to do, but he couldn't help himself. He laughed.

Which made her scream like he was murdering her.

His mother came running into the room and pulled up short as she saw them entangled, half dressed on the bed. Yeah, this was awkward. He was wearing his short military briefs and Felicia's gown had ridden up so that it looked like some kind of sex game. Her face turned bright red.

"Ma!" he shouted as she beat a hasty retreat. "Come back. It's not what you think."

She spoke around the doorframe. "Should I ask what it is, then?"

"Tell Felicia who Jayne is."

"Jayne Erixour?"

"Yeah. 'Cause I don't think she's going to believe me if I tell her." He slid off Felicia.

Shoving her gown down, she glared at him as his mother returned to the room.

Galene bit her lip. "Oh dear gods, what did Jaynie do now?"

"Who is she, Commander?" Felicia asked.

"My best friend. Talyn's other mother."

Felicia frowned. "What?"

Talyn picked his pillow up and returned it to the bed. "Remember when I told you I had a teacher take me home and watch over me until my mother was released from the hospital?"

"Yeah."

"Jaynie."

"No," Felicia said, shaking her head. "Play her message back and tell me *that* sounds like a teacher, mother figure."

Inwardly cringing, he rubbed a hand over his face. "Gah, I can just imagine. Aunt Jayne is a unique individual. Unlike any you've ever met. The fact they ever let her into a classroom says a lot about the Hyshian educational system." He pulled his link to him and listened. And with every word, he screwed his face up harder. Yeah, okay, he'd beat him, too.

He handed the link to his mother for her to hear. She sighed heavily. "Yeah, that's Jayne." She handed it back to him. "What did you call her about?"

"The security for Felicia that you'd mentioned." He passed a dry look to her. "That's my 'girl problem' she's referring to."

"Why would a mother figure call you sexy?"

"It's Jayne," he and his mother said in unison.

Galene nodded. "She's been calling him sexy since he was in grade school."

"Really?"

Talyn scratched sheepishly at his ear. "I went to school with Hyshians, Licia. I felt like a hideous freak, all the time. Jayne started calling me that so I'd feel better about myself. Didn't really work since everyone else looked at me like a diseased flea that was about to give them an incurable, alien disease, but it was her way of trying."

Still sitting on the bed, she drew her legs up to her chest and wrapped her arms around them. Peeking at him over her knees, she gave him a most adorable pout. "Sorry. But you have to admit, that call was pretty damning."

"Yeah. Vintage Jayne."

His mother laughed. "Since there's no murder going on, I'll leave you two to sort this out." She made a quick exit.

Talyn hesitated. "Is it safe, or do I need to gird my loins for battle?"

"You might want to gird a bit. I'm still mad about the other matter. . . . Did you really call Jayne about security for me?"

"Of course, I did. And Jayne's the one who rescued me from Onoria. Hadrian, who you met, is her husband. They have kids together. You would have met her, too, but she had to jettison for other obligations with The Sentella while they were bringing me home."

Now she felt utterly stupid. While she'd known Hadrian's wife had been with them, no one had mentioned Jayne by name.

She crooked her finger for him to come closer.

Talyn hesitated. He wasn't real sure of her mood. Because he hadn't spent much time around anyone other than his mother, Jayne, and her husband, he wasn't real good at reading others' emotions.

And, well . . . Jayne and his mother made it easy. When they were pissed, they launched into highly hostile verbal assaults that ended with an ass beating and restriction. As for Jayne's husband, Hadrian was extremely even-keeled and showed as much emotion as a statue, most days.

He inched toward her. "Should I remove projectiles?"

"No," she said sullenly. "Come here, Talyn."

Bracing himself for the worst, he obeyed. "Yes?"

She toyed with his ear. "I'm sorry. For everything. Just not used to caring this much about someone else. Twice now, I've had to sit in a hospital because you were seriously hurt. And I've seen what you look like after a fight. It's not pretty." She gestured toward the bruise on her face. "And now that I've been hit, I have a whole new appreciation for what you go through. How do you stand it?"

He shrugged nonchalantly. "I was an Andarion in a Hyshian school. I couldn't get into trouble because if my mother was called in for counseling, she'd be punished by the military for it. The other students knew I couldn't fight back, so it was open season on me. Same for the teachers. They were scared of me and it made them vicious. When I came home, I couldn't let my mother know about it or she'd cry and feel guilty. So I learned to take the blows and hide the bruises. It's all I've ever known." He brushed the hair back from her face. "It only hurts when you're the one attacking me. One mild insult from you is like a dagger through my heart."

She pressed her cheek to his. "I love you so much."

"I love you, too. There's nothing I wouldn't do for you."

"Yeah, I noticed. Only a special kind of idiot would get into a Ring with that lineup."

"Yes, but I'll always be *your* special idiot."

She finally laughed. "When will Jayne get here?"

He shrugged. "She'll be coming in interstellarly, if not intergalactically. Could be a couple of days. I'd call her back, but I'm afraid you might hurt me."

She rolled her eyes at him. "You can talk to your aunt Jayne. I won't say a word."

"You sure? 'Cause I'll toss her right out."

She handed him his link. "Call her, goofball."

"I can't do that. If I call her goofball, she'll kick my ass, and she's not a small woman. Not to mention, she's a trained assassin."

She arched a brow at the thought. "How is a teacher a trained assassin?"

He laughed at her confusion. "She's the daughter of Egarious Toole. He's an infamous underworld mastermind and thief on Hyshia. Jayne was in and out of lockups as a kid. So, as a young adult, right after she married, she tried to go straight for a bit. Ended up getting pulled back into the dark side, and now works for The Sentella."

"Ahh," she said as she finally put it all together. "She's the friend your mother didn't name, but called. Got it."

He nodded. "It's why I know so much about The Sentella. I figured if anyone could help us, it would be they. Anatole won't be able to touch them. They're not Andarion citizens or soldiers. He has no authority over their group."

"They could still be arrested for assaulting a royal. Not to mention, the tadara is no friend of theirs."

"Yes, but Anatole isn't *the* tahrs and he's not worth an interplanetary incident. And while I expect him to try something, Jayne is a goddess of creative solutions. I trust her implicitly."

"Then can't you join The Sentella?"

In theory. But since he knew his paternal uncle was one of their key members, it made it rather awkward. While Jayne had often commented on how much they favored, both he and his mother had laughed it off by saying all Andarions looked alike to Hyshians. But Dancer would know the minute he laid eyes on him that they were related. He shared too many traits with his father and uncles for it not to be obvious.

"I'd have to leave the Ring circuit to do that. And I wouldn't be able to take care of my mother if I was one of them."

"You can't help it, can you?"

"Help what?"

"Thinking of your mother first."

"She has no one else. Because of me. It would be wrong to turn my back on her after she gave up everything to keep me with her. I might not be a lot of things, but I'm never ungrateful."

No, he wasn't. Felicia ran her finger down the stubble on his chin, marveling at how handsome he was even without hair. She didn't even see the scars on his body. Not until he pointed them out.

"Take your contacts out, Talyn."

"Why?"

"I want to make love to you, as you really are. No pretense. No walls. Just you and me."

He took them out so fast, it left her laughing.

"Eager, are you?"

He pulled his briefs off. "I have a beautiful female in my bed, wanting me naked. What do you think?"

"I think you're preciously annoying."

"So long as you consider me doably annoying, I'm good with that."

Rising up on her knees in the bed, she cradled his body with hers. "I will always consider you doable." She fell back onto the bed, pulling him with her. Felicia ran her finger over his eyebrow as she marveled at the fact he was stralen. "You look so different like this."

"Does it frighten you?"

She shook her head. "The only thing that scares me is how much I love you. And how sure I am that the gods are going to do something to take you from me because of it."

Talyn wanted to reassure her, but he couldn't. Not in good conscience. He had the same fear in his heart that she did. The gods had never been kind to him. Rather, he'd been their punching bag from the moment he'd been born prematurely and almost died seconds after drawing his first breath to this moment. "I will never willingly leave you."

Smiling, she kissed his lips and wrapped her body around his. "I know, *keramon*. Same here. I will fight for you. Always."

He laughed at that. "Did you really pull a blaster on a doctor?"

She cringed. "Who told you that?"

"Jayne's husband."

Felicia nibbled at his jaw. "I'm your female, Talyn. Like you, I protect what I love with everything I have."

His breathing ragged, Talyn savored those words that meant the universe to him. Unable to stand the intensity of what he felt for her, he slid himself into her body.

She gasped, then moaned in his ear. Closing his eyes, he ground his teeth at how good she felt in his arms.

Please don't let me lose her.

But no matter how hard he tried, he feared what tomorrow would bring for them. What new shit Anatole would hurl at him.

Most of all, he feared that he might have very well signed his own death warrant in the Ring with those blood matches. Neither his mother nor Felicia knew the whole truth about those fighters.

Even though it hadn't been a blood match at that time, Talyn had taken the Zoftiq title from Slaughterhouse.

Don't get used to it, punk. Next time we meet in the Ring, you're going home in pieces.

This time, Duel Odelus wouldn't be going into the fight as a cocky title holder, he'd be coming into the Splatterdome motivated by vengeance, and craving a death match with every piece of his being.

If I have to lose, let him kill me. The last thing Talyn wanted was to be crippled for the rest of his life.

But he didn't want to think about tomorrow right now. Not while he was with Felicia. His blood racing, he buried his face in her wealth of curls and tightened his arms around her.

Felicia cried out at the intensity of Talyn's passion. Normally, he took his time and meticulously explored her. Tonight, he was ferocious, almost desperate.

She nipped his chin, delighting in the feel of his whiskers. A smile curved her lips as he met her gaze and she stared into his bloodred eyes that held the faintest outline of white around the edges. The total opposite of what they'd been when she first met him.

Out of habit, she started to cup his head, then quickly caught herself. Since they'd shaved his hair, he'd been extremely self-conscious over it. Instead of it being comforting, he would recoil from her touching his head. The last thing she wanted was to hurt him in any way.

Growling in her ear, he quickened his strokes. Felicia sucked her breath in as her body exploded with pleasure.

With the sweetest smile, Talyn kissed her forehead an instant before he came in her arms. His breathing ragged, he stared down at her with the most adoring gaze imaginable.

Until he glanced to the bruise on her cheek. Guilt replaced the happiness as he withdrew from her.

"Talyn?"

He gently brushed his fingers over her cheek. "I'm tired of living in an empire where a female can't even walk home with dinner and not be attacked. Where no one feels safe. This is not what I want to defend. It's not what I swore to uphold when I joined the armada."

"What are you saying?"

He gentled his expression before he pressed his cheek to hers. "I'm just venting. I'll be right back." He kissed her before he went to the bathroom.

Talyn paused at the door to look back at Felicia. She was so beautiful in his bed. So frail and tiny. In all his life, she was the only thing he'd ever craved. The only one he'd ever love.

He could handle anything so long as she was here at the end of the day to lay her gentle hand on his skin. No one was ever going to hurt or scare her again. He'd tear this empire down to ashes before he allowed that to happen.

Making sure to keep it out of her sight, he set his link on the counter and closed the door. Before he could stop himself, he texted her brother.

The party at my house is on. Just let me know the details.

While he'd never thought of himself as a traitor or a revolutionary, he was willing to see the tadara and her entire family in the ground, if that was what it took to keep his family safe. The Anatoles should have known better than to start a war with a Hauk and a Batur.

The day had come to change out the ruling parties. And he was the Andarion to see this through.

He hadn't started this fight. But by all the gods, he was going to finish it.

CHAPTER 21

"What in the name of all Andaria are you doing?"

Talyn froze midswing at Felicia's angry tone, unsure about her confusion over his current activity. Surely it was obvious, given his workout shorts and gloves. "Training."

Her face a mask of fury, she closed the distance between them. "You're supposed to be in bed. It's only been a few days since you were released from the hospital."

Wiping at the sweat on his brow, he returned to swinging at the doublebag. "Doesn't matter. I have to get back into shape as soon as I can. Once I report for duty, I doubt I'll have much training time."

And the first of his blood matches was looming before him.

She moved to block him, and softened her expression. "Honey, I'm a physical therapist. *Your* physical therapist. Your body isn't ready for this kind of abuse. You need to rest."

"Fel—"

"Talyn." She reached up to touch his lips and melt his will

in the process. "Don't argue. Get your hulking butt back in bed. Now!"

A feminine laugh sounded in the doorway. "Wow. It's like watching a tiny little kitten yell at a rhino. I can see why you like her, sexy baby. She's fearless."

Felicia frowned at the foreign female voice until she saw Jayne. Heat stung her cheeks at having been caught chastising Talyn.

Smiling, Talyn peeled his gloves off and went to her. "Jaynie! How's my favorite aunt?" He kissed her on the cheek.

"Doing great. Sorry it took so long to get here. Had another dire situation with a friend that couldn't wait."

By Talyn's expression, Felicia could tell he knew exactly who Jayne meant. "Is he okay?"

Jayne nodded. "He will be. We pulled him out and I left him with Hadrian, then headed straight here."

As they talked, Felicia felt truly inadequate. While Jayne's photo had been attractive, it didn't compare to the live version of the female. With long black hair swept up into a messy bun and wearing a black battlesuit that hugged a body honed by countless gym hours, Jayne was the kind of female most magazines had to airbrush into existence.

And she latched on to Talyn like a mother who hadn't seen her child in far too long. She hugged him until he protested.

"Bruised ribs. Bruised ribs."

Tsking at him, Jayne let go and chucked his chin. "So how's my sexy baby? Your mom said I got you into all kinds of trouble with your girl."

"Yes, you did." He stepped back. "Jayne, meet my Felicia."

Jayne approached her with a piercing stare that said the female took in a lot more than just Felicia's physical appearance. "You look so tiny and harmless. But there's a fire in your eyes that says you would and could kick my ass if you had to. I finally believe Hadrian's story about the hospital."

Felicia smiled at the truth. "If you're going to rattle my cage, you better make sure I'm padlocked in it."

Jayne hugged her. "I love that and I'm stealing it. It's a pleasure to meet you, Tara Felicia." Taking her hand, she pulled Felicia to the door, where Talyn was still standing. "Now allow me to introduce you to your two new best friends. Qorach and Morra."

Felicia pulled up short as the largest male she'd ever seen stepped into the room. Holy gods! Her jaw went slack.

As did Talyn's.

The man was at least half a foot taller than he was. For that matter, he was even broader, with muscles that were every bit as defined as Talyn's. They were just bigger. A *lot* bigger. His head was shaved and held only the tiniest trace of black hair trying to grow back in. Fierce and deadly, he inclined his head to them and stepped to the side to reveal the tiny woman behind him.

Since she was wearing a black battlesuit identical to Jayne's and Qorach's, the only part of her skin that was visible was her neon green face and neck. The vivid color was interrupted by black markings that at first seemed to be painted on. But up close, it was obvious that intricate design was actually her skin, too. Her long, straight black hair was pulled back into a ponytail that hung over her right shoulder.

And she was as tiny as Qorach was huge. She barely reached midchest on Felicia, who was barefoot. Compared to the males, Morra barely reached their waists.

"I know," Morra said with a sigh. "I'm basically here to tie Qory's shoes. They're just too dang far down for him to reach them on his own."

Qorach gave her a droll stare as Felicia laughed at her unexpected comment.

"And to answer the questions everyone has when they first meet me, but those with manners are too nice to ask . . . No. I don't glow in the dark. So don't even think of using me for a glowstick. Yes, I'm this green all over. Even my lips are neon green, as are my nail beds. The red lipstick and nail polish are a personal choice. And no, I have no intention of proving it. You'll just have to take my word for it, as I only drop pants for super hot and sexy green men. I'm a Schvardan from Phrixus. We're the land-walkers, which is what *schvarda* means in Phrixian. And while you might think I'm small, so are the deadliest explosive devices. Think of me like that tiny little bomb that can take off all your limbs and destroy half the city when it blows, and we'll get along fine. . . . And yes, frog jokes are highly offensive to me and I will hurt you for making them. Now, let me go catch a fly. I'm a little low on protein."

Qorach made several hand gestures at her.

"No, I'm not saying that. And no one ever asks about you, anyway. They're too afraid to."

He grinned proudly at that.

Morra turned her attention back to Felicia and Talyn. "He can only speak with Qillaq sign language, and some League. So, I'm his translator for most things."

Felicia cocked her head at that. "How similar are Qillaq signs to League or Andarion?"

"More similar to League gestures than Andarion. You speak League?"

Felicia gestured at Qorach. His entire face lit up as he responded.

Morra slapped at Jayne's arm. "Well hell, I just got rendered useless. Look at them go!"

Jayne nodded. "I'm impressed."

"I'm concerned," Talyn added quickly. "I'm not sure I like this."

"No." Felicia gestured more. "Talyn doesn't sign."

Talyn snorted. "Not true. I know obscene gestures in fourteen languages."

They all burst out laughing.

Qorach began signing again.

Felicia frowned. "But I don't know all of those signs."

Morra smiled. "He says it's an honor to be assigned protective detail to such a generous and intelligent lady. And for Talyn not to worry. While he's pretty sure he could kick Talyn's ass, he knows for a fact that Jayne would cut his testicles off to protect her sexy baby."

Talyn let out a tired sigh. "I'm going to be ninety and you're still going to call me that, aren't you?"

Jayne patted his cheek lovingly. When she spoke, it was in the high-pitched tone reserved for mothers talking to small children or pet animals. "Yes, I will, my sexy baby." She glanced around the gym. "I have to say, this is a nice place. When you first called, I was worried about having space for my team. But I can see that there's plenty of room, even for Qory." She turned back to Felicia. "I know he's huge, but I wanted someone who would intimidate Andarion males and make them rethink any stupid ideas they might have where you're concerned."

"I would say you succeeded admirably."

Jayne winked at Talyn's comment. "It was a tall order, and yes, you walked right into that one. As Hadrian says, my family motto is 'anything worth doing is worth overdoing.' And Morra's orders are to stay with Felicia even when you go potty. It's why I have a female in the mix. Until we get this resolved, they are your shadows, night and day. They will give you privacy inside the condo when Talyn is in residence. Only. When he's gone, Morra will be your new bed buddy. We're not going to take *any* chances."

"Don't worry," Morra said with a bright smile. "I don't take up much room and I don't move when I sleep. My people nest in trees or off mountains. Once you fall out of your bunk or off your shelf, you learn not to be a restless sleeper."

"Shelf?"

"Canopies on the side of mountains. Phrixus is a very dangerous place with a lot of deadly creatures. It's why our races are lethal. We had to be, to survive. And it's also why the Naglfari cowards took to the seas to live. They couldn't cut it on Phrixian land."

Felicia frowned at the unfamiliar term. "Naglfari?"

"They're the pasty repugnant semisentient creatures that most know as Phrixian. They're more human in appearance than the Schvardans. And my race is even more xenophobic than they are."

Deciding to change the topic away from something that was obviously an emotional trigger for Morra, Felicia inclined her head to them all. "I can't thank you enough for agreeing to this. While I don't relish the thought of being shadowed, I don't want Talyn distracted by unnecessary worries for my safety. And honestly, I've been really skittish since the attack."

"She's been completely housebound," Talyn added, "which isn't her nature."

"Well, part of that is I didn't want to leave you while you've been recovering, either." Felicia gestured at the training gloves. "And as we've seen, I can't exactly turn my back on *you* lest I find you into something you shouldn't be." She glanced to Jayne. "While I show Qorach and Morra where to bunk, would you please make sure Talyn stands down from training? I want the gloves stowed and his gorgeous bottom attached to a seat of some kind."

Jayne gave her a sharp military salute. "Yes, ma'am."

"Thank you." Felicia led the other two to the guest rooms she'd set up for them. She showed Qorach to his first, and then Morra.

As she started to leave, Morra stopped her. "Okay, so here's my question that I didn't want to ask in front of Jayne, who would have taken my head for it. But . . . why haven't you chained that luscious piece of male to your bed? Holy gods, Felicia! If I had unrestricted access to *that,* I'd never walk straight again."

Felicia laughed. "It's not easy. I have to admit, I do get frequent spontaneous urges to straddle him."

Sucking her breath in sharply, Morra shook her hand in a gesture of supreme appreciation. "The fact you can restrain yourself at all amazes me." She let out a low whistle. "I'm not normally attracted to other species, but dang . . . you a lucky female to have full access to *that* body."

"Should I be worried?"

Morra laughed. "No. If I was going to make a move on him, I wouldn't be telling you I'm lusting for him. What am I? Nuts? Besides, Qory's the only male I'd ever trust at my back."

"Oh. I didn't even consider that. Would you like to be in the same room?"

"Nuh-uh. That's not what I meant. I love and adore him, but we're family. He's my best friend, brother, and drinking bud. Not my boyfriend or lover. Told you . . . I like my men green. And not just behind their ears." Morra began unpacking an insane amount of firearms and weaponry Felicia couldn't even identify, nor had she any idea the female had strapped that amount underneath her clothes.

"Should I ask?"

"Sentella. We fight hard." She looked up with a wicked grin. "And I fight to win."

"You sound a lot like Talyn. I'm beginning to think I *should* be worried."

Morra laughed. "Relax, sweetie. I have a very strict dating code. I would never take another female's heart. Besides, the way he looks at you . . . he doesn't even know I possess female body parts. Trust me. I could walk in butt naked, shake it in his face, and his only question would be, 'Have you seen Felicia?' "

Snorting, Felicia shook her head. "I know we just met, but I really like you."

"It's the green thing. Me and fungi. We grow on things fast."

"Yeah, right. I'm glad you're the ones Jayne brought. I doubt anyone else would be half as entertaining. . . . I'll let you get settled. When you and Qorach are ready, let me know and I'll show you around."

"Thanks."

Felicia returned to the gym to find Talyn sitting with his back to her and drinking water while he and Jayne had a rather loud discussion.

"Keep the creds, boy. Don't you even insult me with that! You're not taking money from me or my family, and I include The Sentella with that. And I'm not taking money from *you*. Your mother told me they reduced your pay."

"I didn't ask for charity, Jayne."

"And I'm not giving you any. What am I, a stranger?"

"No, but—"

"No buts. You and your mom *are* my family, too. What *you* love, I love. What threatens you, threatens me. It's that simple, T.

So don't argue or I'll put you over my knee and spank you. I don't care how big you think you are."

He laughed. "You've never spanked me."

Smiling, Jayne rubbed his arm. "It's so weird to see you grown now. And with facial hair, no less. I still think of you as that studious little boy who sat so quietly in the corner of my room. Never making a peep. Always doing his work without prompting."

She brushed her hand over the faded bruises on his face. "I know many of the secrets you hide, Talyn. I've seen you stand strong against the maelstrom that would tear anyone else apart. But I also know the toll it takes to do that. While you are stronger than anyone I know, and I include Nemesis in that list, you're not invincible. I've been through and survived torture, too. I know how long it takes to get over the nightmares. Have you been sleeping at all?"

"Not really."

"Anxiety issues? Panic attacks?"

He gave a subtle nod. "Anger outbursts, too, that lead to . . . you know. It's why I was working out. I was hoping to burn it out of my system."

"Have you told Felicia?"

"No."

"She needs to know, Baby T. Nothing heals like the touch of a loved one."

"I don't want to burden her."

"You're not a burden." Felicia stepped forward to let them

know she was there. "Sorry. I didn't mean to eavesdrop. I just wanted to make sure that Talyn was following my orders."

Talyn flinched. "How much did you hear?"

"That you're having nightmares and not telling me about them. What's going on?"

He passed an irritated glare at Jayne. "It's nothing."

"Talyn . . . I'm not going to judge you. There's not a weak atom in your entire body and I know it. But you are Andarion. You are sentient and have feelings. There's no shame in admitting that."

He grimaced at her. "Really don't want to talk about it. Just want to forget it happened. Okay? That's how I deal with things. Can't change it. Move forward. There's no need to dwell on shit you can't fix."

She wrapped her arms around his waist. "Okay. I'll never bring it up again. But if you need me, I am here and I will listen without prejudice or judgment."

Jayne smiled at her. "You found a rare good one, T. Good job."

He frowned at Jayne. "Gah, you still sound like a teacher, who's grading me. Or even worse . . ." He made the noise of a circus animal and clapped his hands together.

Jayne laughed. "Can't help it. And you better be glad I don't have any raw fish to hand-feed you. Or I'd make you choke on it." She popped the side of his leg, then kissed his cheek. "Let me go check in with your mom and let her know that The Sentella has your back."

As Jayne wandered off, his military armband started buzzing.

"What the hell?" Talyn pulled out his link and called in to base.

Felicia could tell by his face that it was another outrageous demand.

His frown deepened. "I'm still under medical leave." He paused to listen. "Yes, sir. I'm on my way."

"What is it?"

"Apparently, my health is fine for a lieutenant's duty assignments. I have an hour to report to post or be considered AWOL."

"This is ridiculous!"

He sighed heavily. "Yeah, well. Can't really argue. They always win."

Felicia ground her teeth as she watched his labored gait. He was still in a lot of pain, though he had thankfully refused meds. Otherwise, Anatole would have him punished for it. No wonder Talyn was so paranoid.

Furious about this, she went to call her brother, who was every bit as pissed off about it as she was.

"Did the doctor clear him for active duty?"

"No. We were there just yesterday and I saw the file myself. The doctor said it would be at least three more weeks before Talyn would be fit to call in and request reactivation."

"Where's Talyn now?"

"Dressing."

"Have him report, and I'll meet him at the base. I don't want to give them any reason to take more action against him."

"Thank you, Lorens."

"Anytime, little sis."

Hanging up, she went to find Talyn pulling on his boots. While he looked gorgeous in his red and black uniform, she hated that he had to wear it. Worse, she had a bad feeling in her stomach about what was waiting for him when he returned to duty. "Where are you stationed now?"

He rose and reached for his beret. "Back to Anatole Base."

Under Anatole's direct command. She wanted to curse. "Barracks restriction again?"

"We're not married, so I have no choice. I don't know what my new schedule is. I'll e-mail it to you as soon as I do." Pulling her against him, he kissed her. "I wish I'd known last night was all we'd have. I wouldn't have gone to sleep."

Felicia blinked back the tears in her eyes. Tears that made her voice thick from the pain she felt over his leaving. "Please be careful."

"You, too. Don't leave without your guard."

"I won't. I wish I could send Qorach to protect *you*."

"Yeah, that wouldn't go over well. Besides, I don't need it. I can take care of myself." He tightened his arms around her. "I miss you already."

Taking a deep breath in her hair, he released her. "Your broker sent over the severance forms yesterday. I was going to give them to you at dinner." His brow furrowed by wistful longing, he twisted his finger in her hair. "You are officially released from their agency. Heads up, there's a nasty cover letter to remind you that if you continue an unsanctioned relationship with me, you will be considered a whore, and they'll be forced to report you as an unlicensed prostitute. They've *graciously,* according to their words, granted you thirty days to reconsider and return to them before they file with the courts. Just FYI, I went to the management office yesterday and transferred complete ownership of the condo over to you."

She gaped at his unexpected gift. "Why?"

"We have no papers or contract now, Felicia. If you're living in *my* condo without them, we'll both be arrested. Since I don't have any personal items here, and my official address is with the armada, it was the easiest solution. You don't have to worry about payments for it. I don't have any. I bought it outright. It's all yours. You can do whatever you want with it."

Agony tore through her at the anguished note in his voice. "This sounds like a good-bye."

He swallowed hard. "I don't know what it is. Honestly. But if something happens to me, I wanted to make sure that you're taken care of."

Her tears fell down her cheeks. "Talyn—"

"Shh." He silenced her with another kiss as he wiped away the tears. "You know I'm stralen for you, Felicia. Your life is far more important to me than mine is. And I understand that you don't have the same feelings for me that I have for you. I accept that. We both know we can't marry. And I'm the armada's and Anatole's bitch. I would never blame you if you left me. It's the smart thing to do. I just . . . I want you to be happy."

"*You're* what makes me happy. I'm going to find some way around this, Talyn. I swear it."

"I wish you luck. The gods know, I haven't been able to think of anything. But I do love you. Never, ever doubt that." He squeezed her gently one more time, then stepped back. "I'll call as soon as I can and let you know what my new orders are."

Unable to speak past the grief that choked her, she nodded and walked with him to the lift. Her heart broke for him. Most of all, it broke for her having to let him go when all she wanted to do was hold on tighter.

And after he released her hand and stepped inside the lift and the doors closed, she fell to her knees, sobbing.

An overwhelming fear that she'd never see him again tore through her. *I can't live without you, Talyn. Please, please don't leave me.*

CHAPTER 22

Talyn forced himself to slide his link into his pocket before he gave in to the ferocious need he had to call Felicia on his way back to post. He had to acclimate himself to not having her in his life.

To making it through the day without her smile in his heart.

It would be best to let her go. For all of them.

Strange, when he'd approached the agency to contract with her a few months ago, he'd never once considered that he might actually fall in love with his companion. He'd just wanted someone to be nice to him whenever he had a few hours of liberty. A female who would help with a simple biological necessity.

He'd assumed that she would treat him like everyone else did. Subpar. And watch the clock until he was gone and she could return to her life and friends.

The last thing he'd expected was a female who looked at him and treated him like he was fully Vested. One who actually liked him and wanted to spend time in his company.

Now . . .

Felicia owned him. Heart and soul. Mind and body. He wasn't really the armada's bitch.

He was Felicia's. Happily so. She was the one thing he couldn't live without. Worse, she was the one weakness that could destroy him.

Damn.

Leaving her was so painful. Like having a limb ripped from his body. *You're an idiot. Just let her go and move on.*

It was the sanest and safest thing to do.

The problem was learning how to live without her again. Which made no sense. He'd lived the vast majority of his life without any knowledge of her existence. She'd only been in his life for a few months.

Yet he needed her in ways he wouldn't have thought possible. For the first time, he was beginning to understand his mother and why she still loved his bastard father after everything he'd done to them. If she'd felt one-tenth of this for Fain Hauk, he totally got why she wouldn't let him bad-mouth the male who deserved it. Why his mother had never looked twice at anyone else.

Yes, some of it was the stralen. But even before it'd set in, Talyn had been viciously drawn to Felicia against all sanity. Honestly, he'd fallen in love with her picture before they even met. There had just been something in her eyes that had reached out to him and made him burn for her. Made him want to sink himself inside her warmth and hold her until time ended.

Talyn started to pull out the link and call her, until he realized it was too late. They were pulling in to base.

Damn it! He should have been talking to her the whole time. There was no telling when he'd have a chance to speak to her again.

If ever.

I fucking blew it. He could kick his own ass for being so stupid.

The transport stopped as the guard approached his window. Talyn rolled it down and handed over his security badge that had yet to be updated with his new rank. "Reporting for duty."

Without a word and with a curled lip of repugnance over Talyn's bald head, the guard returned his ID, saluted him, and stepped back.

Out of habit, Talyn returned the salute before the transport carried him to the duty office. With a tight knot in his stomach, he got out to see what fresh hell awaited him.

As soon as he entered, the DO contacted Anatole to let him know that Talyn was there. She then showed him into the colonel's office, where Anatole sat with a smirk on his face.

This was the first time Talyn had seen the bastard since he'd been at their mercy. And it took every ounce of will he possessed not to attack him. Or to kick his desk straight into his chest.

Don't do it.

He's not worth a death sentence.

That's what his common sense said. His sense of justice,

however, begged him hard to do it, anyway, regardless of consequence.

The repugnant asshole hesitated before he returned Talyn's salute. "You're on KP and GP, janitorial duties. I trust neither of those will interfere with your recovery, *Lieutenant*."

"No, sir."

"Then welcome back. So nice to have you here again." His voice dripping with derisive sarcasm, he shoved the orders at Talyn.

Talyn picked them up, saluted, and left immediately before he gave in to his suicidal urges. But as he looked over his new orders, he wanted to turn around and shove them down Anatole's throat.

Whatever. He'd had worse, and this was leaps above what they'd done to him at the palace. At least the KCO wouldn't torture him.

He hoped.

Heading straight for his new assignment, Talyn reported for duty in the hot, stifling mess hall where they were already preparing the night's meal.

At first the major in charge sneered at him. Until he saw Talyn's name on his file. He expected the light of recognition had come from his fighting fame.

Shockingly, that wasn't the case.

"Batur . . . you related to Colonel Galene Batur?"

"Yes, sir. But she's a deputy commander now."

He skimmed Talyn with a frown. "Are you her boy?"

"Yes, sir. Proudly so."

His frown melted into a friendly smile. "You don't remember me, do you?"

There was something vaguely familiar, but Talyn couldn't really place it. "No, sir. Sorry."

He brushed it off. "You were just a small mite back then. I was the one who brought flowers to your mother while she was in the hospital after she'd been shot, protecting Cairistiona."

Talyn nodded as he remembered the male finally. "You helped me with my homework, while we waited for her to come back from testing."

"Aha! It really is you. Yeah, I did." He glanced down at the orders and scowled again. "This puts me at one hell of a moral dilemma, Batur."

"How so, sir?"

"I was told to expect a smart-ass, disrespectful lack-Vest bastard. A coward. And that I should make sure you regretted whatever it is you did that caused you to lose rank and be sent to the mess hall. But I owe my life to your mother. She took three blasts for me and the tizarah while everyone else scattered to save their own asses. And you didn't seem disrespectful then, and you damn sure don't look the part now. Who did you piss off?"

"I'm not at liberty to say, sir. I signed a nondisclosure on the matter."

He cursed under his breath. "That answers it. Can you cook at all?"

"I can run a household MU and boil water. Most of the time without catching anything on fire."

The major laughed. "That's useless. . . . Tell you what, change into your ATUs, and I'll set you on refill duty and counter cleanup for the night."

"Thank you, sir." Talyn stepped back and saluted.

He returned it and dismissed him.

Grateful his new ACO didn't hate him, Talyn headed for his barracks. While he didn't relish refilling the meal stations, it could have been a lot worse.

As he reached his barracks, he was stopped by Captain Raohul. "Where you going, Batur?"

"My bunk and locker . . . sir."

The captain snorted derisively. "You don't belong here. You're not a pilot anymore. You've been busted back to the gen-deck. Your belongings are in lockup there, pending your reactivation. Don't forget to change out your rank before you put on your uniform. It's a court-martial to misrep rank."

Of course it was. Like he'd forget that?

But the captain wasn't trying to be kind. The prick's eyes gleamed with cruel satisfaction. "Thank you, sir, for the reminder."

When Talyn stepped back, the captain grabbed his arm. "Did I dismiss you, Lieutenant?"

Talyn ground his teeth. "No, sir."

"Then you stay planted."

"Yes, sir."

Glaring at him, the captain broke into Talyn's personal space. Something that was much more offensive to an Andarion than a human. "Are you giving me attitude, Lieutenant?"

"No, sir."

"No?" He all but touched his nose to Talyn's. Of course, he had to stand on his tiptoes to do so. "I think I see rebellion in your eyes."

"No, sir."

"Captain!"

Sneering, he moved back, then gasped as he saw Felicia's brother heading toward them with long, angry strides. He immediately fell into a crisp salute.

Lorens narrowed his gaze on the captain before he returned it. "Are you all right, Batur?"

"Fine, sir."

"Then, at ease." He slid his gaze back to the captain. "You're dismissed. . . . Batur, walk with me."

"Yes, sir." Folding his hands behind his back, Talyn followed Lorens.

As soon as they were alone, Lorens relaxed his formality. "Felicia told me that you were called in. I got here as fast as I could. How's it going?"

"It is what it is, sir."

Lorens snorted. "Gods, you *are* military. You probably bleed red and black." He paused to face Talyn. His gaze went to Talyn's epaulettes that bore his new rank. "I'm going to get you back on palace duty. We need someone in there."

"I wish you luck with that, sir. I really do."

"Commander?"

Talyn flinched as he heard Anatole's nasal voice. Locking his jaw to keep from saying anything, he turned and forced himself to salute the bastard, even though what he really wanted to do was plant his fist in Anatole's haughty face.

Anatole completely ignored him to salute Lorens, who was obviously put out by his appearance. His gaze slid to Talyn before he snapped his attention back to Lorens. "May I ask why you're here, sir?"

"That's no concern of yours."

Anatole sputtered. "I'm his CO . . . sir."

"And I'm the second-in-command of the entire armada. I don't believe I need *your* permission to speak with Batur."

He panicked. "Whatever he's telling you is a lie. I don't know if you're aware of it, but this is retaliation."

Lorens arched an intrigued brow. "For?"

"My aunt, the tadara, busted his rank for insubordination. So the allegations he's making against me are all lies."

"All allegations made by any officer, regardless of rank, must be heard and fully investigated. You know that." Lorens tried to lead Talyn away from Anatole.

"I didn't touch his whore!"

Talyn froze where he stood as those words went through him like a hot, searing knife.

No . . .

No, he didn't . . .

It's death to strike a member of the royal house. . . .

Fuck it.

Whirling, Talyn gave in to the demon inside him. He slugged the bastard with everything he had. And he would have done more had Lorens not pushed him back and blocked his access to Anatole as three provosts rushed forward with weapons drawn on him. His breathing ragged, Talyn tried to push past Lorens without hurting the male.

"Talyn!" Lorens snapped as he put himself between them. "Get ahold of yourself! Their weapons are set to kill, *not* stun!"

That finally sank in. Still craving blood, Talyn held his hands up and fought the urge to kick the bastard, who was laughing as he wiped the blood from his lips.

"You're going to pay for that, *Lieutenant*. With your life. Then, I'm going to find out for myself if your whore was worth it."

Talyn went for him again, but the guards blocked his path.

"Take him to lockup!" Anatole ordered.

"Halt!" His face mirroring Talyn's rage, Lorens turned back toward Anatole. If the idiot had an ounce of preservation, he would have seen the fury in Lorens's eyes that matched Talyn's, and run for cover.

"Is he talking about Felicia?" Lorens asked Talyn coldly.

Trying his best not to leap again for Anatole's throat, Talyn gave a subtle nod.

"What happened?"

Talyn ground his teeth. This was not how he'd planned for Lorens to find out about the attack. Of course, the plan had been for him not to find out at all. Felicia's explicit order was to keep her brother out of it since they didn't know who had done it.

Now . . .

"I order you, Batur. Tell me what he's talking about!"

"Someone attacked Felicia on her way home, and tried to pull her into a transport. She said it happened so fast, she didn't know who it was."

"The bruise on her face that she told me came from a doorjamb?"

Overwhelmed by rage at the reminder, Talyn went for Anatole again. One of the guards shot at him, narrowly missing his head.

"Stop!" Lorens ordered all of them.

"He's lying!" Chrisen snarled. "I didn't touch his whore!"

Lorens lunged.

This time, Talyn stopped *him*. "Think of your children. Since I'm already going to jail. Let my execution be for his murder."

"Oh, I'm going to avenge my sister." Lorens glared at Anatole. "You motherfucker! No one touches a member of my family! How dare you!"

Anatole paled. "What?"

"Felicia is *my* sister, you stupid whoreson! Talyn hadn't even mentioned *you*. Contrary to what you think, you are not the center of anyone's universe except the sorry Andarion bitchtress who shit you out!" Lorens pointed to Anatole. "Arrest him!"

The guards did so without question.

"You can't do this!" Anatole snarled. "I'm the tadara's nephew!"

"And my paran sits to her right hand. How do you think he'll react when I tell him you attacked his youngest daughter, you son of a bitch!"

Anatole gulped audibly.

Lorens sneered at him. "If I were you, I'd pray for the mercy of facing Talyn in the Ring. Gods help you if my father gets his hands on you!" He stepped back. "Take him to the brig before I let the lieutenant have him with my blessings."

Once they were gone, he turned on Talyn. "How could you keep this from me?"

"I promised Felicia I would let her tell you. With the exception of the one bruise and being shaken up, she was unharmed. Had I known *he* was the one who did it, I promise you, I'd have ripped his throat out. She kept that knowledge from both of us."

"And you left her unprotected?"

Talyn growled at him. "Hell, no! What kind of Andarion do you think I am that I'd leave my female alone to be harmed?"

Only then did Lorens calm down. "Who's with her?"

"She has Sentella guards. Two of them. One even larger than *me*."

"Really?"

"Of course. I'd have gone AWOL before I put her in harm's way."

Finally calming a degree, Lorens stepped back. "Are the guards why you agreed to those additional fights I heard about on the news?"

Talyn looked away, unsure of what to say.

"I want the whole truth of what's going on. I'm her brother, Talyn. Granted, we haven't always gotten along or been close, but I am the head of our generation. She falls under my direct protection. It is my honor and duty to ensure her safety."

"Then why did you allow her to become a companion?"

Rage darkened Lorens's eyes. "Don't you dare take that tone with me, soldier! I didn't know what she was doing. She didn't come to me before she signed up for it. Not that I owe *you* an explanation. But that's the truth. Now you answer *my* questions."

"I agreed to those fights to pay off her contract so that her agency couldn't force her to sleep with Anatole or someone else she didn't want to."

Lorens gaped. "Excuse me? Are you saying that my sister is living in your home without a legal contract?"

How stupid did Lorens think he was? "Relax. It's her home now. My name's off the lease. Completely. I'm not an idiot. I gave her the condo, free and clear. She's in no kind of legal danger. I've been doing everything I can to protect her."

"Except call me."

"She's my female," Talyn snarled. "It's *my* responsibility to keep her safe."

"But she's not your female, Talyn. Not without blood or contract."

Talyn ground his teeth and clenched his fists to keep from punching Lorens for speaking a truth that shredded his heart. Lorens was right. For Talyn to go near her now risked a jail sentence for both of them.

In that moment, he hated Fain Hauk more than he ever had for denying him his birthright.

A tic started in Lorens's jaw. "You really gave her that condo?"

"I don't need it. Really didn't think I'd live long enough to see it again, as I was sure I'd punch Anatole when I got here." He flexed his bleeding hand. "And look," he said drily. "I did."

Lorens snorted. "You got balls, Batur. I'll give you that. Short on brains, but long on balls." Hands on hips, he faced Talyn. "How much did buying her contract set you back?"

"A little over half a million."

Lorens let out a low whistle. "You paid that and demanded nothing in return?"

"I love your sister."

"Well gods, I would hope so, considering the fact that you've given up several million dollars and are paying who knows what for her security." Lorens narrowed his gaze on Talyn. "You really have Sentella guarding her?"

He nodded. "Two of their best. A Qillaq and a Phrixian."

With a stern frown, Lorens scratched at his chin. "Good choice. Two races Anatole won't be able to intimidate."

"And both have diplomatic immunity from the Caronese embassy for anything they might do to the royals in their protection of Felicia."

"How did you swing that?"

"I know people in low places who know people in high ones."

He snorted a short laugh. "You must. I had no idea you had any connection to The Sentella or the Caronese royal house."

Talyn shrugged. "I don't give up secrets."

"No, you don't. And that's a rare thing, indeed." Lorens sighed. "I'm putting you back on leave until I have a doctor's clearance in my hands."

"Commander—"

"You want to be on duty?"

"Not really. But—"

"Go, Batur. Take the leave until I get this sorted out and your rank restored. By attacking Felicia, Anatole finally made a strategic mistake I can use against him. Our job is to figure out how best to exploit it so that we all get satisfaction from his stupidity."

"I can answer that easily."

Lorens quirked a curious brow.

"Let me have him in the Ring. Five minutes. That's all I need to legally put him out of everyone's misery. Forever."

A calculating gleam darkened Lorens's gaze. "You up to a fight that brutal?"

Talyn scoffed. "You seriously underestimate me, Commander. Trust me, both legs and one arm broken, I could still hand-feed that quim his entrails."

"Then I will see it done. Now go home, Talyn. I don't like hearing the sound of my sister weeping in my ear. We'll figure something out about the contract. If anyone catches you in the condo, just say I sent you there under orders to protect her after her attack."

Talyn stepped back and gave him a sharp salute. "Yes, sir!"

As he walked toward the gate where transports usually waited to pick up soldiers, he slid his gaze toward the brig where Anatole had been taken. *C'mon, Lorens, don't fail me with those orders.* If WAR wanted to bring down the royal house, Talyn was more than willing to personally escort Anatole straight to their gods. That only left three others from that generation who could inherit the throne.

Jullien, Merrell, and Nyran.

They should have never made this personal. Never threatened Felicia. But now that they had . . .

There would be a party at the Batur house all right. One that wouldn't end until there was blood on the walls and three hearts in Talyn's fist.

Jullien went ramrod stiff. "What do you mean, Chrisen's been arrested?"

Merrell raked a sneer over Jullien that, had it been witnessed by anyone else, would have caused Jullien to have him punished. Cousin or not. But since they were alone, he allowed the insult to pass. "That whore he went after? She happens to be the youngest daughter of Saren ezul Terronova."

Jullien cursed *that* unfortunate luck.

"Exactly. And after the attack on his other daughter and son, Terronova's demanding Anatole blood from Eriadne. And this time, he's notified everyone, and made sure he had an audience when he made his demands. Bastard's learning. We were blindsided so badly, there was no way to do damage control." Merrell paused with a frown. "What are you doing here, anyway? Aren't you supposed to be at your father's?"

Jullien growled in anger at the reminder of what had brought him back to Andaria. Last thing he'd expected to hear from his secretary on arrival was that his favorite cousin and cohort was currently jailed, and there was nothing he could do to get Chrisen out.

Making sure the guards were out of hearing range, Jullien closed the distance between them so that he could whisper and only Merrell would hear. "I saw *the* bastard. He still lives."

Merrell had the same reaction Jullien had in the restaurant on Verta. He went pale, then his cheeks turned bright red with his fury. "What?"

"It gets better. He was with Kiara Zamir. Having lunch in an Andarion restaurant, of all things. In broad daylight."

"The Gourish princess?"

Jullien inclined his head to him. "I don't dare contact her father, personally. He hates me. So, I came back for you to light a fire under her father's ass and get him to execute the hybrid before someone else realizes who and what he really is, and rains bombs all over our parade."

Merrell leaned in to whisper in the lowest audible tone possible. "What are the odds of anyone recognizing him as your brother?"

Jullien clenched his teeth tight and spoke furiously through them. "He looks just like our father. Anyone will know at this point. You can't miss it. Even with the scars on his face. It's worse now than when we were in school with him."

Merrell started to step back, but Jullien caught his arm to keep him by his side and finish his report. "There's more."

"What?" Merrell growled.

"He was dressed in Sentella gear. He's one of *them*."

"That explains the hard-on they've had for us for so long."

Jullien nodded. "Doesn't it? And that's why I came home. We have got to get rid of Nykyrian, one way or another. The last thing we need is for that bastard to hook up with the Gourish princess. We would lose everything."

Merrell growled low in his throat as he digested what Jullien was telling him. Damn it all. Why was Nykyrian still alive? Their grandmother had paid well for his childhood demise.

Now . . .

"The Probekeins still have a contract out on Kiara's life, and her father is dealing with that distraction already. We can use some of our special guard to attack and make it appear as if they're the ones after Kiara."

Jullien nodded. "I can contact Bredeh—I went to school with him and his brother, Arast. He wants the bastard dead even worse than we do."

Merrell dug his index finger into Jullien's shoulder to emphasize his point. "You do that. Because if your mother or aunt *ever* learns that hybrid is still alive . . ."

"Trust me, I know." They would personally kill Merrell's mother and demand the tadara's head. "You think I should tell my yaya that I saw him?"

Merrell paused to consider that. While the queen had been the one who'd originally used Merrell's mother to pose as Cairistiona to get rid of Nykyrian, the tadara was a capricious bitch. There was no telling how she'd react to this news that her grandson was still alive. The gods knew, she'd been furious when she'd found out Nykyrian had gone to school with them and they had failed to kill him then. The queen had as much to lose in this as they did should Nykyrian ever come forward.

But Eriadne wasn't that big a fan of Jullien these days either. She saw him as the weak hybrid coward that he was. Yet even so, she still preferred to see her direct blood on the throne than that of her sister. Which meant both he and Chrisen were forced to kiss Jullien's repugnant ass.

All these years, Merrell had been hoping to eliminate Jullien from their lives before the mutant troll spawned an heir. So far, they'd at least succeeded in keeping Jullien from marriage and procreation.

It hadn't been easy. Both he and Chrisen had bloody hands from it. And if Jullien ever found out, he'd kill them himself.

Hating that he had no choice except to kowtow to the creature he hated most, Merrell growled low in his throat. "Let me address this in private with her." And while he did it, he planned to use this as a way to get permission to eliminate Jullien from succession as well. It was time for the throne to shift from Eriadne's Anatole branch to Merrell's.

Time for serious Andarion change.

Jullien nodded. "I'll go make a few calls and see what I can put into place."

"And I'll stir the pot with Keifer Zamir. If Nykyrian really is with his daughter, it should be easy to make that paranoid bastard want his life for it. I'll tell him that you suspect the hybrid raped and is abusing her."

An evil smile curved Jullien's lips. "Good."

Merrell watched Jullien leave while his thoughts whirled.

Things were unraveling fast. Sadly, he might have to sacrifice his younger brother to Chrisen's stupidity. But that was Chrisen's own fault.

This time, Terronova was out for blood.

If they fed Chrisen to Terronova, that should appease him for the time being. It would also quell the unrest with the nobility that was beginning to call for a restriction on royal power. Something they'd all taken a hand in causing, lately.

And once the nobles were distracted, Merrell would be able to go in and clean house.

Starting with the entire ezul Terronova line and ending with Eriadne's life and that of both of her two remaining daughters.

CHAPTER 23

Felicia set a drink down by Talyn as she smiled at his patience while teaching Qorach how to play squerin—an old Andarion game. She was quite stunned at how fast and easily Talyn picked up both Qorach's native language and his signs. Her male was exceptionally intelligent and quick.

As she met Morra's gaze, the elevator pinged unexpectedly. Something that *never* happened.

Assuming it would be Galene, she turned to welcome her. Instead, Aaron stepped off first and was quickly passed by a group of eight enforcers who had weapons drawn and aimed at them.

Morra and Qorach held their hands up immediately and laced their fingers together behind their heads. The light in their eyes said they were debating if they could take their attackers, and what the cost of fighting them would be. Felicia was a little slower to move. For one thing, she couldn't believe this was happening.

Homes didn't get invaded on Andaria. Not like this.

Talyn didn't move at all. He kept his hands on the table, in plain sight. "What is this, Aaron?"

"I showed them the lease and told them that you were friends with Tara Orfanos and that you and your other friends were here, visiting."

"Shut it!" an enforcer snarled as he pushed Aaron aside. "Talyn of the Winged Blood Clan of Batur. You are under arrest for an unsanctioned carnal relationship with Tara Felicia Orfanos."

His features stone, Talyn slid his chair back slowly. "Says who?"

They all kept their weapons trained on him as if expecting the Hammer to attack.

The enforcer who'd been talking came forward cautiously. He extended a warrant toward Talyn, but kept enough room between them that he could withdraw fast should Talyn lunge at him. "It's a royal decree. From the tahrs himself."

Felicia felt her knees go weak. "This is ludicrous! It's retaliation for my brother having Chrisen Anatole arrested!"

"It doesn't matter," Talyn said drily. He handed her the warrant. "Call my mother and let her know."

"Talyn—"

"Shh," he said gently. "We can't fight that warrant. Not unless you produce contract papers for us."

Her heart broke at the hopelessness in his eyes. "I'll get you out of this. I swear it!"

Talyn put his hands behind his back and allowed them to cuff him and drag him from the condo. With one last apologetic grimace, Aaron went with them.

Fury tore through her as she read through the warrant. She'd suspected her agency as being the one who'd filed the report and had the prince sign off on it. Instead, it was Tahrs Jullien himself who accused them.

And as she skimmed the allegations and details, she realized why Talyn hadn't fought it. Unless he pled guilty to blackmailing her into the relationship, or produced legal contract papers for them, she would be seized for a DNA swab to see if she'd had sexual contact with him. If confirmed, she'd be arrested, too.

Tears filled her eyes. She handed the warrant to Morra and went to get her link and call his mother and her father to tell them what had happened.

Felicia held Galene's trembling hand as her father and brother discussed the best way to get Talyn out of jail before Jullien deported him again.

So far, her father had been able to keep him in the downtown lockup, but either Eriadne or Jullien could have Talyn moved. And at any time.

Morra cleared her throat to get their attention. "I admit that I don't understand Andarion law. At all. But . . . from what I'm hearing, all you need is a contract that says Talyn is allowed to have conjugal visits with Felicia, right?"

Her father was less than pleased with how she phrased that. His eyes blazed fury at the small Schvardan. "In short, yes."

"Then produce a contract."

Her father rolled his eyes. "It's not that simple. It would have to predate the allegations and they would have had to have filed it within seventy-two hours of signing it."

"Filed it where?"

"The legal repository, at the palace."

Morra scowled. "Is it automated?"

"Of course." Her father scoffed at the question. "No one could possibly read through everything that's filed on a daily basis. They do eventually review it, but it's a six- to eight-month backlog."

Morra winked at Felicia. "That's it, then. Get me a copy of what one of these things looks like and I'll forge you one. Take about an hour. We'll have him home in two."

Lorens laughed bitterly at her arrogance. "It's not that easy."

"For you, maybe." Morra cracked her knuckles. "For me? I need a sample and an hour. I promise, I can get this done."

Felicia shook her head in denial. "My brother's right. It's not so simple. Nor is it just paperwork. You have to have a licensed overseeing agent or agency. And unfortunately, the enforcers will demand to interview the designated agent before they allow Talyn his freedom."

Crossing her arms over her chest, Morra considered that. "How do you form one of these agencies? Could I be an agent?"

Felicia shook her head. "They can only be established by an Andarion with a minimum of twenty years in the industry."

Qorach signed to Morra, who smiled in response. She turned toward Felicia. "Didn't you say your mother was a companion?"

"Yes."

"Could she be an agent?"

Felicia took a minute to run the scenario. "She could have been granted a license to begin one. Yes."

"Could you be her first . . ." Morra slid an uncomfortable look toward Felicia's father. "Offering?"

"In theory. Why?"

"Can you get her to lie to save Talyn?"

"I think so."

Morra pulled her link out and set it up on the table. "Then tell me what I need to do and what systems I have to tap. Believe me, there's no security that can lock me out. It's why The Sentella hired me. Only two creatures alive are better at this kind of forgery than me, and both happen to work for The Sentella." She passed a happy gasp at Qorach. "Oh look! And one of those two just happens to be sitting beside me! What luck is this?"

Snorting at her enthusiasm, Qorach pulled out his own link and began feverishly tapping.

Galene passed a worried frown to Felicia. "Talk to your mother and tell her that if she does this, I will make sure nothing happens to her. Ever. And let's pray." She touched Morra on the shoulder. "While you work on it, I'll see if I can get to Talyn before he confesses to save Felicia and gets in so deep we can't get him out."

Talyn felt the air around him stir as someone neared his cell, but he didn't bother to look up or move. He was in too much pain for that.

"Baby?"

He savored the unexpected sound of his mother's voice. Bracing himself for the pain, he slowly sat up.

She gasped as soon as she saw him. "What did they do?"

He wiped at the blood on his cheek and winced. "Interrogated me. Since they have no real evidence, they were hoping I'd make their job easy and confess."

Tears welled in her eyes. "What did you tell them?"

Talyn snorted at her question. "Not a damn thing. If I had, they'd have stopped. Maybe. But you know me, Ma. I don't like to answer questions. From anyone. And my relationship with Felicia is none of their damn business. She's my best friend and that's all they need to know on the matter."

Her brow knit with furious concern, she reached through the bars to brush her hand against his throbbing jaw. "Don't worry. She's getting everything together to set you free. As soon as she can reach her mother and get the file number, they'll take it to the repository and have a copy made of your contract."

Talyn had no idea what his mother was talking about. She had to be high. But, he wasn't quite dumb enough to contradict her when he was sure they were being watched. Probably recorded.

Nor was he dumb enough to indict himself on anything. Hence the beating they'd given him. If his childhood, and Ring training, hadn't taught him how to endure pain, his armada basic training had. Name, caste, rank, CO. That's all anyone was entitled to. And it was all they'd ever get out of him. Which had pissed them off to no uncertain end, and made him quite happy with being their personal barnacle.

Talyn glared up at the camera in the ceiling outside his cell and smiled. "I know why I'm here and who's responsible for it. One day, we're going to meet in the Ring, you coward, and I will bathe in your blood. Probably your urine first, as I'm sure you'll piss your pants in fear. So keep hiding like a scared human bitch. It only makes me that much more determined to have it out with you, Andarion style."

"You shouldn't taunt them."

He shrugged. "What are they going to do? Beat me? Ooo, so scared of that," he said sarcastically. "Besides, they're all a bunch of quivering cowards, hiding behind their mamas. I am a Batur and an Andarion officer. I don't fear lesser beings, no matter what blood they believe flows in their veins. Personally, I think they should be tested to make certain they have the lineage their mothers claim. Surely those impressive families couldn't produce such inferior pansy stock, and if they did, then it's time to clean their gene pool. One fatality at a time."

She winced at his growled words. "What happened to my baby who would never say more than three words, and never anything so harsh against anyone?"

Talyn fingered his swollen lips. "He got tired of being force-fed shit."

The door behind his mother opened. A huge mountainous Andarion walked in and eyed Talyn. For several seconds, Talyn expected the bastard to haul him back to the interrogation room for another fun-filled round of I-ain't-telling-you-shite.

Instead, the guard applauded. "You're bold, boy. Stupider than hell, but bold. And you ain't got nothing compared to the fight in your female."

Talyn scowled at him as a sick sense of dread went through him. If anyone had harmed Felicia, he wouldn't rest until he'd slaughtered them where they stood. His back tingled with a fierce warning of the hell he was about to unleash. "How do you mean?"

The guard turned on the wall monitor and stepped back to let Talyn see the screen.

"All the stations have been playing this on a loop. Your female has started one serious firestorm."

Talyn's frown deepened as the scene went from two anchors to Ferrick and Erix at a press conference he'd forgotten was being held today about his upcoming fights. It had Andarions from every major news agency and even species from other planets. All hungry for information and stats on who would kill whom in the Ring.

Dressed in Talyn's custom fighting robes and carrying the Warsword Talyn used for his Ring matches, which looked gigantic in her delicate hands, Felicia made her way to the podium to address the bemused crowd.

Stunned and a little scared over her actions, he met his mother's gaping stare that said she'd had no idea Felicia had planned this.

After leaning his Warsword against the podium, Felicia lowered the hood and stared out at the swarm of reporters. "Obviously, I'm not the Iron Hammer. But I am here with important news." She lifted her hand that held a link and pressed it. Immediately, it began playing the call from Chrisen where he insulted Talyn and boldly propositioned Felicia.

Growling, Talyn charged the bars and glared at his mother. "Why didn't you tell me what that putrid bastard said to her!"

Before his mother could respond, Felicia spoke again. "All of you have come to ask about Talyn, and I'm here to tell you that, right now, this very instant, *Major* Talyn Batur, the Iron Hammer and a national Andarion hero who, as a fighter pilot, has bled in protection of his homeworld and for all of us, sits in jail. Not for a crime *he* committed, but over a personal vendetta started by a royal coward who has refused Talyn's repeated invitations to handle it like a true Andarion . . . in the Ring." She enunciated each word slowly.

A group of soldiers started forward in the crowd, but were stopped by Sentella members who emerged to form a barricade and protect her.

Felicia adjusted her mic. "Before you arrest me and drag me off into banishment as you've done so many other innocent Andarion citizens whose only crime was breathing, I want Andarions, and the rest of the Nine Worlds, to know the truth about our ruling lineage. I am not a rebel. I'm a mere college student who's studying pediatric and physical medicine at North Eris. I never asked to be a tool for certain members of the royal family to use to cripple an Andarion warrior as noble and honorable as Talyn Batur. I didn't believe what I thought were the lies spun by those who hated our government and tadara. This is not the Scythian Age. Or the time of Justicale Cruel. Who in their right mind would believe such crimes could happen in this day and age? I didn't want to believe that Merrell Anatole killed my brother to marry his wife. Or that his brother raped my sister and then forced her to sign a nondisclosure or be killed for it. Nor that Chrisen Anatole would try to kidnap me in broad daylight, outside my own home—just to strike at Talyn for a grudge he holds against Talyn's parents. Those things happen on human worlds. They don't happen here. Not to *our* race."

She pressed her link again. This time, it was Merrell and Chrisen blatantly discussing their crimes and laughing over them. Anger rose up from the reporters.

Felicia nodded. "It's in their own voices. Check your inboxes. Each one of you has a copy of these recordings, and more that have been unencrypted and delivered to your e-mails, and to every news agency in the Ichidian Universe, as well as that of The League prime commander. It is time for these criminals to be held accountable for the atrocities they've committed against their family and us! Are we cowed humans to be terrified of standing up to such tyranny? Or are we not the same warrior race that birthed a family of thirteen brave males and females who, united by blood and determination, held back an invading army to protect our brethren?"

A cheer of support went through the crowd.

Felicia struck her heart with her fist and raised Talyn's Warsword high—the Andarion sign of honor, and a challenge to enemies. "Andaria forever! I know Chrisen Anatole went to school with humans, but it's time our royal family member is reminded that he is supposed to be one of us! Not one of *them*. Get in the Ring, Anatole. Be the Andarion you claim to be! Set Talyn free! Death to all tyranny!"

The crowd began chanting the words with her.

Talyn stared with total incredulity. Proud and awed, he couldn't believe that Felicia would do something like this for him. Why would she risk her life and future?

If that wasn't shocking enough, the guard opened the door to his cell and stepped back to make room.

Unsure whether or not this was a trap, Talyn hesitated and eyed the guard.

A tic worked in the guard's jaw. "Those cowardly bastards have issued a League contract out on your female's life. We have two of our own and Sentella with her, but we know you want to protect her yourself. Like the decent Andarion you are. Good luck, Hammer. Gods travel with you. Get him in the Ring and feed him his teeth." He saluted Talyn.

His mother met his shocked gaze. "I have a transport waiting."

Felicia chewed her nail as her father and brother paced the living room, yelling at her for what she'd done with the media.

Her father glared at her with his white eyes. "You should have cleared this with me. What were you thinking?"

She lifted her chin proudly. "That I'd had enough of Talyn being punished for nothing."

Morra's green cheeks darkened. "Sorry, my lord. I didn't realize when I showed Felicia the files we unencrypted that she'd run off half-cocked to the media. She seems so laid-back and sweet. Innocent, even. Who knew she was a sleeping lorina?"

"I could have warned you," her father scoffed. "She's her mother's daughter."

Felicia opened her mouth to remind her father that he liked that about her mother, when all of a sudden, the elevator pinged. Expecting it to be another attack, she spun, ready to fight.

It was Talyn and his mother. With a happy shriek, Felicia bolted off the sofa to assault him.

Talyn let out a slight groan as Felicia literally launched herself into his arms and wrapped her body around his. He staggered back at the unexpected reaction as she rained kisses over his face. Closing his eyes, he savored the sensation of holding her. Of feeling her body pressed flush to his.

Until she pulled back and saw the bruises. She gasped before she gently fingered them. "What happened?"

"Nothing, but I am seriously pissed at you."

"For?"

"Putting yourself in danger. What were you thinking?"

Rolling her eyes, she slid out of his arms and groaned out loud. "Oh my God, you sound like my paran!" She sighed heavily and pulled Talyn into the room. "Talyn meet my paka. Paka, Talyn."

Talyn hesitated as he finally saw the elder nobleman. For some reason, he'd forgotten how much younger Felicia's mother was than her father and the fact that Lorens was older than Talyn's mother. He gave a slight bow to the politician who had the bearing of royalty. "My lord."

Saren snorted. "Please, don't be so formal." He patted Talyn on the back. "We're practically family. Especially given what all you've done for my Felicia, who should *never* have put you through any of this."

She hung her head.

Talyn's temper snapped. "She's done nothing, other than bring utter happiness to my life." He cut a teasing glare at her. "Maybe not right this moment with the death threats on her head . . . everything else was never her fault."

She smiled at him and hugged him close. "Love you," she whispered in his ear.

He inhaled the scent of her hair and trembled at the fear and love he felt for her.

His mother's link went off. Excusing herself, she went to answer it.

Saren turned the sound up on the monitors where the news was playing. "I do have to give her credit . . . we were never able to get anything into the hands of the media. By hijacking your press conference, Felicia accomplished more in five minutes than all of our members combined, over the last fifteen years."

Talyn frowned. "Excuse me?"

"My father is the leader of WAR," Felicia whispered in his ear. "He took over after Rhys was arrested."

Talyn gaped at that unexpected nugget. Apparently, Lorens was as good at keeping secrets as he was.

His mother returned to the room. "Tylie just heard about the civil unrest. She and Cairistiona are off-planet. They were on their way to rendezvous with Emperor Aros at an undisclosed location, when all this started breaking loose. Given the current political climate, and those demanding royal heads roll, Tylie intends to remain in the Triosan Empire until the dust settles."

Talyn didn't like the sound of that, or what it would mean

for his mother. Although, it might be for the best to get her out of the empire until this ended. "Are you being recalled?"

She nodded. "Cairie's hysterical about everything. Tylie's hoping I can calm her down before they sedate her into a coma. I need to leave immediately."

Saren narrowed his gaze. "What she's planning to do about her mother?"

"Knowing Tylie, she'll try to stay out of it and keep her sister safe. You have to remember that all their siblings murdered each other, and their children. The only one who ever protected Tylie and risked her own life to do it was Cairie. Now, Tylie is done with the senseless violence. All she wants is an Andaria where she and Cairie can live sanely and in peace."

Galene sighed heavily as she slid her link into her pocket. "You wanted the monarchy destroyed, and I can understand your disgust. But let me ask you this, aseseran. Who will run this empire when the Anatoles are gone? Have you any idea of the bloody civil war all of you are about to ignite between the high-Vest families? Do you really think the other ten noble bloodlines are going to step down peacefully for an appointed plenumus? Or what of the twelve high-Vest warrior clans? What if one of them rises up to seize power in the wake of this upset?"

Saren shook his head. "You're a Batur. You know what the Anatoles did to your entire family. They slaughtered them down to your direct nest because they feared the strength of your warriors. The same for the Hauks and the Xus. I refuse to stand by and let them do to my family what they've done to yours."

Morra whistled. "Tempers, guys. C'mon. We're not at war

here. And remember that some of us aren't Andarion. Could someone please explain this blood clan thing to me?"

Felicia moved over to Morra's link to pull up the family crests of the highest-ranked noble and military lineages. "Centuries ago, Andaria was divided into unorganized tribes who fought each other for territory and resources."

"Like most worlds. That I get." Morra gestured at the crests. "I take it these were the main tribes?"

"What's left of them. Back then, the warrior clans were our leaders. Until the Oksanans attacked and we had our first invasion from an alien race. Sadly for them, they marched through a family farm of War Hauks."

Morra cocked her brow. "Hauk?"

"Yes," Talyn said. "The same family tribe of The Sentella member you're thinking. Dancer Hauk is named for the sole Andarion survivor of that battle. His family single-handedly saved our world."

Morra nodded as she digested it. "Sounds like the Hauk I know and love."

"While the father and children fought," Felicia continued, "their mother ran to warn the other tribes of the invading army. It was the first time Andaria united as a single nation."

Saren nodded. "Knowing that we could be invaded again, at any time, we held our first *plenum* shortly thereafter."

"He means bloodbath," Talyn said with a bitter note in his voice. "Not the council meetings they hold today, where the first families pitch the laws that govern us all to our tadara."

Morra screwed her face up as she tried to follow. "Blood-bath, how?"

Talyn glanced to Felicia's father before he explained. "It was a melee where the strongest of each clan fought to see who deserved to be our leaders. There were twenty-four survivors of that match, who then drew lots to see who would become a politician and who would create our military. The caste order of bloodlines and families was then determined by where their ancestor had finished in the match."

Lorens nodded. "Until they got to Dancer Hauk, who had won every match. He drew a politician's lot and refused it. He ended up trading his lot with the first Anatole, who had drawn a military slot . . . Anatole had finished second in the battle."

Her father sighed heavily. "And that began the feud between the first family of the aristocracy and the first family of the military that lasts to this day."

Morra's scowl deepened. "Why?"

Talyn clenched his teeth as age-old bitterness choked him. "Because every Andarion knows that Dancer Hauk and his descendants are the ones who should have been our ruling family. And the Anatoles have spent the last four thousand years waiting for one of the Hauks to rise up and throw them out, and take the throne they're technically entitled to."

"But they haven't."

"No, but they, alone, could, and the Anatoles know that. Most of them fear it."

Morra glanced at Saren. "So where does your family fall in this mess?"

"My lineage is the third of the noble clans. Anatole is first, Nykyrian, then Terronova."

She looked at Talyn. "Yours?"

"We're military. The Baturs are ranked second only to the Hauks."

"So technically the Terronovas are the biggest threat to the queen?"

Lorens shook his head. "No. Because Andarions are warriors, the direct descendants of the Hauks and even the eldest Batur socially outrank the noble bloodlines, except for the ruling family of Sovereign Anatoles."

Morra pressed her hands to her temples as if fighting a headache. "It's like playing shuffle cards."

Felicia laughed. "To you, maybe. Since this is our heritage, we know it intimately. And now you understand why the tadara and Chrisen are so hot for *my* bottom. My paka is the eldest child of the third noble family. My mother is second-born of the ezul Nykyrian lineage and it was her cousin who married the tadara and fathered Cairistiona and Tylie. So I'm a paternal cousin to the tizarahie, while Chrisen and Merrell are nephews of the tadara herself. With me involved with a Batur . . . For them, it's a social nightmare waiting to happen. And because I'm of the Nykyrian and Terronova lineages, if Talyn and I had a legally sanctioned union, our children would be in line for the throne over even Chrisen and Merrell."

Talyn met his mother's gaze and smirked. Until now, he hadn't known the lineage of Felicia's mother. Given her birth caste, if he could claim his father's bloodline, their children would be higher than anyone's, other than the royal heirs. They would even have been styled as honorable tizirans and tizirahs.

"Nykyrian, huh?" There was a strange note in Morra's voice.

"Yeah, why?" Lorens asked.

"Nothing. Just weird . . . we have a Nykyrian who works for The Sentella. He's the only one I've ever known who had that name."

Felicia arched a brow at that. It made sense. Nykyrian wasn't a common name, even on Andaria. "Really?"

"Yeah, but it's his first name. And he's part human."

Galene paled. "Come again?"

"What?" Morra blinked innocently.

Her jaw slack, Galene met Saren's puzzled gaze. "What are the odds of there being two human-Andarion hybrids named Nykyrian?"

Saren sat down slowly as the news sank in.

"What?" Morra repeated.

Saren shook his head. "It's not possible . . . Is it?"

Morra looked back and forth between them. "Andarions, really. Could you catch the off-worlders up?"

Galene let out a nervous breath. "Cairistiona had a son who supposedly died in a fire when he was a boy. She swears that he lived, and that he'll return one day to claim the throne. He was a hybrid—half human, half Andarion—named Nykyrian."

Morra exchanged an exaggerated drop-jaw expression with Qorach, who gestured at her. "Good question. Who was Nykyrian's father?"

"Emperor Aros of the Triosan Empire."

Morra typed it into her link, then let out a nervous laugh. She handed it to Qorach. "It's him . . . I mean, the emperor's older, but that's our Nykyrian. Same facial structure. Same blond hair. I'd bet my life on it."

Nodding, Qorach handed it back to her and gestured more.

"What Qory said. Nyk is even the same height and build as the emperor. At least if these stats for the emperor are correct. As you said, Commander, what are the odds?"

Talyn let out a nervous laugh. "Cairie was right, then. Her son is still alive . . . somehow." He met Morra's gaze. "Where is your Nykyrian?"

"I don't know. I answer to him, not the other way around. But he's a close friend of Jayne's. She'd have to know how to reach him. They've been close friends for years."

Galene gaped. "You're kidding me?"

Talyn ignored the question, since it was a typical Jayne thing to do. No doubt Jayne had been protecting her friend. "You think she knows he's the missing heir?"

"Heir?" Morra choked.

Galene nodded. "Nykyrian was firstborn. He is the legal heir to both the Andarion and Triosan empires."

"Bullshit! For real?"

"If he really is Nykyrian eton Anatole. Yes."

Morra continued to gape.

Galene approached Saren. "We have to get to him. If we restore him to the—"

"Wait!" Saren said sternly. "We know nothing about his character. What if he's worse than the tadara and Jullien combined?"

Morra bristled at his question. "Please! Nykyrian Quiakides is one of the fairest men I've ever known. Loyal. Decent."

Qorach signed to her.

"Yeah, okay, he is a lethal SOB. And was a trained League assassin. But he went rogue when they ordered him to murder a mother and child. I don't know of anyone else who'd throw away the sterling career he had for his morals. He doesn't have many friends, but the few he has, he's known for years and they'd all lay their lives down for him. What does that tell you?"

Galene nodded in agreement. "If it's the same one, I knew him as a boy, and he had a good, fair heart. Not to mention, Jayne wouldn't be his friend if he was anything like Jullien. She's very selective with the individuals she lets near her children and husband."

Saren took a deep breath. "I don't know about this. On the one hand, it'd be easier to put another Anatole on the throne. Especially if it was the firstborn son. But I'm not sure I want to risk it." He looked at Morra. "What was his League rank?"

"Command Assassin, First Order."

Talyn let out a low whistle. Very few assassins lived long enough to make any Command Assassin rank. First Order . . . less than one percent of one percent made that rank, and given the fact Nykyrian would have to be younger than Lorens . . . "Impressive."

"Yes, he is. I've seen him plow through enemies like the Iron Hammer in the Ring with his Warsword." She winked at Talyn.

Lorens folded his arms over his chest. "A true, full-blooded Anatole heir would keep the others from rising up. But

Cairistiona would have to be sober to identify him. And Tylie would have to concur. As well as a DNA test to confirm it."

"There wouldn't be a problem with that." Galene locked gazes with Saren. "If he really is the tahrs, we have Eriadne by the throat. If we can prove she sent him off to die as a child . . . she'd be exposed as a liar who turned on her own grandson. A child who isn't just *our* heir, but the Triosans' also. The political backlash on her would be horrendous."

"She'd be forced to abdicate." Saren glanced to Lorens.

Galene nodded. "I'll call Jayne and find out where this Nykyrian is and what she knows about him while I rendezvous with Tylie and Cairie."

Talyn moved to block her from leaving. "It's too dangerous."

Morra stood up. "I'll go with her, and once she's safe with them, I'll return."

"You sure?"

She gestured toward Qorach. "Felicia can communicate with Qory without me, and you'll need him to protect her. I won't be gone long. Be back in two shakes of a frog's tail."

Talyn laughed. "Thank you, Morra."

As Galene started to leave, Talyn stopped her again. He couldn't speak past the fear that was knotted in his throat.

Her gaze softened as she reached up to cup his cheek. "I'll be careful. Tough times never last. But tough Andarions do. It'll take more than an Anatole to bring down a Batur. You know that. We weren't given our caste standing. We earned it."

"Don't make me have to slaughter the entire royal family, Matarra. You know if anything happens to you, I will."

"Ever my dutiful soldier." She pressed her cheek to his. "I love you, Talyn. I wish your father were here to see what a magnificent son he gave me."

Instead of soothing him, those words only agitated him more. He hated whenever she complimented his father. "May the gods go with you."

"And with you."

Talyn swallowed as he watched his mother and Morra leave.

Felicia moved to hug him. "She'll be fine, Talyn. She's the strongest female I've ever known."

Her father let out an offensive curse before he handed his link to Lorens for her brother to read. His expression dark and lethal, he met Talyn's gaze. "The Anatoles have responded to your challenge."

Lorens's curse matched their father's.

Dread choked her. "What?"

Shaking his head, Lorens looked as green as Morra. "Both Anatoles and Jullien have challenged Talyn to the Ring."

"Good."

"No, Talyn," Lorens said in a deep, earnest tone. "It isn't. As royals, they're invoking their right of proxy. You're not fighting *them*. You're fighting the Mortician, Widowmaker, and Slaughterhouse. In one night."

CHAPTER 24

Felicia couldn't breathe as her father's words slammed into her. "What?"

Talyn moved toward them to see the link. His features stoic, he gave a solemn nod. "As long as they agree to the historic terms of the Ring, I've got no problem with that. I win, the Anatoles submit to the court and pay the tithe."

Felicia was aghast at his blithe acceptance. "Talyn . . . you can't. There's no way you can fight all three of them in one night. Are you out of your mind?"

"I can do it."

"Your mother will kill you. *I'm* going to kill you!"

Qorach gestured at him.

"And Qory says he'll sit on you until you see reason."

Scoffing, Talyn pulled her against him and rested his chin on her head as he held her in the shelter of his arms. "I can do it," he repeated.

She wanted to beat him.

Her father sighed irritably. "Arrogance like that will get you killed."

Talyn shook his head at her father's dire warning. "They have no idea what I'm capable of when motivated. You want them removed from power, this will do it. Trust me. What they're too stupid to realize is that I come from the Open league. Marathon matches were routine there. Not to mention what Anatole did to me while he was my CO . . . Unlike my Vested opponents, I'm trained for this and I am motivated by a personal grudge."

Felicia stared at her brother. "Lorens! Talk sense into him!"

Lorens locked gazes with Talyn. "I wouldn't want to walk into that Ring with that lineup. But having seen you fight . . . I still think you're an idiot."

Talyn snorted. "Thanks."

"What do you want me to say? I agree with Felicia. This is suicide. I can think of a lot less painful ways of killing yourself than this."

"I challenged them. They accepted. There's no way I can bow out."

"You challenged *one* of them," Lorens reminded him. "Not all three. At once."

"Doesn't matter. I will not back down."

Lorens let out a frustrated breath. "You survive this noble act of blatant stupidity, and I'll foolishly reward it by making sure you get a commander's rank out of it."

Felicia was aghast. "You're not seriously going to reward his idiocy, are you? Really?"

Frustrated, she stepped away from Talyn to approach Qorach. "What would it take for me to get you to break Talyn's arms and legs?"

He laughed.

Unable to stand it, she headed for the bedroom and slammed the door.

Talyn hesitated. "I didn't mean to upset her."

Her father smiled sadly. "She loves you, boy. Females are not like us. They don't understand that sometimes duty and honor have to come above love."

"This isn't about either duty or honor." Talyn pulled out his left contact to show her father his real eye color. "It's only about love, and keeping her safe from all threats."

Her father let out a low whistle. "There are only three Andarion families that carry that gene, and none of them are Baturs."

Lorens paled. "What are you saying, Paka?"

"His father is Fain of the Warring Blood Clan of Hauk."

Talyn mentally cursed Felicia's father's intelligence. He hadn't even thought about the fact that anyone who knew the history of stralen would be able to put it together so fast. Truthfully, not even Talyn had known it was solely in three lineages. The only reason he knew the Hauks carried it was due to the legends of their family.

"Are you sure?" Lorens asked his father.

"Positive. Fain's the only one in the three carrier families who's been disowned." Saren held Talyn's gaze. "Tell me I'm wrong."

Qorach gaped. Most likely, he knew Talyn's uncle Dancer,

since Dancer would be one of Qory's Sentella bosses. He probably knew Fain, too.

Talyn swept his gaze over them. "I'm trusting all of you to keep it a secret. For Felicia's sake. And my mother's. No good can come of anyone knowing my father's identity."

Saren cursed under his breath. "The gods certainly screwed you, boy. You should socially outrank everyone in the empire but the tadara and her children."

Lorens let out a bitter laugh. "How did I miss it? Now that I know, I see it clearly. You look just like your father . . . and uncles."

Talyn shrugged it aside. "We make our own realities. See what we want to see."

Lorens shook his head. "Given the blood flowing in your veins . . . I pity the morons about to unknowingly walk into the Ring with you. Nothing in this universe is deadlier than a War Hauk protecting their own."

"Yes, there is. A Winged Batur out for blood."

Saren clapped him on the shoulder. "It is my honor to have you as part of our family."

But Talyn could never be legally tied to their lineage, and they all knew it. Still, it was enough that her father accepted him. It was much more than Talyn had ever expected from either of them.

He put the contact back in. "Thank you, *mu aseseran*. Now if you'll excuse me . . . I have to go grovel to your daughter and make amends."

Saren laughed. "Your mother taught you well, boy."

• • •

Felicia wiped at her tears as Talyn sheepishly entered the bedroom. He approached the bed slowly.

The moment he saw her tears, he sat down and pulled her into his arms. "I'm sorry, Felicia."

"Then don't fight. It's not worth it."

"If I don't fight them, I lose everything. Even you."

She scowled at him. "What are you talking about?"

"You didn't read the challenge, *mia*. Merrell has named your contract as his prize if I bow out or lose. While I might be able to get out of Chrisen's challenge, I can't legally dodge Merrell's. Not without losing you in the process."

Sick to her stomach, she cupped his cheek. "What is Jullien's challenge?"

"My life or freedom. His choice."

She sobbed. "I did this! Oh gods! Why did I challenge them? I was trying to protect you and instead . . ."

"Shh," he breathed against her hair. "You stood up for me, Felicia. Publicly. Never apologize for that." He removed his contacts before he kissed away her tears.

"You should hate me for this."

His eyes darkened as he slid his hand beneath the hem of her shirt. "I could never hate you. Your smile and the taste of your lips are what I live for."

Felicia choked on a sob as he kissed her breathless. How could he be so understanding? She wanted to kick her own butt for doing this to him. "I love you so much, Talyn."

Smiling down at her, he slid her panties off then pushed her skirt up so that she was bared to his hungry gaze. "I love you, *couriana*. I always will."

He nudged her thighs apart so that he could taste her. Gasping, she laid her hand against his cheek as he tormented her with pleasure and drove all her anger away. As he licked and teased, she lost herself to the sensation of his tongue and lips. And when she came, she cried out in pleasure.

His breathing ragged, Talyn entered her and drove her orgasm even higher and made it more fierce as he thrust against her with hard, furious strokes. Cupping his cheek, she stared into his eyes to watch as he lost himself to his own pleasure. In that moment, she wanted to be his wife so badly, it burned like a bitter ache inside her. More than that, she wanted his children. To be able to scream out to the universe that he was hers alone. It wasn't right that she couldn't claim him the way she needed to.

But in her heart, she knew the truth. She would always be his. No one else would ever make her feel the way he did whenever he held her.

In his eyes, she was beautiful.

She clasped him to her, then frowned as she realized he was still mostly dressed. "Oh my God, Talyn! You're still wearing your boots and pants? Really?"

He bit his lip in that adorable way that was uniquely his as color darkened his cheeks. "You didn't seem to notice. Besides, you're still wearing *your* clothes."

Laughing, she nipped his chin. Then more horror consumed

her as she realized something else. "My father and brother are right outside! How am I supposed to face them after this?"

"I don't know why you're freaking out when I'm the one they're likely to shoot. Or geld."

She laughed again until there was a sharp knock on the door. Stark cold terror and embarrassment filled her entire body. Had they heard them?

"Talyn?"

They both cringed at the sound of Lorens's voice. Talyn slid from the bed and pulled his pants up, then fastened them while Felicia quickly straightened her clothes and the bedcovers.

With a sheepish look at her, Talyn cracked open the door. "Yeah?"

"We have a massive problem. Someone just made an attempt on the tadara's life and they're blaming *you* for it."

"What?"

Lorens nodded. "We've got to get you out of here. They have a massive contract out for both you and Felicia." He held Qorach's link and played a message from Jayne.

"Hey, sexy mountainside. Let Baby T know that I just got word The League is moving in massive forces to deal with the mess on Andaria. Queen bitch is claiming someone named Talyn Batur has made an attempt on her life because he doesn't want to meet her grandson's challenge and was demoted in rank after assaulting members of the royal family. I'd come personally, but we've got one of our major players MIA. And we're all, including me, being charged with the kidnapping, rape, and the murder of Kiara Zamir. My fear is I'd bring more problems right now than solutions. When it rains, it pours like a beast. I have Sentella coming in as backup ASAP. In the meantime, we need to move my sexy baby and his female to a safe zone. Love you all. Don't get hurt."

Felicia gasped as she heard the message. Talyn saw red. Before he could think better of it, he grabbed his contacts and headed for the lobby.

Felicia scowled. A bad feeling went through her as she watched the fierce, determined way Talyn moved. She followed him through the condo, and when he headed for the foyer, she knew it was about to become worse.

"Qory! Stop him!"

Qorach tried, but Talyn dodged and twisted, and was in the lift so fast, she could barely follow his actions.

Terrified of his intentions, she ran to catch the next lift. By the time she stepped out of it, Talyn was outside the lobby, on the sidewalk, surrounded by media. She started for him, but Qorach caught her arm and gestured for her to stay back.

Through the glass, she could see and hear everything.

Talyn glanced at her over his shoulder, before he returned to the reporters. "I had nothing to do with anyone attacking the tadara. Had I wanted her dead, she'd be dead. By *my* hand. Unlike the Anatoles, I don't move in secret or hide like a bitch. As for the challenge? I accept. Name the time. Name the Ring. And you better bring body bags. You're going to need them, 'cause after I mop the floor with your proxies, I demand to face all three of you in the Ring. Warswords bared."

The reporters erupted as Talyn moved to withdraw. An

instant later, blaster fire broke out the lobby glass. Screams echoed as everyone took cover.

Ignoring the glass, Felicia ran toward Talyn.

Talyn grabbed her and used his body to shield hers while Qorach drew his weapon and searched for their assailant. After a few seconds, he motioned them back into the building.

"League?" Talyn asked Qory.

He nodded and gestured.

Felicia stood on wobbly legs as she translated Qory's signs. "He says that he doesn't know how many there were. He just saw one, but he's sure there are more. And he thinks you're an idiot for calling out the tadara like that."

Qory sputtered.

"Okay, he didn't really say that last part. *I* did. Are you insane?"

"I'm not letting the lies continue. She wants a fight, she picked the wrong Andarion to challenge. Baturs don't back down."

"Maybe," Lorens said as he joined them. "But you need to withdraw before one of those assassins takes out this building. C'mon. We have a transport waiting in the back deck."

"Take Felicia."

Before she could protest, Lorens did it for her. "She won't be any safer apart from you than with you at this point. They know she's your female. It makes her a target. You might as well stay together so you can watch her and not make us all crazy with your most-founded worry."

Talyn wanted to argue, but he knew Lorens was right. Besides, the last thing he wanted was to be away from her. "Where do we go?"

"We'll decide that once we're in the transport. C'mon."

Talyn made sure to keep Felicia covered as they moved through the building to where her father waited.

The moment they left the back door, the assassin opened fire. Talyn grabbed a blaster from Qorach and shoved the giant toward Felicia. "Get her out of here. Don't worry about me."

"Talyn! No!"

The sound of her panic tore through Talyn. But Qory didn't hesitate. He threw her over his shoulder and ran to the transport. Lorens started toward Talyn.

He shook his head. "Felicia first. I'll be in touch."

Lorens hesitated until the assassin opened fire once more. He ran to the others while Talyn fell back, drawing the assassin away from them.

As Talyn entered the building again, he ran straight into a group of Andarion enforcers. They pulled their blasters on him.

"Talyn Batur! You're to be remanded into custody, pending your royal honor match. Any attempts to flee will be seen as treason."

Talyn dropped his blaster and put his hands on his head. As they moved to cuff him, the assassin came in and drew up short. The head enforcer glared at the League soldier. "Your services aren't necessary. This is an Andarion matter. The League has no business here."

By the look on the assassin's face, it was obvious he wanted to argue, but there was too large a crowd.

And media.

He didn't dare make a move on Talyn's life. But the cold expression on his face said that he didn't like this, at all.

And he wasn't through with this pursuit.

Talyn allowed them to pull him out and put him into a prisoner transport. He considered fighting, until he saw Officer Hawas.

Hawas offered him a sad smile. "Sorry about this. But it's the only way we could keep you safe until the match. We knew the tadara would kill you if she had a chance. She's put a five-million-credit bounty out on your head with The League. We intend to make sure no one collects it."

Talyn glanced over to the others in the transport with them. "I'm still a little fuzzy on what's going on here."

Hawas grinned. "As of an hour ago, Tizirah Tylie has taken the throne and ordered her mother arrested for egregious crimes against her family and the empire. Until Tadara Eriadne's cleared of these charges, we aren't under her command. Like your female said, we're not humans to blindly follow orders. And we aren't sheep to be led to slaughter. The ruling family is down to ten members. There are a lot more of us than there are of them. We will not be abused another day. Their tyranny ends. All hail Andaria."

Talyn inclined his head in gratitude. He was just starting to relax when something slammed into their transport and tore it apart.

His hands still cuffed, Talyn couldn't really catch himself as the transport rolled. Blasts struck the craft until it came to rest, upside down.

No one moved. Bodies were strewn everywhere. Talyn smelled fuel and knew the vehicle was about to explode. Pain seared his body as he tried to free himself.

The side window was kicked in by someone on the outside. For a moment, he thought he was being rescued, until he was hauled out and shoved onto the ground at the booted feet of the assassin who'd fired on him at the condo.

Talyn tried to fight, but with his hands cuffed behind his back there was nothing he could do. Before he could blink, he heard the blaster's recoil.

CHAPTER 25

Talyn cursed as blood ran into his eyes from the wound. It wasn't until he heard his name, and gentle hands rolled him over, that he realized it wasn't his blood, after all, and that the additional pain he felt came from the assassin falling on top of him.

Stunned, he stared up at Felicia's tear-filled eyes. "Licia?"

She shook terribly as Lorens freed his hands.

His face ashen, Lorens stared at his sister in total disbelief while Qorach and Saren went to check on the others.

Talyn realized Felicia held a blaster in her hand. After rising to his feet, he pried it from her trembling grip and gathered her into his arms as she wept against his chest. Startled, he met Lorens's gaze in an effort to confirm his suspicions.

"She grabbed my blaster and shot him before he could fire on you."

Felicia pulled back to inspect his body. "Are you hurt?"

"Skinned and bruised, but nothing serious."

Her tears fell even harder as she sobbed and sobbed. "I-I thought he was going to kill you. I didn't think we'd make it to you in time."

"He *was* going to kill me. You saved my life, Felicia."

She winced as she saw the assassin's body behind him. "I can't believe I killed someone," she whispered.

"It's okay." Talyn scooped her up in his arms so that he could protect her. "Don't think about it." He made sure to keep his body between her line of sight and the assassin on the ground.

Saren inclined his head to them. "Lorens, get them to safety. We have help on the way for these men. We'll stay and render what aid we can."

Still stunned to the core of his being over what she'd done for him, Talyn carried Felicia to their transport and put her inside while Lorens took the controls. As sirens drew closer, they drove off.

Lorens glanced at them in his mirror. "She wouldn't let us leave you. We had to circle back to the transport to keep her from clawing out my eyes."

Talyn smiled at Felicia. "Ever my ferocious *mia*."

She took his hand into hers. "Ever my heart."

Those words choked him.

They headed out of the city, toward Saren's summer home, but since the route was clogged by rioters and those trying to flee the overpopulated war zone, hours went by. No matter which way Lorens tried, they ended up blocked.

Talyn's link started buzzing. He pulled it out and answered.

"Where are you?" his mother demanded without preamble.

"Matarra?"

"Yes. I'm seeing all kinds of horrifying things on Andaria about riots and arrests, and looting. About you being arrested for treason!"

"We're okay at the moment. Where are you?"

"I'm onboard the *Royal Tiakara*, with Tylie and Cairistiona. Have you heard the news?"

"Enforcers told me that Tylie had seized the throne and demanded the arrest of her mother. Is it true?"

She didn't answer his question. "Who's with you?"

"Lorens and Felicia."

"Saren?"

"No. I was attacked by a League assassin and the enforcers with me were seriously wounded during the altercation. He and Qory stayed behind to render aid. Given that I have League assassins after me, we thought it best to immediately vacate the area."

"Put me on speaker."

He switched it over. "Okay, Ma. Go. You're live in the transport."

"We were right earlier. The Sentella Nykyrian *is* the missing heir."

"What?" Lorens asked as he made a left turn.

"It's true. By the time I rendezvoused with the royals, Cairistiona and Tylie had already met him and confirmed it. Independent of my report. It's why Tylie overthrew her mother and ordered her arrest. They're getting ready, right now, to have dinner with him and his wife, Kiara Zamir. Cairie wants to reinstate him to the line of succession."

"What?" Lorens repeated as if he couldn't wrap his head around it. Not that Talyn blamed him. He was having a hard time himself. "She really found her son?"

"We don't have the DNA results back, but it's definitely him. I saw the photos. And he told them both that he remembers everything his grandmother did to him as a boy. He's furious at the royal family over it all. Tylie said no one could fake his indignant rage. It's why he's never come forward in the past. He doesn't want the throne. Or anything to do with his family, Andaria, or our politics."

Talyn could definitely understand that.

Lorens sucked his breath in sharply. "Yeah, well, if he's a decent male, we need him."

"That's what Tylie's trying to stress to him. Maybe they'll have success at dinner. His father will be there, too. With luck, they'll talk sense into him. Oh, and get this, Nykyrian married the Gourish princess and she's pregnant with his child. That is definitely confirmed. If we can get him to agree to reinstatement, this will change *everything*."

Yes, it would. And it would get rid of Chrisen and Merrell, and their power over the Andarion people, permanently. Talyn met Felicia's stunned gaze.

Lorens gasped. "He's really married to royalty, and has an heir on the way?"

"Yes. With Triosan backing, Tylie immediately filed a

temporary injunction removing her mother from power and Jullien from succession. There's no telling what's about to start over this. Eriadne won't leave quietly."

Neither would Jullien.

"Are you safe, Matarra?"

"We are. Aros isn't taking any chances with Cairistiona's life, and neither is Tylie. In addition to Andarion Guard, we're surrounded by Triosan troops. What about you?"

"We're fine."

"Lorens? Felicia? Is my son lying to me?"

Felicia pursed her lips. "Not lying, per se. Perhaps painting the facts in an optimistic light."

"We should be fine," Lorens inserted. "I think the royals have bigger things to concern themselves with right now than Talyn's challenge. In fact, in lieu of what you just told me, I'm taking Talyn and Felicia to Command. With Tylie in charge, it'll be the safest place for them."

"All right. Keep me posted." She hung up.

Talyn wasn't sure what to think about all of this. It was happening too fast. "Are you sure about Command?" he asked as Lorens headed them back into the city.

Before Lorens could answer, his link buzzed. "Lieutenant Commander ezul Terronova."

"Commander, this is Acting Tadara Tylie of the Most Sovereign Blood Clan of eton Anatole. I'm sure by now you are well aware of the political upheaval taking place in the empire, and the fact that my mother has been deposed."

"Yes, Majesty."

"As a result, I have issued orders that have removed Prime Commander ezul Aysu from his post, pending investigation. A copy of that has already been sent to your inbox. My trusted allies have sworn that I can put my faith in you. Do I have your oath of loyalty?"

Talyn held his breath. If Lorens gave it and the tadara happened to be reinstated for any reason, Lorens would be viewed as a traitor for siding with Tylie against her. That was something the old bitch would never let go.

He would be executed immediately.

Lorens glanced at them in the rearview mirror before he answered. "Yes, Majesty. I am forever loyal to you and your cause to remove the former tadara from power."

Talyn respected him for standing by his convictions. That single statement was a declaration of war against Eriadne.

"Then it is my honor to make you the acting prime commander of our armada until the new monarchy is established and a permanent prime commander is formally appointed. Do you accept the position and the responsibilities?"

"It will be my honor to serve you and my empire, Majesty. I shall give you only my best."

"Thank you, Commander. Your loyalty and service will not be forgotten. In the meantime, I am forwarding your new position to all our military. I'll be in touch with an update on the ruling monarchy later tonight."

"Thank you, Majesty." He hung up.

Stunned, Talyn leaned forward in his seat to clap him on the shoulder. "Congratulations, Prime Commander."

Lorens snorted. "Don't congratulate me, Lieutenant Commander Batur. I'm appointing you as my second-in-command. I fall. *You* fall."

Talyn sat back, completely slack-jawed as that sank in. He wouldn't have been more stunned had Lorens shot him in the head. "Pardon?"

Lorens glanced at him over his shoulder. "There truly is no one else I'd put at my back right now. No one I trust more. We win this overthrow, and your rank will be permanent."

Her face a mask of fear, Felicia swallowed hard. "And if we lose, both of you will be executed for treason."

Talyn tapped at the markings on his neck. "I'm already branded a traitor. I've publicly insulted them all, and with their challenge, they've made it clear they want me dead. In the goriest way possible. You think if Eriadne retakes her throne she won't be coming for me, anyway?"

Felicia wanted to deny it, but she knew the truth. "You are all that matters to me, Talyn." She placed her hand on Lorens's shoulder. "And you are my family. My blood. I don't want to bury either of you."

Talyn winked at her. "Don't worry. I don't lose. Haven't you seen my fighting record?"

Rolling her eyes, she didn't appreciate his lame attempt at humor. "You're not funny."

"But I am funny-looking."

She laughed in spite of the terror inside her. "You stole that from me."

"Hope it's not the only thing of yours I've stolen."

She stroked his jaw with her hand. "It's not. You stole my heart the first day I met you."

Lorens cleared his throat. "All right. Knock it off, you two, before you make this any worse on me. I am the big brother, you know? No *gru-gru* in the backseat or I might gut Talyn myself. Geld him, at least."

Talyn laughed as he put a little more room between them. "So what are our first orders, Commander?"

"Put a two-Andarion space between you and my sister on that seat. Then establish ourselves at the command center. We need to make sure our troops see their leaders and know who we are."

Felicia hesitated at the sight of Talyn in his formal uniform. Her heart pounding with pride and fear, she brushed her hand over the lieutenant commander epaulette badges Lorens had loaned him. Two stars and two stripes for his new rank, and the winged skull with a dagger through it that marked all Andarion military designations. In that instant, one of their first conversations went through her mind.

All Talyn had wanted was to make a commander's rank.

"Does this mean you're going to retire from the Ring?"

A slight smile hovered at the edges of his gorgeous lips as he looked down at her through hooded lashes. "Only if you stay with me."

"I have no intention of leaving."

"Then once I fulfill my current contracts, I'll retire, and never look back."

Those words choked her as she remembered that *she* was the entire reason he had those upcoming fights. But for her, he'd be done with it now.

"Don't," he breathed as he fingered her lips. "You are *the* only reason I'll be able to stop fighting this year. Without your brother, I'd still be Lieutenant Batur. Not a lieutenant *commander.*"

"You earned that rank. Had Anatole not been a bastard, you would have made it by now."

"Maybe. But don't look over your shoulder, and don't dwell on what we can't change. Keep your eye on the horizon and focused on what we need to do now. Upwards and onwards. Always."

"Spoken like a true fighter pilot."

He winked teasingly at her. "And a Ring fighter."

She smiled then and kissed him. "Good luck."

Closing his eyes, he held her against him for a moment longer. With a deep breath, he forced himself to step back and meet Qorach's gaze. "Keep her safe."

Qory inclined his head.

Talyn left her to head toward Lorens's office, down the hall from the prime commander's lounge where Felicia was being guarded by Sentella.

He just "adored" the way the other soldiers' gazes went from his rank to his bald head and back again. It was obvious they wanted to comment, but didn't dare since he was now second only to Lorens in rank . . . he even currently outranked his mother.

And it took all his willpower not to self-consciously brush his hand over the light dusting of hair that was just starting to grow back. He refused to give them the satisfaction of seeing how much their judgment stung. They weren't worth it.

Scanning his hand, he half expected the door to not open. To everyone's surprise, including his, it did, and admitted him into Lorens's office, which was still in perfect order from the last Andarion who'd held it. Nothing had been packed or removed from the room.

Talyn frowned. "You're not moving?"

Lorens shook his head. "I doubt my rank advancement will be permanent."

"Why?"

"Just thinking that if Cairie and her son are returned to succession, your mother will be the next prime commander."

Talyn scowled at his assumption. "What makes you think that?"

"She's the one they trust most, which is why they're keeping her close to them in this time of crisis. They don't know me or my loyalties. Not really. I would choose your mother over me, were I they."

Made sense. But Talyn found it hard to believe that Lorens was so complacent. "You're okay with that?"

Lorens smiled. "I'm the second-highest-ranking member of the armada, of course I'm okay with it. Personally, I don't want the responsibility that comes with the PC's office. I would take it if I were appointed, but I like the rank I held. Adjutant to the prime has been good to me." Lorens handed him a small link. "Your access clearances are all in place. This runs on a secured network that only three of us can access. Me, you, and the ruling house. Which at this time is Tylie."

He threw his hand up and the walls illuminated with news feeds for Talyn's view. "Most of the riots have been quelled. The League is still after you, but I've notified them that they are to cease and desist, or be held in violation of our treaties. Unfortunately, that doesn't mean they'll listen."

True. Still, it was better than nothing. "Where's the former tadara?"

"She's fled with her personal guard. At this time, her exact location is unknown. The Sentella is after her, too. Jullien is also off-grid, as are Merrell and Chrisen. Last we heard, Jullien was headed toward his father's empire. The rest of the Anatoles and ezul Nykyrians are in lockup, awaiting the return of Tylie and her court." One screen lit up.

Talyn scowled at it.

"Finally . . . that's the location of Merrell and Chrisen. They seem to be hiding on their father's back property, on the outskirts of Eris. Would you like the honors of arresting them?"

He quirked a sarcastic brow. "You have to ask?"

Lorens laughed. "Make sure you take a team. Anything happens to you and I have to face my little sister. No offense, she scares me more than you do."

Talyn snorted. "She scares me, too."

Relishing this task, he left immediately to carry out his orders. He paused in the hallway as he caught sight of Syndrome's little brother. "Captain Pinara?"

He snapped to attention and saluted Talyn immediately. "Sir!"

Talyn returned the salute. "At ease . . . You're Farina's youngest brother?"

Swallowing hard, he nodded. "Yes, sir."

"Then I think you'll enjoy our assignment. We're out to arrest Chrisen and Merrell Anatole."

The vicious, hungry light in his eyes was one Talyn understood all too well. "Thank you, sir."

"Grab an assault team you trust and meet me in the hangar."

"Sir! Yes, sir!" The captain ran off to comply.

Talyn froze as he caught sight of himself in the window's reflection. He barely recognized it. No matter how hard he tried, he couldn't get used to not having his warrior braids. His mother had plaited them on his fourteenth birthday on their way home from his Endurance. Like all Andarions, he'd worn them as a source of pride.

You're still a warrior. Still a Winged Batur.

Still a War Hauk.

No one could ever take away his will to fight. That was an integral part of his being.

And it was time for payback. Quickening his stride, he went to suit up for a mission he was definitely looking forward to.

• • •

Talyn adjusted the link in his ear as he listened to his men surrounding the royal compound. "There are three small signatures in the front room. From their size, I'm assuming children or females. The two we're after are in the rear left quadrant with what appear to be three large bodyguards."

"Copy that, Commander. Eight targets confirmed. Weapons to stun."

Talyn hesitated. He glanced over to the female on his right. "Lieutenant Veryl? Let's try to gently extract the smaller targets before we rush the males. I don't want innocent blood on anyone's hands. Are you up for it?"

She removed her helmet and gave him a look of approval. "Yes, sir."

He spoke into his mic. "Cover the lieutenant."

She walked up to the door and knocked softly.

The female who answered the door was Merrell's wife—the same female who had been married to Lorens's brother Merrell had murdered.

Veryl talked to her for a moment before the female paled and called the two children over. By their age, Talyn assumed they were more likely related to Lorens and Felicia than the Anatoles. With Veryl and two males covering their retreat, they headed across the yard to a transport.

"Merrell Anatole's wife and her two children are secured."

"Good job, Lieutenant. Protect them." And with that, Talyn gave the order to move on Chrisen and his brother.

Talyn led his troops into the house. Cautious and alert, he made his way down the back staircase, until he heard them watching the news, and commenting on what they intended to do to Cairie, Tylie, and Talyn's mother once this "nonsense" ceased.

His gaze turning red, Talyn moved in first. One of their bodyguards started to draw on them, until he realized how many soldiers were with Talyn.

The guard fell back.

As they swarmed in, Talyn saw that it was four bodyguards and Merrell. One target was missing.

"Where's Chrisen?" The words were barely out of his mouth before he felt something hot slide in through the plates of his body armor and pierce his side.

"Right here, you son of a whore!" Chrisen growled in Talyn's ear. Still, there was no sign of the male. Nothing that registered visually or through their equipment.

"Cloaking device," Talyn gasped as he staggered back. Unwilling to risk one of his soldiers being harmed, he latched on to Chrisen and held him fast so that he couldn't escape or wound another.

Chrisen twisted the blade, but Talyn wouldn't allow him to pull it out of his body. His sight dimmed.

And as Chrisen tried to knock Talyn away, Talyn grabbed his head with one hand and wrenched the helmet off, exposing Chrisen for the others to find in the event he passed out.

Yet that was all he could manage before his legs buckled. His soldiers closed rank and subdued Chrisen as they called for medics.

Talyn had been wounded enough in his life that he knew how bad this wound was. Blood poured out of the injury, like an artery had been nicked. Everything swam as he tried to focus and maintain consciousness. He sprawled on the floor and rolled to his back. The room tilted even more. Darkness was coming so fast, he wasn't sure he'd make it to the medics' arrival.

He pressed his voice dial and called the one person he needed most.

"Talyn?"

In spite of his pain, he smiled. "Hey, baby." He pressed the link deeper into his ear so that he could savor every syllable of her precious contralto.

If he had to die, he wanted the last sound he heard in this life to be Felicia's tender voice.

She hesitated. "What's wrong? You don't sound right."

He groaned as the medics arrived to cut open his armor and they pressed against his wound. "Love you, *mia*."

"Talyn!" Felicia shouted as she heard the chaos over his link. Tears blinded her. "Baby, if you can hear me . . . I love you, too. Please be okay!"

Suddenly, another voice came over the link. "Who is this?"

"The commander's female, Felicia. Who are you?"

"Ger Tarra, I'm a medic. He's wounded and we'll be taking him to North Eris ER."

"I'll meet you there. Thank you." Her hands shaking, Felicia hung up and told Qory what had happened.

Lorens met her in the hallway of the command center. "You heard?"

She nodded. "Talyn called me. What happened?"

"Chrisen was cloaked. Coward ambushed him. He would have probably taken out more of our men, but Talyn, even wounded, subdued the slimy bastard. C'mon, I have a transport at the entrance."

She ran to the front of the building as fast as she could.

Once she was inside the transport with Lorens and Qory, Felicia started to call his mother, but didn't want to upset her until she knew more details about Talyn's condition. Terrified, she clutched her link and prayed as they rushed through the streets that were still littered with remnants of the political shift in power.

Much of the rioting had stopped once word of Tylie's official ascension had reached their media. While no one shed a tear for Eriadne or Jullien, many respected both of the tizirahie. Tylie because of a vicious attack her own sister, Irenie, had made against Tylie when Tylie was only thirteen, and Cairistiona for being the one who'd saved Tylie's life by brutally slaughtering Irenie for her treachery.

Now all that appeared to be left of the overthrow was the cleanup.

As soon as they reached the hospital, Felicia ran inside. She reached the nurses' station at the same time the doors opened to admit Talyn and the medics who were trying to save his life.

She rushed to his side.

A soldier started to push her back.

Talyn held his hand out to her. "Felicia?"

Only then did the soldier let her pass. Tears blurred her vision as she took his hand. "You've got to find a safer, saner occupation."

He choked on a laugh.

"I love you, Talyn."

He squeezed her hand. "Love you." And then they took him into the OR, leaving her there to stare after them and pray.

Lorens pulled her against him.

She wanted to cry. But this wasn't the time for tears. Felicia forced her emotions down as she called a nurse over. "We have the same blood type. If he needs a transfusion—"

"No need, Ger Tarra." The nurse jerked her chin toward the door. "We already have a list of volunteers, with more calling in even as we speak."

Dumbfounded, Felicia gaped at the sight of thirty-five Andarion soldiers in the waiting room who'd followed the medics in. And as her gaze swept them, they offered a salute. At first she assumed it was for her brother, until one of the soldiers came forward and removed his helmet.

He bowed before her. "It is an honor to meet the commander's female. If you need anything, Ger Tarra, let us know."

Scowling, she glanced at Lorens. "I don't understand."

The soldier straightened. He glanced at the others before he spoke. "Before we moved in, the commander, who has more reason than any to want to brutalize the entire royal family, secured their innocents without conflict. Then after he was assaulted by a coward, he held the knife in his side to keep the rest of us from being harmed. Commander Batur is the most honorable Andarion I've ever served under. We are here to guard both of you with our lives."

A tear slid down her cheek. "Thank you, Colonel . . ."

"Verrus."

"Verrus. It is my honor to meet you."

He gave both her and Lorens a salute before he took up post at the OR doors.

This time, Felicia didn't have to wait long before a frazzled orderly came rushing through the doors.

"Is there a Tara Felicia here?"

Felicia sighed as she realized what must have happened. She rose and went to him. "I'm Felicia."

"Are you squeamish?"

"No. I'm a med student."

"Thank the gods. You've got to do something with your male! He's impossible."

She suppressed a smile as she followed the female through the doors, down the hallway, and to the table where the doctor was attempting to treat Talyn while he cursed them for it. She heard him long before she saw him.

"*Keramon*?" Felicia chided in a patient tone. "What are you doing?" She moved to stand by his side.

"Tell them to stitch the damn wound and give me Prinum!"

Felicia narrowed her eyes at him before she glanced to the images on the monitors of his injuries. She looked over to the doctor. "Are those Talyn's?"

"Yes. As you can see, he has a lot of tissue damage—"

"Stitch the damned thing closed! Now!"

She tsked at Talyn's shout. "Are you a doctor?" she asked him like a mother to an angry toddler.

"No," he said sullenly.

She met the gaze of the anesthesiologist. "What all have you given him?"

"Enough to choke a rhino. I can't believe he's still conscious."

When she looked at Talyn, she saw the raw determination in his gaze.

"I need to be on my feet, Felicia . . . please."

She stroked his whiskered cheek. There was no missing the feral determination in his gaze.

Finally, she relented. "Give him Prinum and stitch the wound."

The doctor sneered at her. "You're a student—"

"Who knows your patient. Trust me, Doctor. If you don't do what he wants, when he wakes—and he will—you won't be happy. The Iron Hammer is an Andarion with a steel will and terrifying temper. The Prinum will heal him."

Growling in anger, he obeyed.

Felicia teasingly touched the tip of Talyn's nose. "Now play nice and don't bite the doctor." As she started to leave, the doctor's voice stopped her.

"Don't you dare step one foot outside this room until I'm done with him. You're the only one he listens to."

She snorted at that. "He doesn't listen to me, either. If he did, he wouldn't have been hurt."

Talyn reached out for her.

She took his hand and kissed his open palm. "You really are more trouble than you're worth."

He ignored her playful chastisement. "Did you call my mom?"

"No. I figured you only needed one female yelling at you at a time."

"Thank you." He grimaced as the doctor began stitching his wound.

Felicia sucked her breath in sharply. "Please tell me you took a local."

"He refused it," the doctor mumbled. "Apparently, he likes pain."

She sighed heavily. "What am I going to do with you?"

"Keep loving me . . . I hope." He held such a sweet, vulnerable look in his eyes that she had to smile.

"Always that."

His grip tightened on her hand.

"I wish you'd take something."

Talyn shook his head. "So long as Eriadne and Jullien are on the run, you, my mother, and your family are in danger. I will not lie in a bed and sleep until I know you're all safe from harm."

The doctor gentled his touch. "Is that why you've been so difficult?"

Talyn nodded.

The doctor glanced over to his assisting nurse. "Give him thirty RTs of Strisassin."

"What is that?" Talyn growled.

Felicia stroked his hand to calm him. "It's a local that won't make you drowsy."

"But it will numb the pain until the Prinum works." The doctor grimaced at the depth of Talyn's wound. "You're lucky the medics repaired your artery. I'd still rather have you on the table, yet I understand why you want back into battle, and I commend you for it. I lost my sister to the Anatoles." He met Talyn's gaze sincerely. "I'll have you on your feet within an hour. . . . And next time, son, don't just growl at us. Let us know why you're being an ass."

Talyn let out a stern growl as he lifted his jacket so Felicia could examine his ragged wound. He needed to rendezvous with her brother and get a status update. While he adored her, he needed to go.

Fast.

She cast a nasty glare at him before she kissed the skin above the wound and slapped his ass. Hard. "Mess with me and I'll shoot you myself to keep you home."

Snorting at her empty threat, he straightened his uniform and sealed his armor over his healing injury. "Satisfied?"

"Not even a little." She handed him his helmet.

The sad fear in her eyes gave him pause. Cupping her cheek,

he offered her a smile. "It's Jullien we're after now. He won't attack the way Chrisen did."

"How do you know?"

"He's not that smart or that brave." He gave her a deep kiss that conveyed his own fear for her safety. Then, he gently rubbed his nose against hers. "I want you naked in my bed on my return," he whispered.

She nodded. "Don't shatter my heart, Talyn."

He swallowed hard against the sudden lump in his throat that was caused by those words. It was said that when two Andarions were really in love and divinely unified, if one of them should die, it shattered the heart of the survivor. It was why stralen males seldom lived more than a day after the death of their wives.

Trembling with what he felt for her, he took her hand in his and led it to his chest so that she could feel his heartbeat through his red armor plate. "I will forever be your bitch, *couriana*."

She rolled her eyes and pushed playfully against his chest. "And here I thought you'd say something sweet in return. I should have known better."

Talyn started to leave her on that note, but stopped himself. This could very well be the last time he ever saw her in this life.

Before he could think better of it, he pulled the glove off his hand and took hers. He lifted her hand so that he could kiss her palm. Felicia's gaze fell to his fingers.

A sharp scowl lined her brow as she pulled his hand closer

so that she could see the small, intricate tattoo that encircled his unification finger. "What's this?"

"My caste forbids me from tattooing your lineage on my arm." It was something only married Andarion males did to honor their wives and vow their eternal fidelity. "Nor does it allow me to buy a pledge ring." He tightened his grip on her hand. "This was the only legal way I could let the universe know that you are, and will always be, my one true heart."

Felicia bit her trembling lip as she read the Andarion words that encircled his finger. *Forever Felicia's.* Tears blurred her vision at his very public and extremely defiant declaration to everyone that he loved her. "When did you do this?"

"A few days ago while you were visiting your mother."

"How did I miss it?"

He smiled. "I was careful to keep it hidden."

"Why?"

"I wanted to surprise you with it for your birthday."

A tear ran down her cheek until he kissed it away. Only Talyn would remember something so trivial in the midst of this chaos.

"I don't deserve you," she whispered.

He laughed at that. "I know. You must have *really* done something awful in a former life to get stuck with me in this one."

She laughed in spite of her tears. "Be safe."

Stepping back, he saluted her. "Yes, ma'am." He placed the helmet over his head, completely shielding his face from her. He was so huge and fierce in his suit. So invincible in appearance. But she knew the truth.

Talyn wasn't. He bled, and he could die doing this.

Even worse, he was heading into an extremely dangerous situation. While Jullien might be a coward, Eriadne wasn't. She was a feral bitch who'd murdered half her family to take her place on the throne.

Now she was cornered and losing.

Eriadne wouldn't go quietly into history. She'd take as many of them with her as she could. Something she'd proven an hour ago with an attempt on Felicia's father. It was why Felicia was so heavily guarded and what had motivated Talyn even more to return to active duty.

If they didn't secure the remaining royals ASAP, this would turn into a bloody civil war that could go on for years. They needed a lightning strike to put them down.

Immediately.

Another tear slid down her cheek as she feared for Talyn. Eriadne and The League had a staggering price on his head. The only ones who wanted his throat more were the Tavali.

All of them would be after the bounty on Talyn's head.

No matter how much she wanted to believe otherwise, she couldn't find a happy ending in this. WAR had been trying for decades to put Eriadne down, and like some supernatural beast, she always returned to power.

And this time if she returned to the throne, the bitch would claim the lives of everyone Felicia loved.

CHAPTER 26

Talyn hesitated as the soldiers he passed kept saluting him, which, given his new rank, wasn't *completely* unexpected. But what made him so uneasy was the way they looked at him.

With respect.

Ever since he'd led them in after Chrisen and Merrell, everything had been different.

Everything.

The guard captains who were stationed at Lorens's door even opened it for him.

Yeah, Andaria was definitely coming to an end. This had to be the sign of some impending doomsday.

"Is something wrong?"

He turned toward Lorens before he remembered he was supposed to salute him.

Lorens returned it with a frown. "What's got you so skittish?"

Talyn removed his helmet and brushed uneasily at his neck.

"Just not used to Vested looking at me with anything other than contemptuous sneers on their faces. It's scaring me."

Lorens laughed. "I have our top advisors in the war room. You ready?"

Talyn nodded, then followed him into the adjacent conference room where the elite of the Andarion armada—at least the ones Tylie hadn't relieved of their posts—waited. They came to their feet and saluted Lorens, who quickly had them retake their chairs.

Lorens gestured for Talyn to occupy the seat on his right. "For those of you who haven't met him yet, my new adjutant is Lieutenant Commander Batur."

Now there were the derisive snorts Talyn was used to. And the sneers that had him lifting his chin as he defied them with a hard stare.

"Bastard lack-Vest," someone mumbled loud enough to be heard.

Lorens glared at each commander in turn. "If anyone in this room has an issue with my chosen second-in-command, then you have issue with me. You will give him the respect he's earned through military service and loyalty, or I'll allow him the honor of having you in the Ring. Any takers?"

That effectively quelled them.

Satisfied, Lorens turned on the monitors that showed various stats and updates on what was happening on Andaria and in their territories. "Now, let's get to business. Jullien eton Anatole was arrested an hour ago when he assisted mercenaries in the kidnapping of Tizirah Kiara eton Anatole."

They sucked their breaths in.

Even Talyn let out a low whistle at that particular brand of stupidity. While he didn't know Nykyrian personally, he knew from Jayne how lethal the male could be. And he knew exactly what *he'd* do in Nykyrian's place.

It was a wonder Jullien was still breathing.

"Tizirah Kiara?" Commander Nazaru asked from the other end of the table. "Who is she?"

Lorens glanced to Talyn before he answered. "The pregnant wife of our soon-to-be Tahrs Nykyrian eton Anatole. Acting Tadara Tylie has reinstated his standing in the royal lineage—"

That set off a round of blustering.

"Who is he?"

"Did the plenumus approve?"

The outraged questions blurred together until Lorens held his hands up. They quieted down instantly.

Lorens called up the picture of the male who looked every bit as fierce as his reputation claimed. It was one of Nykyrian in his League uniform. His long white hair was braided down his back, and in typical League fashion, a pair of obsidian sunglasses obscured his eyes. Numerous scars marred his features, including two nasty ones around his mouth that appeared to have been made by a gag of some sort.

"Tiziran Nykyrian was the firstborn twin of Tizirah Cairistiona that Eriadne attempted to murder when he was a small boy. While it is true he was raised among humans, he was a League assassin. A Command Assassin of the First Order. And he is currently a key member of The Sentella. An organization that was set up for the same reason as The League. To protect those who cannot protect themselves from any person or government corrupted by power. Acting Tadara Tylie has assured my father and the plenumus that Tiziran Nykyrian exemplifies everything Andarion."

They exchanged interested looks at that.

Nazaru cleared his throat. "Do you believe we can trust him?"

Lorens rubbed at his chin. "I haven't met him, but I trust the opinion of those who have. As soon as he learned that Jullien had aided in the abduction of Nykyrian's wife, he reacted in true Andarion fashion and almost killed his brother. He and a Sentella strike force are currently en route to save her, and he won't be stopped until she's safe. . . . If she's not, Nykyrian has vowed to return and destroy Tiziran Jullien with his bare hands."

They nodded in approval at an action any of them would take.

"For Jullien's actions against his brother, Tizirah Cairistiona herself has ordered him taken into custody. As of this minute, we have all the royal family in custody, except the former tadara. We've had several leads on her location, but so far none have panned out."

Commander Pinara, who was a cousin of Farina's, sighed heavily. "So long as she remains at large, she's a major threat to us. She still has allied nations who might come to her aid."

Lorens nodded. "We've contacted all of them, and none of them have heard from her."

"Yet," Nazaru added. "Doesn't mean they won't."

Pinara agreed. "Or that they're not lying to you, biding time until they attack to gain back her throne for her."

As they continued to argue, Talyn leaned over to whisper into Lorens's ear. "I have an idea, Commander. I know exactly how to find her. But I'll only tell it to you."

Lorens sat back in his office chair while he and Talyn watched Talyn's plan unfold on his smallest monitor. He laughed bitterly. "Boy, you *are* brilliant. How did you know?"

Talyn shrugged. "A wounded lorina always returns to its den. With her family arrested, and no one Parisa can trust with her safety, the only place for her to go is to her aunt."

"I respected you before this, Talyn. Now . . . I'm glad you're my top advisor, and I hope you never turn your battle skills against me. You *are* formidable."

Talyn didn't comment on that as he watched Chrisen's mother, Parisa, "escaping." Little did she know, she'd been implanted with the same tracer Andarion soldiers all bore. They could track her through anything except extreme electromagnetic fields.

Under Talyn's orders, they'd sent in a group of supposed patriots to free her. In the ensuing escape, Parisa had been shot in the arm with a blast that masked the injection of the chip. She was bleeding, but not so much as to keep her from fleeing.

She hadn't even tried to save her sons during her escape. All her attention had been on her own freedom.

That said it all about their family.

Lorens frowned as they traced her headings. He double-checked to make sure it was correct. "That's Tavali territory she's entering."

Yes, it was.

Talyn cursed as he realized what it had to mean. "So all this time, Eriadne was working with them against our people?" There was no other reason for Eriadne to be hiding there. Given the decades they'd been at war with each other, the Andarion queen would have never gone to the Tavali for shelter.

Unless they'd been secret allies.

Otherwise, the Tavali would have murdered her on sight.

With a stunned expression, Lorens met his gaze. "She had to have been. Shit. What do we do now? There's no way to extract her from a Tavali portbase. They'll annihilate us."

"Nice optimism." Talyn considered their options for a few minutes.

Most ended in utter destruction. But the more he thought about it, the more a radical idea began to take form.

A slow smile spread across Lorens's face. "I know that look. You have a plan."

"Yeah, I do. Hang on and let me check on something." Talyn headed back toward the prime commander's lounge, which was actually a small condo set aside for the PC's use whenever they were under threat, such as now.

He opened the door and froze as he found Felicia teaching Qory how to bake in the small kitchen area. What the hell? The giant had flour smeared all over his face while she patiently instructed him. Had the moment been less dire, he'd have laughed his ass off at the sight.

As it was, Morra laughed at Talyn's expression. "I looked the same way a few minutes ago when I first got here and saw them."

Qory made a rude gesture at Morra that Talyn didn't need to have translated.

Lorens pulled up short behind him and burst out laughing.

Felicia glared at her brother. "At least he's trying to learn. You'd starve if you didn't have someone to cook for you."

Lorens held his hands up in surrender and wisely checked his tongue.

Talyn closed the distance between them. "Qorach? Didn't you tell me that you had friends in the Tavali?"

He nodded.

"Close friends?"

He gestured a response.

"Like a brother," Felicia translated. "Why?"

"Is he a member of the Porturnum group?"

Qory let out a sound of scornful amusement.

"That would be a serious negatory." Morra was the one who translated his words this time. "Neither he nor Chayden are welcome among the Porturnum Nation. Their leader hates their branch and, in particular, their Tavali father."

So much for his plan. But Talyn wasn't quite defeated. "Do they have any allies among the Porturnum? Or someone who can deal with them? One who can get me and a small team inside their Port StarStation base?"

Qory made a quick gestured response.

"Maybe." Felicia narrowed an irritated glare at Talyn. "You're not thinking of doing something stupid, are you?"

By that tone, he knew a *yes* would get him severely cock-blocked. "Um . . . no. I would *never* do something stupid."

Felicia rolled her eyes. "At least you don't try to lie to me so that I don't know you're actually lying." She sighed heavily. Cleaning off her hands, she came around the kitchen island to glare up at Talyn. "Qory . . . Go with him and beat him as I would if he does anything too stupid."

Qory smiled at the thought and gestured to Morra.

"He says your terms are acceptable."

Talyn shook his head. "I'm not leaving you without protection."

Felicia arched a brow at him. "I'm in the middle of the armada's command center, with my older brother sitting on top of me like a rabid lorina with its sole-surviving kitten. I assure you, I will be fine."

Even so, Talyn wasn't convinced. He had a bad feeling in his gut. And it wasn't over *his* mission. "I don't like this."

"Guess no one's happy, then. You think it thrills me to have you go into the heart of beings I know have already shot you down and wouldn't hesitate to do so again?"

Talyn offered her the charming grin that had gotten him out of much trouble with his mother while growing up. "If I guess correctly, do I get a bonus?"

Growling, she shook her head. "You're so impossible. I have no idea why I love you."

" 'Cause I'm cute and fluffy, and I don't bitch when you rip the covers off me at night."

She laughed at that. "Go on, get out before I make good my threat to shoot you in the leg."

Talyn paused at the door to glance back at Felicia. The sad light in her eyes made his stomach lurch. "I'll be back, *couriana*. Promise."

"You better be."

His heart heavy that he'd made her sad, Talyn led Morra and Qory toward his office while Lorens stayed behind to console Felicia.

Morra used his link to place a call to her ally. When the man answered, he wasn't what Talyn had pictured as a Tavali. At all. With dark auburn hair, he looked more like an aristocratic politician than a ruthless pirate. In fact, the man bled refinement. But that being said, his manner of dress was a careless casual, something reflected by the fact he hadn't shaved in a couple of days.

The only clue to his real nature was the cold-blooded ruthlessness in his sharp blue eyes. "Lady Deathblade," he said in greeting to Morra. "It's been quite some time since I've had the privilege of seeing your beautiful face."

She snorted. "Ryn, Ryn, Ryn . . . you're such an outrageous flirt."

"Can't help it. I've always been attracted to the ladies, especially when they're lethal." He winked at her. "And since I know you so well, I know you're not calling to pass the time. What can I do for you, my lovely?"

"I need a huge favor. Where are you?"

Ryn tsked. "Not at liberty to disclose. I'm on official business for my mother. Why?"

Morra deflected his question with one of her own. "Any chance you're going to be near the Porturnum's Port Star-Station base anytime soon?"

The amused grin on Ryn's face said that he knew she was being evasive on purpose. "And again, I ask why."

She introduced Ryn to Talyn. "I'll let Talyn take over."

Talyn inclined his head to Ryn. "We have it on good authority that Venik is harboring our deposed tadara, and Parisa Anatole, a wanted fugitive. I want to go in undercover as a Tavali to verify it, and extract them if they really are there."

Ryn arched a brow at that. "Have you any idea what happens to someone wearing Tavali gear when they're not entitled? We have grave issues with posers."

"And I have grave issues with the Andarion tadara trying to kill her own grandson and then using the Tavali, who are supposed to be our enemies, to hide her from our justice."

Morra cleared her throat. "By the way, that grandson he's talking about . . . it's Nykyrian Quiakides. Someone near and dear all our hearts, who has a grudge against both the queen *and* Parisa."

Ryn's other eyebrow shot up. "Really?"

Morra nodded. "So long as they're free, Nyk's wife is in danger."

"You just trotted out the magic name to the game, little

sister. I owe Nyk for protecting my brother. There's nothing I wouldn't do for him. Even bring my mother's clan into war." Ryn turned away for a second as if considering his next course of action. "Fine. I'm already here at their Andarion base. And this explains a lot of what I've been overhearing since my arrival. Y'all come as my guests and I'll sponsor you. Let me know if you have any trouble getting in."

"Thank you," Talyn said.

"Peace be the journey." Ryn cut the transmission.

As Talyn straightened, the knot in his gut drew tighter. Something bad was about to happen. "Can we trust him?"

Morra nodded. "That brother he mentioned? It's Darling Cruel."

"The Caronese prince?"

She nodded. "They have the same father."

And Darling was the Sentella friend Jayne was always trying to protect. She thought the world of the man, and Jayne trusted almost no one.

Ryn wasn't what Talyn felt, then. But something was off. He could sense it with the part of him that had never failed to be right.

If only he knew what his gut was trying to tell him.

Qory gestured to Morra as they left to head to the landing bay.

"What?" Talyn asked.

"He's reminding me that we need to dress you like Tavali. You walk in there in *that* uniform . . . well, I'm always up for a good fight, but if you get hurt, Felicia will kick my ass and

Jayne will help her." She chucked Talyn on his arm as they boarded their Sentella ship, and Qory left to head for the flight deck to do preflight checks. She pulled Talyn to a private room on board. "So follow me and drop those pants, cutie. This is going to be fun."

For her, maybe.

As minutes went by and Morra used Talyn as a living doll, he knew what caused the lump of dread in his stomach. She put him in things that crawled into areas of his body that the gods had never meant fabric to touch, while Qory took over flying them out of the station and heading them into space.

Talyn had no idea what he was in for until he looked into a mirror. He cringed at what he saw. "Sentient creatures really dress this way?"

Morra laughed. "They do, indeed. And I have to say, you wear Tavali well. There's just one thing we need, that you should love."

"A bag over my head so that no one knows it's me?"

"Close . . . and stop bitching. Being Andarion, you should be used to having your face painted."

Talyn bit back the pain she unknowingly caused him. As a bastard, he wasn't allowed to paint his mother's lineage on his face. It was something that had been a bitter pill for him every time he'd had to go to temple for high holidays. And why he'd never gone to any kind of Andarion festival. It was just too embarrassing to be the only one in the crowd bare-faced.

He sat down for Morra to reach his head, and paint his features in true Tavali style . . . a skeletal design that highlighted his white eyes. She pulled a scarf over his mouth that matched the hood he wore over his head. It completed the skeleton design.

"Just stay covered and they'll never know it's you." She took the mirror from his hand and returned it to its drawer before she headed to the flight deck.

Talyn stood and adjusted his blasters and Warsword before he went to join them.

Qory did a double take, then smiled approvingly.

Talyn's link buzzed. Clicking it on, he didn't bother checking ID. "Commander Batur."

Felicia's sweet voice sent a chill over him. "Hey, baby. I know I only have a few minutes before you'll be in Tavali territory and they might pick this up. I just wanted to wish you luck and tell you again that I love you. That I'm proud to be your female, and that you better stay safe."

He savored every syllable. "I will, *mia*. Everything's in place. Don't worry . . . I love you, too."

She made a kissing noise in his ear before she ended the transmission.

Morra smiled at him.

He started to respond, but his attention went to the screens, where a massive Tavali strike force was falling into place.

Morra sobered instantly before she took over communications. "Crimson Tavali, this is Green Fire from the Black Flag Nation, copy?"

"Copy. We need confirmation. Who's your father?"

"No father. We're Rogues who fly under the mercy of Hermione Dane. Code name Kirren . . . hail the Wasturnum, forever. We've come on a peaceful mission to rendezvous with the favored son. He can verify my identity and cause."

Talyn stepped forward as the Tavali armed their weapons.

Morra held her hand up to signal him to hold position. "Problem?"

"No problem. Identify all heat signatures on board."

"Morrtalah Cheho'vitastamiutstoh speaking. I fly with Qorach Rohrtag and Andor Enre."

Talyn arched a brow at her alias for him. They'd not discussed it, but he made sure to commit it to memory.

The ships powered down their weapons systems. "Hail Tavali and welcome, sister. You're cleared to land in the station, under escort."

Talyn ground his teeth as he realized just how tight security was for the Tavali station. Since they were close enough for echoing scanners, he didn't speak. Anything they said from this point on was subject to being picked up by Tavali devices. This was where he envied Morra and Qory's ability to communicate solely by hand gestures. He had no idea what they were saying to each other right now.

But by the frenetic way they moved their hands, he figured they had the same concerns he did.

As soon as they landed, Morra extended the ramp, then opened the door.

There was a "welcoming" party waiting as they disembarked. Talyn crooked a smile at the fear that immediately darkened their gazes as they took in the size of him and Qory.

A small blue-skinned human approached them. "Who's the captain?"

"I am." Morra gestured at them in turn. "Both of my muscle are mute. Their voice boxes were damaged in fights."

"You're the one with the name no one can pronounce?"

She grinned at him. "Morra Deathblade is what it translates to in Universal."

He made a note of that in a small e-ledger. "Captain Dane is busy right now, in a meeting. We're to show you to his quarters to wait for him."

As their Tavali escort led them through the bay, Talyn kept his senses alert. The station was a lot bigger than he'd thought from the reports he'd read about it. And there were a lot more Tavali here than he'd ever guessed. No wonder they'd been able to attack Andarion freighters and fleets so viciously, so often.

Just where would they have put the Andarion tadara?

For the first time, he was beginning to doubt their intel. Maybe Parisa hadn't come here, after all. Not to mention, he was now doubting his own sanity. Perhaps they should have come up with a Plan B, C, D, or even E and F.

Yeah, definitely F, because they were starting to look fucked.

They turned down a corridor and were met by a group of pilots scrambling. Talyn and Qory stepped aside as they ran past, headed toward the bay.

"What's that?" Morra asked as she stared after them.

Their escort checked with his e-ledger before he spoke.

"Sensors picked up a group of Andarions hiding in the shadow of a moon. We're assuming they're there to attack us."

Talyn cursed the luck and wished he had some way to warn his troops.

"Come to think of it . . ." The Tavali jerked the lower mask off Talyn's face.

When he started to draw on him, Talyn kneed the man, grabbed his blaster, and knocked him into the wall.

Morra quickly came between them. "What the hell?"

The Tavali curled his lip. "He's Andarion!"

She snorted. "Yeah, he is. So's your boss, Venik. What's your point?"

"How do I know he's not a spy for the others?"

Morra gently tilted Talyn's head back to expose the prison mark Chrisen had placed on his neck. "They let branded traitors in their armada?"

When the Tavali moved to touch the mark, Talyn let out a guttural sound that made him jump back.

Morra crossed her arms over her chest. "Wise move. He's not quite tame."

A bead of sweat rolled down the Tavali's face. "Yeah, okay. Just keep him leashed."

"Then don't attack him. You move on him, and I'm not liable for his actions against you."

"Hey, Tres?"

The Tavali froze at the call, then let out a relieved breath at the sight of their contact. "Dane. Thank God! I surrender this group to you, brother." He beat a hasty retreat as Ryn Dane closed the distance between them.

Just over six feet in height, and muscled, Ryn had dark red hair that was brushed back from a handsome human face.

He narrowed his gaze at Talyn before he glanced to Morra and Qory. "Anyone speak the Trassel dialect of Caronese?"

They all three held up their hands.

Ryn smiled. "Excellent. No one else here does." He inclined his head to Talyn. "You must be Jayne's sexy baby."

Talyn let out an irritated breath before he nodded.

Ryn laughed and clapped him on the arm. "Don't worry. My mother still cuts my meat for me, too."

Morra jerked her chin toward Ryn before she explained his job to Talyn. "He's the Tavali Ambassador."

"Yeah," Ryn sighed. "I'm the only one of the few who can legally parlay between the Tavali groups and sovereign empires."

Talyn frowned. "Why is that?"

"While my mother is Hermione Dane, notorious Tavali leader, my father was the Caronese governor, Drux Cruel."

Talyn remembered Morra telling him as much. "I'm surprised Jayne didn't send your brother over for this, too."

"She probably would have, but he's lending aid to Jayne and crew, while they go after Jullien eton Anatole."

Which brought Talyn back to his earlier concern. "Is our intel correct? I thought Jullien was in custody?"

Ryn gave a subtle nod. "Only *very* recently. . . . Now follow me."

They'd just started down a hallway when another group of Tavali came marching toward them.

Ryn motioned for Talyn, Morra, and Qory to stop. "There a problem?"

"Venik wants a word with your friends." The Tavali's gaze narrowed on Talyn. "In particular, the Andarion."

"That'll be hard to do since he's mute."

"Look, Dane. We're just following orders. Whatever High Admiral Venik wants, High Admiral Venik gets. Right now, he wants your friends. Hand them over."

Ryn let out a disgusted sigh. "Venik can kiss my hairy ass." Faster than anyone could follow, he pulled his blaster from its holster and opened fire. "Fall back!" he ordered Talyn and Qory.

Where? Talyn stared at two corridors, unsure of which one to take.

Just as he started to ask, Ryn grabbed Talyn's sleeve and hauled him toward the one on their left. "The queen and her niece are in the last room on the right."

Morra and Qory ran for that room.

Talyn laid down cover fire for them. "Great," he said to Ryn, who was helping them escape, "but I feel compelled to point out that we're a little outnumbered right now."

Ryn didn't respond. Rather, he tapped the link in his ear. "This is Ambassador Dane summoning all of the Wasternum in range. Venik's men have attacked me and busted truce. Notify the clan! I'm in the northern corridor and require immediate assist. Again, all Wassies, full on, brothers and sisters. The Favored Son is under attack!"

Three doors opened behind them.

Talyn swung around and took aim. Until Tavali poured out to fire at the ones after them and cover their retreat. "How do I tell the enemy from your guys?"

Ryn snorted. "If they shoot at you, shoot back. If it's one of my people, don't worry about blasting one by accident. Jayne would kill them anyway for endangering you."

With the others engaging Venik's people, Talyn and Ryn rushed to where the queen was staying.

He and Ryn covered Morra and Qory while they rewired the locked door. Their enemies were quickly cutting through Ryn's men.

Worse, Talyn was almost out of charges.

Just as he squeezed off the last round, the door opened. They headed into the room a heartbeat before he heard the dreaded sound of a trip wire.

Shit.

Qory slammed into him an instant before the bomb detonated.

CHAPTER 27

Talyn groaned at the pain in his body as debris settled around them. There was a crushing weight on top of him. Smoke dimmed his vision, making him choke and cough.

Had half the station fallen in on him?

That was what it felt like.

Ryn let out a feral curse. Covered with ash and pieces of the ceiling, the Tavali wheezed and choked.

Talyn shifted as he heard Morra coughing next to him. "Morra?"

She ignored him as she gasped. "Qory?" Her voice was thick from her tears. "Oh gods, no! Qory, answer me!"

It was only then that Talyn realized the weight on him was from Qory. The giant had grabbed him and Morra and used his own body to shield them from the blast.

As gently as he could, he rolled Qory onto his back. Burns and cuts covered the man. "Qor? You're still with us, right?"

Blood trickled from the corner of his mouth as he blinked.

"Don't move!" Morra snapped as he tried to sign to her. "You just lie still and I'll get help for you."

Talyn sat back on his haunches as his sight cleared enough to see a shadow rushing past him. It took a second to realize that had been the tadara, saving her own ass.

Typical.

Rage dimmed his vision. His only thought on killing her, he pushed himself to his feet, in spite of his pain, and ran after her.

But no sooner had she entered the hallway than several recoils from Tavali soldiers bounced around her. Shrieking, she fell to the floor and placed her hands on her head in surrender.

Talyn reached her first. Luckily, she hadn't been injured during it all. She was whole to stand trial for her crimes.

Even though his blaster was empty, he angled it at her. "Eriadne eton Anatole, in the name of the Andarion Empire and by orders of Acting Tadara Tylie, I remand you into custody to face your charges. May the gods render mercy to you."

She spat in his face. "I will not be taken in by some lack-Vest bastard!" She tried to rise, but Talyn held her in place.

Talyn wiped the spittle from his cheek. "Bitch, please. You're not only being taken in by a lack-Vest bastard, you were brought down by one. Chew on that." He pulled the binders from his pocket and used them to restrain her.

Until a blaster appeared at his temple.

Talyn froze as Eriadne laughed.

"Kill the bastard upstart!" she demanded. "I want to feel his blood on my skin."

He heard the sharp click as the setting was switched from stun to kill.

"Don't do it, Venik," Ryn growled from the other side of the corridor as he slowly closed the distance between them. "That Andarion is not only under my protection, but that of the Caronese and Sentella. You kill him and it won't be my blast you have to fear. Nemesis himself will be gunning for you, with Jayne leading him in."

Still the blaster remained at Talyn's temple. "Have you any idea what you've done, Cruel?"

Ryn snorted. "In Tavali Canting, I'm not a Cruel. I'm a Dane. And unless you want the full wrath of my mother to fall down on your ass, I suggest you call off your rats and let's part as friends. Or do you want the shitstorm that will follow?"

"We had a deal!" Eriadne shrieked. "Kill him, and I'll make you a tiziran!"

For one heartbeat, Talyn was sure Venik would pull the trigger.

Instead, he holstered the blaster. "As tempting as that is, I've seen what you do to your own. So I think I'll pass, before I end up as an unflattering stain on the floor."

Talyn looked up to meet the older Andarion's bitter stare. Dark-skinned and well muscled, Brax Venik was not what Talyn had expected from the Porturnum Tavali leader.

And his half-breed status was obvious. No wonder Venik hated Andarions. If they'd been as *kind* to the Tavali leader growing up as they'd been to Talyn, he more than understood the hostility the Porturnum leader bore the Andarion race.

Venik glanced to Ryn. "While I hate to lose my alliance with the Andarion tadara, Eriadne's *maybe* isn't worth angering your mother or splitting the Tavalis into another bloody clan war. Which is a sure thing if I start killing those under Dane Canting, especially her only son. . . . Tread in peace, little brother. Give your mother my best." He called off his men and left Eriadne to them.

Talyn scowled as Venik walked away as if nothing had happened. He handed Eriadne over to Ryn before he moved to check on Qory and Morra. "How's he doing?"

"I've got the bleeding stopped. I just need the damn medics to get here!"

They arrived a few seconds later.

Talyn stepped back while they tended Qory. There were several bodies in the room of beings who'd been caught in the blast. He whispered a prayer for their souls.

But those words scattered as he realized that one of the bodies was Parisa's.

Damn. Venik was right. Eriadne hadn't even shed a tear over her own niece, or even thought about her. At all.

Hell, even Talyn felt a twinge of guilt for the part he'd played in putting Parisa here. He couldn't fathom how the former tadara could be so cold.

Not that it mattered.

As he started to tell the medics to take Qory to Andaria, his link buzzed. "Commander Batur."

"T-T-Talyn?"

His stomach shrank at the terror in Felicia's voice. "Baby? What is it?"

"Awww, how sweet and touching."

Talyn reached out to brace himself against the wall as his entire world tilted. It was Chrisen. "What are you doing with her?"

"What do you think? And if you ever want to see her alive again, I suggest you cut the throat of the tadara, and return my mother to Andaria. You will back my mother in her rise to power or I'm going to record the sounds of your female screaming your name for help as I skin her alive."

Talyn couldn't breathe as those words sank in and horrified him. He had no doubt they'd carry out that threat.

But Parisa was dead. . . .

Everything turned hazy. A metallic bitterness stung his tongue as his ears became warm and buzzed. His back burned like fire. It was the same frightening sensation he'd had as a small child whenever his emotions had spun out of control.

Why he'd had to learn to control them very early in life. To let no one ever push his buttons. To keep every part of himself leashed at all times.

Now . . .

The beast inside him craved blood.

"Don't you touch her! You hear me, Anatole? If she so much as stubs her toe in your custody, there will be no hole in hell you can find small enough that I won't come for you and drag you screaming from it."

"You don't scare me, lack-Vest. You have two hours to show my mother taking the throne. After that . . . this ezul Terronova bitch won't be so pretty to look at."

Morra froze as Talyn made the sound of a rabid animal.

Worried about him, she started to reach out to touch his arm. He threw his head back and let out a savage roar. It was so deep and raw, she felt it through her entire body.

All movement stopped instantly.

His breathing ragged, Talyn turned toward her. His eyes glowed a fierce red that was made more sinister by the snarl on his handsome face. An instant later, massive black wings unfurled from his back.

Holy shit.

He spread them wide.

"What the hell," she breathed.

Falling away from Talyn, Ryn passed a shocked gape to Morra. "Anyone else know Andarions had wings?"

"You're all supposed to be dead!" Eriadne snarled. "I made sure of it."

Talyn laughed malevolently in the former queen's face. "You missed one, bitch."

During the "purging" of the Winged races, Eriadne had tested, by law, every member of those lineages to see who held the recessive gene. If the test came back positive, the Winged carrier had been executed. Every familial member. But because his mother's family was medical, the Baturs had found a way to fool the test and save themselves.

Now, Talyn was one of the extremely rare Winged gene carriers left on Andaria. It was why his mother had taught him well to control his emotions and keep his wings concealed.

No matter what.

This was the first time he'd ever publicly shown them, and

the first time they'd been out since he turned eight and his mother had threatened to surgically remove them if she ever saw them again.

It was also how he'd known that he and Jayne were related by blood. The day he'd first seen her wings, while staying with her and Hadrian, he'd learned that she was not only part Andarion, but that her Andarion grandmother had been the younger sister of his mother's grandmother, who'd fled Andaria to avoid the purging.

They *were* family.

Talyn closed the distance between him and Eriadne. "Just so you know, that was Chrisen. He wants me to cut your throat and return his mother to Andaria to be proclaimed tadara in your stead. If I fail to do so, he's going to kill my female." He pulled out his tactical knife, and ran his fingertip along the black blade. "The first half of his terms are acceptable to me."

He stepped toward her.

"Wait!" Eriadne fought against Ryn's hold. "Spare me, and I can tell you how to get your female back."

"You have three seconds before I trim your lineage."

"The same way I tricked Nykyrian." Eriadne glanced down to Parisa's body. "She and Cairistiona are almost identical in looks. Put my daughter on the throne and he won't know the difference. I promise you. It'll give you time to find your female and save her."

"Why should I trust you?"

Eriadne lifted her chin. "Because my blood turned on me. If Chrisen wants me dead, I won't rest until I stand over his rotting corpse."

That Talyn fully believed. He also knew that Chrisen would never release Felicia. That slimy bastard had a plan and it didn't include allowing Talyn to live to seek his own revenge. Nor would he suffer Felicia to go free after what her father and brother had done to them.

Sometimes it's better to bed down with the devil than the devil's handmaiden. The old Andarion proverb played through his mind.

His fury barely leashed, he moved to stand over Parisa's body. Eriadne was right. She bore a frightening resemblance to Cairistiona.

Talyn watched as they carried Qory away on an air stretcher and Morra followed in his wake. Rage pounded through him. So many had already been lost in this fight.

Even more injured.

It was time for it to stop.

He shoved Eriadne back toward Ryn. "Do you have a brig on your ship?"

"Yeah."

"Keep her in it. Knock her out if you have to."

As Talyn started to leave, Ryn's voice stopped him. "I also have a fighter. It'll get you home a lot quicker than a ship. It's yours if you want it."

Never had Talyn been more tempted to kiss a man. "Thank you."

Ryn inclined his head in kinship before he led the way to the bay where his ship was docked.

It took Talyn only a few minutes to get into the fighter and acclimate to the controls and unfamiliar language. Basically, they all ran alike. So long as you knew where the key controls were, you were relatively safe.

At least he hoped that was true.

Talyn launched and headed home. After he set his coordinates, he called his mother to make sure she was still all right in the midst of this chaos.

"Oh thank the gods!" His mother wept. "We heard the command center had been overrun and taken by loyalists. I was terrified you were there."

"What happened, Matarra?"

"Ironically, the same plan you had for Parisa. Once they heard she'd been set free, a group of loyalists decided to follow the lead and break in to release Chrisen and Merrell from their cells."

Talyn cursed himself for his stupid plan. He'd never dreamed that another group would play copycat. "What happened to Lorens?"

"He was badly wounded when . . ." Her voice trailed off as if she'd caught some slip. "He's in surgery."

"I know they have Felicia. Chrisen already called me."

"I'm so sorry, baby."

"Do we have their locations?"

"No. They removed their chips. We have no way of finding them."

Talyn felt his back tingling again. Forcing himself to stay calm and control his wings, he focused on what needed to be done. "Is Cairistiona sober and alert?"

"Yes. Why?"

"I have a favor to ask."

"It's a bad time, Talyn. Nykyrian was almost fatally wounded while extracting his wife from his enemies. He's in surgery, too. And the prognosis isn't good. They don't expect him to survive the surgery."

While he could appreciate that, Nykyrian wasn't the most important thing to *him*. "It's to save Felicia, Mom. Please don't make me bury her."

"What do you need?"

"A miracle."

After the loyalists had retaken the command center and Lorens had been seriously wounded, the remaining WAR soldiers had withdrawn to Anatole Base, where the majority of weapons and ships were kept. Talyn headed straight there. His plan was to mount a two-soldier mission, just him and Ryn, to get Felicia back.

The last thing he'd expected was the mass of troops who surrounded his fighter the moment he surrendered controls to the tech op on landing. Since his engines were locked down, there was nothing he could do.

He was completely at their mercy.

Disgusted at his luck, he opened the canopy and descended to the waiting mob he was sure would take him into custody.

They didn't. Rather they stood back to allow a colonel, who was a few years older than him, to approach Talyn.

The colonel saluted him.

Talyn returned it as he cast his gaze around the others, watching for any sudden moves.

"What are your orders, Commander?"

Talyn blinked twice as those words registered. He was tempted to look behind him to see if someone else was there. But actually, it made sense. With Lorens in surgery, he was their XO.

Yeah, that screwed with his head, too. He was the youngest commander in Andarion history, and that responsibility settled on his shoulders like a gravity-dense planet.

Finally recovering from the initial shock of their respect, Talyn cleared his throat. "I need stat reports."

"The command center is still in Anatole hands. We have strike teams in position and snipers on the surrounding rooftops. If they step one foot out, we're ending lineages."

Talyn considered that as he led the colonel toward his new office. "Shoot to stun or wound. Let's not kill anyone for being an idiot. Or for being loyal, even if it is to a fractured crown." Honestly, had Chrisen not made this personal, Talyn wasn't sure which side he'd have been fighting for. "But if it's Chrisen or Merrell, I give full pardon to anyone who puts them in a grave."

The colonel relayed Talyn's orders before he returned to his updates. "We still have no bearings on the escaped tizirani, other than Jullien, who is in Triosan custody. The other two pulled their tracers out before they ran."

"Do we know who released them?"

"From video feeds, yes. We have the names of several traitors."

"Has anyone checked to see if *their* tracers are working?"

A light of respect shined in the colonel's eyes. "No, sir. But we will now." Colonel Tievel issued that order, as well.

When Talyn reached Chrisen's former office, the majors on duty opened the door for him. A weird, uneasy feeling danced up his spine as he entered, not for discipline this time, but for command.

It was the first time in months that he'd entered this office without a sick lump of dread in his stomach. And the weight of his new position and responsibility hit him hard. In the past, only his life had been on the line.

Now . . .

He held the life of every soldier who believed in Tylie and Saren in his hands. The lives of his mother and Felicia. Of Tylie and Cairistiona.

The future of the *entire* Andarion empire. It was all up to him.

Don't fuck this up.

Gods, when I said I wanted my life to change, this was not what I meant. He ran his thumb around the finger that held his homage to Felicia, and let an image of her in his mind soothe his trepidations.

Had he caused all this by daring to defy the gods and take something for his own? Was this his punishment for trying to be happy?

No, he refused to believe that. Just as he refused to believe he would never see Felicia again.

You're no longer alone. He glanced around at the soldiers who were standing by his side.

Everything he'd ever wanted was on the line now. Even his life.

I won't go back.

He'd fought too hard to get here. No slimy little whoreson was going to take his life or his female from him. Not without a brutal fight.

And brutal fights were what Talyn Batur specialized in. *Bring it, bitch. With everything you have.*

The only thing different was that this time, he wasn't fighting for respect or rank. He wasn't fighting for himself.

He fought for the only thing that currently mattered in his backwards, screwed-up life.

Felicia.

And he was going to end this. Once and for all.

Felicia wanted to cower and cry as she struggled futilely against the chains that held her to her chair. Before Talyn, she wouldn't have hesitated to fall apart and beg Chrisen for mercy. But one of the two things she'd learned from Talyn was how to keep her head up in the face of those out to harm her. She would never allow them to take her power from her and make her weak.

They weren't worth it.

The other was that she wasn't alone in this universe. There were Andarions out there who stood up for victims. Andarions who wouldn't let evil win.

Talyn was one of them and he would come for her. He wouldn't let her down.

And when he got here, he would kill every one of them for taking her. She knew it with every beat of her heart.

"There's only fifteen minutes left," Chrisen said as Merrell changed the broadcasts, looking for news about their mother and the queen. "You think he'll do it?"

"Kill the tadara? Absolutely. Free our mother . . . I don't know." He paused on the coverage over what Nykyrian Quiakides had done to Aksel Bredeh and Aksel's base. They flashed to a picture of his weeping, pregnant wife sitting in a hospital waiting room between Tylie and Cairistiona. "At least we don't have to worry about one of our hybrid cousins on the throne. Jullien will never inherit now that his parents know what he did to his own brother. And it looks like Nykyrian will die of his injuries."

"Good. Then the right order of inheritance is ensured."

Merrell nodded. "As it should have been. A true Andarion on our throne . . . me. Not some hybrid piece of shit." He cast an evil smirk at Felicia. "It appears your lack-Vest bastard doesn't love you, after all." With a sickening saunter, he closed the distance between them and pulled her hair back from her face.

Felicia jerked as far away as she could. Since the gag in her mouth kept her from speaking, she growled at him.

Merrell buried his hand in her hair and jerked her head back. "You think you're tough? I can't wait to hear that fight turn into screams for mercy."

"Mer, look!"

They both turned toward the monitor to see Parisa being led into the palace by a group of soldiers. Since the news was still showing Cairistiona in the hospital where Nykarian had been taken, they knew it wasn't her.

Their mother was finally free.

"Unbelievable," the commentator said. "In a stunning and unexpected move, Tizirah Tylie has agreed to abdicate her power."

They cut to an interview with the princess in the same hospital, where Cairistiona was sitting in the background.

"My mother will be sorely missed. And the last thing I want is to see another member of my family venture into eternity. Nor do I want another innocent Andarion to suffer. While we are a warring race, the time has come to live in peace with ourselves and only fight against invaders. Those who would do us all harm. It is my honor to step down and allow peace to reign and a new tadara to ascend to her rightful place as our leader." And with that, Tylie left the reporters who were shouting out questions. She returned to take her sister's hand in the hospital, as their guard pushed the reporters back and closed the doors in their faces.

Merrell let out a sound of utter disbelief. "I'll be damned. Batur did it."

Chrisen shook his head. "So we let her go?"

Merrell laughed. "Of course not. Our mother's about to be tadara and we will be the new heirs." He glared down at her. "The only question is, which of them do we gut first?"

Before Chrisen could answer, Merrell's link buzzed. He checked the ID and smiled. "Matarra?"

Chrisen went to his side. "Put her on speaker."

Merrell obeyed. "Can you repeat that for Lord Dull and Boring?"

"We're planning the coronation within the hour. I need both of you here for it so that everyone can see you take your rightful places in our world."

Felicia jumped as someone touched her bound hands. It took her a second to realize they were signing to her in her palm.

You're safe. Talyn is with me. We're cloaked.

Tears stung her eyes as Talyn brushed a tender caress against her cheek to let her know he was with her. She felt the air stirring as he moved to stand between her and the Anatoles.

Morra loosened Felicia's hands so that she could free herself. She patted her arm encouragingly.

Felicia still couldn't see them, but just knowing they were here . . .

Never had she loved Talyn more.

"How did you get free?" Merrell asked his mother.

"Batur arranged it. Tell me where you are and I'll send an entourage to escort you both to the palace."

"We'll come on our own. See you shortly." Merrell hung up.

Chrisen gasped. "What are you doing?"

"Something about this doesn't feel right. I don't trust that bastard lack-Vest. Do you?"

Chrisen glanced back toward Felicia. "No, but he loves his female. For her safety, I think he'd obey us."

"Then she's coming with us." Merrell moved to take her and collided hard with Talyn.

Talyn immediately decloaked. In full battlegear, he reached for Merrell. "You should have just gone on." He slung him against the wall, then pulled his blaster out and angled it for Chrisen. "One excuse to pull the trigger. Please!"

Chrisen held his hands up.

The expression on Merrell's face said that he wanted to be stupid. Until he realized Talyn wasn't alone. One by one, six more Andarion soldiers decloaked.

Both Merrell and Chrisen went down on their knees and surrendered.

Talyn clicked his blaster from kill to stun before he shot each of them.

Twice.

Morra arched an inquisitive black brow at him.

He pulled his helmet off and handed it to the soldier on his left. "I want them kept unconscious until Cairistiona orders their deaths. Otherwise, I'm going to be executed for murder." Talyn turned to Felicia and knelt down by her side to gather her into his arms.

Felicia buried her face against his neck. "I knew you'd come for me."

"Always." Trembling from the relief of finding her, he kissed her with everything he had.

Felicia gasped as Talyn stood with her in his arms. "I can walk."

"I know."

She scowled as he refused to set her down. "Talyn?"

He tightened his arms around her. "I came too close to losing you. Right now, I'm not sure I'll ever let you out of my sight again. Definitely not until all the dust settles from this shit."

Smiling, she laid her head down on his shoulder. "Okay, then. But this might get awkward when I have to go to the bathroom."

He laughed as he carried her down the hallway. He paused to look back at his men. "If you want to drag those two bastards out of here by their ankles, instead of getting hernias carrying them, I'm all right with that. And if you bang their heads into everything you pass along the way, I'll consider expedited promotions."

The soldiers laughed so hard, they actually did drop them.

Morra clapped the one closest to her on the arm. "Not used to management with a wicked sense of humor, are you?"

"Not used to one with any kind of humor. Period."

Felicia snuggled against Talyn.

Until they were outside. Talyn locked gazes with her. She had no idea what the expression on his face meant.

"No more hiding," he breathed an instant before a huge set of wings expanded out of his back.

Gaping, she reached hesitantly to touch the soft texture of them. "You're winged?"

"Stralen isn't the only recessive gene I carry."

She kissed him. "And I love every molecule of you. Recessive and otherwise."

Talyn glanced to the other soldiers with him. One by one, they released their own wings. He grinned at her stunned expression. "Cairistiona and I reinstated the Winged divisions for the armada. She's extended her protection to us. After all, we're an endangered species now. The very last of our kind."

Morra grabbed the largest Andarion male who didn't have

a prisoner to carry. "I have to say, I'm beginning to have a fine appreciation for these non-green species."

Felicia laughed as the soldiers took flight.

Talyn hesitated on the ground with her. "You ready for this?"

"I trusted you with an airbike. I think I can handle it."

But instead of joining the others, he stared down at her. "I love you."

She rubbed noses with him. "Love you, too."

He tightened his arms around her before he took flight. Felicia's stomach fluttered as the ground rapidly receded. She wasn't quite as brave as she'd claimed. The only thing that kept her fear at bay was the knowledge that Talyn would never willingly allow any harm to come to her. That here, finally, she was completely safe.

Funny how she'd always thought of love in the most childish of terms. She'd assumed being in love meant someone would lavish her with attention and gifts. Spoil her blind. But that wasn't true love. True love was placing someone else before yourself. Giving without the expectation of getting anything in return, because their happiness meant more to you than your own. She totally understood that now.

And love was only right when the one you were with felt the exact same way about you. That was why they spoiled you and why you spoiled them in return.

No, she didn't know what the future would hold for them. But whatever disaster or challenge life threw at them, they'd get through it the same way they'd gotten through this.

Together.

EPILOGUE

Felicia shot to her feet as Duel Odelus knocked Talyn to the Ring floor with a brutal punch.

Lorens wrapped his arm around her. "It's all right, Felicia. He can take it."

Yes, but she didn't want him to. More to the point, *she* couldn't take him taking it.

Glancing at Morra and Qory, who were sitting beside her, she winced as Talyn was struck again and again. This was why she'd never wanted to see any match Talyn was in. Why she'd always stayed in the locker room during the fight.

His blood and pain were more than she could take. But this was their anniversary and she'd promised him that she would sit Ringside with her brother and nephews, and their friends.

Little had she known how hard this would be.

When Talyn came to his feet, his gaze went straight to her. By that, she knew how much he appreciated her being here.

For him.

It was the least she could do, since she was still the reason he was getting the snot beaten out of him. This was the last fight he'd contracted for to free her of her contract. How she wished she could go back in time and change things.

But then, if she hadn't contracted with her agency, she would have never met him.

That part was all she didn't regret.

"It'll be all right, Aunt Felicia." Gavarian handed her his drink.

She took a sip to settle her nervous stomach as she ignored the crowd that cheered Talyn getting beaten. Even Qory cheered with various signs while Morra made loud shouts of encouragement for Talyn to rip out Duel's spine.

For a moment, she thought he might. It was what he'd done to Chrisen in their fight a few months back. Something that had made Ferrick deliriously happy and unbelievably rich.

Shaking her head, she tried not to think about any of that.

So much had changed over this last year. Completely sober, Cairistiona was now the beloved Andarion tadara, with Nykyrian and his son, Adron, as the crowned heirs behind her in line for the throne, Eriadne, Jullien, and the remaining Anatoles were in prison or exile. Galene was the prime commander of their armada. Lorens was Galene's adjutant, and Talyn was now the commander at Anatole Base. As such, he was in charge of their primary fighter corps, and a lead advisor to his mother and her brother.

While she and Talyn still couldn't legally live together or marry, they did have a contract, courtesy of her mother and

Morra. It wasn't as good as unification, but it was the best they could hope for under current Andarion law.

And since it allowed her to remain with Talyn, it was more than enough for her.

Felicia winced again as Duel slammed Talyn to the ground, again and stomped him. "How can he stand that?"

Lorens snorted. "Your male is one tough SOB."

Erix shouted something at Talyn. With a fierce roar, Talyn came off the floor and laid into Duel with an unbelievable fury. In a matter of minutes, he had Duel trapped.

The victory buzzer went off.

Thank the gods, it was over. She could finally breathe again.

When the announcer reached for Talyn, Talyn took his mic. Pulling the mask from his face, he spat out his fang guard. "I have an announcement to make." His breathing ragged, he met Felicia's gaze through the bars that separated them. "Tonight is a special anniversary. Two years ago, on this day, I met mu Ger Tarra Felicia. Not long after that, I made a promise to her that once I became a commander, I'd retire from the Ring. And with this, my last contracted fight, I'm keeping my word to her and surrendering my title."

Felicia couldn't breathe as tears blurred her vision. He'd really done it.

Unbelievable! No one walked away from a career like his.

No one. Except a male whose integrity meant more to him than titles. He'd given her his word that he would quit before they killed him.

And he'd kept it.

Tears choked her.

As soon as the cage walls went down, Talyn left the Ring and came straight to her seat.

Hesitating, he held his hand out to her . . . as if she would *ever* deny him anything.

Felicia threw herself into his arms and kissed him.

"I'm disgusting," he said with a laugh.

"No. You're beautiful. Even the gross sweat." She nipped at his lips. "You didn't have to do this."

He cupped her face in his wrapped hands. "I have ulterior motives."

"And those are?"

"I don't want another night where I'm nursing bruises, instead of making love to you."

She tsked playfully at him. "Then what will I do without those boo-boos to kiss?"

A devilish grin curved his lips. "Oh, I think I can come up with something else that needs your attention."

Laughing, she pulled her hand from his face. As she opened her mouth to speak, he gasped, seeing the tattoo on her finger.

Talyn choked on the raw love he felt as he read the words she'd placed on her flesh. *Forever Talyn's.*

She smiled up at him. "My anniversary present for you."

Tears filled his eyes. "You know what this means?"

She nodded. "That I am, and will forever be, of the Winged Blood Clan Batur."

"No. It means you have to keep me. There's no getting rid of me now."

"And I would have it no other way." She kissed him then, knowing that while the rest of the universe might not recognize their unification, they didn't need them to. They didn't need the blessing of the Andarion courts or anyone else.

She was his and he was hers.

No one and nothing would ever again divide them.